DON'T
TELL
ANYONE

For Susie, my sister-in-law and friend.

DON'T TELL ANYONE

A GRIEVING MOTHER...

A MURDERED DAUGHTER...

A FORBIDDEN RELATIONSHIP...

ELEANOR GRAY

MIDNIGHT INK
WOODBURY, MINNESOTA

FIRST EDITION
First Printing, 2016

Book format by Bob Gaul
Cover design by Ellen Lawson
Cover art by iStockphoto.com/87150337/©Armin Staudt
Editing by Nicole Nugent

Midnight Ink, an imprint of Llewellyn Worldwide Ltd.

Library of Congress Cataloging-in-Publication Data
Names: Gray, Eleanor, author.
Title: Don't tell anyone: a mystery / Eleanor Gray.
Description: First edition. | Woodbury, Minnesota: Midnight Ink, 2016.
Identifiers: LCCN 2016026046 (print) | LCCN 2016035234 (ebook) | ISBN
  9780738750224 | ISBN 9780738750996 (ebook)
Subjects: LCSH: Murder—Investigation—Fiction. | Mothers and
  daughters—Fiction. | GSAFD: Mystery fiction.
Classification: LCC PR6119.E973 D66 2016 (print) | LCC PR6119.E973 (ebook) |
  DDC 823/.92—dc23
LC record available at https://lccn.loc.gov/2016026046

Midnight Ink
Llewellyn Worldwide Ltd.
2143 Wooddale Drive
Woodbury, MN 55125-2989
www.midnightinkbooks.com

Printed in the United States of America

Acknowledgments

Family has always been immensely significant, by its absence when I was growing up and by its glorious presence with a loving husband, five children, their partners, sons-in-law, and now grandchildren in my adult life. In short, this is a story with family placed at its very heart and in which not even death can break the love between mother and child.

I'm grateful to Broo Doherty, my agent, for knowing me well enough to suggest that I write this kind of book. As ever, my thanks to the team at Midnight Ink for their enthusiasm for the novel, most specifically Terri Bischoff, Nicole Nugent, and Katie Mickschl. I couldn't have done this without you.

One

"I HATE YOU. I HATE YOU. I HATE YOU."

"Tara, sweetheart, I know it's a shock and I realise you're upset, but it really will be all right." Archie wore his best caring voice, the one he used at the hospital. Low and calm, it was ever so slightly patronising. Not a good tone to adopt with a thirteen-year-old, and certainly not in these circumstances.

"How can it ever be all right?" she hissed. "You and Mum are getting divorced—"

"Separated," I interjected. It was the first word I'd spoken since Archie had delivered his spiel. He'd pitched it in such reasonable tones that I was almost deceived into thinking my life would stay exactly the same. Three words changed all that: *People grow apart.* I felt as if someone had excavated my internal organs.

Tara swivelled her ferocious brown-eyed gaze on me as if it were my fault. Deep down, I knew she was right. I'd been the mug who'd introduced Archie to the lovely Kristina Beaumont at one of the gallery's exhibitions for an up-and-coming American painter. Still in shock, I couldn't remember the damn guy's name.

"Whatever," Tara said, vermillion spotting her cheeks. "Phoebe's parents did exactly the same. You guys will split. I know it."

I stared at Archie, hoping that he would offer a denial and give me a glimmer of hope, but he stayed stubbornly mute. So Tara was right about that, too. Scared, I crossed the floor of our tiny kitchen and put an arm around her tight, pointy shoulders. There was no give and I had a fleeting memory of Tara as a toddler, rigid and resistant in her pushchair, tummy braced and facing the sky while I attempted to squeeze her middle and strap her in. My daughter, so like her father in looks, had always been feisty and spirited in a way I'd often envied and only sometimes regretted. Now I clung to her, more for my benefit than for any comfort I could give.

I don't know for how long we huddled together in the intolerable silence. It was like standing in the tattered remains of a location after the film crew have packed up and gone. Archie had his back to the worktop, his head slightly turned away, shy and uncomfortable. The pale, washed-up light fell across the left side of his face, accentuating the planes of his cheekbones framed by precision-cut sideburns and thick dark hair. His mouth was very slightly open, his full lips pink beneath a soft moustache. I'm an art historian and, for a moment, he reminded me of Caravaggio's portrait of Christ. After fifteen years of living together and thirteen years of marriage, Archie could still knock me out. Had he been a woman, he would have been deemed beautiful. Through fortune and genes, he'd passed this dormant beauty on to Tara. I idly wondered whether it might be more a burden than a blessing.

"Will we stay here?" Tara jutted her chin in the direction of a kitchen cupboard that I'd once lovingly painted. Now it looked chipped and tired, a bit like me. She'd said it like she wanted to. That it was important to her. In need of TLC, our house was still her home, which was, frankly, disturbing. On my wage from the gallery it was unlikely we could afford to stay unless I got a second job or took in a lodger, something for which I wasn't queuing up. Archie didn't earn a lot at the hospital and, although he'd assured me that he would "see me right, financially," I wasn't so certain. Not that Archie would ever have to worry about money. Kristina was loaded.

I cleared my throat, about to speak, but Archie spoke for both of us. It occurred to me that he did this often "That's the plan," he said, brightly avoiding my gaze.

"And you." Tara glowered at him. "Where will *you* go?"

I took a breath. Archie and I had agreed not to drag Kristina into it even though she—the Bitch from Harp Hill, as I'd malevolently nicknamed her—was the reason Archie had ripped out my heart, but my daughter was no fool.

"Around."

"Around?" Tara's husky voice bristled with indignation.

"Here in Cheltenham, not far away. I'll pop back to see you often, you'll see."

"Pop back? I'm not one of your sick fucking patients."

Normally, I'd have asked Tara to mind her language, but I was with her. *Fucking* was an apt description in the circumstances.

Archie pursed his lips, pained. I hoped he was in hell. That's the trouble with affairs when you act out a fantasy, I wanted to say. It has a nasty habit of crashing into the real world, leaving all kinds of devastation in its wake.

"I didn't mean it like that," he muttered.

"What did you mean, that you'll check in when you can bear to tear yourself away from Krissie?" She said it in a *ha, take that* tone.

Krissie? I snagged inside. Is that what he called her? How did Tara know? Had she overheard? When? Where? My arms dropped to my sides. It was my turn to look venomously at Archie. Sorry this is such a royal pain for you, darling, but these are the consequences of shagging someone else when you are already attached.

"I..." he spluttered. I felt a hot thrill of triumph as I watched him squirm, but Tara wasn't done.

"You've chosen her over me, over us," she raged.

That's my girl. He was on the ropes, nowhere to hide, and Tara was piling in. I should have let her finish him off with a knockout blow, but an annoying sense of fair play assailed me. If I were honest, I hoped that if I stayed calm and played nice, Archie would find me attractive again and realise that he'd be mad to leave me for someone as shallow as *Krissie*.

"Look," I said, "let's all take a step back and calm down."

A grateful smile raced across Archie's lips. Well worth me prostrating myself, I reckoned. We couldn't sit in our cramped kitchen so I marched through to the sitting room, hoping the others would follow, which they did. I sat on the sofa and patted the seat next to mine. Tara threw herself down and tucked her long legs up underneath her. *My* girl. *My* daughter. It was Saturday and she wore a simple navy printed dress with a round neck, the curve of her collarbone exposed like shiny white seashells on a sandy beach. She wore a braided skinny belt and her toenails were painted dark blue. Archie sat in his favourite chair. I grimaced at the thought of him taking it with him. As long as it sat in front of the fire, it remained a solid presence. If it left, I could no longer pretend that Archie would come home.

4

I grabbed Tara's hand and squeezed it. "This is a horrible situation," I began.

"Not for him," Tara growled, jaw flexing.

"It's tricky for all of us," I managed to say, playing Mrs. Magnanimous and wondering what my family would make of it all. My sister Tiff would threaten to punch Archie's lights out. My mother was a different proposition altogether. Her live and let live philosophy resulted in three daughters with different fathers. I'd been born during my mother's "respectable" period and brief marriage to a salesman who sold windows and doors. Tiffany was the result of a rebound marriage to a bloke called Bob who lived around the corner from my mum's old house in Gloucester, and Calypso was the issue from a fling with Norman during her "ganja and dreadlock" era. Norm had returned to live in Trinidad and Cal had sensibly joined her dad. My mother, currently sunning herself with a new man called Ron in Margate, would not find it in her to condemn Archie, who she'd always loved for his looks but thought was "a bit of a knob."

"Grace is right," Archie said. That was the other thing about Archie. He never referred to me as Mum. From when Tara was small, he'd encouraged her to call us by our Christian names. To his dismay, it had never caught on, mainly because I'd done all in my power to subvert it. Tara needed parents, not best mates. "It might even work out for the good of us all," he said.

My jaw fell slack. How could he possibly see an upside for us?

"In what way?" Tara said tentatively. I noted that some of the heat had died down. Her body was more relaxed, less like she'd been soaked in saltwater and left to dry out in the sun. Archie, damn him, had piqued her curiosity. Next he would beguile her as he'd once beguiled me.

"For a start, you could spend part of the week with us."

I blinked. *Us* meant Archie and me, not Kristina and him. I opened my mouth to protest, but Tara sniffed at the bait.

"Where exactly?"

"At Kristina's home. You could have your own room."

"Now, hold—"

Tara cut me off. "How big is it?"

"A double with its own bathroom."

I gaped. I'd always longed for an en suite. Our bathroom was downstairs and off the small utility. Tara shivered with delight next to me. Archie was shamelessly courting her and she was seduced.

"Won't Kristina have something to say? You can't make that kind of decision. It's not your house." I hated the tone of my voice, which was preachy and critical, not like me at all.

"It's already been discussed." I thought he was bluffing, but Archie spoke in such a dismissive, matter-of-fact way that I knew I was snookered. I wanted to pursue it, but Tara pitched in.

"Would my friends be able to sleep over?"

Archie beamed, glad no doubt to be out of isolation and back in the rehabilitation ward. "Of course."

Someone had inserted chipped ice into my blood. Our house was tiny. It had never been conducive for more than three people. Kristina ran an interior design business from her home on the hill. I'd heard from others that it was vast, a showcase home, swags and Travertine flooring, underground heating, and a kitchen in which you could hold a cabinet meeting. Horribly, I realised that Tara and Archie were involved in high-level domestic negotiations.

And they didn't involve me.

Tara glanced sideways, visibly perked up, and grinned. Her eyes shone with sudden excitement, as they had when she was little. Then the object of her enthusiasm would be a new bike or an invitation to a party, not a change of lifestyle and a new bloody bedroom. "Wait till I tell Thea and Amy," she bubbled. A mean bit of me cursed my daughter for being so easily bought.

"I think we need to slow this right down," I said, mainly because everything and everyone was sprinting away from me. I'd lost Archie. I could not, would not, lose Tara.

"Sure," Archie said, impossibly laid-back, "but I think we all agree that we can work it out."

I'm not very good at being nasty, but I hurled my best *drop dead* stare at Archie, who was oblivious, it seemed, to what he was demanding of me. Did he really believe that he could trade me in for another and keep the comforts and advantages of his previous existence? I blanched at the thought of Tara used as a pawn in a tug of love between us. Maybe I should do them all a favour and walk under one of the Goldline buses that regularly ran from Cheltenham to Gloucester. Tiff's voice rang in my ear: *Don't be such a frigging drama queen.*

"Right," Archie said, slapping his thighs and standing up, job done. "Fancy a Coke, Tara?"

I frowned big-time. We never kept cola in the house. What had come over Archie? Even in small ways, he'd changed over the past twelve months. I could see it now. Six months ago I began to seriously suspect. A month on, I knew. Even then I thought we'd work it out, but every conversation took a circular route in which Archie insisted separation was the only option. Must be Kristina's poisonous influence. I should have spotted the signs a long time ago. What really rankled, he was treating his declaration as though it was cause for celebration. *Let's crack open the champagne, why don't we?* And Tara had bought it.

"Mum?"

I looked up at her in confusion. To her credit, the shine had worn off a little. She looked less buoyant, more small sailing boat and less ocean-going liner. Pathetically grateful, my eyes filled with tears. She crouched down in front of me, her limbs so lithe and flexible, and took both my hands in hers. A dark curl fell across her face, a vision of blossoming beauty. My heart ached and tore.

"It will be all right," she said, coaxing and trying to cheer me up. And then she broke into an enchanting smile, almost mischievous.

"What?" I said, forcing myself to reciprocate.

"Life is random." Her favourite phrase, she'd often tease me with it.

It certainly seemed that way. Never in a million years had I ever thought I'd be a divorce statistic. Not severed from Archie, from us, from our lovely life together. I squeezed her hand and said the first thing that was in my heart and on my mind.

"I love you."

"I love you, too, Mum."

In that brief moment of time, I felt okay.

"And besides," Tara said, still with the playful expression, "it could be worse. Nobody died."

I didn't know why, but cold sweat exploded over my body. Fear squatted deep within. It was as if someone had opened the door wide and summer had fled, bleak winter sweeping in.

Two

Four years later

"Do you find the defendant, Jordan Dukes, guilty or not guilty of the murder of Tara Reeves Neville?"

"Guilty."

"Is that the verdict of you all?"

"Yes."

"Thank Christ for that." Tiff closed her pudgy hand over mine and squeezed. "At last the little snail-brained shit will get what he deserves. It's over, Grace."

How could it ever be over? The best part of a year ago I'd entered the death zone. There was no chance I'd ever find my way out.

I stared straight ahead at Tara's boyfriend in the dock. Dressed in a suit with a white shirt and tie, he looked more grown up than his nineteen years. On the three occasions I'd seen him, he was dressed in jeans and a T-shirt, usually with something offensive and challenging emblazoned across the front. Straightaway when Tara first brought him home, I understood her attraction to him. It wasn't the tattoos or the smooth, pale coffee–coloured skin or eyes that were more black than brown or the rather delicate features. It was his swagger and style, his quick wit—in spite of Tiff's remark—and the way he had a cheeky answer for everything. I still found it incredible to think that he had plunged a knife into my daughter's heart and left her for dead.

I came to as the judge thanked the jury for their speedy two-hour delivery, then dismissed and adjourned the court. Without an appeal, he warned that sentencing would be carried out that afternoon. It would go badly for Jordan. Having put in a plea of innocence at the outset, he'd shown no remorse and stayed improbably silent throughout the entire nine-day trial. Even his own defence team had labelled him a pathological liar. I noted this with detachment, in the same way I noticed the wood panelling, the dark robes and wigs, the fusty smell of dust and old books and dry "courtly" air. I wasn't sorry for Jordan. I was sorry for me, for the way grief had doubled me up and bent me out of shape. I was sorry for Tara, for smashed dreams and hopes and a life extinguished, and for Archie, grey and drawn, seated less than a metre from me. I hoped I'd done justice to our agony in the victim impact statement set before the court. I must have written it a dozen times. The final version still didn't express or convey the magnitude of our loss. A helpless part of me wondered whether it would even make a difference.

Tiff tugged at my sleeve. "Come on, let's get a drink."

I nodded absently. Drinking too much, I promised myself that I'd get it under control. Soon. After the funeral, I'd said, but that milestone had already passed. Next I vowed to pack it in when I returned full-time to work, but the stress of functioning and talking to others had made me seek solace in the bottle all the more. Lately I'd told myself that I'd stop when I could prevent myself from bursting into furious tears and crying and crying and crying. I'd stop when I could bear to feel the heat of the sun on my face and smile without feeling guilty.

No chance.

I got up and shuffled sideways and felt a set of eyes fasten onto mine. I looked and saw a man who'd sat through every day of the trial. Pitched forward, intent, lean with misery, he had short, close-cropped blond hair flecked with grey, astonishingly brown eyes and skin burnished permanently by the sun. Not because he spent time in foreign climates, but because he worked outside in England's green and pleasant air. Nobody told me who he was, but I'd worked it out. *My dad's a builder,* Jordan had mentioned once when life was good and uncontaminated by murder and grief and interminable pain.

"Come on, Grace," Tiff nagged. Four years younger than me, the same age as Kristina, Tiff was more like an elder sister. Born bossy, she had challenging hooded eyes, like her dad; a light-olive, slightly weathered, porous complexion; a wide nose; and, as I often reminded her, a big mouth. Not that she gave a damn. "By the time we get out of here," she complained, "it will be time to come back."

"Right, sorry."

By now we were at the back of the court. I didn't remember getting there. The family liaison officer, a stolid woman with curly rust-coloured hair and protruding front teeth, exchanged a few words with me, but I couldn't tell you what she said or what I said back. It was as if I were entirely absent from what was going on around me.

Through the fog of my own private grief, Detective Inspector Dunne, the senior investigating officer, emerged. Deep in conversation with a court official, he looked across at me and mouthed *Good result.* I winched a smile onto my lips, turned away, and sought out my mother, who was milling about with her latest squeeze, a big bloke called Doug who had dodgy dealings in scrap metal and, I suspected, stuff that fell off the back of a lorry. He hailed from West Bromwich in the Midlands but had a holiday home in Spain from which they'd flown for the trial.

Graham, Tiff's on/off boyfriend was already slipping out a packet of cigarettes, desperate to get out into the open. "Taken the day off from the fish stall at the market especially," he muttered as I stumbled past. Of Archie, there was no sign. Probably lurking round a corner with Kristina. According to Archie, she'd taken Tara's death and the ensuing police investigation badly. Was there any other way she could take it? I'd asked testily. He'd opened his mouth to elaborate a defence and, uncharacteristically, I'd cut him off before a word formed itself in his voice box let alone passed through his lips.

Welcome to the new me: mean, can't be bothered, what's the point?

We tramped outside into a bright cold day. To be honest, every day had been cold and hard since Tara's death. I couldn't see that ever changing, for when your child dies, hope and reason for living die, too. My life had become an unbearable mess in the last eight months, punctuated by random and unpredictable bouts of weeping.

I felt a hand grab mine. It was my mother, big hair stiff with hairspray so dense it made you sneeze if you got up close, pastel eyeshadow on her lids, red lips, and pencilled eyebrows that always made her look surprised. At least her hair was coloured professionally nowadays. As a child, when we were hard up, she'd been known to resort to shoe polish to cover the grey. She had a thing for make-up and what she called serviceable clothes. Today she wore a dark navy suit teamed with a frothy, fuchsia-coloured blouse that had weird ruffles at the neck. In what I could only describe as a pincer movement, Doug slipped into step on the other side of me. His big camel overcoat with velvet collar gave him an odd air of respectability that didn't sit particularly well on his thickset shoulders. He had a penchant for gold bracelets, necklaces and chunky rings. Underneath the bling he sported a number of tattoos. A rough diamond was how my mother regarded him. I privately thought him heavier on the rough than sparkly gem. Nevertheless, it was nice to have a big bloke batting for me. Doug had a unique aura that made other men think twice before approaching him. At sixty-eight years of age, he'd still be pretty good in a fistfight, I reckoned. I never used to think like this, but sudden, violent death had changed me and every belief I'd ever held. I could no longer tell what exactly life might strike me with next.

Did it really matter, I wondered? What could be worse than this?

"You all right, chick?" Mum said as we walked, or rather hobbled, side by side. I'd had to slow down because Mum was wearing impossibly high heels that caught on the uneven pavement.

"'Course she is, Doll." Doll was not Doug's pet name for my mum. She'd been christened Dolly Saunders. Rumour had it that she was a beautiful baby, like a doll, hence the name. Wasn't neuroscience.

I thought it best to say nothing. I was not all right. I would never be all right. Since the day I received twelve missed calls on my mobile, how could I ever attain that unassuming, go-along to get-along, almost karmic state that most people take for granted? My daughter's death date would be forever imprinted on my heart as surely as her date of birth.

Again my habit of tuning out ensured I remembered nothing of the journey to the pub in Westgate. Graham held the door as we all trooped in. As I passed him I caught a heady whiff of haddock and nicotine.

"So what will you all be having?" Doug said expansively, a thick chain bracelet jangling on his wrist as we pitched up at the bar. "Gracie, love?"

13

"Tonic water," I said.

"Tonic water," Doug repeated to the barman. "With a gin in it."

"I don't like gin," I protested.

"Make that vodka," Doug corrected. I didn't have the strength to argue and drifted away to find a seat in an area that looked as if it were set to serve school dinners. Graham pulled up a chair next to mine. Sharp-featured, his thin sandy hair clung to his skull for dear life. It sounds like someone trying to be funny, but his best features were his ears, which were small and pixie-like. Graham clearly concurred, because each lobe had several piercings to better display a selection of hoops and studs. Now I came to think of it, I was the odd one out in my choice of men. Archie wouldn't have been seen dead with an earring or a bracelet. He'd never even worn a wedding ring. Maybe he should have done.

"All right?" Graham said.

I wished I could have had a quid for every time someone asked me that. I nodded, feeling a familiar tug in my chest that told me my body begged to differ.

"Nearly over now," he said, twirling an unlit cigarette between his fingers. I nodded again. He looked relieved that I'd agreed with him, probably because I made a nice change from Tiff, whose purpose in life was to argue. Graham turned his attention to my mother, who'd scraped back a chair to join us. "You all right, Doll? Nice holiday?"

"Lovely, Gray," she said, using Graham's annoying nickname. *Gray* could just as easily refer to Grace. I started every time I heard it.

"Bostin," Doug said, a term meaning "brilliant" in both Birmingham and the Black Country. I was fluent in the lingo because our family had spent my formative years in Oldbury in the West Midlands before we'd moved with Bob, Tiff's dad, to Gloucester when I was ten. We always knew when my mum had had too much to drink because she'd revert.

Used to crack me up.

Would I ever experience spontaneous laughter ever again?

The barman staggered over with our order: pints for Doug and Graham, G&Ts for Tiff and my mum, and vodka and tonic, whether I liked it or not, for me.

Graham struck up a hesitant conversation with Doug, who fell in although I could tell he had his mind on other matters, plotting his next "bit of business," probably.

"Room for one more?" Tiff said, squashing her stocky frame in between Mum and me.

"Ouch!" I let out.

"Jeez, Gracie, I barely touched you."

"You dug into me with your elbow." My sister worked at a riding school and spent her entire day mucking out and exercising other people's hacks. People who "had too much money for their own good," according to her. Consequently, she had muscles like pile drivers.

"Need more meat on those bones, Gracie," Mum said. She sounded disapproving, but I knew that this was only because she worried about me. I'd lost a staggering amount of weight since Tara's death.

"Yeah," Tiff said. "We'll need to walk around with magnifying glasses if you get any thinner."

I didn't comment and sipped my drink. Unable to eat breakfast that morning, I felt the lovely warm fizz and glow that only hard spirits on an empty stomach can produce. I'd pay for it later.

"So what do you reckon? Life sentence?" Tiff said.

Graham took a decent swig of his beer and wiped the foam away with the back of his hand. "Bound to be."

"No *bound to be* about it. Depends on whether the judge is one of those soft liberal bastards," Tiff said.

"Are you out of your tree?" Doug said. "Judges are not put on this earth to be soft, only to be arseholes." The way he said it gave me the impression that Doug knew, from personal experience, what he was talking about.

"Whatever happens, it won't bring back Tara," I murmured. Hot tears pricked my eyes. Oh God, here I go, I thought, all kinds of vile feelings swelling inside me.

Mum reached behind Tiff and rested her small hand on my shoulder. "You're right there, lovey," she said softly. "We all know that."

Noise at the other end of the bar made me bat away a stray tear and swivel round. I wasn't the only one.

"Well, what do you know, the harpy from Harp Hill," Tiff muttered in my ear.

I wasn't looking at Kristina. I was looking at Archie, whose pale face and shattered eyes said it all. Like a couple of cowherds, they'd done the equivalent of entering hostile Native Indian territory and discovering that the Sioux were having a powwow. What to do? Sound the retreat or front it out? I caught his eye, forced a smile, and nodded. He smiled back and took a step forward despite the fact that Kristina was doing her best to drag him back out into open country.

As I made to get up, Tiff clamped her hand on my coat sleeve. "What the hell are you doing?"

"I'm going to talk to Archie."

"Why?"

Because he looks like he could do with a hug, because he's in pain, because he's as lost and desolate as me. I knew what Tiff was thinking because she'd been vocal on the subject: *None of this would have happened if he hadn't run off with that stuck-up tart.*

There was no point in arguing with Tiff. I'd only come off worse. "Won't be a sec."

"Well, don't be long," Tiff grumped.

Automatically, Kristina inserted herself between Archie and me. God alone knew why. With her long blonde hair, effortless beauty, and slim figure undisturbed by childbirth, I posed no threat to her. She reminded me physically of one of those floaty women you see in paintings by Botticelli. If this weren't enough, she wore her smooth sophistication with the same ease as her killer heels. Coming from good breeding and money, Kristina knew how to behave. Her culture was absorbed, probably from her mother's amniotic fluid; mine was studied and learnt. In this regard, Archie was like me, although his societal transition had been from the opposite direction. Not long before we met he'd had an enormous row with his mind-blowingly wealthy parents, who owned a boatbuilding company in the New Forest. He'd walked out, been disinherited, never to return. Aside from his sheer physicality, it was one of the things for which I'd loved him—for making a stand, for not being trapped by the accident of his birth. I always suspected that, somewhere along his family line, there had been the odd duke or prince. Maybe that's what he and Kristina saw in each other. Maybe that's why they'd meshed. People tend to gravitate to their own kind. I'd always been an impostor.

"Hello, Kristina," I said.

"Hi, we were looking for somewhere to have a break, but there probably isn't time now."

"I think you'll be okay." I looked at Archie. "We're not due back for another forty minutes. You know what judges are like. Long lunches and all that." Aware I was gabbling, I forced a tight laugh that stuck like a crunchy piece of gravel in the back of my throat.

"Yeah," Archie agreed with warmth I hadn't seen in ages. "Get you a drink?" I looked back, gestured that I already had one. "Krissie, order me a Scotch, would you, darling? I want to have a quiet word with Grace."

Kristina's dark blue eyes turned a shade lighter. Her mouth tensed and tightened. Unforgivably, I was pleased, thrilled even. Whatever else Kristina had going with Archie, this was not her territory. It didn't matter how much she and Archie jogged together and did posy press-ups and bend stretches in the park, or declared their loved-upness in public. Tara had been *our* bundle of love, *our* child, *our* daughter.

I moved away a little. Archie kept his voice low, his look furtive. "How are you doing?"

"Okay," I lied. "You?"

He shrugged. "You're awfully thin, Grace." A little downturned at the edges, his eyes drooped with concern.

"So everyone keeps telling me."

"I worry about you."

I felt giddy. Archie had an intense way about him. It was the first thing I spotted when we'd met at a party in London, where I'd been studying for my degree at Goldsmiths. Archie, a nurse, was based at St. Thomas's Hospital. When he spoke to me, it was as if I were the only other person in the room. It used to make me feel so cherished and loved. Some nuance in his expression now reminded me of Tara. My nose prickled, a prelude to tears that I did my level best to head off.

"Think Dukes will go down for a long time?" he said.

"Certain of it." I'd feverishly trawled the Internet and compared similar cases to find out what the likely sentence might be. The closest I'd got was a young man sentenced to twenty-four years for stabbing to death his girlfriend in a hairdressing salon in front of her clients. Lots of witnesses and he'd openly brandished the weapon. Nothing like what had happened to Tara. There were no witnesses and the weapon had never been found.

And, oh yes, I'd done my homework on Dukes. A member of the notorious Stringers gang based in Gloucester (their soubriquet earned because of the type of thin vests worn come rain or shine, and more commonly seen as the must-have gym item), Jordan had a reputation for being short-fused although I'd never witnessed it. It was always *Mrs. Neville* and *please and thank you*. One of his mates, I discovered, had been jailed for life for possession of a loaded pistol. Another had been found to have two thousand pounds worth of crack cocaine stashed in his home. Not that the jury would be told about the company Jordan Dukes kept. Early on I'd worried that circumstantial evidence would not be enough to convict him, but DI Dunne, a man with a forehead like the Grand Canyon and a nose you could ski off, had put me straight. *Dukes's DNA was found at the crime scene, his fingerprints fits a bruise on Tara's arm. He changed his statement twice. A knife, pretty much identical to the blade used to kill Tara, was discovered hidden under a floorboard. That little lot should be enough to persuade a jury.*

I reminded Archie of this again.

"That's good. Good," Archie repeated, wan and listless. Not that it made him any less attractive, I thought, as I looked into his gorgeous, mesmerising eyes. Prior to Tara's death, we'd had a reason to stay in touch and it pleased me. If I were honest, and silly as it was, I thought there was a chance that we would get back together. Throughout the past long months, Archie and I had maintained close contact by phone and occasionally in person when planning the funeral. We'd sometimes compare notes, usually on our experiences with the police. Once sentence had been passed, all that would cease. A bubble of panic rose up inside my chest. Would Archie miss the connection as much as me?

"And afterwards?" he said.

I frowned. There was no afterwards.

"We're taking a short luxury break. You should do the same."

I opened my mouth to say that a) I couldn't afford it, and b) Where would I go on my tod?

"If money is an issue ... "

"It's not." I still had some pride. "Thank you." I smiled quickly. "It's kind of you."

"Are you sure I can't persuade you to change your mind?" Archie wore his *sweet little boy, nobody can put a dent in me* smile. It reminded me of the first time he'd invited me to go back to his place. At first, I'd declined. Then ...

I dug my fingernails into the soft palms of my hands. "No, I'll be fine. You'll see."

A great gale of laughter erupted behind me. Archie glanced over my shoulder. "Your family," he chuckled. The one that welcomed you with open arms, the one that treated you like a son because you had no family of your own, a little voice inside my head whispered. "Some things never change," he added. I tried to laugh with him, but it wouldn't come. A shadow fell over us. Archie darted an anxious look in Kristina's direction.

"Was there something else?" I said.

"Erm ... yeah." He cast a quick glance over his shoulder, opened his mouth and closed it again.

"Spit it out," I said with a jittery laugh.

"No, it's fine," he said, snatching a smile.

"Archie, you can't just—"

"Really," he said, his smile wider than wide now. "Nothing, me being silly, really."

"But if—"

"God, how long does it take to get served around here?" Kristina bore down on the pair of us like a drone primed to hit a target. "I suppose that's Gloucester for you."

I bit my tongue. My mum had taught me well: only pick fights worth expending energy on. "Right then, have a good break if I don't see you after the hearing."

"We're only going for the weekend," Archie said, a bit defensively, I thought.

"A long weekend," Kristina said emphatically. "You really should follow our lead, Grace."

I hate the word *should*, which probably explained why I said what I did. "Actually, I'm going back to work tomorrow."

"On a Friday?"

"No point moping around. Take care of yourself, Archie," I said, squeezing his arm.

He issued another flat smile, but his eyes said *we need to talk.*

"We're so looking forward to it, aren't we, Archie?" Kristina's tone was brittle, bright, and barbed. "I've booked in lots of spa treatments, hot stones, and aromatherapy. You should try it some time."

"I'll think about it," I said. "Good. Great."

Archie looked at me once more in silent communication. We'd both been drowning since Tara's death, but he suddenly looked like a man who had been pushed into the Hoover Dam. Wondering what he'd really wanted to say, I backed away and joined the others.

Three

Jordan Dukes was sentenced to a minimum of eighteen years. For the first time in two weeks, I saw a reaction in his eyes: numb disbelief. So now we were on the same page, I thought grimly.

Predictably, Graham and Tiff didn't think the sentence stiff enough. "Life should mean life," Tiff sniffed. "Lock them up and throw away the key." Doug, I noticed, was strangely quiet on the subject. Me, I didn't feel the sense of triumph and closure I'd hoped for. A brief exchange of looks with Archie told me he felt the same. I hoped he might talk to me once more, but Kristina, all business, quickly spirited him away.

Against my better judgment, I returned to my mum's, a swish four-bedroom bungalow fourteen minutes out of Gloucester. Doug had paid $460k cash for it, she'd told me in a gushing moment. The cherry on top was the fact that it had a double garage (even though she didn't drive), a Sky Satellite dish, three bathrooms, four lavatories, and a conservatory. I couldn't blame her pride. Falling on her feet had been a long time coming. For years we'd lived in one cramped dwelling after another, depending on whom she was sharing a bed with at the time. God alone knew how I, "the clever one," as Tiff constantly reminded me, had managed to stay in one place long enough to receive any education, never mind absorb it. Out of our little band, I'd been the only Saunders to go to university. I'll never forget my mother's joy and the shine in her eyes at what she regarded as the pinnacle of her achievements.

The gathering at the bungalow took on the air of a wake. Aunts, uncles, neighbours, and extended family in the form of relatives and friends of lovers—my mother had a habit of keeping cordial relations years after a relationship had faded or she'd moved on—congregated to express their satisfaction at the outcome. Only Bob, Tiffany's dad, a bear of a man not too dissimilar to Doug in appearance, came straight over, wrapped his arms around me, and enveloped me in a massive hug to the point that I thought I might lose it. At Tara's funeral, an event so surreal I'd floated above the surface of the entire proceedings, he'd done exactly the same, and I had.

Calypso called from Trinidad and sent me "big love and hugs." I stayed for a couple of hours, made polite conversation, stuck to orange juice only because I was driving and, when somebody put on a CD, murmured in Mum's ear that I was off. She slipped her arm through mine and drew me close.

"You can always stay. Tiff won't mind." Tiff spent more time at my mum's than she did at Graham's. "You know you'd be welcome. Might do you good."

I patted her hand. "I'll be all right. Promise."

She threw me a look that said she didn't believe me. Recognising the streak of stubborn that ran through my veins, she wisely didn't argue. "All right. You'll phone the land line when you get back?"

I knew text messaging to be a waste of time. My mum was pathologically immune to technology and rarely switched on the mobile phone Tiff and I had bought for her. I promised that I would.

It took me over forty minutes to extricate myself. Tiff was the last to say good-bye.

"Now don't you be locking yourself away," she said squarely. The thing I hated most about Tiff were the things I also loved about her: her honesty and directness, oh, and her laugh, which was the filthiest on the planet. Tara had loved Auntie Tiff like no other, even when Tiff had given her a hard time about taking up with Jordan Dukes. How I wished now that Tara had taken her aunt's advice.

Tiff was still lecturing me. "Remember, if you do, I'll come looking for you to winkle you out." And I knew she meant it. At my darkest hour, when I couldn't communicate with anyone, Tiff had virtually broken into my apartment to rescue me. Since then, she'd had a key "just in case," although in case of what we never discussed. "It's high time you got your mojo back."

Others would have been horrified by her blunt approach. Not me. This was my sister and I knew she loved me, maybe even more so than my mother.

"And for God's sake, do something about your hair."

"Coming from the style queen of the stable, that's rich." Tiff's dark hair was cut by none other than herself, with unpredictable results.

She waggled a finger at me. "You know what I mean." I did. I had a mop of ash-blonde and used to sport a choppy bed-head look, the hairstyle equivalent of ripped jeans. It had complemented my Bohemian taste in clothes. Now it was mid-length, unstyled, unhighlighted and middle-aged. I'm quite tall and had a thing for soft scarves and long, flowing numbers. Fine when I was younger, but now I wasn't certain, less certain about everything in general.

"And Mum's right. You could do with carrying more timber. You used to have such a lovely curvy figure."

"Now you're starting to worry me."

"Fuck off."

I hugged her and, several inches taller, ruffled her hair, which I knew would piss her off.

"Remember what I said," I heard her say as I sped down the drive.

———

I was back in Cheltenham by nightfall and managed to squiggle my second-hand Mini into the only parking space a couple of streets away from where I lived in a garden apartment in Lansdown. I'd moved there with Tara twelve months after Archie moved out. If you have to make hard choices, there has to be a major, overriding advantage and, to our minds, there were many. A triumph of style over substance, impractical, ridiculously small with nowhere to park, the flat was perfect and we'd fallen in love with it on sight, a bit like I'd done with Archie. Immediately I was reminded of his odd behaviour in the pub. Was I reading too much into it? Weren't we all entitled to be a little strange in the circumstances?

A flight of stone steps took you down to a small courtyard and impossibly high walls that seemed to reach up to the heavens. Our place, with its churchy windows and hidden corners, had the timeless feel of cloisters. The best thing about it was that, once inside, you felt safe, as if you were unassailable. Even when the unthinkable happened, my home had never let me down. I'd grieved in it, got drunk in it, howled and cursed in it. Serene and calm, it had listened to me, never judging, constant, like the best friend you could ever have. And it was filled with my beautiful things, a small Nic Joly piece that I'd saved up for as a housewarming present to myself, the Lenkiewicz limited-edition print Archie bought me in an extravagant gesture when Tara was born, loads of books on painters and painting, and Tara's collection of vintage teen magazines, mainly American.

I let myself inside, closed the door behind me, and leant back against the solid oak. I longed for cool air to touch my skin and seep into my bones. I wanted to let my heart rate settle. Instead, I ached with a deep nagging pain that I knew would never leave me, a hurt that reached into the core of my being, like an aggressive cancer that held my entire body for ransom with no demand for payment. As I closed my eyes, I pictured Tara as a toddler, as a little girl, as young woman, and felt the sheer pointlessness of my life without her. I wished I'd gone properly insane, not this weird, unpredictable flitting in and out of madness followed by bouts of extreme, unvarnished lucidity. It would have been easier.

Shaking myself out of self-pity, Archie's face drifted in front of mine. I recognised every expression, every facet, whether he was sad, ecstatic, turned on, silly, or playful. Like me, he was slow to anger. I'd known him as boy and man. Which was why I knew something was up, something he wanted to tell me and didn't want Kristina to know.

Something bad.

Uneasily I wondered what the hell that was.

Four

Some time later, I slipped off my coat and shoes and whacked up the heating. The big disadvantage of losing weight was my tendency to feel the cold more keenly, but at least my little home was easy and cheap to heat. Deciding to change into a pair of cosy pyjamas, I stripped and briefly surveyed my naked reflection in the mirror. My body didn't really look like mine anymore. My collarbone jutted out and my sternum and ribs were visible beneath the skin. My tummy, once softened and rounded by pregnancy, was almost concave, and my thighs were slimmer than they'd been when I was seventeen. Without muscle tone, my sudden weight loss didn't suit my build. Archie once told me that I had Nordic looks. I could see what he meant. I was quite even-featured and my forehead was wide, with few lines, my skin fine and fresh despite the wasting away I felt beneath. I'd seen photographs of my dad and I looked a lot like him. My mum always reckoned he was the best-looking of all her conquests. I pulled a grin, noticed how the bridge of my nose wrinkled up into lots of little creases. Lines at the corners of my blue eyes deepened and my cheekbones were sharper, more pronounced. My teeth were pretty good and, as I relaxed into a false smile, I thought, yes, I could look warm and friendly and approachable.

I slipped into my pyjamas, remembered to call home, and spoke briefly to my mum, who I could tell was borderline tipsy.

"I love you, Gracie, you know that, don't you?"

"Yes, Mum."

"Now you take care of yourself. You know where we are. Anything you want, you only have to ask."

I smiled sadly.

"Did you hear me, Gracie?"

"Yes, Mum. Thanks," I said through a voice thick with anguish.

Afterwards, I wandered into the galley kitchen, where I took a glass from the cupboard, resisted Mr. Russian Standard, and settled for milk. Sipping it carefully, I opened the door to Tara's bedroom and crept inside.

I felt exactly the same as the first time I'd entered after her death: as desperate as a woman who knew her prayers could never be answered. Would I ever feel otherwise?

As part of the investigation, the police had gone through my daughter's stuff, taken her computer away, and searched for evidence. Routine, they'd said. Grave robbers, I'd thought, and hated them for it. Since then, I'd put her things meticulously back where they belonged, her shoes in three neat rows—flats, sneakers, and trainers at the front; high heels and party shoes in the middle; boots at the back. I'd tease her that she had more shoes than Russell & Bromley. There was a single rack on which hung five pairs of jeans and a dozen summer dresses. Her perfume, Light Blue by Dolce & Gabbana, remained on her bedside table alongside a collection of nail varnishes in shades of black and blue and indigo, together with assorted items of makeup. A fan of chick-lit, she'd been reading Sophie Kinsella's *Can You Keep a Secret?* at the time, the bookmark still in place on page 248. Beside the table were her school bag and bag containing a new swimsuit that she had never worn for a holiday she would never go on. A box underneath her bed contained her favourite childhood toys, a Zhu Zhu pet—a kind of digitised hamster—and her Crayola Girlfitti set with which she'd played for hours when she was little. A thin IKEA storage unit housed her massive collection of CDs and reflected her changing and evolving musical tastes. I half smiled at the memory of her sitting me down and, in excited tones, telling me to listen to her latest music fad. It was rap, and I'd nodded and clicked my fingers and pretended to like it because I knew that Kristina, much younger than me in outlook and opinion, would not only rave about it but would understand it, too.

I'd dusted and swung a vacuum cleaner around Tara's room every week since her death. Obsessively, I'd changed the linen on her bed even though she was asleep somewhere else, far away and out of sight. When I'd told Tiff this, she stared at me as if I'd lost the plot and, ever practical, advised me to turn Tara's room into a study or a second sitting room, but I couldn't. Not yet, no more than I could imagine my daughter rotting in the distended earth, her bones silvered by decomposition and decay, crumbling away to nothing.

Shakily, I put the glass down and sat on Tara's bed. A montage of photographs covered most of the facing wall. Among shots of Tara and her friends, some were of me, some of Archie, several with the three of us together. There were no pictures of Kristina, for which I was glad, although, like it or not, Tara had always got on well with her. *She's such a laugh*, she used to say. It had driven me crazy and I'd often tortured myself with the thought that Tara kept photographs of Kristina in her other bedroom at her other house. Lots of outdoor shots with Kristina sunning herself in the massive garden, or interior photographs of "the girls cooking together." No doubt if I'd had a range cooker the size of Birmingham I'd have been caught on camera, too.

My favourite snap was one Archie had taken when Tara was fourteen. She had large hoop earrings in her newly pierced ears (an issue we'd argued long and hard about). Dark hair swept back from her face, a couple of strands escaping carelessly from a left-side parting. She must have nicked my lipstick because she normally wore neutral lip-gloss and here her lips were the deepest shade of pink. She wore her favourite jacket, pale blue, padded with two button-down pockets and a furry collar. But these were only trappings. With her head tipped lightly to one side, her brown eyes sultry and half closed, as if she were focusing on something else, it was possible to glimpse the blossoming woman inside the girl. Full of possibility and promise and…

Oh my God.

I crumpled onto her bed, stretched out, feeling my bones crack, and buried my face in covers that no longer smelt of earth and fire and song, and had long ceased to remind me of my daughter. Instead they were redolent of Archie and my mind helplessly hooked on his betrayal. Tiff had not been so far off the mark. Maybe if he hadn't deserted us, Tara might not have taken up with Jordan Dukes.

Screwing my eyes up tight, I tried to obliterate the thought. No good would come of thinking like that. Blame was such a pointless emotion.

I wasn't sure how long I stayed there. Could have been minutes, could have been much longer. When truly bad things happen, hours,

30

days, and weeks have no meaning. You don't eat. You barely sleep. When you do, it's patchy and inadequate at best; at worst, crammed with horrible visions, terror, and screaming. I'd often fall asleep for a few minutes, jolt awake, remember it all again and weep until, exhausted, I'd fall asleep, only to repeat the process like some mythological figure punished and in torment for eternity. You quickly discover that chronic fear is not sharp-edged or smothering. It burns and engulfs and incinerates you from the inside out. It withers, rots, and reduces you to a nothing. It's also soft, creepy, and insidious, like a sadistic lover's embrace. My lover assailed me now. For the millionth time I thought of Tara's shock, fear, and pain as the tip of the knife pierced first her clothing, then her skin, and then her heart.

What does that feel like?

Do you feel pain before terror, or terror before pain?

Hot tears blistered my eyes, springing into the corners, travelling down my cheeks like tributaries of a river and trickling underneath my chin. I sobbed as uncontrollably as when I'd first heard the news and my heart shattered.

Five

―――――――――――――――――――――――――――

"*K*ristina says I can have a party at her house."

Tiff stiffened and I did a double take. It would have been comical had I not been so horrified. I also noted that her house took precedence over their house.

"Well, we can hardly have one here," Tara said in response to my expression, which was gob-smacked meets freaked out.

"I could hire somewhere," I said, trying to tamp down the anxiety in my voice, "a village hall, or something." I was so sick of hearing about the big house at Harp Hill with its en suite bathrooms, offices on the top floor, and bloody great gardens.

"Yeah, right," Tara said, clearly unimpressed.

"No need to be like that, Tara," Tiff said, wading in. "Your mother's only doing her best."

I glanced gratefully at Tiff, my secret weapon to be wheeled out as backup when the need arose. Trouble was, as soon as Tiff exited, things between Tara and me often disintegrated.

Tara flushed and chewed her lip. "I know," she said quietly, sloping off to her room. "Soz," she added, her shorthand version of sorry.

"I'll put the kettle on." This was Tiff's prelude for straight talking. Tea made, she launched in.

"You've got to learn how to play this better. Don't try to compete. If Miss Posh-chops wants to throw a party for our kid, then let her."

"But—"

"I know it's hard, Gracie," she said, clamping one hot hand over mine, "but you've got to put Tara first."

"I am putting Tara first. I don't want some rich bitch up the road buying my daughter's affection with cheap gestures and gifts."

"Cheap?"

"Well, flipping expensive."

"Not that old record," she exploded.

I pitched forward and ran my fingers through my hair, which was as knotty as I felt inside. "Am I the only one who sees it, or am I delusional?"

"God save us, for someone who's bright, you can be thick as dog shit."

"I don't think—"

"Nobody doubts Kristina's agenda. I've only got two GCSEs, not a frigging degree in Art History, but even I can see that. It's textbook stuff straight out of the evil stepmother files."

I pulled a face. "I wish you wouldn't refer to her like that."

"Why not? It's true." As they weren't married, stepmother was entirely inaccurate but I didn't argue the point. "You know what your problem is?"

I sighed.

"You're too nice. You want everyone to like you, so you roll over like a puppy. Not everyone is going to tickle your tummy, Gracie, and especially not the Wicked Witch of the West."

I smirked and then laughed.

"Better," Tiff said with a grin. "'For Chrissakes, loosen up. You're involved in open warfare and you've got to put your smart hat on, not one of those horrible flowerpot things you usually wear on your head."

"It's called a cloche, you muppet."

"A cloche is something you put over outdoor plants. Tara loves you," Tiff motored on. "She's doing what kids do: going after the main chance. She's no fool and she's got more sense than you and Archie put together. Let her have her party and anything else she can grab with both hands. She'll soon see what Kristina's really made of and then she'll realise which side of her bread's buttered."

"Jesus, Tiff, you sound like Mum." Our mum's platitudes and trite little homilies that meant bugger all in the real world were legendary.

Tiff blew across the surface of her tea and took a slurp.

"What if you're wrong?" I said, careful to avert my gaze. "What if, by letting her go, giving her freedom, Tara thinks I don't care?"

"She won't think like that." I didn't remind Tiff that she had no children of her own. "I know Tara and I know you," she continued, as if she'd read my mind. "Kristina Beaumont will never come between you. Archie would never allow it." She glanced away, took another shallow sip.

"What?" I said.

"It's nothing."

"Rot. Give."

"All right," she said, with a bullish gleam in her eye. " If anyone needs watching, it's Archie."

"Archie?" I burst out, thinking it preposterous.

"Tara has always been a daddy's girl. How do you know he isn't pulling Kristina's strings from the sidelines? How do you know it doesn't suit him for them to be so pally?"

I scoffed, told her Archie didn't have a manipulative bone in his body.

I remembered this the following morning while forcing down a piece of toast. After that particular conversation there had been other obstacles with which to contend—a whole menagerie of ponies, cats and dogs, endless sleepovers with Tara's mates. The "insanely happy era" had lasted over a year.

And then things changed.

I glanced at the clock, dropped the rest of the toast in the bin, bolted down the rest of my orange juice, and cleaned my teeth. The gallery didn't open until ten, but I liked to be there half an hour early to give me enough time to grab a coffee, catch up on what was happening in the art world, and generally settle.

Sweeping up my coat and bag, I headed into town. Michael said I didn't need to go in, but working was better than staring at my own four walls, in spite of feeling mostly comfy and secure inside them.

I set off on my thirteen-minute journey through the streets to the Promenade. A March wind gusted into my eyes. Overhead, the sun was high in a sky with a cloud formation that resembled soapsuds.

They had been great at work. We're a small team. I know that Lexi's mum is recovering from breast cancer, that Vron secretly fancies Seb, who is married to a woman called Arabella who treats him badly. Michael, the gallery's manager, is a keen figurative artist. His lovers are his muses. Consequently, I can never keep up with his private life, although I can usually gauge what's going on depending on how many paintings he has on the go at any one time. Search me how he can hold down a full-time job, but that's Michael. The point is that my work colleagues know how to treat me. They'd seen me through my divorce and now this. What was awkward in the beginning (everyone tiptoeing around me and being too solicitous—I lost count of how many cups of tea and coffee were made and plates of biscuits left on my desk) had reached a quiet level of unspoken understanding. They never asked questions or pried, but they never avoided me either, like some had done, as if what had befallen me was contagious. Bit by bit I'd talked, probably more to them than to my own family. It seemed easier, somehow. I could be the woman I was rather than the woman I had been.

Modern and light, set on three floors, the gallery had a massive glass front in which currently sat a collection of work by Bob Dylan. We did a lot of stuff like that. I'd once had a local artist berate us for it. *Flaming pop stars, they all think they're Renaissance men. They should stick to what they're good at, not ruin it for the rest of us.*

I went inside and straight upstairs. Michael was already at the desk, parked in front of a computer. He didn't seem like an artistic sort, if there was such a category. Slim, urbane, clean-shaven with prematurely grey hair, he had an authoritarian air about him that suggested he might be a high-flying solicitor or barrister and, believe me, I'd studied enough of the breed lately to identify one of those when I saw him.

He looked up with a crooked smile that women found enchanting. "Are you supposed to be here or did I drink too much wine last night?"

"Thought it was better than moping around at home."

"You could go for a walk in the park, read a book…"

"You don't want me?" Please don't do this, I thought. I need to work, to do, to exist, to live. I tried to keep the plea out of my voice. I succeeded because Michael followed it up by arching an eyebrow and pouting his full lips.

"You really expect me to answer that?"

"Easy, tiger." I relaxed, shrugging off my coat. "Coffee?"

"Love some and then we can talk about drumming up interest for the Rayner exhibition."

I slipped into our backroom cum kitchen and storage facility, stowed my bag, and made up a cafetiere using the particular brand Michael insisted upon.

"I've gone through our database of clients I think would be interested," Michael said. "Mainly people who've already bought pieces."

"Shall I do a ring-round?"

"That would be great. Check out the publicity blurb and run the conversation along those lines, you know the drill. Make a note of those who'd be free to attend and then we'll organise invites. Right," he said, slipping out his mobile. "I'm popping downstairs to sort out a little problem."

My turn to arch an eyebrow; Michael's little problems usually involved a woman, occasionally an irate husband.

"Work." He grinned. "Not pleasure, regrettably."

Most people think that working in a gallery is a lovely way to earn a living. Occasionally we get tricky customers. "Something I should know?"

"Only if I need a hand with it." He dithered, made to go, and then turned back. "You all sorted then, Grace?"

"Fine."

"Good."

He dithered a bit more then turned away.

"Michael?"

"Yeah?" he said, spinning round.

"He got eighteen years."

I had the benefit of his full green-eyed gaze. "I'm guessing that's a result." The upward inflexion in his voice let me know that Michael understood that, whatever justice had been done, nothing would bring back Tara.

"The most I could hope for."

"Yes, I see. Is Archie pleased, if that isn't too crass a question?" Michael had always rather liked Archie. I think he was genuinely sorry when we split up.

"I imagine so."

"Give him my best when you see him next."

I paused, wondering for the zillionth time what Archie had wanted to tell me, not sensing but *knowing* that it mattered. "I will, thanks," I said hurriedly.

He did that thing that people do with their faces when they want to reach out but don't quite have the courage to do so. It consists of a quick, thin-lipped grin and a narrowing of the eyes, almost like an *ouch!* A trademark of his style, there's a TV and screen actor, whose name I forget, who adopts it all the time. I'd become as much a specialist in body language as I had in hangovers over the past several months. I flashed a quick reciprocal smile of gratitude, turned back to the list and, under the guise of bracing myself to rejoin the real world, punched in Archie's number on the office phone. As soon as it went to voicemail, I remembered his weekend away with Kristina and hung up.

Twenty minutes later, Michael emerged with a troubled expression. He waited while I finished my call to a client then pitched in.

"Could you bear to drop over to Pittville?"

"Haven't got the car with me."

"No problem, I said someone would be along in an hour. Gives you plenty of time to get yourself together and walk there. Vron's due in any minute and she can take over the ring-round."

"Are you really so intent on getting fresh air into my lungs?" I said with a smile.

"I wish." He let out a heartfelt sigh.

"What's the matter?"

"Brigadier and Mrs. Smith-Arrow dropped in at the beginning of the week and wanted three pieces by Jackson Mantle." A Midlands artist, Mantle's pieces, extravagant seascapes full of gorgeous light and colour, sold for upwards of £6,000. Larger pieces were nearer £10k. Decent business.

"They took them home to try out against their existing décor," Michael explained. This was not as off-beam as it sounded. Lots of our high-end clients viewed work in their own surroundings before committing to a purchase. "Originally, they were happy and we came to a deal, but it seems they can't make their minds up about where to hang one of the paintings and I'm concerned they'll call the whole thing off and pull out."

"You want me to go over and play interior designer?" More up Kristina's street, I thought, grimly unable to help it.

Michael looked pained but nodded. "I'd go myself but—"

"You don't like the client."

"Is it that obvious?"

"Only to me."

"She's all right, but he's an arse."

"What's the address?"

Michael told me.

I let out a breath. The property he referred to sat adjacent to the park. There were about half a dozen similarly monster-sized houses. Very elaborate. Very chichi.

"Will you be all right?"

He'd handed me a poisoned chalice, but I didn't really mind. I was often asked to troubleshoot because, unlike the others, I was a bit older, a year younger than Michael's forty-five, and, according to everyone who knew me, calm, pleasant, and diplomatic. "I enjoy a challenge," I assured him. "Can we make the deal more attractive?"

Michael wrinkled his nose. "I've already worked out a fairly tight profit margin."

"No wriggle room at all?"

He puffed out his cheeks. "Offer them another two percent, lowest I can go, frankly."

I smiled thanks, collected my things, and headed out as Vron was coming in. "Hey," she said. I liked Vron a lot. She was everything I wasn't. Short, petite, and highly groomed in a *must have my nails manicured professionally every week* way, Vron spoke with a light Southern Irish brogue and was mad as a musician on speed. If there were any cock-ups, Vron was usually responsible. Despite this, privately, I thought Seb would be better off with her than with his wife Arabella, who, as Tiff would crudely say, spoke with a plum in her mouth and acted as if she had a banana up her arse.

"Hey, gotta dash, Vron. Michael will explain. See you later." And off I trotted down the Prom and straight through by North Place and onto the Evesham Road.

Thank God for work.

Six

The Smith-Arrow house was a late Victorian, sashes and swags, detached villa. Must have at least six bedrooms and probably a staff flat, I deduced, gazing up. On the upper elevation there was a beautiful arched stained glass window.

I wasn't like either of my sisters when it came to other people's property or possessions. I didn't resent it and my blue eyes did not turn a ghoulish green. Good luck to anyone who could acquire such wealth, although Archie never agreed with me because wealth was what he'd turned his back on. Consequently, I'd never met his parents or any member of his family. He wouldn't let me, said they were poisonous to anyone he took home. The closest I'd got was a secret late-night visit to a colossal house on the edge of the New Forest in Hampshire. Dressed stone, impressive grounds, and a swimming pool and tennis court in the garden, his father's reward for working day and night in a company manufacturing luxury yachts.

"He never got the fact that I had no interest in the business," Archie once told me. "Thought I was a pussy because I wanted to go my own way." Archie had paid a high price for his independence: cut off without a penny.

I stood back, straightened up, and, taking a deep breath, walked into the Smith-Arrows' large circular drive, up the six stone steps to the putty-coloured front door, and rang the bell.

A woman dressed in a black suit and white shirt emerged. She had dark hair, which was swept severely from a face that displayed Mediterranean features.

"Are you from the gallery?" she said in accented English. Spanish, I guessed.

"That's right." I stuck out my hand, which she didn't take.

"The Brigadier and Mrs. Smith-Arrow will receive you in the drawing room. Follow me."

Very *Downton Abbey*, I thought, letting my hand drop, pursuing her into a large hall with a Harlequin patterned floor.

In a strictly professional capacity, I'd entered numerous houses like this and they always seemed to contain the same furnishings and design. The highly polished walnut console table, the type you see in hotels with visitor's books; original artwork on the walls, often with African artefacts; the sweeping grand staircase with a banister made from walnut and that stretches up four storeys and you can't help but think would be fun to slide down; and not forgetting the mirrors, though search me why a vast area needed to appear larger. The Smith-Arrows' home, with its old-world colour schemes, obeyed convention in every aspect, even down to the smell: wax polish mixed with fresh flowers and expensive room spray. As a study of how the rich lived in their natural habitat, it provided a perfect example.

Almost before we got to our destination, there was a shout followed by a bark of disapproval and raised voices. Next the door flew open and a teenage girl wearing school uniform I heart-stoppingly recognised flew out. Flinging a "fuck you" over her shoulder, she stormed past, her face pinched with rage and framed by long flame-coloured hair.

"Ruby, come back this minute," a woman's voice yelled, too late.

My guide broke stride only for a moment, giving the impression that this was a regular occurrence.

"Leave her, Zara. I'll deal with her later." Straightaway I identified the male bark of disapproval, probably belonging to the Brigadier. By now we were at the open doorway, me hovering awkwardly behind by a few paces.

"Don't just stand there, Rosa, show the man in," I heard him say.

I cleared my throat. Rosa stepped aside and I glided into an opulent drawing room with chandeliers, Tantalus, sofas with Regency stripe, and high-backed chairs that looked ancient and expensive. What was more unusual was the dazzling array of military artefacts and memorabilia, including framed medals and what appeared on a first glance to be signed treaties. In front of the open log fire, two black Labradors snoozed flat out.

Mrs. Smith-Arrow, a lean elegant woman in her early fifties, stayed seated, or rather perched, knees together, small feet clad in flat shoes neatly side by side. She wore slacks, not trousers, that were too short, and a cashmere sweater with a silk scarf at her throat. Her husband, a tall, thin man, older than his wife by ten years or so, wore a blazer over a shirt and tie, salmon-pink jeans, and tan brogues. Bony-featured and with piercing eyes that looked as if they'd spent too much time squinting at the sun, he had a raptor-like appearance. His hair was military-grade short, cut high above ears that had exceptionally long lobes. He and his wife were both suntanned to within an inch of melanoma and the lines on his face indicated a tendency to drink more Krug than was good for him. Even if Michael hadn't muttered a word, I'd have known that this man, a walking study of disdain, was trouble. My mum would have had something to say too: never trust a man whose eyebrows are not the same colour as his hair.

My smile felt wonky on my face. I was still recovering from the shock of seeing a walking reminder of Tara's schooldays. "Grace Neville," I announced and stuck out my hand for a second time. For a second time, it was ignored.

"Where's Michael?" Smith-Arrow barked. The expression on his face was not so much penetrating as excoriating.

"He couldn't come, I'm afraid. Unavoidably tied up in a meeting."

"So he sends you?" Honestly, if he'd said *the monkey* or *the oily rag,* he couldn't have been more offensive.

"That's right," I said breezily. Was this the time to tell him that I had a first-class honours degree? Probably not. "So which painting aren't you quite sure about?" I surveyed the room as if it might materialize out of the woodwork.

Not so fast, his look implied. "Are you in a position to offer us a better deal, or do I have to pull Michael out of his meeting?"

There are some clients for whom "the deal" is the key factor and the art subsidiary, an investment, nothing more. In a rare moment, I'd once complained to Tiff that the clients with the most money could be tight when it came to loot. Always keen to bash "the toffs," she'd surprised me with her response: *That's how they got to be rich as Croesus, you twat.*

"As a senior member of staff, I'm fully authorised," I said smoothly.

Mrs. Smith-Arrow spoke for the first time. "Well, at least that's something, Roland."

Smith-Arrow twitched his lips into a smile, all image and no light or warmth. It made him look so hideous that I preferred him when he was nasty. At least then I knew exactly where I stood.

The next two hours could be described as the most arduous of my life. They had me scampering from one room to another, Smith-Arrow issuing orders as if I were a raw recruit on a parade ground for the very first time and cocking it up. "Up a bit, down a bit, along a bit. No, not there, but there." This followed by much sighing, hands on hips, shaking of heads, and distressed expressions. I was clearly trying their patience. Not content with attempting to find a home for the one painting that seemed to be the problem, the other two were now up for discussion. After an hour and a half of switching paintings and travelling down corridors from which I thought I might never find my way back, I doubted very much if any deal could be struck and didn't much care. The house, for all its fabulous proportions and possessions, had a staged, empty feel. It was like an internationally acclaimed model shimmying down the catwalk, cold-eyed and poker-faced. The home lacked soul or a personal signature, and it was hard to imagine anyone ever loving, laughing, debating, or even breaking their hearts within its haughty walls.

About to urge them to make a decision—we had returned to the expansive drawing room by now—Ruby, their daughter, flounced in and threw herself onto the nearest chair. Both hands resting on the arms, legs apart, leaning back like a boxer taking a break between bouts, the epitome of surly youth.

"Not now," Smith-Arrow growled.

"Aww," she said, shrewdly targeting her mother with an appealing look. "It's really, really important."

"You heard what your father said." Mrs. Smith-Arrow glanced nervously towards her husband and, keen to defuse a potential scene, at me. "Daughters," she said, rolling her eyes. "Do you have children, Mrs. Neville?"

I opened my mouth to say yes and then remembered. Crushing sadness washed over me. I don't quite know what happened. A hot, burning sensation unexpectedly fled across the pit of my stomach and gathered pace, lighting me up from inside. Uncontrollable, it spread up and out, enveloping me like a firestorm. A vein inside my temple pulsed. There was a high-pitched whine in my ears. In answer to their blank, disturbed looks, I gabbled a response that made no sense. Even to me. The back of my hand covered my mouth to stifle a shout and then I was stumbling and running, the heels of my shoes clattering down the patterned hallway, as if someone had bombed the house and I was trying to find my way out of the explosion before the next one detonated. Tears streamed down my face. I had to get out. I had to run and hide.

Wrenching open the front door, I tore down the stone steps and was across the drive when a voice behind me cried, "Stop!" Next a hand grabbed my arm and spun me around.

Ruby held my handbag, which she dropped onto the gravel in the same way a cat drops a mouse at the feet of its mistress. Launching herself at me, she clung, holding me tight, and made a shushing sound. "It's all right. It's okay. Please," she said. When I drew away, hugely embarrassed, her face was a picture of concern. I don't know how or why, but my sobs became less frequent and I felt the demon fire inside me extinguish.

Retrieving a tissue from my pocket, I wiped my swollen eyes and blew my nose. Ruby studied me closely. She seemed older than I'd previously thought, or perhaps it was connected to the grown-up way she'd hurled after me. I dimly registered that she was fifteen, maybe nearer sixteen, although it was always tricky to tell.

"I'm so, so sorry," she said. It wasn't a variation of the trite response to which I'd become accustomed. She looked absolutely sincere, as if she really meant it.

I glanced over her shoulder and anxiously towards the open front door. "Your parents, whatever will they think?"

Her eyes sharpened. "They're too retarded to think. Don't worry, leave them to me."

"But I was horribly unprofessional." God, Michael would kill me for screwing up.

"It doesn't matter."

It did. I wanted to smile at her for her glorious naivety. Instead, I shifted from one foot to another in an agony of indecision while Ruby regarded me with something approaching awe. "Are you really that girl's mother, you know the one in the newspapers, the one whose boyfriend…?"

I chewed my bottom lip. Would I always be known as "that girl's mother"? I nodded feebly.

"That's so, so sad," she said, her eyes welling up with sudden tears. Endearingly, I noticed she used *so* a lot. *So* like Tara. "She went to the same school as me. All the older kids talk about her."

"I really ought to go back inside," I said, not wanting to discuss it and really not wanting to return.

"Don't. They'll only be embarrassed and that will make things worse." She dropped her voice conspiratorially. "Not good at feelings," she confided.

My spirits sagged. I'd done the emotional equivalent of setting loose a tornado, leaving devastation in its wake.

"Okay, but I'd better call my boss." I fished out my mobile.

She frowned. "Will you get into trouble?"

"Quite possibly."

"That's not right." She adopted the same feisty tone she'd used with her parents.

"Not your problem." I mustered a smile. "I'm sure it will be fine," I said, more in hope than conviction.

"You'll be all right then?" Ruby glanced back at the house. She seemed quite torn.

I assured her I would. "Run inside. You'll catch cold." I watched her go and, walking away a little, pulled out my phone to contact Michael, immediately noticing that I'd had two missed calls from Archie. Shaky, I phoned him straight back, frustrated by the sound of his recorded message. I waited for it to finish then said, "Archie, it's me, Grace. Returning your call. Pick up when you can."

Please.

Next I phoned Michael and explained as best I could what had happened. I didn't tell him that I was assailed with dread and inexplicably afraid.

Seven

Michael was decent about it but insisted I take immediate leave. "And I don't want to see you back until you're ready, however long it takes."

"But—"

"No argument."

I trudged back home. It was midafternoon and any remaining sunshine had checked out for the day. Depressed and worried by whatever it was that Archie wanted to tell me, and feeling guilty about screwing up the art deal, I changed out of my work clothes and slothed around in jeans and a sweater, watched teatime television, and opened a bottle of wine earlier than I should have done. I was halfway down it when Michael called.

"I've received a mother of all bollockings from Smith-Arrow."

"Michael, I can't apologise—"

"No need." He snorted a laugh. "Christ knows what came over him because not only has he coughed up the full amount, he enquired about another piece."

Ruby, I thought, almost passing out with relief. "Wonderful," I burbled.

"Got any plans?"

I looked at the bottle furtively. "No."

"Be kind to yourself and make some."

Tiff had the same idea. She phoned as I dumped the empty wine bottle into the green recycling box. "Me and Gray fancy a night out tomorrow. Thought you'd like to come along."

Tiff's idea of a night out had never coincided with mine. I like ambient surroundings—not slick exactly, but stylish, with good food and wine that didn't give you a hangover. Not fancying a ratty pub that smelt of greasy food, served wine on tap, and belted out tacky popular music, I declined.

"Why?"

"Because I'm not in the mood."

"Bollocks to that, we'll soon cheer you up."

I flashed with irritation. Tiff spoke as if I were getting over a job loss.

"It's Saturday night. You can't stay in."

I hadn't considered a Saturday night out as critical to my enjoyment for a long time. I burbled something to that effect.

"So what *are* you going to do?"

"Watch TV, I guess."

"And drink?"

"I might have the odd glass."

"So why not drink with us? Doug and Mum are coming. It will be a laugh."

Tiff meant well. I knew she did, but I could summon neither the desire nor the energy. "I'm fine here, honest, Tiff."

"You don't have to get dressed up or anything."

"It's not that."

"Well, what is it?" Her voice had an ugly, frustrated edge. I stayed quiet because I didn't want to admit that I was secretly waiting for Archie to call again. I also didn't wish to confess to what was travelling through my mind, namely that Tiff's urgent desire to rehabilitate me was borne out of guilt.

"Look, Grace, it's been nearly a year."

"It has not."

"All right, eight or nine months."

"No time at all."

Either she didn't agree or wasn't listening. "Dukes has been put in the slammer and won't be coming out anytime soon. You've got to get your life back."

"I will." I won't. I can't. This was what I really felt.

"So make a start."

"I'm not ready." How could I explain?

She let out an irritated sigh. "Do you want to wind up like one of those sad women who live their lives backwards?"

"I don't understand what you mean." I did.

"Stuck in the past?"

But my past is all I have. I have no future whatsoever.

"Leave it, Tiff. I hear what you say, but everyone moves at a different pace." And I'd hardly moved from the agony of raw grief to whatever lay in wait to devour me next.

"You keep saying that."

"Because it's true." I failed to hide the exasperation in my voice. I'd read about people like me, whose lives have been destroyed, marriages wrecked, careers damaged, with addictions to booze and drugs to numb and keep the pain at bay, for when a parent loses a child by violent means, there are so many unintended and undreamt of consequences. At least, I supposed, forcing a bitter smile, my marriage could not be destroyed.

"Aren't we good enough for you?"

"What?"

"You heard."

"You know very well that's not the case."

Tiff mimicked me and continued, "We've all been running around, trying our best to make things right for you."

"How can you make things right?" I spoke tersely, as if ejecting a pip from a lemon.

"Mum is worried sick."

"Then I'm sorry." Eyeing up the wine rack, I registered that I had one bottle left.

"You know what, you've got well above yourself ever since you married Archie."

I was speechless. Others would have exploded in outrage. Like I said, it wasn't my way.

"Think you're better than us, don't you?" The rise in Tiff's voice indicated that she was very cross indeed. My sister has a terrible temper and is not always logical in her thinking. She was venting her frustration on me for something entirely different. I braced myself. "You sold out a long time ago, Grace. You betrayed your roots."

I hung up. If wanting to do well, hold down a decent job, and have nice things around me was considered treachery, I'd willingly sign up for the title *traitor*. Automatically an action replay of my conversation with Archie whistled through my mind.

"Was there something else?" I said.

"Erm ... yeah ... No, it's fine ... Nothing, me being silly, really."

"Nothing" meant something.

Something that was scary.

And with that thought revolving around inside my head, I opened another bottle of wine.

Eight

A desperate cry—mine—woke me the next morning. I lay still, the agony of loss snuggled next to me, eyeball to eyeball, nose to nose, as smothering as it had ever been.

I contemplated getting up, going out, and walking through town on the busiest day of the week. Always something to distract: buskers, shops full of people, office workers, folk running to get a bite to eat, life in all its vivid colour as I'd once known it. I'd stroll among them gladly, anything to crush the images of knives and blood and death, but it no longer worked. Booze, too, had lost its efficacy. Tiff was right. I had run away from my upbringing and my family, but I could not run away from this. My heart was broken and could not be mended. If we'd had another child, perhaps then there might have been a chance of recovery, although I wasn't certain it really worked like that. One child is, surely, not a substitute for another.

A steaming, head-reverberating hangover assailed me. My skin felt clammy. Deciding to spend the day in bed, I rolled over and pulled the duvet tight underneath my chin. The phone had other ideas. Before nine on a Saturday it could only mean one person: my mother. I would have happily stayed hidden in the dark all day, but Mum soon put paid to that fond thought.

"Come for Sunday lunch tomorrow, Grace."

This was not an invitation, but a proclamation. I scrunched up one eye, trying to focus on where the pain was worst.

"We'll be eating about half past two, as usual." To give Doug and Graham enough time to get a few pints down their necks first.

"Mum," I protested feebly.

"Gracie, love, Tiff told me what happened. She said some very silly things and she's sorry." This was standard operating procedure. Whenever Tiff and me had a spat, which was often, my mother would get to hear of it, usually via Tiff, and would then take all necessary steps to intervene and broker a peace. "And there's no need for you to worry about storage," she said in firm tones. "You can leave your things in the garage for as long as you like."

I propped myself up on one elbow. My head spun and my stomach lurched with excess acid. I could virtually smell the slightly fruity aroma of ethanol leaking from my pores. Worse, panic dug its sharp nails into my heart. "Tiff didn't say anything about storage."

"Oh, didn't she? Must have got the wrong end of the stick." Mum gave a nervous giggle. "Anyway, it isn't a problem."

Clearly it was, and I knew why. Tiff spent so much time at my mum's she thought it a grand idea to give up her council flat. Trouble was, she had a lot of stuff and planned world domination of the double garage. Part of Tiff's dastardly plot entailed getting rid of my belongings, the landmarks of my life, the things that told my story and proved that it was real—that I had loved and given birth, that I had once been a wife and mother. And there were Tara's possessions, too. The average teenager acquires an amazing amount of kit. We couldn't take it all with us when we'd moved to the apartment from our three-bedroom home, so we'd spread it around the family. As soon as Doug bought my mum's bungalow, she offered to have it all under one roof. One day I'd have to sort through it all, but I didn't want to be railroaded into it and I didn't envisage sorting it anytime soon.

Mum was still prattling on. "We're family, Gracie, and when times are rough families stick together." Cue music for *Eastenders*, my mother's favourite soap opera. "So you'll come?"

"Yes," I said weakly.

"Good girl."

———

"All right?" Tiff had her sulky face on. Wearing jodhs and an old pullover with leather patches on the elbows, she stood in our mum's kitchen with arms crossed, eyes flickering, her back to Mum's pride and joy—a double oven cooker with eye-level grill.

No, I thought, I'm not all right. Archie needs to talk to me and, even though I don't know why, I'm terrified. It's amazing how you can lose your sense of perspective when you're stressed out to the eyeballs.

I nodded. She gave me a stare back that said *You look like shit.* Normally Tiff would have voiced this, but she didn't dare in front of Mum. Anyway, I had to agree with her. I'd spent Saturday tucked up until the afternoon, mooned about, started drinking again, and ended up with another hangover. Two doses of painkiller coupled with pints of water, energy drink, and coffee had done little to reduce the seesaw effect of rampant nausea. You can disguise a hangover when you're twenty-four, not when you're forty-four.

Sweet meaty smells pervaded the kitchen. My mum, bless her, had prepared my favourite roast beef with all the trimmings. Since she'd taken up with Doug, she cooked without annihilating it or turning meat into fifty shades of grey, a vast improvement. As a child, I'd chomped my way through roast dinners that bore a strong resemblance to cured shoes. It was only when I met Archie that I was introduced to food that was cooked with a lighter touch and at a lower temperature.

Mum bustled into the kitchen like a cherub on amphetamines, gave me a hug, told me to help myself to a drink, and donned a pair of oven gloves.

"Shift, Tiffany, will you?"

Tiff did and pulled a face at me.

Checking the beef and peering into saucepans to see that everything was rolling at the right speed, Mum glanced across at Tiff with an expression that said *make more bloody effort* and sped out to open the front door to Doug and Graham.

I guess every daughter thinks a mother is, in the nicest possible way, uniquely strange. My mum was no exception. As any grandmother would react, she was devastated by Tara's death. She'd heard the news from Tiff, who told me afterwards that Mum had sat with a hand clamped to her mouth crying *oh God, oh God* over and over. The first time I saw her, after the police had visited, she walked slowly forwards, with arms open wide, composed in a way that was desperately important to me. I couldn't have coped with my mum going to pieces and, even though I knew it cost her, she didn't. Not when I threw my arms around her, not when I held her so tight I thought I'd crack one of her ribs, not when I broke down. A woman of many life experiences, she knew how to meet and manage its vicissitudes. While she could weep buckets at having her heart mashed up by a man, I never saw her cry over Tara. A model of dignity, she reserved her tears for when she was alone, when she thought nobody could hear, and I loved her for it.

Doug bowled in, loud as ever, and Graham followed. A huge fan of Doug's, probably because he was scared of him, Graham was ho-hoing at one of his more off-colour jokes.

"Christ, Gray, who got you dressed today?" Tiff said.

I didn't blame her. More often seen wearing biker leathers when he wasn't dressed for the market, Gray's look could easily be described as bizarre. Taking sycophancy to a brand-new level, in imitation of Doug's dress sense, he wore a lemon and grey check sweater over a pair of navy slacks and what looked like spats.

"Don't you like it?" Graham glanced down as if he wasn't sure what he'd put on that morning.

"You look as if you're about to fucking tee off."

"Language, Tiffany," Mum said.

"He looks a right tool," Tiff persisted.

"Leave the boy alone." Doug winked at me and helped himself to a generous glass of red wine. "Want one, Gracie?"

I raised my orange juice and gestured that I was fine. For once, Doug didn't try and bamboozle me into having a "proper" drink, which came as a relief.

"Can I do anything to help, Mum?" I said.

"You could lay the table in the conservatory."

I glanced across the kitchen and headed Tiff off with a warning expression. Last time I'd obliged with table-laying duty, Mum had cooked a three-course dinner and Tiff had got funny about how I set out the knives and forks. I don't really argue, but I'm not averse to bickering with my sisters. When Tiff starts to lose an argument she swears more than usual and her nostrils flare. She excelled herself on that occasion by blowing her stack. *You're a bloody social climber.* To which I'd replied with cold, deafening silence.

This time she offered to help and, amazingly, under my instruction. I regarded it as my sister's way of offering an olive branch.

Lunch ready, we trooped through and sat down. In spite of my foul constitution, I brightened. Motor-mouth Doug was on form and kept the conversation flowing at a jaunty pace. When he talked his teeth, numerous and small and crammed into a large mouth like a shark's or barracuda's, glittered with gold. Maybe that's why he looked sinister sometimes, although I don't think my mum saw it. With Doug, she was the happiest I'd ever seen her.

My mum looked pleased that she'd got Tiff and me back on speaking terms. Tiff relaxed and got sozzled on my mum's Liebfraumilch. Doug had it crated in by the lorry load. I suspected under strict instructions from my mum, nobody talked about the trial, nobody asked awkward, direct questions like, *What the hell are you going to do with the rest of your life?* The word *Archie* remained taboo.

"Bum a fag off you, Gray?" Tiff said, after we'd finished.

"No smoking in the house, Tiffany," Mum warned.

"I know the rules," Tiff said, grabbing her all-weather jacket that smelt of wet horse and dog, and sloped off outside. Not before giving me the look that said *Come on, we need to talk.*

I duly followed and we ended up leaning over the garden fence that overlooked an expanse of green fields inhabited by sheeplike bundles of soggy yarn. Tiff balanced her glass on the lawn, pressed a roll-up into her mouth, and lit it with Graham's lighter. Her round cheeks sucked in and out, reminding me of a captain of industry chugging on a cigar. After coughing a bit and flicking a flake of tobacco from her tongue, she launched in.

"Thing is, reason I got narky—"

"I know why you got narky."

I had a bad habit of interrupting people and she reminded me of this by wagging a finger and poking me in the chest.

"Sorry," I said.

She took another drag and shook her head. To my surprise, my big tough younger sister's eyes welled with tears. "It was my fault," she mumbled.

"What was?" I knew but I didn't want her to think I did.

"It," she said to which I pulled a frown worthy of a pantomime dame. "Tara. What happened." She dropped her voice and looked around the empty garden as if something or someone might materialise from behind the trees. "The murder."

"Tiff, it was nobody's fault. Random," I said, thinking Tara would be *so* pleased with me for choosing that word.

"But if I hadn't tried to play auntie, you know, taking her to the pub and that, Tara would never have met Jordan Dukes."

Yet you did and she had. How I'd silently cursed Tiff for dragging Tara to the Black Dog, but now was not the time to remind her. "Law of unintended consequences," I said, attempting to sound brave.

Her thick eyebrows drew together. "Law of what?"

"You know, you do one thing and then another follows that you had no intention of happening."

"Like you and Archie splitting up?"

Was this my cue to open my mouth and tell my sister? Should I confess that I had a strange gut feeling that there was stuff going on, *bad stuff*, that I couldn't put my finger on? Is this what sudden violent crime does to the mind? Does it mean that, forever afterwards, you live in fear, that you only see the bad in events and people instead of the good? "Yeah," I mumbled, tamping down my more extreme thoughts.

"Mmm, I get it, but I still feel terrible."

I put an arm around her shoulder. "We all feel terrible, but there's no point dwelling on it." I broke into a shaky laugh. "Good coming from me, huh?"

She smiled sadly. "I'm sorry, Gracie. I didn't mean to give you a hard time. I want the best for you, no matter how it comes out. I'm not clever with words like you. You know I love you."

Not given to sudden declarations, she was obviously pretty drunk, yet in that rare moment I understood she meant what she said with all her being, and it made me feel a rush of raw emotion for her. For all her foibles, she was the most loyal, constant, and straight person I knew. "Love you, too, you chump, even if you drive me potty."

"What you need is a new man," Tiff said, carried away on a wave of sentiment. The warm feeling dissipated. Truth was, I was still in love with Archie. Always would be. I laughed and shook my head. "I'm serious, Grace. All you need is a makeover."

"Thanks very much."

"Nothing a trip to the hairdresser won't fix. Hey, we could go shopping," she said flushing with excitement, or booze, or both. "We could buy you a brand-new look."

To go with my brand-new status as "that girl's mother." "Tiff, it's a lovely idea but—"

"When's your next day off?"

"Don't know," I mumbled. "Frantic at the gallery at the moment. Big exhibition coming up. You know how it is. Gets a bit silly." I felt only moderately sneaky for not revealing my new non-working arrangement.

"Check your diary and let me know. We can do that thing, what's the word? French or something . . . "

"*Liaise*," I said.

"That's right." She had a silly grin on her face as she repeated it in an exaggerated fashion.

I smiled weakly. Trapped.

Nine

First thing on Monday morning, before I lost my courage, I phoned Archie and was met with the same maddening message. This time I was bold. "Hi, it's me, Gracie. Just wondered how you are, how the weekend went. If you need to chat about anything, anything at all, you know I'm here." Embarrassed and feeling a bit of a clown, I cleared my throat and signed off. Then, as a preemptive strike, I booked myself into a hairdresser's for the following morning and set about cleaning the apartment, paying attention to all those little things I usually skipped. In between, I obsessively checked my landline, double-checked my mobile. Nothing. Deeply dissatisfied but, with the weather fine, I drove to Leckhampton Hill, parked, and set out along the Cotswold Way.

The views from the top are spectacular. You can see the Malverns and the Brecon Beacons as well as Cheltenham landmarks, like the "donut," otherwise known as GCHQ and Britain's third intelligence agency, the ugly former Eagle Tower building jutting up from the Bath Road and punching a dirty great hole in the skyline, churches and stately homes and castles and lots of dwellings embedded Lego-like in the landscape. Cows and sheep like dots and people Lowryesque. I didn't feel alone or invisible here in the way that I often did when in a room full of people.

Following the path along a beautifully crafted section of dry stone-wall, I gazed down on deserted quarries, walked through wooded areas, and stumbled over ancient burial mounds. Sick of my own interior monologue, I didn't think or assess or analyse or conclude. I borrowed a day pass from Buddhism and existed entirely in the present. I consciously didn't think of Tara. I didn't think of Archie. I didn't think of me. I simply placed one foot in front of the other, exchanged greetings with walkers, stroked the odd dog skittering ahead of its owner, and revelled in the wind lifting my soon-to-be-cut hair and *lived*. Only when I came down from the hill and climbed back into my car did I remember Tara with a dull thud, and, by association, Archie, and next Tiff's bonkers idea that I should date.

Musing on it in the same way one might think about winning the lottery, companionship appealed, but I couldn't offer anyone anything more intimate and it would be unfair of me to ask someone to comply with my narrow expectations. Truth was, nobody could fill the yawning chasm in my life and nobody could stand in for Archie. I wasn't blind to his faults. God, the man had deceived me and broken my trust and my heart, but Archie had done so much to make me better than I thought I could be. He had imbued me with confidence. He had aided my escape from the back streets of the West Midlands and then Gloucester and helped in my transition—Tiff was right when she'd called me a social climber. Archie had helped me to live big instead of living small, and sharing my life with him made me open my eyes to possibilities. I'd felt blessed. Ironic that, in the end, he'd visited a curse on me.

Unsure what to do next, I drove down the hill, picked up some flowers from a fruit and veg shop at the top of the Bath Road, and went to St. Peter's church where Tara lay buried.

I don't have a religious sinew in my body, which is not the same as saying I lack a spiritual core. I think most people are like that. Since Tara's death I've thought more about the suffering in the world—those held in appalling conditions in totalitarian states, families running for their lives from men who would casually butcher them, cruelty meted out on the weak and the old and the young and vulnerable, all those corners of the earth ripped apart by famine and disease. Whereas pre-Tara, I couldn't name those places and people properly, now they trip off my tongue. I *live* them. I *feel* for them.

Embracing the solitude of the graveyard, I laid a bouquet of stargazer lilies on Tara's grave and murmured the words on the headstone. At once, sunshine faded behind a belt of cloud and a bitter wind with evil designs buffeted underneath my jacket. Against my will and best intentions, my mind flipped back to the big change in my daughter's behaviour, the silent era in her life after the honeymoon period faded.

"Tara, your dad will be here any minute. Are you ready?"

"I'm not going."

I popped my head around her door. Still in her dressing gown, Tara lay on top of her duvet. "What's up?"

"I'm not feeling well."

"What's the matter?"

"Tummy ache."

"Period?"

"Um, yeah."

"Doesn't mean you can't go on holiday."

"I told you, I don't feel well."

"Budge up." She did and I sat down and placed a hand on her forehead, which was cool and smooth. "You're not running a temperature."

Tara scowled as I studied her, attempting to tune into what was really wrong. "I've changed my mind," she insisted.

"The flight and hotel are all booked. Your bags are packed."

"I don't want to go. I want to stay here with you."

Secretly I was elated. Ashamed, I forced it down and did my best to behave in, as Archie would term it, a civilised manner.

"That's lovely, darling, and I'm going to miss you terribly, but you'll have such a smashing time. I know you will. Dad wants to take you water skiing and …"

She sat up straight, bounced off the bed and tore into the sitting room. Bewildered, I followed.

"Tara, has something happened?"

Sullenly she said, "No."

"You really don't want to go to Italy?" I said, smiling and teasing her. I'd have been doing cartwheels for days if my mum had suggested two weeks in a foreign country. A holiday for us was a week in a caravan on the Welsh coast in the rain.

"Not yet," she said, tight and prissy.

"But Dad will be so disappointed."

"Not my problem."

Her resistance amazed me. "But you always have such a great time."

"That was before."

"Before what?"

She shrugged and took an avid interest in a stain on the carpet. I repeated the question.

"Doesn't matter," she mumbled.

"Look, Tara, sweetheart ... "

"What?" Her head snapped up. Never had one word in the history of mankind ripped with so much aggression.

"Have you two fallen out?"

"No."

"It wasn't anything to do with him ticking you off for smoking?"

"Are you tapped?" Her eyes blazed with fury.

"What's changed?"

"Why do you have to keep banging on and on?"

"Because I'm trying to understand."

"Well, don't. I haven't had a row, all right? I JUST DON'T WANT TO GO." She stood red-faced and panting. Like most teenagers, Tara could be stubborn, yet I sensed something bigger in play.

I counted to ten and said in a quiet and restrained voice, "You're really sure?"

"Positive."

"What do you want me to do?"

Spotting my weakness, she immediately relaxed and brightened. "Phone and explain."

"Explain what?"

"That I want to stay with you."

I could well imagine how that would be received. "I can't. It wouldn't be kind." Actually, it would be misconstrued and I'd be blamed.

"All right," she said, as if I were the most pathetic person on the planet, "then I'll do it."

And, to my astonishment, she did. It hadn't gone down well and, as I'd prophesied, Kristina had accused me of manipulation and worse.

Fondly imagining that we were going to share quality mum and daughter time, I'd organised to take as many days off as possible from work, not easy at such short notice. But Tara's mood only briefly lifted. It didn't really improve when Archie and Kristina returned, although they never mentioned the holiday or held her impulsive decision against her. If anything, it heralded a new epoch in which Tara would rant and bash me over the head with Kristina's opinions. Next, amid much drama, which I hated, Tara would flee back to Harp Hill or, as I believed, was lured back to Harp Hill. On good days, Tara was quiet, less carefree, and secretive. *Typical teenage behaviour,* my mum told me at the time. *Remember the strops Tiff used to get in?*

But I never got to the bottom of Tara's strange and unpredictable behaviour.

As I stood in the graveyard, my hand resting on cool marble, I asked myself with a shudder, *Before what?*

Ten

"Hi, Grace," Archie said tentatively, as though he thought it a bad time for him to call, which it was because I was on my way out of the graveyard, a sudden sting of tears streaming down my face. "Sorry, I didn't get back to you. Been rushed off my feet since our return."

"Good break?" I said, my voice thick with crying.

"Very nice and restful, thanks. Are you okay?"

"Fine," I said. "Right," I added, gathering myself, taking a firm, deep breath, "just wondered if everything was all right. I mean … erm … obviously things are not exactly normal, but, well … "

"Is something wrong?" Archie's voice was sharp, not like his at all. "Nothing's happened, has it?"

"No, no," I swallowed. "I thought, well, wondered really, that last time we spoke, I thought you wanted to tell me something."

"Did you?" He sounded astonished.

"Yes."

"No," he said, drawing the word out. "Nothing I can think of."

Crushed, heat surged in my cheeks. Had Kristina got to him? Had I imagined the whole thing? Did I not know him anymore? "Oh, I must have got the wrong end of the stick. Never mind," I said, hating the false trill in my voice.

"Work all right?" he said.

"Fine," I lied.

"Good."

"You?"

"Like I said, busy."

Feeling a chump, I scrunched my eyes tight. "I'll let you go." I was running on empty, running on fumes.

"Bye, Grace."

"Bye, Archie."

Why don't I believe you?

———

My days had no rhythm and roll. Without the routine of work, everything took place in slow motion. Each time I looked at my watch the hands had barely moved. Look outside, the clouds were stationary, trees still, no rustle in the leaves. Everything inert. Such a contrast to the early days of the police investigation with so much going on around me and numerous people visiting; colleagues and friends phoning; relatives, police officers, victim support, counsellors, and vicars I'd never clapped eyes on before; Archie lost and desolate; Kristina inconsolable. And all the while I was sinking, mute and helpless, as if up to my knees in quicksand in the middle of a desert alone. I don't know how I got through that acutely bleak period. I didn't, really, simply blundered blind, smashing against and tearing myself on every sharp-edged corner. I didn't want to give in to that again, that sense of being spun out and senseless, thoroughly done over and crucified by life.

With this thought pinned rigidly in my head and all thought of Archie swept aside, I set out for the hairdressers and what I hoped would be the first step on a rocky road to rehabilitation. I'd chosen a different salon deliberately. Like Tiff said, I needed a fresh look and new start. I wanted to go some place where I would not be known as the woman whose daughter was murdered.

Warm air, as if I'd strayed inside my mum's new fan-assisted oven, gusted towards me together with a lovely smell of expensive shampoo and conditioner, punctuated with the more astringent whiff of hair-lightening agents. A bright-eyed young man with a thin moustache and foreign accent greeted me, checked my name, took my coat, and gestured towards one of the squishy leather chairs.

"Callum will be with you in a moment. Would you like a drink? We have tea, Earl Grey, Indian, or, if you prefer, camomile, peppermint, rosehip and apple ..."

"Coffee?" I said hopefully.

"Straight, latte, cappuccino, macchiato, espresso?"

"Um ..."

"We also do mocha and hot chocolate."

I felt a brief but distinct surge of panic. What had happened to the confident me? He was only asking what I wanted to drink, not my opinion on the European Union. "Cappuccino would be lovely," I said, immediately wishing I'd ordered an espresso.

"Water? We have sparkling, still, Hilden or—"

"Tap would be fine."

Lightheaded, I slumped into the soft leather, picked up a magazine, and trawled through photographs of the great and the good and aristocrats with alliteratively imaginative double-barrel surnames.

My coffee arrived on a tray with a doily, a single slim wafer biscuit and a glass of Severn Trent water. I fleetingly wondered how much it would all cost and returned to the magazine. Engrossed, I barely noticed a tall bony guy in black jeans and T-shirt who looked like a dead ringer for the singer-songwriter Paul Weller.

"Grace?"

I looked up.

"Hi, I'm Callum."

With a louche, *hey man* smile, he pulled up a chair on wheels, sat down, crossed his long legs and pitched forward with one elbow balanced on his thigh, a hand cupped underneath his chin. "So what are we doing today?"

His gaze locked onto me, which, frankly, I found unnerving. I had a horrible feeling that I was going to get voodoo with my haircut. "Open to ideas," I said shakily. "Obviously it needs cutting and seems to have darkened a fair amount during the winter months."

He scooted towards me and raised both hands. "May I?"

"Erm … yes."

Like a chef sifting flour, his fingers ran through my hair with a practiced touch, not entirely unpleasurable. Making strange coded noises that didn't really indicate what he thought, he said, "It's got great body and, with a few highlights, we could sex it up. How radical do you want to be?"

"Um, I don't really know."

"Well," he said, grasping a clump. "This does nothing to frame your face."

"You'd cut it all?"

"Definitely."

A sudden vision of Edward Scissorhands skipped through my mind. "Right," I said, bullish, Tiff's voice strident and encouraging in my ear, "and the colour?"

He scooted across the floor, swiped what appeared to be an encyclopaedia from the reception desk and whizzed back towards me. Choosing lowlights or highlights was a minefield I'd never negotiated before. I decided that it was a lot easier choosing paint. In the end, I caved in under the weight of Callum's enthusiasm. God help me if he were a bull-shitter. "Go for it," I said, thinking it was not the worst thing that could happen even if it went wrong. I could always wear the cloche, I thought, half smiling at what Tiff would make of that.

Three hours later, my hair had been wrapped in tin foil, bleached—Callum said that they didn't use that process anymore, although it still smelt the same and made me sneeze—heated up, washed, cut, styled, and blow-dried, or as they now termed it "blasted off." My new sleek cut looked amazing and took ten years off me. With no change from over a hundred pounds, I paid and gazed in wonder at the new me and felt a vague stir of hope marred only by the fact that Tara was not around to view it. She would have loved the transformation, I thought, abruptly sad.

Callum kissed me warmly on both cheeks. "You look great." It was the nicest thing anyone had said to me in ages, and I trotted back home with an approximation of a smile on my face and a tear in my eye.

Eager to share my new look with Tiff and take up her offer of a shopping trip, I picked up the phone and punched in her number. The line went to voicemail, indicating that she was out on a hack. Undeterred, I left a jolly message, hoping that she would catch the spark of excitement in my voice.

I hadn't eaten all day and, feeling hungry, a novelty, went through to the kitchen, made a cheese and pickle sandwich and cup of tea, and devoured both while flopped on the sofa. Unsure what to do next, toying with dropping into work to show off my new hairdo, I decided to go through my wardrobe and ruthlessly chuck out anything I hadn't worn for the past two years.

I'd hardly got cracking when the doorbell rang—one of those old-fashioned mock antique door pulls I'd picked up from a reclamation centre for five quid. Guessing it was someone trying to flog me fish or cleaning materials for which I had no use or canvassing for donations, I posted my prepared "thank you, but no thank you" speech on my lips, and opened the door. One look and the air punched out of my body.

"Sorry, you are Mrs. Neville, aren't you?"

My jaw slackened, mouth opened. No words. They'd got lost.

He shifted awkwardly from one foot to the other and peered at me. It had a galvanising effect.

"What the hell do you want?"

"I almost didn't recognise you, sorry. Look, I know how this must seem, but I'd really like to talk to you."

"You have nothing I want to hear and I have nothing I want to say."

"Please, I'd be so grateful if you'd give me a few moments of your time."

"I can't. I'm busy and it would be … " I hesitated, unable to find the right word, and grabbed the first that was close enough. "Inappropriate." For God's sake, I thought, it's been less than a week. We've had a trial with a judge and jury and your son has been found guilty.

"I wouldn't ask if it weren't important."

"I don't want to appear rude or heartless, but I'd like you to go away. Now."

"Mrs. Neville, I'm begging you."

"You have no damn right to be here." I realised that I was shouting. To my ears, my voice sounded like the roar of a wounded lioness. "If you don't leave, I'll call the police." I made to close the door.

"If it were your boy imprisoned for a crime he didn't commit, wouldn't you do everything to save him?"

I stopped, breathless and bewildered. His brown eyes locked onto mine. His hands, gnarled from heavy outside work, shook. The freshly pressed trousers, textured twill shirt, and highly polished shoes, designed to create an impression of respectability, were betrayed by two nicks on his cheek where he'd cut himself shaving, no doubt in his anxiety about seeing me. Blood stained his collar.

"There has been a terrible miscarriage of justice, Mrs. Neville."

He shrieked desperation. The unfamiliar heat of fury inside me died down. I suppose it was for that reason that I said to the father of the man charged with the murder of my daughter, "Best come inside."

Eleven

I listened.

Allan Dukes didn't ask for pity. He didn't plead that Jordan was misunderstood, a victim of misfortune, that, due to a difficult childhood, he'd gone off the rails. In a low voice that only an astute ear would identify as emanating from Gloucestershire, he spoke briefly of Jordan's mother, a woman who'd upped and returned to Jamaica when Jordan was seven and never came back. Allan Dukes mentioned youth offending teams, case managers, referral and community and youth rehabilitation orders and ASBOs (antisocial behaviour orders) only as a means to create context. He expressed deep remorse for not doing a better job of bringing up his son. It was obvious to me that, in common with most parents whose children fail, he shouldered the blame for Jordan falling in with "a bad lot."

These facts emerged surreptitiously and I accepted them. What I could not accept was Allan Dukes's strong defence of his son's activities on the night he plunged a blade into my daughter's heart.

"He's headstrong and wayward, but he's not a murderer, Mrs. Neville," he said. "He would never hurt anyone, especially not Tara. He loved the girl."

"Then how do you explain the mark on her arm?"

"The day before her death they'd been out in Gloucester city centre and Tara stepped off the kerb. Jordan grabbed hold to steady and prevent her from getting hit by a car."

"How do you know?"

"Because he told me."

"Why didn't the defence team mention it?"

"Because Jordan didn't tell them."

"Why not?"

"The same reason he kept quiet about where he really was that night."

It took me a few seconds to process the implications. I pitched forward. "What exactly do you mean?"

"Jordan wasn't with Tara because he was somewhere else, doing something he shouldn't."

"What?"

"Ripping off a rival gang, most likely."

I frowned. "You don't know?"

"He won't say."

My frown deepened. I could feel lines tugging at my mouth. "You'll have to help me out." What I really meant was that he'd have to do better than that.

"Jordan is covering for someone."

"You mean that if he discloses his alibi, he'll point the police in their direction?"

"Exactly."

Bristling with frustration, I said, "With the greatest of respect, Mr. Dukes—"

"Call me Allan."

I had no intention of calling him Allan. This man needed to be kept as far away from me as possible. "Who exactly is this mysterious person he's allegedly protecting?"

"Someone in the gang."

"You know that for a fact?"

"It's what Jordan told me."

"When?"

"Two days ago."

By which time he would have had a nasty introduction to prison life. "But he wouldn't say who?"

"As I've explained, he refused to say."

"Because he can't or won't?"

Allan viewed me with a hounded expression. He'd come full of hope and I had deconstructed his bullet points one by one, reduced his argument to fragmented pieces and stamped all over them.

"Do you know anything about the Stringers?" he said quietly.

"Yes."

"Then you know what they're capable of."

"Aren't you forgetting a tiny detail?" I was barely able to contain my sense of reason. "Your son was and is a member."

"He never did any of the really bad stuff."

The last thing I wanted was to get into a debate about morality. From where I was sitting, everything they did was *really bad stuff*.

"Mrs. Neville, don't you see he's afraid to speak out?"

My eyes widened. What could be scarier than doing time in prison? I didn't buy any of it and it must have shown in my expression.

The lines around his eyes deepened. He was a big man, not fat, but well built and muscular, yet in that moment he shrank a little and seemed small. I realised then that he was as terrified as he was despondent. It occurred to me that we were both victims, perversely connected by our children, if for very different reasons. For that I was genuinely sorry.

"What if I could find out?" he said, an urgent catch in his voice.

"If you discover new evidence, you must take it to the police." I could not contain the stiffness in my voice.

"You'd be in favour?"

"Of course," I said, thinking it irrelevant anyway. Allan Dukes was never going to find a reason to clear his son because a reason didn't exist. "Why wouldn't I?"

He shrugged. "Some might think that if you dance with the devil, you get everything you deserve, whether or not you're guilty "—he paused, looked me straight in the eye—"and particularly if you're a young mixed race kid."

Was he intimating that I was a racist? "I'm not one them," I said stonily.

"Didn't think you were, but you never know. The cops, police, I mean," he said as if he'd forgotten his manners, "had it in for Jordan from the start." He seemed to be talking almost to himself. Silence clogged the room and I badly wanted him to leave. I still didn't really understand his desire to speak to me. He didn't need my permission to prove his son's innocence. Perhaps he was sounding me out, to see if I had doubts about the trial. As if I would. I wanted what passed for closure. Needed it.

"I believe my son, Mrs. Neville."

I let out a sigh. How could I blame him? What parent wants to believe the worst of their offspring? "I'm sure you do," I said, as gently as I could.

"And I believed you had a right to know."

"Kind of you."

"I thought," he stumbled, "that if you talked to Jordan, he might tell you what he won't tell me."

"What?" Fear gnawed a fresh hole in me.

"What with you being a woman," he said solicitously, "and Tara's mum."

"Have you any idea what you're asking of me?" Blood pulsed through my cheeks. The sudden rage that had consumed me, without warning, flared right back up. "Your son has destroyed us with a pain and sorrow that no parent should endure."

He swallowed. "I understand ... "

"No, you don't," I said, my head hammering, "I'm not proud of it, but there was a time when I'd have gladly plunged that same knife your son used to butcher my daughter into *his* chest."

Most men would have backed off. Allan Dukes remained calm and resolute. "Which is why I believed you should be the first to know that Jordan is innocent and that the man who killed your girl is still out there."

I had a sudden image of Edvard Munch's *The Scream*. It wasn't possible. There had been a trial that had lasted for over a week, evidence given, a judge and jury. Twelve men and women couldn't be wrong.

Could they?

The thought stuck fast in my heart like a rusty blade.

I gaped at him and struggled to my feet. "Get out," I cried. "Get out of my house."

Twelve

"I want to know. I need to know." I stared at Detective Inspector Dunne and gave the sodden tissue in my hand a further twist for emphasis.

"There was no sign of sexual assault."

I thanked God for that small mercy.

"As I've already said, we have a suspect."

"Jordan. But why, why would he do it? It doesn't make sense."

"We think Tara wanted to finish the relationship. Jordan wasn't happy and lost his temper. It's a common enough scenario."

"Tara never said she was unhappy. I thought she was in love with him." Dizzily so, as only a teenager can be.

Dunne raised his eyebrows. They disappeared into the creases in his forehead. "Kids never tell a parent everything, do they?"

Mine did, or so I thought. "What about DNA?"

Dunne frowned again. "Not sure I follow you."

"You said that Jordan's DNA was found on Tara. Well, it would be. What about other DNA in the room?"

Dunne sucked in through his teeth, which were stained. "DNA is a bit of an issue, actually. The hotel room hadn't been cleaned very well. Less than hygienic, you might say. Not the most salubrious of establishments."

"So there was more than one person's DNA present?" I imagined a human soup of previous guests.

He nodded and confirmed what I'd already worked out. "But the point is that we have arrested the right individual."

"And what does Jordan say?"

"No comment."

"He's guilty, you think?"

"Without doubt. An open-and-shut case, Mrs. Neville."

I could replay only fragments of conversations like the one I had with Dunne. I have no clear recollection of the content or sequence of events and I've often lain awake at four in the morning struggling to piece them together. My overriding concern was that I'd missed something critical. Feverishly I ran through it all again now.

It had been a Friday night and Tara was staying over at Archie's. The rest of the weekend she was to spend with my mum and Tiff, or so she'd said. With nothing unusual about it, I never challenged her. True, I knew the risk that if Tara were in Gloucester she might also find a way to see Jordan Dukes, but I took the view that if I spoke out too strongly, I'd only drive her closer to him and create a barrier between us. As far as my sister believed on the weekend in question, Tara was with me.

On Sunday morning I'd visited a girlfriend who was having marital problems. She lived in a street where the mobile signal in her house was poor. I hadn't bothered to switch on my phone from the previous evening and only did so when I returned home. (In a cruel twist, my landline had been temporarily out of action due to a fault on the line.) Imagine my panic at so many missed calls. As soon as I saw the text from my mother, someone who rarely communicated like this, I knew something catastrophic had happened. It was like one of those world events that remain with you for a lifetime, like the Twin Towers crashing down.

Only this was different.

This was no shared shock and awe.

This was my life, my precious daughter, as personal as it got.

Before I had a chance to respond, two police officers arrived at my door. That's when I knew for sure.

There is no easy way to break that kind of news. I think one of them said something like, *I'm really sorry to inform you that your daughter was found dead in the early hours of this morning.* Other words followed: *murdered, stabbed, Jordan Dukes.* I grabbed at them in the same way a drowning refugee grabs for a life belt and misses. I learnt more from the ensuing police investigation and trial than I ever did from that conversation. Even if I'd been told at the time, I doubt I'd have taken it in. It's simply not possible to absorb that sort of news in one go.

Shock does strange things to memory. On overload, I blotted the more graphic detail out. Since then, I've learnt to assimilate it, not because I wanted to, but because I owed it to my daughter to know the truth. I'd given birth to her and it felt only right that I understood the nature of her death.

What I discovered scalded me. It struck me then that you only truly know a person after they're dead. Secrets might be taken to the grave, but they are rarely kept there.

She'd been found in a cheap hotel down a ratty street close to the train station. It was alleged that she and Jordan had used the thirty-pounda-night room many times, which was how a male receptionist was able to identify Jordan entering around eight the Saturday evening before, although he couldn't swear to see him leave or return. There was no CCTV to corroborate either version of events. An alcoholic often known to sneak outside for a drink or a cigarette, the unfortunate receptionist had his witness statement ripped apart by Jordan's defence team, not that it had done any good.

A guest in the floor below heard screams around half past one on Sunday morning, some five and a half hours after Tara and Jordan checked in. He didn't report it because he thought it was someone fooling around, or, as he put it under intense cross-questioning, "having rough sex." Only when blood seeped through the ceiling onto his bed a couple of hours later did he think there was more to it, and by then it was too late to save Tara. Diverted from a nearby location, paramedics arrived at the scene within minutes of the alarm being raised, found Jordan Dukes in the room clutching Tara, and inadvertently trampled over and contaminated the area in a doomed endeavour to restart her heart.

According to a pathologist, Tara died as the result of a single stab wound, the trauma immediate and catastrophic. She had taken a few steps before collapsing. Archie informed me that it was probably too late for her from the moment the blade struck. When Jordan Dukes ripped into my child's heart, he ripped into mine, too. And now Allan Dukes was picking at the scab and reopening old wounds.

I remembered how Archie behaved the moment he found out. As devastated as he was, he took over. He asked all the questions I'd thought of and many I hadn't. He identified Tara's body. With his nursing experience, it was a given. I didn't feel sidelined; I felt grateful. He swung into clinical mode, at which I marvelled, although later on there were times when I thought him cold and distant. I only recently appreciated that it was his way of protecting himself.

Against this context, I thought again about Allan Dukes's strange visit. An urge to call Tiff was now superseded by a stronger instinct for survival. Feuds between the families on her council estate were not uncommon. Telling her about Allan Dukes would be like priming a weapon. Who knew how she might react and where it might lead? I knew my mum would understand and give me a sympathetic ear, but I didn't want to upset her. And Archie? Shouldn't I tip him off in case Allan Dukes came tapping at his door? I phoned him straightaway. This time I got through and without obfuscation.

"Are you all right to talk?"

"Sure, about to fix something to eat before I go on shift, but no worries."

"I could phone back later."

I heard Archie take a few steps, followed by the sound of a door closing. "No, it's fine."

"Has Allan Dukes been to see you?"

"Good God, why on earth would he do that?"

"He believes there's been a miscarriage of justice."

"You're joking. How does he work that out?"

I told Archie what Allan had said, word for word. Archie's reaction was similar to my own. In fact, I'd rarely heard him so cross. Livid, he didn't buy it, either. "Isn't there a law against pestering victim's relatives?"

"He wasn't pestering."

"I've a mind to call the police and report him for harassment."

I paled. If I never saw a police officer again I wouldn't be sorry. "I really don't think he meant harm. He's desperate."

"You sound as if you're sympathetic to him." Archie had an accusing, critical note in his voice. Not for the first time, I thought it not like him at all.

"It's not his fault, Archie."

"That's debatable. Perhaps if he'd done a better job of bringing up his son, Tara might still be alive."

Dismay lodged in the centre of my chest. It felt hard and obstinate and distilled, like grief. I wondered what I'd started. Floundering, I said, "If he contacts me again, I'll do something about it."

"You'll let me know?"

"Yes."

"Promise?"

"Archie ..."

"Promise me," he said, softening his voice, more caring and less stern.

Vows, I thought, those we keep to ourselves and those we keep to others—except Archie had betrayed his. "I promise," I said, stinging as Kristina's voice, high and clear, piped, "Archie."

"Sorry, Grace. Gotta go. Kristina needs me."

Needs you. What about me?

Choking down a sudden flood of jealousy, I told him I wouldn't hold him up.

"Great. Thanks," he said as if in a hurry.

Thirteen

The next day I turned it over in my mind. Allan Dukes was deluding himself. Jordan had spun his dad a line. He'd bought it and he expected me to do the same. Simple.

But what if Jordan really had been somewhere else?

What if he hadn't killed Tara?

What if?

Too bizarre to contemplate, I lay in bed wondering what I was going to do for the next fifteen hours. Spooked and unsettled, I decided to get out of town and go for a tame meander around the Cotswolds. I'd have coffee in Stow-on-the-Wold, grab a sandwich in Moreton-in-Marsh, and visit an art gallery there that had a fine selection of work by Russian painters. If the weather held, I'd nip to the touristy little market town of Chipping Campden. I liked it because it was where Bob and Mum had once taken Tiff and me as a treat when we were little.

Sorted and determined to forget about Allan Dukes and his ludicrous ideas, I dozed for an hour and then got up. A glance in the mirror reminded me that my new hairstyle was the best decision I'd made in ages. Some of the confidence buoying me yesterday returned. I dressed warmly in jeans, a favourite sweater with a cowl neck, and tan boots absolutely right for covering miles of pavement. I spooned bioactive yogurt into my mouth for no other reason than I thought I should eat something healthy, cleaned my teeth, and eased myself out of the flat.

Patches of blue sneaked through the clouds, promising fine if chilly weather. Jumping into the Mini, I drove out of Cheltenham and picked up the A40, turned off onto the A429, and arrived in Stow thirty-five minutes later.

Finding a handy parking space in the main street, I set about doing touristy things. I peered into antique, butchers, and sweet shops selling homemade sweets and fought off an urge to buy a bag of coconut mushrooms, Tara's favourite, the memory bittersweet. Eyeing up tiny but exquisitely built cottages that I'd never be able to afford, I sucked up the ancient Roman architecture, took a spin around the Red Rag gallery with its eclectic collection of British contemporary art, and finished up in the next-door coffee shop, where I ordered a latte. Solo again, without the advantage of displacement activity, my thoughts skittered like fruit flies partying in Majestic.

Allan Dukes.

Archie, his voice, his tone, lies and promises, promises.

Hindsight is a great thing. With the advantage of 20/20 vision, you can reel the footage back and see an affair and all those little telltale signs of betrayal in Technicolor. The increase in text messages, the phone calls taken in private, the willingness to do more shifts at work, the absence of desire to spend time together, alone. And, of course, Archie had the perfect cover. I'd been sympathetic when he'd lied about the pressures and demands of working in an oncology unit and the need for solitude. What a mug I'd been. The only benefit, I reflected as I sipped my coffee, was that his mercurial moods had stood me in good stead for Tara's teenage volatility. She could never seem to make up her mind about whether she hated spending time at Harp Hill or whether she loved it. One moment she'd call, demanding I pick her up, the next that I take her back. I'd teased her once that there was a reason there was a moan in the word *hormones* and she'd almost snapped my head off. I'd often felt as if we were characters in a foreign art house film, all those moody looks and weird camera direction. My friends assured me that they were enduring the same with their teenage daughters. One mother of adolescent boys told me to be grateful. *At least she engages. I'm lucky to get a word out of the pair of them. Spend their entire lives in their bedrooms in the dark. I swear I've bred a couple of bats.* Thankfully Tara's baffling behaviour screeched to a halt a couple of days after her sixteenth birthday.

After a demoralising shopping trip in search of the perfect dress for her prom night, we'd taken a breather in Café Rouge in the main square.

"I've met this boy," she told me.

"What's his name?"

"Jordan."

"Jordan who?"

"Dukes." Her eyes shone with adoration. "He's lovely, Mum. Got a gorgeous smile, dark brown eyes, and skin the colour of hard toffee, just like Auntie Calypso."

"I wouldn't bandy that about, Tara. It's not very PC."

"Jordan wouldn't mind. He's mixed race and proud of it."

"As he should be," I said. "Is he still at school?"

"Works with his dad. He's a builder in Gloucester."

"Is that where you met?"

Her gaze shifted from me to the table. "Yes, at Auntie Tiff's."

"Oh?"

"Well, not strictly at Auntie Tiff's, but when I was over there."

Tara was concealing something, but I was reluctant to stop her flow. I'd get the full gen from Tiff later. "How long have you known him?"

"A couple of months." So that accounted for the frequency of Tara's visits to see my mum and sister.

"Has Auntie Tiff met him?"

"Um, yeah."

"And?" I said, arching an eyebrow. "What does she think?" Tiff had a nose for people. Whereas I always saw the good in them, Tiff had a habit of spotting the dark side, as she put it, probably because she had a dark side of her own.

"She doesn't know him." Code for she doesn't like him.

"Do I get to meet Jordan?"

"Yeah." She brightened. "If you like."

I did like, and, what I saw of him, I liked, too. It did not prepare me for our next conversation a few days later.

"I want to go on the Pill."

"Tara, you're only sixteen."

"So?"

"You hardly know Jordan. It's a big step to take."

"That's rubbish. All my mates are on it."

"It's not like getting a new brand of phone provider." I thought this might make her laugh. She didn't see the joke.

"All right, I'll get pregnant then."

My heart skipped. Was there an inherited gene for falling pregnant with alacrity? I thought of my mum and scrubbed out the thought and the baggage

89

that went with it. "Have you talked to Dad about it?" Tara had no boundaries when it came to discussions with her father. To my surprise, she hadn't.

"Please, Mum. I really, really like Jordan."

"Was this his idea?" It came out more sharply than I intended.

"It was mine."

"What about STDs?"

"For God's sake, Mum. Chill out. Jordan isn't like that."

"It's not a matter of pick and choose, Tara. Has he slept with other girls?" Older than Tara, I wouldn't have put it past him. His engaging personality and good looks ensured he would never be short of female company.

"A couple," Tara huffed. "If you want me to nag him to get checked, I will."

"Deal," I said, ignoring the belligerence in her tone. "But, let me make it clear, you will not be sleeping with him under this roof."

"Aww, Mum."

"Your father would go mad with me," I said, applying the Get Out of Jail Free card that divorce can occasionally hand you. "I'll make an appointment with the doctor."

She'd thrown her arms around me as if I'd promised her a lifetime of blessings. How wrong could she have been?

I drank up, drove the short distance to Moreton, drifted around, bought salami and cheese from the deli in the high street, and finally finished up at the Manor House Hotel. The conservatory dining room with its ecclesiastically styled windows was sprinkled with ladies that lunched. I settled for a sandwich and small glass of white wine in the Beagle Bar, all greens and tartans.

At home you can eat a meal alone without blinking, even if deep inside you miss a person with whom to share dinner and conversation. In public it's less easy to carry off, as if my single status were on show for the world to see and judge. Maybe that's why my mind played along to a different soundtrack, coruscating with childhood memories and stuff I'd long forgotten or buried. Mad, bonkers moments when my mum had whisked us off to a funfair when we should have been at school. The time she found fifty quid stuffed down the side of the sofa and fished it out, roaring in triumph. She'd fed the gas meter and treated us to fish and chips and mushy peas and we thought we were made. Less appealing, I recalled endless moves, never having a place to settle, always saying good-bye to friends you'd only recently gotten to know. I thought of a little brother, stillborn and unseen, perfect and beautiful but without life or breath, of the rift that grief had caused between my mum and Bob, and of a world of shrouded silences, stifling misery, and strong, occasionally vicious words that could never be taken back. In that regard, Mum and me shared something in common. We had both loved and lost. In the garage, the baby clothes bought for her much-wanted son sat in storage alongside Tara's baby clothes.

Had I missed something?

Was Allan Dukes right?

Had the wrong person been convicted?

I ate my sandwich without pleasure, paid the bill, and arrived in Chipping Campden in time for the sky to break. Rain poured as if an unseen power had turned on a faucet. Shoppers scattered, some sheltering from the cloudburst, while hard men in short sleeves and T-shirts strode impervious to a soaking and having their hair plastered matte and black to their faces. I smiled at first as a gaggle of schoolchildren tore through every puddle, shrieking at the tops of their voices as if a monsoon had finally arrived after a period of drought.

And then my heart bled.

From the sanctuary of my car, I watched them all and experienced a strange, guilty sense of longing for a life lost and so different to the one I now led.

When the weather finally settled, I ventured out and drank in the heady smell of fresh rain on medieval limestone and walked the high street, through the cobbled Woolstaplers' Hall, along by the alms-houses, and inside a lovely cutlery shop on a corner that I always visited, although I'd never bought so much as a teaspoon there.

After the storm, the streets were as quiet as dawn in winter and, as I wandered without aim or purpose, I wondered how many buildings had yet to relinquish their secrets and ghosts.

Did Tara have secrets?

Were there ghouls in her closet that I didn't know about?

Was someone else responsible for her death?

I'd only once visited the hotel, if you could call it that, where Tara died. Others had made the pilgrimage and left flowers and teddy bears outside the entrance. Standing there on a still day without sunshine or breeze, staring up at chipped walls, flaking paint, and a Sky Satellite dish protruding from an upper elevation, I'm not sure what I expected—or if I expected anything at all. A place that had teemed with other people's stories had suddenly seemed bereft of narratives and answers.

Wasn't that odd?

Troubled, I climbed into the Mini and took my place in the great exodus of workers eager to return home and eventually walked through the door to the apartment without a glimmer of either attainment or adventure.

Immediately I knew something was wrong.

With a small property, you tend to notice more readily marks on the paintwork, stains on the carpet, a picture that has been bodged and hangs crookedly on the wall. My garden was a courtyard with containers. Not much of a gardener, I had plants that I could not kill—roses and shrubs, a bamboo that had a mind of its own, and an olive and Christmas tree planted three years before that, astonishingly, had not yet given up the ghost. There was no lawn, no turf, and no grass. Yet, straightaway, my eyes zoomed onto a single fresh green blade on the mat by the front door.

Puzzled, I pushed the deli food into the fridge and shrugged off my coat. I checked the windows, which were locked, and then carried out a forensic search. Nickable items like my laptop and television were still in the sitting room—my magazine was still open where I'd left it. Nothing appeared taken from the kitchen, my bedroom, or the bathroom. Likewise, in Tara's room, nothing appeared disturbed or stolen. Perhaps Allan Dukes had trodden grass in during his visit the previous day, although, judging from the state of his shiny shoes, I doubted it. If he'd parked his car around the corner, he would have made the journey to my place on foot over pavement. However, I had to admit it was possible. He could have strayed onto the green in front of Lansdown Terrace.

None the wiser, I turned to go and froze. Tara's shoes. A knee-high boot had keeled over. Not so strange, perhaps, but less easy to explain, a pair of sneakers had changed places with a navy pair of open-toe sandals. A charge ran through my body like an electric current. Turning slowly round, I noticed other things. The pots of nail varnish were out of sequence, too. Diving to the floor, I looked underneath her bed and noticed that a lid on one of the storage boxes was askew. Dragging it out, I checked the content, which were mainly school exercise books, notepads, and keepsakes. I stared at the rape alarm I'd given her when she started coming home late. Fat lot of good that had done. I got the impression that her books had been tampered with, although, weirdly, nothing was missing. And I would know. Definitely. Unquestionably.

Rocked, I realised that someone had been here, in my daughter's room, my shrine to her, and yet there was no sign of break-in.

Only Tiff had the key to my apartment.

Fourteen

I phoned Tiff early the next morning.

"Are you kidding? I've spent every waking hour this week at the stables."

"Right," I said, dejected.

"Has something happened?"

"Of course not." I was sure my high-pitched laugh was a dead giveaway.

"You sound weird, Grace."

"Do I?" I trilled, falsely bright. "Spending too much time on my own and imagining things." As soon as the words escaped my mouth, I wanted to claw them right back. I hadn't mentioned my enforced sabbatical.

"Are you calling from work?" Tiff said suspiciously.

I sidestepped. "Honestly, Tiff, it's fine. *I'm* fine," I said with emphasis.

"Hmm. Look, I'd better go. Got to finish mucking out. I'll phone Gray and we'll come over tonight."

"It's okay, I've plans."

"Really?"

"Yeah," I bluffed. "Thought I'd go to the cinema."

"On your own?"

"Yes."

"What are you going to see?"

"Haven't decided yet."

"Well, if you're sure."

I was and said good-bye. I couldn't work it out. Someone had definitely entered the flat and gone through Tara's things, but not mine. What was he or she searching for, and why? Then I had another idea. It was so blindingly obvious I don't know why it hadn't occurred to me before.

"Archie, it's me," I said, leaving a message on his phone. "I know this sounds slightly strange, but did Tara leave a key to the apartment at yours? If you could call me back, I'd be really grateful."

He returned my call as the two o'clock news on the radio finished. I guessed he'd come off shift or was on a break.

"Tara never left a key here. What's it all about?"

I prevaricated. "It sounds so silly."

"Try me."

I explained. Archie listened then floored me. "It's obvious."

"Is it?" I was always astounded by the way in which Archie could cut to the heart of a problem while I seemed to get distracted and ensnared in its permutations.

"Who was the last person to visit your place?"

"Allan Dukes."

"There you go."

"But Archie, how did he get back in?"

"Maybe he stole a key. Have you checked?"

I scratched my head. I hadn't. "All right, well, say he did. What was he after?"

"I don't know, something that he thought he could use."

"Use?"

"To disprove that his son killed our daughter." Archie was bitter. I couldn't blame him, but Allan Dukes's behaviour didn't stack.

"Archie, he was with me the whole time. He came through to the sitting room. I never left him alone. We sat down, I heard what he said, and then asked him to leave."

"Are you sure?"

"What do you mean, am I sure? I know what happened."

"You hadn't been drinking or anything?"

Irritation prickled my skin. "No," I said in a wintry tone. "I had not."

"Then I don't know what else to suggest, other than you go to the cops."

I must have let out a groan.

"Or I could report it for you."

"I don't want you to. Nothing was taken."

He didn't sound pleased but he acquiesced. "Actually, I'm glad you phoned, there's something we need to discuss."

Hell, I was right. I knew it.

"Yeah?" I said, pleased that I could read him so well.

"I would have mentioned it before," he said, mildly clearing his throat, "but it didn't feel right, what with everything going on."

Like Kristina hovering over you?

Relieved, I didn't even feel critical of his earlier denial. It had to be important, I realised. "Fire away," I said.

"Actually, I'd prefer to talk face-to-face."

Did Archie know something that would throw light on Allan Dukes's claim? No, don't be silly, I thought, of course not. There was another possibility. Thrill charged my entire body. "When?"

"How about later, say five? Could you do that?"

"Absolutely. Where?"

"Do you know the Strand?"

"Around the corner from Cambray Place?"

"On the High Street, opposite the Swan."

"I'll be there."

I spent the next hour deciding what to wear and wondering why Archie wanted to meet. Sharing my life with Archie had always been sexy and dramatic and unpredictable. Did he have news? Was there a change of heart? Had loss and the culmination of the trial finally changed him? Had he found out that living with Kristina had been a huge mistake? Had lust dissipated, withered, and died? My mind raced on madly ahead. Could he now see her for the shallow, self-obsessed woman that she was? My God, I hoped so. Almost sick at the thought of that possibility, I kept busy.

Firing up the laptop, I Googled the electoral roll for Gloucester and filled in Allan Dukes's name. A single entry came up. Occupants at his address were listed as Jordan and Dionne Dukes. Tara had mentioned Jordan's younger sister, who'd now be around the same age Tara was when she first took up with Jordan. Next I trawled the Internet for small builders and stumbled across an advert for Allan Dukes's business. *We are a small, friendly, well established Gloucester-based building firm with thirty years experience. All aspects of masonry undertaken and we only take on one project at a time.* A number of testimonials vouched for his craftsmanship, honest pricing, and courteous service. Did this sound like the man who had blagged his way into my home in order to steal? *You're so gullible,* Tiff had often told me.

I dressed with care. I wanted Archie to realise that I was holding it together, that I was confident, that my feelings for him had never changed. He'd always maintained that our love was timeless. *Wherever you are in the world, no matter what you do or who you're with, there will always be a special place for you in my heart,* he'd said. It had nearly killed me. Less easy to assimilate, he'd declared it in the same breath as *It's over.* Above all, I wanted to remind him of those first words and prove to him that we shared too much life experience, the great and the very worst, to give it up. I wanted him to understand that I would gladly have him back.

With this in mind, I settled on a slate grey pair of jeans, a green tailored shirt that accentuated my figure, and short black boots with a small heel. I'd invested in a brand-new trench coat a month or so before Tara's death but had never had the heart to wear. Now would be the right time.

I took great care with make-up, striving for a natural look without appearing dowdy. Mocha-coloured eye shadow highlighted the blue in my eyes, a slick of pink on my lips, and a dab of cologne behind my ears. Leaving in time to ensure that I was fashionably late, and not too eager, I strode down the high street, the epitome of confidence. For the first time in a long time, I noticed second glances of appreciation. Tiff was right. I had to get on. I had to carve out a new way. And I could do it. With Archie.

Forget about Allan Dukes and his wild assertions. Forget about that stray blade of grass on the carpet. Forget everything...

Sleekly handsome in a tailored jacket over a navy open-neck shirt and pale ice-blue jeans, Archie was already at the bar sipping a pint. He turned as I walked in and threw me a smile that made my chest ache.

"What will you have?"

Vodka, I thought. "Do they do coffee?" I said.

"I'm sure they will." He caught the eye of a barman and ordered.

"What are you drinking?" I said, viewing his glass. It was a silly thing to ask, but I didn't want to launch straight in with questions. I wanted to seem relaxed, a woman of the world, in control, not in the least bit needy.

"Draught Moretti. It's good." He took another sip and smiled admiringly. "I love your new hairstyle. It really suits you."

"Thanks." I swelled with warmth and confidence. Surreptitiously, I undid the buttons of my coat and let it fall open to reveal my more up-to-date image. "I thought it was time to make a break, to try and move on."

Again the smile. "Couldn't agree with you more."

My coffee appeared. Archie suggested that we decamp to a table. Quiet at that time in the pub, we could take our pick. Archie selected the cosy one for two in the corner near the window.

"Old times," I said, with my warmest smile.

"Indeed." He snatched at his drink and his left knee twitched. I suddenly realised that he was shy, nervous, really unlike him. Endearing.

"First of all," he began, "I wanted to ask if that man has bothered you again?"

"Archie," I said, pulling a face, "it's been twenty-four hours. I think he got the message."

"Only if he does—"

"Is that the only reason you got me here?" I tried to quell my alarm. "I thought I'd made it perfectly clear."

"Yes, yes, you did. Sorry. Concerned for you, that's all. I don't want him digging everything up again."

How sweet of you to care. "And neither do I. There's no need to worry. I have it nailed."

He nodded vacantly and reached for his glass.

"So," I said lightly, "what did you want to talk about?"

He waited a beat, as if marshalling his emotional resources, and fixed me with an expression that I knew so well. When he reached across and placed a strong smooth hand over mine, my brain turned to mush. I leant in towards him. At that distance, I could smell hops and heat and Archie's expensive aftershave.

"I'm going to marry Kristina," he said.

Everything constricted, including my throat, my heart, my stomach. Nausea coursed through my body. There was a strange humming sensation in my head, as if all my energy powered down through my body into the tips of my toes before shorting out, wasted. The room didn't move; it spun. I must have looked as dumbfounded as I felt because Archie repeated it.

I stared at his hand as if it were a false widow spider, and arched back. "Congratulations," I said thickly, as if my tongue was drenched in paraffin oil. I needed to escape, get up, flee, run all the way home, but the muscles in my legs felt atrophied. I couldn't move. I couldn't even fall to the floor and crawl on my hands and knees because I couldn't flicker a hair or sinew. Some bastard had disconnected the nerves that sent impulses to my brain.

"You look shocked, Grace."

"No," I said, hoping my eyes didn't gleam with tears. You've ruined me, I wanted to shout. How could you be so cruel? Why inflict this on me now? You could have sloped away and done it and told me afterwards. It wasn't as if you needed my blessing. As badly as my spirit was crushed, I stirred with a sensation that was alien to me: anger.

"We'd been thinking of it for some time. Had a few problems, to be perfectly honest ... "

I flinched. "Problems?"

"Yeah, you know, relationship stuff. We were on the verge of splitting a few years ago and then, you know ... " He broke off, coughed, and stared into the depths of his drink.

"Tara," I said. "Our daughter," I added, as if he'd forgotten and needed to be reminded. No, not *simply* reminded, *bloody* reminded.

I must have tossed my head back in defiance because Archie looked at me as if I'd stripped naked in the middle of the pub.

"I know it's difficult and perhaps the timing could be better," he said meekly.

"Don't give it another thought." I spoke through my teeth and lifted the cooling coffee to my lips. When I put down the cup, it clattered against the saucer.

"There's something else," he said. The concerned expression in his eye had morphed into one of worried anticipation. Had I been Tiff, this would be the entree before I blew my stack. But I was not Tiff. I was Grace, dignified and serene, no matter the provocation, or so people said. I sat up straight, braced for whatever Archie was to impart. Please God, don't let Kristina be pregnant.

"We're moving away."

"Selling up?"

"Yeah."

"The house is on the market?"

"Not yet, but it will be."

Blindsided, I gaped at Archie, who sat or rather twitched opposite. "Where?"

He cleared his throat for the umpteenth time. "We don't know yet. We simply want a fresh beginning, like you said." He eyed me as if it had been my idea.

"But what about your job?"

"I can get another. Nurses are always in demand."

"I see." Except I only half saw.

"It's not been the easiest decision to make, but it's the right one."

"How does this fit with Kristina's plans?"

"She can work pretty much anywhere," he said with a proud smile.

"Right then," I said, jumping awkwardly to my feet. "Better be off. I hope you'll both be very happy with your new life."

"Grace, I—"

"Good-bye, Archie." And with as much poise as I could manage, I strode out of the bar.

Fifteen

Humiliation and heartbreak are a toxic mix. Heads swivelled in astonishment as I openly sobbed through the streets and tore across roads, my face hot and seared with tears. Gawping at me as if I were the victim of a road accident, one driver almost mounted his white van on the pavement. I wanted to scream my pain at all of them and shriek, "My daughter is dead," for although Archie had broken my heart for a second time, it was Tara for whom I wept.

By the time I reached my road, my steps had shortened and my crying ceased. Spent, all that remained was a tight, impossible-to-loosen knot of fury. I flung myself into the flat, paused by the door, checking for further signs of incursion—there weren't any—and slumped down on the sofa, exhausted.

Replaying the conversation with the intractability of an obsessive, the point that had stuck—and which I hadn't pursued—was Archie's confession that he and Kristina were on the verge of splitting. *A few years ago,* he'd said.

Roughly around the time Tara took up with Jordan.

If I were honest, their teenage relationship caused more waves at Harp Hill than with my family and me. I had concerns, which I made plain, but I didn't rave and rail against it as Kristina and Archie had done. I'd put it down to the primeval possessiveness of fathers, Archie unwilling to relinquish his daughter to any man. Perhaps this explained problems within the relationship with Kristina. I'd heard from friends in second marriages that rows between partners were often the result of disputes and disagreements concerning children, and rarely due to difficulties within the marriage itself. Not that any of it mattered now. In the end, Archie had had the drop on me. He'd been right to be suspicious of Jordan Dukes.

I changed out of my clothes—they didn't feel right anymore—and made myself a sandwich because I couldn't be bothered to cook. Turning the television on, I watched a programme on wildlife, although I didn't absorb a word of commentary. I kept thinking about the break-in, Archie's revelation and his decision to move away, so out of character and unexpected. Stranger still, he'd been the only person I'd told about Allan Dukes and then the very next day someone lets himself in and hunts for … what?

Muddled with thinking, I went to bed early, fell asleep quickly, and awoke three hours later. A searchlight snapped on in my brain and my mind homed in on the unthinkable.

What if Allan Dukes was right?

What if someone else *had* killed Tara?

What if that individual feared that, from the grave, Tara could somehow expose him?

Tara, I realised, held the key. Somehow, I had to disinter her past and reclaim it.

I turned over, willing myself to relax, to be positive, to think of nice things that made me happy. I couldn't think of a single one. Sleep evading me, I got up, made myself a cup of tea, and took it back to bed with my laptop.

Didn't the police conduct a thorough search of Tara's stuff? Hadn't they studied her computer, viewed every message on her phone? If she'd had blood diamonds tucked into her knickers drawer, they would have unearthed them. Despite Jordan's dubious social activities, there had been no sign of drugs, not so much as a packet of cigarettes or a bottle of booze. But...

I powered up the laptop and found Allan Dukes's work number on the website. Then, for reasons with which I didn't want to fully engage, I looked up and jotted down the number for Paragon Boatbuilding, the Neville family business in the New Forest, the family from which Archie was estranged. Content, I fell asleep.

———

I lost my nerve the next morning and drove straight to the stables. It was a vile wet day and I found Tiff in the indoor school astride a horse called Jackman. An odd transformation occurs when my stocky sister takes to the saddle. In tune with her mount, she becomes at one and as one, attains an elegance of grace and movement impossible when on two pins instead of four. I watched, transfixed, as horse and rider effortlessly scaled a triple jump combination at heights that made my pulse stammer.

"Hiya," she shouted, red-cheeked, her steed cantering around the circuit and screeching to a dusty halt in front of me. "Good film?"

"Sacked it off."

Thought you might, her expression said. "Shouldn't you be at work?"

"Not today."

Tiff threw me a quizzical look, scrunched both reins in one hand, swung one leg round, and dismounted with a bounce. "Come on," she said, "walk with me and you can tell me all about it."

While Tiff took off Jackman's tack, groomed him to within an inch of his life, and gave him a bucket of bran mash, I told her about Archie's pronouncements. I kept back the visit from Allan Dukes and didn't breathe a word about someone entering the apartment. Two revelations in one day were enough for my quick-tempered sister to get her head around.

"Had to happen sometime," she said. Fiercely loyal and hating Archie for leaving me, she was frighteningly restrained and, dare I say, reasonable. I'd expected, and frankly hoped for, a more robust response.

"Which? Getting married or moving away?"

"Mmm," she said. "Moving away, that's the part I don't quite get."

"Me, too. Kristina's built up a lucrative business in town. She has a reputation. I mean, where will they go, for heaven's sake? London?"

"New York?"

I gawped at Tiff. "You don't really think so, do you?" Not that it should make any difference to me. New York or New Malden, the result would be the same: no more Archie. "It seems madness for her to want to up sticks."

"Maybe she doesn't. Maybe she's falling in with Archie's plans."

"Do you really think so?"

"You give that man too much credit," Tiff flashed with reproof. "What Archie wants, Archie gets. The sooner he crawls out from underneath your skin, the better. You're well rid of him."

Chastened, I drove back home.

Again, the apartment seemed intruder-free, but, with a thud of alarm, I realised that if someone had a key to my place they could enter my home at will, at any time and while I was in it. I sent an email direct to a locksmith in town. Ten minutes later, I received a reply. An hour and a half after that, the lock had been changed and I had a new set of keys.

Feeling more secure physically, I steeled myself mentally. It took me a long time to rehearse exactly what I was going to say, longer still to summon up the courage to pick up the phone, which I did twice, slamming it back down before I eventually thought, to hell.

It rang for a long time. I almost gave up and then a weary voice, thin and brittle with age, came on the line.

"Hello, Digby-Neville speaking."

As part of Archie's escape to freedom, as he put it, he'd dropped the Digby part of his surname. *A pretentious load of old cobblers,* he'd once said. It seemed strange to hear his father use the family name now.

"Is it possible to speak to Mrs. Digby-Neville?" I believed a woman-to-woman conversation would elicit more information.

"She's in the garden."

"Oh," I said. From what Archie had told me, their land went on for miles.

"If you don't mind waiting, I can get Blount to go and find her. Take a few minutes." A high-pitch whine whistled down the line, followed by the crackle you normally associate with a radio on the blink. Hearing aid, I realised.

"If it's not too much trouble," I shouted.

"Yes, I can hear you. Who shall I say is calling?"

"Archie's ex-wife—"

"Good God, Kristina?" he barked.

Mentally, I skipped several beats. "Grace," I said, shaken.

"Ah, yes, I see," he said in a manner that indicated he didn't have a clue.

Those were the slowest few minutes of my life. When had Archie been in touch with his parents? How did they know about Kristina? Had she been introduced while I, his wife of thirteen years and the mother of his child, had never set one foot over the threshold? For all the time we'd been together Archie had been keen to go his own way, rebel against his structured upbringing, escape his destiny, ditch his inheritance rather than comply with his parents' wishes. There had been a family dispute, he told me. He—

"Hello?"

Almost the same register as her husband's, the voice was scratchy and cultured, the speaker clearly of a great age. Archie had said that his mother was forty when she had given birth to her only son. Flummoxed by Mr. Digby-Neville's reference to Kristina, I barely knew where to start.

"Thank you for talking to me."

"Yes, I'm a little confused. Baz said that you're Archie's wife."

"His ex."

"I see, yes." She said it as if she'd rummaged through a drawer and fished out, quite by chance, an important document. "Archie mentioned you."

Mentioned? How good of him.

"And I understand you had a daughter who died."

Emotion flooded through me. I wanted to snap MURDER, but realised it was not her fault. I trotted out my prepared lie. "I've lost contact with Archie, I'm afraid, and wondered whether you had his number."

"I see. Well, I'm not sure that's possible. I'd have to talk to Archie first."

"Right," I said uncertainly. "Archie and … erm Kristina are moving, aren't they?"

"Correct. We're downsizing to our cottage in the grounds to allow them to live in the main house."

I clung to the table to steady myself.

"Although what this has to do with you, I've not the faintest idea."

I laughed nervously. "I'm not stalking him or anything." God, what had possessed me to say such a thing?

"I know very well what you're up to."

"Excuse me?"

"You're after his money. It's plain as the nose on my face."

"What money?"

"The money we put in trust, his inheritance, and I can tell you now, we'll fight you all the way through the courts, if we have to."

"But—"

"And don't come the wide-eyed innocent with me, missy. I may be old, but I'm not senile."

The phone went down and I was left standing amid the wreckage of Archie's lies. Tumbling with questions, I asked myself when he had reconciled himself to his family. Was it recently, or years ago? Chillingly, I wondered whether he'd led a double life. What kind of man was he, really, and what the hell else had he lied to me about?

Sixteen

"*That's a pretty dress. Did Dad buy it for you?*"

"*Kristina.*"

"*She took you shopping?*"

"*Yeah.*"

"*Where?*"

Tara threw me a spiky look. "In town."

"*When?*" *Acting like an arch inquisitor, I couldn't help myself. Pressing Tara about Kristina was like scratching an itch. Every time I got an answer I didn't want to hear, I bled.*

"*Last Tuesday when you were working.*"

I slunk off to my room and howled. Kristina had it all—beauty, poise, a relationship that worked with my Archie and my daughter, and the type of double-jointed flexibility when it came to her working arrangements that I couldn't compete with. Damn her.

This streaked through my mind as I charged off to Harp Hill, my foot dangerously on the accelerator, flat out, as I sped up Hales Road.

I screamed across the tarmac drive and parked side-on next to Kristina's black Porsche Cayenne 4x4, Archie's more modest Audi nowhere to be seen. Didn't mean he wasn't home. The vehicle could be hiding in the triple-fronted garage.

Stomping up the steps to their Grade II villa with its ceiling roses, cornicing, fireplaces, and original fucking features, I rang the bell.

Kristina opened the door. She didn't look astounded. She looked as if I'd shot her. "Grace," she burst out. "This is a surprise."

"Isn't it?"

She was casually dressed in sloppy sweater and straight leg jeans. Her slender feet were bare, toes waxed, toenails highly manicured a pale shade of coral, heels buffed and smooth. Her bloody feet offended every fibre of my being.

"I want to speak to Archie," I said.

"Is something wrong?"

"Is he in?" I said, ignoring her. This was between me and him.

"No," she said, tossing back a lustrous lock of long blonde hair.

"I don't believe you."

She took a single step towards me, blocking any view I might have of the spectacular hallway where it seemed that even the dust particles were collected, polished, and rearranged. "If you tell me what it's about, I'll pass on a message."

Kristina was the same height as me but looked taller because of her slim, I called it scrawny, build. However I had the advantage when it came to weight, despite my new thin look, so I simply shoved past her, skirting the grand staircase on my left and careening down the wide corridor and into the drawing room on my right.

"You can't barge your way in," I heard her shout after me.

"I just did," I said, locking eyes with Archie. He had his back to one of the double aspect windows, through which there was a fine view of a walled garden. Cornered, his gaze flickered from me to Kristina, now standing level with my shoulder. Fury and frustration pulsed off her in waves.

"It's all right, Krissie," Archie said in a melting voice. "I'll handle it."

"This is outrageous." She didn't stamp. Her voice did the job for her.

I turned and fixed her with a level look. "For once, I agree with you."

"Please, Krissie," Archie said in a coaxing *sweetie, darling* tone.

Darling stalked out and Archie invited me to take a seat. I had a choice: two sofas, two easy chairs, or a footstool that nestled by the gigantic fireplace. "I'll stand, thanks."

"Mind if I sit?" He was incredibly calm. I guessed as soon as his mother slammed down the phone, she'd called her precious son to warn him.

I shrugged as if I didn't give a damn either way, which was true. He sank down, legs splayed, nice and easy, leaning right into a caramel-coloured leather Chesterfield. He tilted his head toward me.

"Why did you lie about your parents?"

His eyebrows drew together, shocked it seemed that I had made such a wounding allegation. To help him out, I said, "I asked you where you were going and you said that you didn't know."

"I didn't want to hurt you. Is that so very wrong?"

"What's wrong is that you've done the equivalent of Photoshopping me and Tara out of their lives."

He let out an expansive, *must you fuss so much* sigh. "It wasn't like that. You know the deal I had with my parents."

"The *cutting off without a penny* deal, the *I never want you to darken my door again* deal, the one when you jettisoned the family name and did your own thing? Are these the same parents who never wanted to

112

meet me and their granddaughter, or are these alien parents parachuted in from Mars?"

Awkward did not cover Archie's expression. First he looked amazed by my reaction and then mortified. I was glad.

"I know how it must seem. You had to put up with so much of their crap—"

"No, I didn't. I had to put up with *your* crap, and to think I let you whinge on about your poor-little-rich-boy upbringing. No doubt, you'll be reclaiming your roots and calling yourself by your proper name too: Archibald Digby-Neville."

The sheepish expression on Archie's face told me all I needed to know.

"They're getting on, Grace. Dad's not well."

"Is that why you deliberately misled them about our daughter's death?"

His olive skin turned the colour of grouting. "It was a kindness to them."

"What about kindness to me? What about honouring Tara? I suppose you told them she'd had cancer."

A thin blue vein ticked in his neck and his mouth froze into a short straight line. "Now you're being ridiculous."

"Am I? And when did this magical reconciliation take place? Last year, the year before, or did you never really part company?"

"Long after we divorced, if you must know," he said, too smartly to my mind.

A charge of revelation grabbed at my chest. I pictured Archie, in secret financially involved in the business for years, in which case our divorce settlement was not what it should have been. I don't know whether Archie read this in my eyes, but he quickly laid out his defence.

"Mum contacted me after Dad first got sick a couple of years ago. We struck up an accord. Now he needs someone to take over the running of the business."

"You're going to give up nursing?" Everything you care about, everything you stand for, everything that made me care and fall in love with you? "What the hell happened to you? What about your ideals, all those things you believed in?"

"It wasn't an easy decision. I feel guilty about it."

I was dumbstruck. I could no sooner imagine Archie managing his dad's business empire than working in a corner shop. Then I twigged.

"Is this Kristina's idea? The lure of serious money must be right up her street. Bitch."

"Grace, that's not—"

"Don't you dare say it," I hissed, "you spineless, double-dealing shit."

The man had seen me in all my facets, or so he thought. He'd witnessed my happiness, my joy, my sadness and desolation. In all the long time he'd known me, he had never had a ringside view of my rage. Not ever.

"You know what? I don't believe a word of it. You've been plotting this for ages."

"If this is about the money—"

"How dare you," I ranted. I was guilty of many things—wanting to be loved, mostly—but I wasn't a gold digger. I didn't have it in me. He stayed silent and his brow wrinkled into lots of tiny hurt lines, injury in his eyes. When he finally opened his mouth to speak I was in no mood to listen. "You're a liar and a user. I'm glad you're going."

And, with these my final words, I strode through the house with my head held high, flung open the door, hurled down the steps and into my car, and drove away.

This time, I did not cry.

Seventeen

"Have you seen how much they're flogging it for? Over a million and a half quid."

I'd spent a miserable weekend on my own. Since I'd fled from Harp Hill, Archie had besieged me with phone calls. He, as much as I, didn't like conflict and definitely didn't like anyone thinking the worst of him. We still shared that much in common. But, in the light of my latest discovery, I was in danger of succumbing to paranoia. It was good to hear a familiar voice again.

"How do you know, Tiff?" I said. "It's not even on the market yet."

"Doug told me."

"How the hell would he know?"

"Contacts in the property trade."

Doug had contacts everywhere but I doubted in Cheltenham's thriving property market. Sounded more like an educated guess. I told Tiff about Archie and Kristina's grand plans to move back and take over the family business.

"You're joking."

"No, I had a horrible conversation with his mother on the phone." Which led me to question all sorts of things about my ex.

"You?" Tiff snorted. I, apparently, didn't do "run-ins."

I explained the Nevilles' firm belief that I was set to challenge the original divorce settlement. "'As if."

"Why not? Get yourself a good lawyer and bingo!"

"Tiff, It would take money I don't have. Lawyers, good or bad, don't work for nothing."

"Doug would help out."

"Only if he thought there was something in it for him." Had Tiff morphed into Graham? He never stopped banging on about Doug this, Doug that.

"So you're going to roll over as usual?" The challenge in her voice was crystal.

I let out a weary sigh. With Tiff clamouring for action, I felt under siege.

In the absence of a reply, Tiff gave up and rang off. This was standard sisterly operating procedure. Almost immediately, the phone rang again, but it wasn't Tiff. The display revealed an unknown number. Rattled, I broke the habit of a lifetime and picked up.

"Grace?"

I winced. What the hell did DI Colin Dunne want? Then I realised Archie must have made good on his threat to report an intruder in the flat. It took a feat of will not to let out a groan.

"Hi, Colin," I said jauntily.

"How are you doing, Grace?"

"Oh, you know. Getting along."

"Glad to hear it. I know this is out of the ordinary, but I wondered if I might pop round."

I jolted. "Has something happened, fresh developments? New evidence emerged?"

"Good grief, whatever makes you think that?"

"Oh, nothing," I said, backtracking faster than a government minister on a policy statement.

"I can assure you," he said with a fat laugh, "the right man is serving time."

"Yes, of course."

"You didn't doubt the conviction, did you?" Now he sounded worried.

"No," I said shakily. "When would be convenient?"

"In the next quarter of an hour? I won't take up too much of your time."

"See you in fifteen then," I said, wishing I were at work.

Dressed in a smart grey suit, pale blue shirt, and silk tie, Colin Dunne, with his expensive aftershave, groomed hands, and neatly cut hair, bore a passing resemblance to a highly skilled PR guru. Only his craggy, reddish complexion gave the game away. Even in repose, poor man, his default expression was belligerent.

I ushered him through to the sitting room, where he sat down, undid the button of his jacket in a practiced manner, and laid his tan leather briefcase on the sofa. My mind flashed back to previous visits: updates on the investigation, which had taken place at breakneck speed, the likelihood or otherwise of a guilty plea being entered, and the mystifyingly slow and arcane workings of the court. Often Dunne's information would double up and tally with the family liaison officer's.

Sometimes, it didn't, which only served to confuse me. Whatever, I'd deduced that Dunne was a conscientious sort.

He smiled warmly around the room and then at me. "Looks like you're getting your life together." I didn't comment. People often mistook my seeming capability for strength. He could believe what he wanted. "Which is why I thought you might be the very person to get involved in a new initiative on knife crime."

My gut reaction was an immediate and resounding NO. A great idea, for sure, but I was not the person to promote it. Too raw, I couldn't see a way ahead in which I wouldn't always feel this way. Unwilling to disappoint him immediately, I forced a smile, which, unfortunately, as often happened with people, Dunne mistook for interest.

"Four knife-surrender bins are to be placed in designated areas in Cheltenham and Gloucester," Dunne continued. "We want anyone who carries to feel secure that they can get rid of weapons without the threat of prosecution." I nodded my strong agreement. "Part of a wider initiative with West Mids, the slogan is *Get a life, bin that knife.* Good, isn't it?" His muddy coloured eyes were shiny with enthusiasm.

"I can see it working well. Not sure where I fit though."

"We're asking people like you to distribute leaflets."

Like me? "Where exactly?"

"In the town centre."

"To passersby?" The thought appalled. Chuggers of every denomination already dominated the high street. Going shopping was like navigating an obstacle course. I'd become an expert in cultivating a look that said *do not disturb.* What really riled, Dunne perceived me as no different to them and yet I was different to them in countless, unimaginable ways.

Dunne fixed me with an expectant, toothy smile. He had sharp incisors, I noticed. Colour raced across the tops of my cheekbones. "I'm not sure that's quite me."

"You'd be in touch with other mums who've suffered a similar experience," he said, diving into his briefcase and drawing out a sheaf of papers. An image of the victim support woman flashed before my eyes. She'd meant well with her phone numbers, names of people, names of organisations, websites, and white noise. He handed me a wodge of information.

"Can I think about it?" I said.

"Course you can."

In his mind, he'd got a result. I thought he'd get up and go. He didn't. "Grace, what you said earlier about Jordan Dukes."

I did my best to assume a vacant expression, as if I'd no idea what he was talking about. Dunne's large, sloping nose emerged from his jagged face more prominently than seemed possible. "You expressed doubts about the conviction."

"Did I?" I said, trying to make light of it.

"That boy was bad right from the moment he emerged from his mother's womb. Rotten to the core, always will be." Dunne reeled off a list of Jordan's crimes, from minor misdemeanours to the more serious stuff. To his credit, Allan Dukes had been truthful. He'd never played it down.

"I know all that," I said, unthinking.

Dunne's dented brow deepened. "How?"

I held his stare. "What I mean is that I'm not surprised."

"We've been trying to bang him up for a long time. Your daughter's death created the perfect opportunity for us."

What? I stared at him. Bile flooded my mouth. I could not order Dunne out of my house as I'd done with Allan Dukes, but I wanted him gone, exactly the same. I stood up, flicked a cold smile, and glanced at the clock over the fireplace. Dunne followed my eyes and took my lead.

"You'll give the initiative some thought?" he said, pausing in the narrow hallway.

"I will."

"Take care of yourself, Grace."

I nodded numbly and watched him cross the courtyard. After I shut the front door, I dropped the leaflets in the log basket ready for burning.

———

What are the odds of a miscarriage of justice? How many times do killers stalk the universe while others do their time, or, under other more extreme judicial systems, pay the ultimate price? The thought undid me, which was why, when Archie called again an hour later, I answered.

"Grace, I really don't want us to—"

"Never mind about that," I said. "Colin Dunne came round this morning."

"What the hell about?"

"Doesn't matter. The point is I've got a bad feeling about the cops. They were gunning for Jordan. He's been in their sights for years."

"And with good reason."

"There's a difference between drug running and murder."

"One often leads to the other, Grace."

He was right. How naïve of me. "I don't know. I can't explain. I want it to be all over, yet I don't feel it is. What if the police were blinded by a need to get a conviction, any conviction, at any price?"

"You're stressed," Archie said in his most soothing tone, the one he reserved for work. Oddly, it irritated me.

"That doesn't make me stupid."

He let out a gigantic sigh. "Unforgivably, Allan Dukes has put a nasty seed of doubt in your mind."

"Yes, but—"

"Did you mention his visit to Dunne?"

"No," I said in a quiet voice.

"Has it occurred to you that Tara might have given a copy of her key to Jordan?"

"I hadn't thought of that, no," I admitted. Stupid me.

"Well, maybe that's how Allan got hold of it. Don't you see, by entering your apartment and rummaging through Tara's belongings, it gives credence to what he wants you to believe, that his son is innocent?"

"You mean he set the whole thing up? You really think so?" I was lightheaded with confusion.

"It's the only scenario that makes sense."

My face screwed up in disbelief. "It's a very elaborate deception, isn't it?"

"Desperate measures." Then, as if that was sorted, he continued. "About yesterday, I've been giving it some thought and, well, it was Kristina's idea, really," he said, quite obviously struggling to find the right words, "and we thought, as a goodwill gesture, and a token of faith, bearing in mind … "

"Archie, what are you burbling about?"

"We'd like to offer you a sum of money."

I blinked. My mouth went dry. "For what?"

"I'm not saying you've had a raw deal, you understand, but we think it fair if you accept a gift, say twenty-five thousand."

Twenty-five thousand pounds was a small fortune to me. I should have grabbed it. It's what Tiff would do. "It's incredibly generous," I stammered. "I'm stunned. I don't know what to say, Archie."

"Say yes. Nobody need know."

I spiked inside. Was he buying me off? Were there strings attached? What did he want in return? A more insidious thought inserted itself into my brain, unbidden. Did Archie want me to kill dead the possibility of Jordan's innocence?

Spotting my hesitation, he added, "No sense in being proud."

I told him what I told Dunne: "Thanks, I'll think about it."

And then I called Allan Dukes.

Eighteen

"*We did a pretty good job with Tara,*" *Archie remarked a few months after he'd moved out. "She's a lucky kid.*"

I frowned. Was I being thick? "How do you work that out?"

"She's got three important people in her life—you, me, and Kristina."

I wasn't the violent type. Had I been, I would have laid him out with a single blow to the head.

The conversation flittered through my mind while I stroked a lock of Tara's baby hair, white-blonde and as fine and delicate as a spiderweb. I kept it in a small jewellery box in my bedside drawer. I took it out more often these days, normally at low moments.

This was one of them. I'd opened Pandora's box and I was afraid of what might jump out of it and smack me in the eye.

After Allan Dukes had recovered from the initial shock of hearing my voice, he said that he would be right round. That was twelve minutes ago.

I returned the keepsake to my drawer and poured myself a glass of water. I didn't rehearse what to say because I wasn't sure what I expected or hoped for. Of one thing I was certain: Jordan's dad deserved a listening ear, if only because Dunne's stated bias against Jordan alarmed me at least as much as someone entering my apartment uninvited. Quite where Archie's offer of hard cash sat in the catalogue of awkward coincidences was anyone's guess.

Half an hour later, there was no sign of Allan Dukes. I washed up my glass and squinted out of the hall window with its view of the courtyard and stone steps leading up to the pavement and road. Rain fell in slick sheets, colouring the world grey.

Out of nowhere I heard the frantic cry of a baby. My ears pricked and the sound grew louder and more desperate. Almost at once, Allan Dukes hurried down the steps, boots clicking, head bent, and hugging a mewling bundle to his chest. Taken aback, I opened the door.

"I'm so sorry," he said, speeding inside. Water trickled down his face and his wet blond hair was dark with rain. He said something but I couldn't hear above the noise, which had reached ear-splitting proportions. I edged closer. Over the top of a blanket, I could see a downy head bobbing feverishly, the skin beneath suffused bright pink in spite of the baby's dark complexion.

"He won't stop," Allan said in dismay.

"Here, give him to me." I held out my arms. Doubtfully Allan pulled the shuddering bundle away and handed him over. I was immediately engulfed in the uniquely sweet, yeasty aroma of new baby, mingled with the smell of stale milk, nappy, and damp wool.

I stared in awe. I'd forgotten how little and vulnerable they were, the way the bones in their skulls weren't yet fused, leaving a dangerous gap, and how their limbs were soft and smooth and unprotected. Gazing at him, I cupped the back of his tiny, perfect head in one hand, supporting his fragile neck, and clasped him firmly to me. He quieted, turned, and I felt his little mouth lock onto my bare neck and suck. Silence.

"Jesus, how did you do that?" Allan said, genuinely perplexed. He wore a short-sleeved Polo shirt, as though he hadn't had time to throw on a jacket. The hair on his muscular arms lay flat against his skin.

"Don't be fooled. It's only a matter of time before he starts wailing again. Poor little thing, he's like a vampire after dark. When did you last feed him?"

Allan swung a rucksack from off his back. "Um, a few hours ago," he said vaguely, "I brought his milk with me. Anywhere I can warm it up?"

"The kitchen's through there," I gestured with my chin. In inverse proportion to his size, the baby thrashed about, gearing up for an encore. I gently nudged the tip of my little finger into its mouth to buy time, felt the baby latch on and suckle furiously, and followed Allan into the kitchen.

"Do you have a microwave?" he said.

"Afraid not."

"No matter. I'll get inventive."

I watched as he filled the kitchen bowl with warm water and placed the prepared bottle into it.

"What's his name?"

"Asher. Wasn't my choice," Allan said, smiling an apology. He had a good smile. Wide and honest, it made his eyes sparkle, although nothing could disguise the dog-tired lilac shadows beneath.

"Your son?"

"My grandson. Dionne's baby."

"Dionne's?" I burst out. "She's only sixteen."

"Aye, I know." He flushed with shame. There was an *if only* expression in his eyes. *If only* I'd been a more assiduous father. *If only* I'd had a more lasting relationship with the children's mother. *If only* I'd been more disciplined with my son. *If only* I'd been firmer with my daughter and kept a closer eye on her. I read it all because I suffered from the same affliction.

"I apologise," I said. "I didn't mean to be rude."

He shook his head and gave another sad, *no offence taken* smile. "Don't get me wrong, he's a lovely baby, but it's damned hard work."

"Where is Dionne?"

"At school."

I was amazed. "Surely, you're not doing this on your own? What about social workers, health visitors?"

"Paper chasers, more like."

"Is the father in the picture, or his parents?"

"Don't want to know."

"But—"

"Asher normally goes to a baby-minder but she called in sick today. What with the business and everything …" His voice petered out. He dropped his gaze, dejected. I felt sorry for him. Archie would have said that this was exactly what Allan Dukes wanted, to play on my sympathy.

Asher squiggled and mewled in my arms. Any minute now, his little lungs would fill and the kitchen would reverberate with his hollering. "Is that bottle ready yet?" I said anxiously, dancing from one foot to the other.

"We could give it a go." Allan took the bottle out and ran a drop of milk on the back of his hand to test the temperature. "Yep, that's good."

Despite Asher struggling in my arms, I was reluctant to hand him back. It was so nice to have someone to cuddle again. Allan settled him in the crook of his arm and, instantly, Asher locked onto the teat. "Magic," he said, watching the baby glugging away with the same pride and contentment I'd once observed in Archie with Tara. It was such a joyous recollection that I almost forgot why I'd invited Allan Dukes into my home.

"About Jordan," I began. He glanced up, wary of the mention of his son's name. "I was hasty and upset," I said. "I didn't hear you out properly. I'm prepared to listen now."

He viewed me for a long moment, unsure, it seemed, of my timing, my sudden change of heart. I forced a reassuring smile and he opened his mouth to speak but then thought better of it, worried, perhaps, of saying the wrong word in the wrong way. I realised then how much I'd dashed his hopes the first time. "It might be better coming from Jordan," he said, at last.

I swallowed. Prepared to give Allan Dukes a hearing, I was less certain about direct contact with Jordan. "But you said he wouldn't talk about it."

"Not to me, but he'll talk to you. He said so."

I felt as if Allan were running on ahead. Wasn't he asking too much, and how would it work? Was I even allowed to see Jordan in prison? I posed these questions to him.

"There are protocols," he admitted. "A prisoner has to agree to it and so do the prison authorities."

"Is that likely?"

"I suppose they may view it as a form of restorative justice."

"But that would mean Jordan admitting his guilt."

"Yes," he said, sombre.

My hand flew to my temple. "I'm sorry, are you saying that Jordan killed Tara?"

His eyes flashed with determination. "No."

I glanced at the baby. Milk-mouthed, Asher was fast asleep; his eyelids ringed a delicate duck-egg blue, peaceful and calm. My heart throbbed for what he'd been born into and how his life might turn out.

"Then I don't understand."

"Jordan accepts his fate. It doesn't make him guilty of Tara's murder. It's important to him that you understand that. Would you agree to see him?"

I baulked at the prospect. How would it make me feel? What might it do to me? Would it really help or make things a whole lot worse?

Allan took my silence as acquiescence. "You'll need ID, of course."

Silence invaded the room like an army poised to strike.

"It might provide closure," he murmured.

"I suppose you may be right," I said, more in hope than conviction. "It might be easier all round if Jordan uses my maiden name, Saunders." In a late bid for independence, both my passport and driving licence were held in the same name. I'd no idea why I hadn't fully committed to Archie. I'd loved my new surname, Neville. Perhaps I'd always known deep down that he would leave me one day.

"Thank you," he said awkwardly. I had the distinct feeling he was holding back. Where was the smoking gun, the incontrovertible proof? Agreement to see Jordan at some time in the future didn't seem a very satisfactory outcome and closure wasn't guaranteed. Where does that leave us, I wanted to ask.

He dropped his gaze to the sleeping child. "Jordan was like this once," he murmured, "his whole young life before him. He was a good lad, good at school, too, didn't always run with the wrong crowd, and then ... " He glanced up. "I'm not making excuses, but he hasn't had it easy."

I felt the familiar tug of shared experience. Hadn't I said the same about Tara? Although, by comparison, her life had been charmed—until the very end.

"Once he reached his thirteenth birthday I could never prise him away from the Stringers," Allan said. "That's when I lost him for good. He'd promise me he'd dump them, but they'd always lure him back. In his head they were more his family than the one he had."

"I'm sorry," I said, and I was. His helplessness resonated with me. I understood the way something new and shiny and more exciting would always take priority in a young teenager's mind against boring, dependable, and constant. I'd been there many times. When a child spurns the best you can give, it strikes deeply at the core of you. It's devastating.

"How is he?" I spoke in the same tentative tone people used with me.

Allan dropped his gaze again. Did I see a tear fill his eye? "Not good."

"I hear he's serving time in Bristol."

"Pretty rough in there. Filthy, too. Jordan seems to spend a lot of time in lock-down. Not much to do. And the men in there ... "

I swallowed. Any sane person would berate me for my ability to feel sympathy for the boy. Archie would be furious at what he would see as my duplicity and betrayal. Tiff, if she knew, would threaten to knock sense into my head. I didn't understand it myself. If things had been simpler, if Allan didn't blaze with conviction, if my flat had not been violated, maybe I'd feel differently. But they weren't simpler and I was secretly afraid that the killer was still out there. What if Allan was right and the murderer had got away with it and was possibly primed to kill again?

"The gang," I said, "tell me about them."

Allan visibly relaxed; easier terrain, less personal. "There are three main players—Ruben Monk, Jango Waring, and a girl called Dax."

I expressed surprise. Allan's eyes flickered. "Vicious as sin and a right piece of work. She and Jordan used to go out."

Something cold slithered across my guts. "Used to?"

"Before Tara."

"Who dumped whom?"

"Jordan dumped Dax."

"Christ," I exploded. "Do you think she had a hand in Tara's murder?"

"If she did, Jordan isn't saying. Not to me, at any rate, and I think he would."

I didn't know what to make of it. Surely the police would have checked out the possibility? A bleak thought entered my mind. Maybe they had. Maybe they didn't care. Jordan was always "good for it."

"I've done some digging," Allan said. "Nothing that would get me killed," he added without expression.

"Killed?" I said, startled.

He flicked a smile. "You're not really aware of the risks, are you?"

I don't think he meant the way it sounded, as if I'd lived a cosy, sheltered life, but I couldn't be sure.

Pressure expanded inside my head. What was I getting into? I'd been risk-averse for most of my life and look where that had got me. But this? Into what murky world might it take me? And yet wasn't I already stumbling through a rank tunnel of despair and suspicion?

He shook his head slowly. "These kids could do you serious harm. They've been rolling with knives since they were ten. There are no boundaries they won't cross, Dax included."

"I appreciate your candour."

"It's why you can't get involved."

"Like it or not, I am involved. You did that the first time you knocked on my door."

He dropped his gaze, embarrassed. "Only in so far as Jordan is concerned. You leave the rest to me," he said, glancing up.

I spiked with alarm. The fire was back in his eyes. If he did something stupid or illegal, his children would be without a father and his grandson without an anchor. It hadn't taken me long to work out that Allan Dukes was the centre of the family universe. Without him, the planets would implode. "What are you going to do?"

"Not sure yet. I'll have a clearer idea once you've seen Jordan."

So it all hinged on me.

Silence descended on my small kitchen, overwhelming and smothering, thick as smog. He watched me with an expression I couldn't grasp or read, as if reaching out, but the connection between us was crackly and spasmodic. Finally he spoke without a trace of a smile.

"We're the fallen, aren't we, you and I?" The melodic tone of his voice, the intimacy in his eyes evoked a memory of another time when it was me and Archie and no other. "We're victims of our children's bad choices."

Chill swept into the room. I suppressed a shiver. I knew nothing about Allan Dukes. I'd never assumed people in different walks of life were intellectually or emotionally impoverished but, to my shame, and if I were honest, I'd dismissed him as a low-life. Written him off, as Archie had done, and yet his honesty and eloquence spoke more to me than any fine words Archie had spoken lately. There was much more to this man than I'd given him credit for. I wasn't mesmerised, but he intrigued and spoke to my heart as well as my mind.

"You said you'd been digging. What exactly did you discover?"

131

He viewed me as if weighing up how much more I could stand to hear. "On the night Tara died, a lad was knifed on the outskirts of Gloucester."

"Gang-related?"

"Tyrone Weaver was a member of the Zimba Crew, bitter rivals of the Stringers. To date, his killer or killers have never been found."

My eyes widened. "You think Jordan was involved?"

He looked me in the eye. It was like watching the slow, agonising moment before two cars skid on ice and collide. And then I realised. "But that would mean Jordan was involved in murder," I said thickly.

"Yes," he said, "just not Tara's."

Nineteen

Numbed, I watched Allan Dukes leave. Whatever was exhumed, no good would come of it for Jordan or for him.

"You'll let me know about a prison visit?" I'd said, running my finger lightly over Asher's soft-as-down cheeks as Allan hovered by the front door.

"You should receive a visiting order in the mail."

"Okay, I'll let you know when it arrives."

Then I curled up in the sitting room. Someone had implanted a lump of stone where my brain should be. Had Dax killed Tara for the most basic of reasons, a lover's revenge, or was I way off beam?

But it still left me with a problem. If Dax killed Tara, why would someone enter my home a week after the trial ended?

Unable to settle, I drove over to Mum's. Tiff would most likely be knocking around. She often popped in for a cuppa in the afternoon, if she wasn't teaching, before she went back to the stables to straw down. It would give me a chance to patch things up between us, although I'd no intention of breathing a word about Allan Dukes.

Loud voices from the back garden greeted my arrival. I paused on the drive and heard Doug tearing Tiff off a strip.

"What the fuck did you go and do that for, you stupid bitch?"

"Because what you're doing is sick."

"There's no law against it."

"Yes, there is. Tell him, Mum."

My mum famously never gets into arguments—fine if you're on the receiving end but frustrating if you need an ally. It gave me a sobering revelation of how I often came across to others. Tiff had warned that if I stood in the middle of the road on everything, I was likely to get mown down.

I clicked open the side gate, walked down the paved path, skirted a border, and halted in horror. Held by its claws, upside down, a dead magpie dripped blood onto the lawn. Grasped in Doug's other hand was a hammer, the steel head red and clotted in brain tissue. On the grass at Tiff's feet was an upended Larsen trap, a cage in which a decoy bird is placed as bait, the idea being to trap other birds alive and unharmed. But what Doug did with the birds once in his possession...

I didn't need anyone to explain what had transpired.

Three heads swivelled towards me. Mum's face crumpled in distress. Tiff and Doug, with pinched, hard expressions distorting their features, looked ready to knock the hell out of each other. Spotting a likely supporter, Tiff pounced.

"See, Gracie thinks it's disgusting, too."

"What's disgusting," Doug growled, "is the way them birds wipe out the rest of the bird population. As a countrywoman, or so you say, you should bloody well know that. And they peck out the eyes of newborn lambs."

"Bollocks, Doug. That's an old wives' tale. Why don't you face the fact that you like killing things? You fucking enjoy it."

"Tiffany," my mum waded in, "that's not fair and not true. Now say you're sorry."

"For what, calling him a murderous bastard or letting the decoy bird fly free?" Tiff's cheeks were shot through with crimson. Flared red, her nostrils resembled the fiery mounts she rode. Dangerous. Equally dangerous was Doug's uncompromising stance. In no mood for taking prisoners, his eyes were slits, the angle of his jaw set rigid and his lips curled back in a scowl that would make most shudder.

"Doug, the girl was only doing what she thought best," Mum pleaded. "It does seem a little cruel to cage a bird as bait."

"And that's definitely against the law," Tiff sniped. "I could report you to the RSPB."

Doug's face darkened. His grip on the hammer tightened. For one terrifying moment, I thought he would strike my sister. Instead, he dropped both bird and hammer onto the lawn.

"I'm not going to stand here and listen to this crap." He stalked towards me with a "Ta-ta, Gracie," and sped across the drive, wrenched open the door of his 4x4, and drove off, stone and chips of gravel flying.

"Now look what you've done," Mum said, dismayed and accusing.

"Good riddance," Tiff said, unperturbed. "I suppose you expect me to clear that lot up," she added glancing at the carnage on the turf.

"Well, don't look at me," I said. "Come on, Mum, let's get you inside for a nice cup of tea."

Kettle on, cups and saucers on the table, milk in the jug, sugar in the bowl—these were as important and traditional for restoring order to the Saunderses as the sacraments at Mass.

Glumly Mum threw herself down on a kitchen chair and tapped her manicured nails against the grain.

"He'll calm down," I said, pouring out tea.

She turned her big painted eyes on mine. "Do you think? I hate it when Dougie gets mad. He's got such a temper on him."

"He'll be fine, you'll see."

"I wish Tiffany wouldn't interfere," Mum fretted. "It was nothing to do with her."

"You know Tiff," I said, humouring her. "A one-woman cause merchant."

"She certainly gets a bee in her bonnet."

"Talking about me again?" Tiff rolled in, not looking best pleased. She stamped towards the sink and washed her hands with vigour. "Bloody feathers and muck everywhere."

"Tiffany, please." Mum pressed her fingers to her forehead "I think I'm getting one of my heads."

"Why don't you go and put your feet up?" I said.

She patted my hand. "You're a good girl, Gracie. If you don't mind, I think I'll do that." She picked up her cup and saucer and tottered shakily towards the sitting room.

"Creep," Tiff hissed, eyes narrowed.

"Sit down, shut up, and have a brew. You've picked enough fights for one day."

She gave me an old-fashioned look and grinned. "I thought he was going to deck me."

I grinned back. "*I* thought he was going to deck you."

"Bloody hell," she said with a dirty laugh, merrily pouring out tea into which she spooned two sugars, no milk, black as tar. "Me taking on slippery Doug Davis."

"Slippery and savage. I'd give him a wide berth, if you know what's good for you."

"Don't worry, Grace, I know how far I can push it. Any further, fuck knows what I'd unleash." She viewed me impishly over the rim of the cup. "Anyways, how's tricks with you? Any more royal proclamations from Archie?"

I told her about the offer of money. Fast as a greyhound out of a trap, Tiff asked the same question I'd asked: "What does he expect in return?"

"Nothing." There is no greater lie than the one we tell to ourselves. Was I lying now? I wondered with a snatch of fear.

"To quote our dear old mum, no such thing as a free dinner."

"It's lunch," I said.

"Whatever," Tiff said bemused. "He's a crafty bugger, isn't he? There's probably a legal reason, buying you off, or something like that. At the same time he gets to lighten his load of guilt."

"Guilt?" It came out as a startled yelp.

"Who pissed on your grave? I meant for running back to mummy and daddy. What else did you think?"

"Nothing," I said, taking a gulp of tea and scalding the roof of my mouth.

Tiff threw me a quizzical look. She always knew when I wasn't telling the truth. "If I were you, I'd ask for more. You'd be soft in the head not to."

"Who says I'm going to take it?" Fortunately, my phone rang and cut Tiff off before she could get cracking with a reply. Gratefully I scooped it up.

"Is that Grace Neville?"

"Yes," I said, unable to place the female voice.

"Hi, Grace, I'm Emma Gadzinski on behalf of the *Gloucester Guardian*."

"Who is it?" Tiff mouthed.

"Journalist," I mouthed back, putting it on speaker.

"Fuck," Tiff said, clearly not caring who heard.

"I was wondering whether you'd be interested in giving an interview. We're looking for a human interest piece in the light of the recent trial and—"

Tiff leant across the table and in one swoop, snatched the phone from me and belted out, "No, she wouldn't, you ghoul."

"Erm ... Who am I speaking to?" the voice warbled into the open air as Tiff held the phone between us.

"Her sister, not that it's any business of yours. We've already made it clear to people like you that we don't want to comment. Got that? Now fuck right—"

"As Mr. Neville has already agreed, we thought it would be a more rounded piece if we heard the mother's side of the story."

I have rarely seen my sister thrown off-balance. She has an answer for everything even if it's inappropriate, wrong, or downright rude. Momentarily lost for words, she gaped at me. I gaped back, speechless. Recovering quickly, Tiff eyed me, nine parts concern, two parts rage.

"You thought wrong," she snapped and cut the call.

I covered my eyes with my hands. The world as I knew it had gone crazy. From the moment the murder train got going, we'd all been on board, every one of us, and especially when it came to slimy approaches from journalists, and there had been many. The party line was, nobody talks to the press. Archie, it seemed, had careened off into the sidings. Why?

"You knew nothing about it?" I heard Tiff say, kindness and sympathy softening her voice. Miserably, I shook my head. "Why the fuck would he do that?" she said as I peeped nervously at her before lowering my hands. "What?" she said.

"If I tell you, you have to promise that you'll keep it to yourself."

"Okay." She said it slowly and I sensed that she had the equivalent of her fingers crossed behind her back.

"I mean it, Tiff. You have to promise that you won't act on it, say anything to anyone, or go after anybody."

"I don't much like—"

"Promise me, Tiff." I was as strident as I could manage. Tiff doesn't normally give in to things she can't negotiate her way out of.

"What do you want me to do, spit on my hand?" We'd watched a cowboy film as kids and, to our mum's displeasure, had picked up the dirty habit to seal bargains between us. "Or do you want it in blood?"

"It's no laughing matter, Tiff. I'm serious."

"I knew something was up. You have my word, cross my heart and hope to die."

Collapsing inside, my face fell. A sob escaped from deep in my diaphragm, caught in my throat.

"Shit, Gracie, I'm such an idiot. Please don't cry. I promise. Now tell me. You have my word."

Twenty

I pushed my tears away with the back of my hand and started from the beginning. I told Tiff about Allan Dukes and the disturbance of Tara's things at the apartment.

"So that's why you phoned me?"

"Yes."

I revealed Archie's reaction and then explained about Allan Dukes's subsequent visit. She tried to interrupt four times, and each time I told her to shut up and hear me out. I saw all kinds of reactions in my sister's face. From shock, anger, and suspicion to blank incomprehension, mostly aimed at me.

"You're not seriously going to visit that scumbag?"

"Have you not listened to a word I've said?"

"Allan Dukes has charmed you, God only knows how or why. What did he do, show you the size of his cock?"

My jaw locked with fury. "If you're going to be so bloody crude, forget I ever spoke. I'm off." I stood up.

"No, wait," Tiff said, grabbing hold of my sleeve. "I'm sorry. I shouldn't have said that. I'm gobsmacked, that's all."

Which was a first. I looked down at my sister's hand on my arm with disdain. Whatever she thought, I wasn't going to roll over. "Unless you have something insightful to say, I don't want to hear it."

The bewildered expression in her eye was not dissimilar to Archie's when I'd cornered him at home. I didn't gloat but felt an unusual stir of triumph.

"Sit down, Gracie, please," she said, a plea in her voice.

Slowly I scraped back the chair and sat down with a thump. We were eyeball to eyeball. Tiff flicked an anxious smile. She was probably wondering what had happened to her older sister. Had she been possessed? "Are you certain you weren't mistaken about the stuff in Tara's room?"

"Positive. Things were moved."

"What would someone be looking for?"

I shook my head. "But it supports the argument that Jordan didn't kill Tara."

"One way of looking at it," Tiff said in a way that assured me she believed him guilty. "There is an alternative though—the search could be unconnected."

"Too much coincidence, and it still doesn't explain why."

Tiff fell briefly silent, not at all like her. Shoot your mouth off first, think afterwards was more her line. "You've spoken to Archie, you said?"

"Yes."

"How did he react?"

"Defensively."

Tiff topped up the pot with fresh hot water, still deep in thought. "What about Tara's mates? Do you think she might have lent them a key? Kids do that kind of thing, don't they?"

A cloud of doubt enveloped me and with it a terrible hopelessness. It had taken my childless sister to point out the obvious and I'd been too crazy to see it. Enduring Tara's teenage years, I'd observed the life of the teen from close quarters. In the average adolescent's world, everything occurs with frighteningly heightened intensity. A single word, one look or action can spell disaster or joy, nothing in between. I'd never been able to keep up with the speed with which friends fell out and made up, or understand the impact of social media messages, how they were variously interpreted, misinterpreted, and misunderstood, friendships cast and broken, occasionally destroying the participants. Having never wished to be part of an in-crowd myself, I didn't get it in others. Archie had, of course, and so had Kristina.

I smothered a sigh. Tiff was right. It was not such a stretch to imagine one of Tara's mates having a key. Perhaps there was a boy who, once sweet on her, wanted to retrieve a memento, or a girl who sought a souvenir and reminder of Tara's existence, though why now, after so many months had elapsed, I couldn't comprehend. Then I remembered Dax. Light flared inside me. I told Tiff about Jordan's previous girlfriend.

"Even if she did it, which is a big *if*, and even if she had a key, no way would she risk being seen at your flat, and for what?'" Tiff viewed me with watchful eyes. "See," she said, "mine is a much simpler and logical explanation." I nodded in agreement, dull-eyed. "Is there anyone you can talk to? What about Thea?"

Tara's best friend. "I should have thought of her before."

"Right," Tiff said, as if checking off a tick-list, one down and two to go. "About Jordan Dukes."

"Hmm?" I wasn't really listening anymore. The premise on which I'd built an entire story Tiff had exposed as flaky.

"From what you've told me, he's capable of anything."

I shrugged, disconsolate.

"You're not really going to see him, are you?"

"I don't know, Tiff. I really don't know."

———

"Thea, it's me, Mrs. Neville, Tara's mum."

Thea Molyneux was my second call. I'd phoned Archie first thing and left a terse message on his phone to which I didn't expect a response anytime soon.

"Hello, Mrs. Neville. How are you? I heard about the trial. Must be a relief."

"Yes," I said swiftly. "The thing is, I wondered if you were free to talk."

"I've got to dash out in a minute, sorry, having my nails done, but I could ring back later."

"Have you time to catch a coffee? I'd really like to discuss something in person."

"Oh," she said uncertainly. "Well, if you're sure, I could see you afterwards in town. Might be a bit rammed though."

"Doesn't matter. How about the Muffin Man?"

"The basement café with the bicycle outside?"

"That's the one. What time?"

"Midday, I should be done by then."

I arrived early and found a quiet table for two in a tucked-away corner near the entrance. Declining the lunch menu, I ordered coffee and mentioned I was waiting for someone to join me. Seconds later

Thea arrived. Eighteen years of age, full of bounce and vigour, she wiped me out with a magnificent smile so reminiscent of Tara that I wilted. She slipped down into the seat opposite and flashed her fingers with a rippling motion. Her nails were emerald green with star motifs at the tips.

"Very nice," I said approvingly, my voice flexing with false good humour.

She gave a girly laugh, flicked a lock of red hair away from her face, and fixed me with a green-eyed, *isn't life swell* gaze. Then, as if she'd suddenly remembered who I was, the smile expired, her eyes clouded, concern pinching her lips. "So how's things?"

I didn't lie. "So-so."

She let out a sympathetic sigh. "I still can't really believe it. How long has it been now?"

"Eight months and twenty-three days."

"Must be hard for you, Mrs. Neville."

"Life goes on," I said in a stupendous effort to lighten the tone and mask the lie. In my experience people at ease are more willing to talk. My coffee arrived and Thea ordered a cold drink. She looked at me with expectant eyes: *what have you got me here for?*

"I wondered if Tara had ever given you a key."

"To what?"

"Our home."

Lines crinkled her smooth brow. "Never."

"Would she have lent one to anyone else?"

"Why would she do that?"

"I don't know exactly."

The tip of Thea's tongue peeped out between her lips. "Not very likely. We tended to meet at mine because there was more room. Oh," she said, her eyes flashing with alarm. "Thoughtless of me. I didn't mean it to come out like that. I ..."

"It's okay, Thea. We live in a shoe-box," I said, forgetting there was no more *we*. Now I came to think of it, after the initial euphoria of moving to a smart new pad in the centre of town, Tara rarely brought back her friends because, as she reminded me, it was cramped. Thea had proved the exception, yet her spontaneous response to my question appeared to rule her out as the culprit with the key.

Her drink arrived. She poked the straw into her mouth and took a long swallow.

"Was Tara close to anyone other than you?"

Her fair lashes quivered. "You mean other than Jordan?"

"Yes."

She shook her head.

"Nobody who had a crush on her?" I was riffing, scrabbling around in a hopeless attempt to find something. Anything.

Thea grabbed the straw and took another drink. Instinctive. Defensive.

"Thea?"

"No," she said.

"Are you sure?"

"Yes." She glanced up at a painting on the wall behind me in a clear bid to avert her eyes from mine.

"What about Facebook friends?" The police had trawled through Tara's contacts and hadn't found anything dodgy. Archie had closed the account soon afterwards.

Thea shook her head again.

"However unimportant you believe it to be, can you think of anything significant that didn't stack?"

145

She flashed a hard smile. "That's easy: going out with Jordan Dukes. I never got what she saw in him. Sure, he was good-looking and he could be wickedly funny, but purleese."

Every time I asked a question, all roads led back to the boy. Maybe he had done it. Maybe Allan was wrong, blinded by a father's love for his son.

I tried again. "You've known Tara since primary."

"Sounds like an eternity, doesn't it?" She spoke softly, almost to herself.

"You knew Tara before her dad and me split up."

"Yeah," she said, dragging out the word, uncertain where I was going with it.

"She took it badly, didn't she?"

"That's what happens, Mrs. Neville." She virtually snapped it as if I were thick as well as morally bankrupt. "But she got over it. Wasn't as if she were the only girl in class whose parents were divorced."

"She was pretty moody, right?" I needed her agreement. I needed her to trust me. No use getting hung up on my gold star membership of the divorce club.

"Uh-huh."

"Was anything else wrong?"

She blinked. "Like what?"

I took a deep breath. "Something happened to Tara before Jordan Dukes came along, but I don't know what." I searched her face, saw the lie form on her lips and then die.

"I don't know what happened."

"But ... " I said, my voice a question.

Her gaze downcast, Thea pushed the glass away, struggling, apparently, with either her conscience or a primeval reluctance to speak in other than glowing terms about the recently dead. I waited. Hoped. Prayed.

"Tara changed," Thea blurted out, "became secretive to the point of obsession, moody, like you said, but this was different. It was as if the old Tara had disappeared and been replaced by someone else, an impostor."

My lungs constricted inside my chest. "When did you first notice?"

"Around the time of my fourteenth birthday party. July," she added.

"But that was several years ago."

"You asked me if I'd noticed anything. Well, I had."

"You're sure?"

"Positive. She was proper strange at my sleepover."

"In what way?"

"I can't really explain."

"Please," I said hating the catch in my voice. "Can you try?"

Thea issued a gale of a sigh and tipped back on her chair.

"Was she texting someone?" I said, clutching at the first thing I could think of. Tara had always loved her phone.

"That was what was so weird about it. When I said she was secretive, I really meant it. There were no communications and yet, well, it was as if she'd fallen in love, but not in a good way, if you get my meaning."

Fallen in love?

I sparked with anxiety. Thea tapped the table lightly with her newly polished nails.

"Can you think who that might be?"

The tapping increased to a crescendo. Thea's gaze was hard yet distant, struggle in her expression. She knew, all right, but she was reluctant to tell me.

"Please," I begged again. "I need to know."

With a flourish, Thea put her hand flat down on the table. "I'm not telling tales, and I don't want to say the wrong thing, or you to get a mistaken idea, but, and you probably know this already, but well—" She stopped abruptly.

"Yes?" I squeaked.

"Tara had a really funny relationship with Mr. Neville."

I stared vacantly. The stab of anxiety bloomed into full-blooded, full-throttled terror. "You mean close?"

"Unusually," she said, looking at me square before glancing at her wrist in a theatrical fashion. I'm not entirely sure she was wearing a watch, but Thea claimed she had to fly. She stood up, wove a scarf around her neck, draping it around her shoulders as if it would some-how muzzle her from saying anything else. Leaning over, she pecked me on both cheeks, told me to take care, and fled.

I sat stunned. Archie and Tara, what was Thea thinking? Ridiculous. Perverse. Plain horrible. False. The despicable product of a teen-age girl's overactive imagination, I concluded angrily.

Only as I plodded back home did I wonder what had caused problems between Archie and Kristina.

What if I was wrong?

What if … ?

Twenty-One

Despite my best intentions Thea's insinuation wormed itself into my head with the same determination as a grub burrowing through an apple. However much I tried to kill the thought, it excavated a little deeper.

Everyone has a secret life, a fantasy world in which they are beautiful or handsome and where they can have whoever in whatever way they choose. For all I knew, more men and women acted on their fantasies than those who didn't. Archie and me had always enjoyed sex. In the great spectrum of sexual behaviour, we were healthily adventurous, nothing kinky, no handcuffs. Unwanted, my mind coruscated with sexual encounters. Had there been anything outside the norm, anything unusual, off-limits? Panic gripped me at the memory of one time, only once, and Archie hadn't forced me, hadn't …

Shutting the memory down, I told myself it meant nothing. I never ever suspected that Archie had a thing for younger girls, let alone what Thea was implying. Intimacy, the ultimate connection, only waned with me the moment he clapped eyes on Kristina. I'd mourned his loss of desire for me, wept at the trap he'd sprung which I was powerless to escape. No other relationship could be as intense, as seductive, as full on as my relationship with Archie. Barren of love, I'd felt diminished and dried up in ways that were unimaginable. Overnight I went from sexy siren to crone. Relentlessly, I asked myself how I could have been taken in by Archie's duplicity. When he'd first commented to me that Kristina had lovely looks, I'd thought little of it because we'd gone way beyond the point of getting pissy about my appreciation of good-looking guys and his admiration of good-looking women. Cheltenham was the kind of place where beautiful people strolled down the Promenade every day. It would be hard not to comment. Fool me, for not making the distinction in Kristina's case.

And that led me to another thought. Archie and Kristina were loved up with each other. He would not, could not, have strayed in the way suggested. This is what I told myself. This was what I chose to believe. We all share and accept lies but this wasn't one of them. All of it tumbled through my mind when Archie phoned to apologise about "the press incident."

"Honestly, I'm sorry."

"You broke our agreement, what we'd discussed, what we'd agreed, Archie."

"I know that," he said, contrite. "I thought with the trial over it wouldn't hurt, and Emma was so persuasive."

How persuasive? Is she a kid on a work placement? "Did she turn up at your door?" Is she young and pretty? was what I really thought.

"She phoned. Look, it's sorted, Grace. I've contacted Emma and told her it's off."

"Good."

"I gather Tiff told her where to go," he said, in a weak attempt to humour me.

"Hardly."

"Emma sounded really upset."

"Miss Gadzinski will have to be thicker-skinned than that if she wants to succeed in the world of hack journalism."

"Ouch, that doesn't sound like you." In the absence of a reply, he continued, "So we're square?"

"I'd say so." I paused. "About the money?"

"Still on the table, Grace."

"Does it come with conditions?"

"Conditions?"

"Rules, stipulations, prerequisites, demands?" Silences?

"You sound odd, Grace."

"I'm fine," I said curtly.

"Like I explained, it's a goodwill gesture, a way of leaving things on an amicable footing."

"Very decent of you, only I was thinking forty grand would be commensurate with a fifteen-year relationship."

Whether or not Archie was stunned into agreement or whether through nameless guilt he felt it better to accede, I'd no clue. Either way, he said, "I'll get a cheque drawn up right away. I could drop it round tonight."

"I'll be out," I lied. "Put it through the letterbox, or in the post, if you prefer."

"Right," he said, rattled.

Good, I thought. Screw you. Another scared part of me thought, Why give me forty thousand pounds?

━━━

Easter came and went. I spent Sunday as usual with Mum, Doug, Tiff, and Gray. When Tiff ambushed me in the kitchen and asked about developments, I told her truthfully that I'd taken the money (I didn't say how much), that Archie had dropped the interview with the press and, other than that, nothing to report. I didn't squeak a word about Thea's lurid imagination. How could I find words to describe something I could neither entertain nor imagine?

But if Jordan didn't kill Tara, who did?

What was the motive: retribution, crime of passion, a means to shut her up?

Hairs on the back of my arms stood erect at the grim possibilities.

A day later, and with the unpredictability of a desert storm, the visiting order arrived. Now that it had materialised, I stared at it in the same way an alcoholic on a recovery programme views an unopened bottle of Scotch. *Get behind me, Satan.*

Propping up the opened envelope against the toaster in the kitchen, I didn't call Allan Dukes like I promised because I could only afford to trust myself, nobody else. Not Archie, not Allan, not Thea, not even Tiff. Running out of people, it probably said more about me than them. Instead I called Michael and discussed returning to work on a part-time basis, my duties restricted to minding the gallery. We tentatively worked out that I'd go back the beginning of the following week. If I were to visit Jordan Dukes, it had to be soon. If …

It sounded daft, but I needed something to happen, another indication or a sign that would prove Jordan Dukes guilty. Conclusively. Indubitably.

Nothing happened. No revelation. No communication from the spirit world or any other. Not when I walked along the hill in the sunshine. Not when I strode through town. If Allan Dukes was waiting with a racing pulse for my call, he didn't let me know. Archie's cheque deposited safely in the bank, it would clear in a few days. No strings. No threats.

At a loss, I stretched out on Tara's bed, head resting on the pillow, hands clasped behind my neck. My eyes travelled the room, skimming over her personal belongings and alighting on her CD rack, most of its contents, to my mind, the sort of music used on detainees in black sites. Not all of it, of course; some I actually enjoyed. It sparked a memory of what I'd describe as her Amy Winehouse period. (I'd been bothered at the time because of repeated references to drugs in the song.) There was one track she'd played endlessly, "Back to Black." I closed my eyes, hummed the tune, the lyrics half formed in my throat, something about *going back to her*.

My eyes shot open. Wired, I sat up, swung off the bed and went straight to Tara's music collection, my fingers flying over the sleeves, looking for Amy. I pulled out *Frank*, read the song titles, and put it back, then found *Back to Black*. My fingers shook as I switched on Tara's CD player, slipped the CD inside, cranking up the volume, and went straight to track five.

Tapping out the intro, I listened rapt, as if the words held the whereabouts of the Holy Grail, the truth about the beginning of time, and the lost secrets of the Ark of the Covenant. My skin prickled as Amy's haunting contralto voice sang a long good-bye. When a bell tolled in the final chorus, it sounded as if it were playing for Tara. Was I being fanciful? Had music stirred an emotion and memory that did not exist, or was this a reflection of what was really going on inside my daughter's head at the time? And what did it mean? That Tara had a secret lover, a man already married—*go back to her*—and ...

A kind of febrile sickness storming through me, I remembered a bright sunny Sunday in summer. It had been early morning. I was barely awake. Noise shuffled through my brain, which in my soporific state, I couldn't place. Dragging myself out of bed, I'd found Tara dressed, about to sneak out of the front door.

"Do you know what the time is?"

She turned to me and beamed. "I couldn't sleep and it's such a lovely morning, I thought I'd go for a walk."

"Where?"

"The parks."

"Will you be long?"

"Why?"

"I thought we might go out, do something"'

Her face clouded. "I've got homework."

"Okay," I said, miffed. "Got your key?"

She produced it and waved it in front of my nose with a laugh. Excited, skittish, she was in a funny mood, I thought. A welcome change from melancholy, though.

"Go back to bed, Mum. You look knackered."

I did. Tara returned five hours later.

"Where have you been?" I said. "It's almost lunchtime."

"Chill, Mum. I ran into Thea and we went back to hers."

"I wish you'd phoned, or texted."

"Sorree," she said, dragging out the syllables.

"What have you done to your bottom lip? It's swollen."

Tara pressed a hand to her mouth. "Is it?"

"You look as if you've been punched." I peered more closely. "Is that a rash on your chin?"

"Oh, I remember, we've been eating crisps, salt and vinegar, always makes my lips tingle. You're not really cross, are you?"

"Not now you're back," I said, smiling with relief. I went to hug her.

"Hey," Tara took a step back, palms extended. "Got totally sweaty on the walk. Think I'll take a shower."

"Right," I said, arms dropping to my side. Uneasy, I watched her scoot into the bathroom. She seemed to take a long time to wash the perspiration from her body.

A fist of fear clenched inside me. Tiptoeing in my mind towards the door marked *questions I'd never wanted to think about or answer*, I opened it a crack and peeped inside into the darkness. What if Tara had a lover pre-Jordan? What if that's who she met that sunny morning? What if I'd been stupid enough to miss it? What if Tara and Archie …

I slammed the door shut.

Twenty-Two

Two days later I went to Bristol.

Everything pretty much took place as Allan predicted. Once inside, I showed my identification, received a body search in the form of a pat down, and passed through a metal detector. Two prison officers patrolled with dogs to sniff out anyone importing drugs.

Along with a fleet of mums and dads, girlfriends and husbands and kids, I entered a room set out with tables, four chairs at each, red seats for visitors, plain for prisoners and those on remand. Vending machines stood at one end, a prison warder with a watchful gaze seated at the other. In each corner, CCTV cameras operated like spies in the sky. On the far wall hung a big round clock like the kind you see in train station waiting rooms.

There was a collective swell of greeting and conversation as visitors surged across the room en masse. Jordan Dukes stayed seated when he saw me. He looked nothing like a boy who had coldly thrust a blade into Tara's chest, skewering her heart.

Grubby and tired, with a fresh angry bruise around his left eye, his cheeks were sallow and hollow. He'd dropped pounds it seemed since the trial, his slim build now plain thin underneath a shapeless T-shirt and dirty grey jogging bottoms too short for him. On his feet were trainers with Velcro attachments. In common with his drab clothing, his eyes were dull, no gleam, no spark. He had an air of defeat, his swagger all gone.

I'd thought long and hard about what I should say and how I should say it. Standing in front of him, my carefully prepared speech vanished and I mutated into an amnesiac. I glanced to my left and right, caught the eye of a guy with pitted skin and a surly, threatening expression. My nervous smile, unreturned, froze on my face and I lowered my gaze. I was out of my depth in here. I had no grasp of how things worked. I might as well have been in the House of Commons during a point of order.

"It's good of you to see me. I appreciate it." I scraped back the chair against a floor scuffed by many pairs of previous shoes and sat down opposite Jordan. Cool and polite, he surveyed me, and I surveyed him. I wanted to feel rage. I wanted to feel power. I wanted to feel *this is where you damn well belong* triumph. I felt none of those things. I'm not good at retribution.

"I did not kill your daughter, Mrs. Neville." He did not speak with a voice of defiance. He didn't tip back the chair on two legs, challenging. He did not whine or plead. His dark-lashed eyes blazed with conviction that comes when people speak from their hearts about what they know to be true. If Jordan Dukes was duping me, he was the best con man in the business.

"Then who did?"

"I don't know."

"Or won't say?"

"I don't know," he repeated, quietly emphatic.

"Dax?"

He stiffened. Lines I'd never noticed before appeared around his eyes and mouth. "My dad told you about Dax?"

"He did."

"He shouldn't have."

"Why?"

"Because she'll burn you, burn everyone."

Literally or figuratively? Whatever Jordan meant, I got the drift. "Is she the reason you're keeping your mouth shut?"

He flashed with sudden anger and ripped his gaze away and concentrated on a scratch on the table. Precious seconds trickled through my fingers like fine sand. I'd hardly sat down and we'd run into a brick wall. Panic fluttered inside me. "I can't help you if you don't help me."

He didn't move for I don't know how long. We sat together sharing silence as if it were our last swig of water before crossing a desert without a map or compass.

Eventually he swivelled round, eyes locked onto mine. "Don't you get it? I don't want your help. I want you to know the truth that I never laid a finger on Tara. I loved her. That's all I want you to know."

"But…"

His warning expression scorched me. I glanced at the clock. Three minutes had passed. Fifty-seven remained.

Painfully aware that I needed a different approach, a different angle, I reeled the conversation back to a less contentious footing. "Jordan, what happened in the hours leading up to Tara's death?"

"You were at court," he said sullenly. "You heard."

"I want to hear it from you, in your own words. Again."

He leant back, crossed his arms tight.

"Please, Jordan. I'm not here to judge."

"Aren't you?"

"I'm here because if you didn't kill my daughter, someone else did." Now I'd said it out loud, shock twisted inside me followed by cold, slimy fear.

His shoulders hunched. He placed both palms in front of his face and rubbed furiously. "Okay, okay," he said, letting his hands drop to his sides. "I saw Tara on the morning."

"Which morning?"

"Saturday before she was killed on Sunday," he said slowly, as though I were slow-witted.

"Where?"

"In Gloucester. I was working on a house conversion with my dad, plastering and that. She'd texted me. Sounded upset so I told her to meet me there. She caught a bus from Cheltenham after leaving her dad's."

I knew this. It didn't seem that significant at the time. Now it taunted me.

"What was she upset about?"

"She didn't say."

"Did she tell you what was wrong when you saw her?"

"Nope. Didn't expect her to what with my dad there."

"She didn't mention a row, something like that?"

"Didn't spell it out. I thought she'd quarrelled with someone."

"Who?"

He fell silent.

"A friend, someone at school?"

He let out a sigh, yet his eyes flickered with hidden knowledge. "She never said."

"But you thought you knew. Who?"

"Not rocket science." He shrugged. "Her dad."

Him again. What was becoming a familiar stab of anxiety jabbed me in the gut again. "You've no clue what about?"

He shook his head. "She said something about now not being the right time."

"But you got the impression she was ready to talk at some point later?"

"Yeah, yeah. She said, once we were properly alone, she had a secret to tell."

"A secret? She actually used that word?"

"Uh-huh. A *dirty* secret."

A sour taste filled my mouth. Jordan cocked his head, his eyes penetrating mine, as if he realised that maybe I knew what the dirty secret was. Some horrible skeleton rattling in the family cupboard, a sinister lie maintained for years and passed on from one generation to another. I forced myself to swallow, which was hard because my salivary glands appeared to have packed up.

"What happened next?"

"I told her I'd see her later at our place."

"The hotel?" The dump.

"Yeah."

"What time?"

"I popped in around eight, but we didn't talk then because I had to go back out."

"Had to?"

"Mmm," he said, deliberately vague, I thought. "I told her I'd be back later."

"How much later?"

"I didn't say."

"Why?"

He puffed out his cheeks, tightened the muscles in his arms, flexing the fingers of one hand, cracking knuckles. Resistant.

I repeated the question.

"Business," he said, slow-eyed.

"Gang business?" My narrowed gaze was met with another shrug. "The boy who got stabbed?"

He blinked slowly. Mouth zippered. Face as unyielding as freshly laid stone.

I dropped a tone. "Did you kill him?" Contempt sharpened his features. I glanced at the warder, who was looking the other way. "Did you knife him?" I hissed.

At a speed that made me jump, Jordan leant across wild-eyed, his mouth centimetres from my face. "I did not." The warder swivelled in our direction. Ordering myself to stay calm, I flashed an apologetic smile, praying he wouldn't remove Jordan from the room. Someone else appeared to catch his attention and he nodded at me and looked away.

I told myself that it would be all right. Be patient. Be firm. Play nice and understanding. I softened my voice. "But you know who did and you were with them that night, right?"

Never rat out your mates, his eyes said. Not if you know what's good for you.

I pointed to his eye. "Have you been threatened?"

"Nah, some scumbag tried to jump my bones."

Jesus Christ. "Jordan, this isn't about loyalty. You're looking at throwing away the best years of your life locked in this shit-hole, and for what?"

"You think I don't know that?" he sneered. "You think I like this? Think I'm a real hard man?"

We both glanced in the direction of a young woman, a girlfriend or wife, jumping to her feet and heading for the exit, sobbing. This time I dared not look at the clock on the wall.

"So you went back to the hotel, right?"

"Yes," he said, eyes downcast. "Around three-thirty in the morning." He looked straight at me. "That's when I found her." His jaw clenched and I could see the vein in his neck bulge. I knew the rest. The prosecution convinced the jury that Jordan had murdered Tara, got rid of the weapon, and returned to the room to act out the part of heartbroken boyfriend.

"Do you know anyone who wanted Tara dead?"

"Dax, but she didn't do it."

"She could have ordered someone else."

"Nope."

"You're sure?"

"I'm sure."

I wasn't convinced.

"That's not to say she isn't dangerous," he said, an urgent light in his eyes. I remembered what Allan had said. *Vicious.*

I waited a beat, held his gaze. "What does she have on you, Jordan?"

He briefly closed his eyes.

"Can't you tell the police?"

"Sure," he jeered, "I could talk to Dunne, why not? He'd still find another way to bang me up. Fucking tosser."

"Your dad could talk—"

"Don't even think about it." His voice shrieked alarm.

"But—"

"Hear me out." Desperately, he glanced towards the warder. "He goes snooping around, my dad isn't the only one who's going to get hurt."

"What? I don't understand."

"If anyone so much as asks a question, points a finger, Dionne and her baby get it."

I gripped the table with both hands and muted a cry. The warder shot another look in my direction. Not now, I thought, not now I've broken through.

"Now do you understand?" Jordan said, his eyes level with mine.

In that brief moment, I didn't see a cold-blooded killer. I saw a wronged young man. I nodded. "Does your dad know about the threat?"

Jordan hung his head, chewed on a nail that was already chewed. "Too stubborn to listen. You can explain."

"Me?"

"He likes you."

Does he? I didn't know what to make of that.

"He'll listen if you tell him." *Please*, his eyes said.

I promised I would.

"Thank you," he said softly, with evident relief. "I'm sorry, Mrs. Neville. I know what this must mean to you. When I get out of here I'm going to find whoever and ... " He glanced over his shoulder again, the sentence suspended in midair.

"Jordan, you can't think like that."

"No? Why not?" There was challenge in his voice.

"Because *I'm* going to find the person who did it."

"You?" He flashed an incredulous grin. I might as well have told him I was about to hitch a ride to the farthest corner of the universe. But I meant it with all my heart, if it took me the rest of my life, whatever the price, whatever the consequences. How could I not?

"Ten minutes left." The warder's voice sliced through the room like a cutthroat razor. I was fast running out of time.

"Were you aware of Tara having many rows with her father?"

"Asking the wrong person, Mrs. N. I wouldn't know what was normal. Me and my dad, well, sometimes we don't see eye to eye."

"Did you ever go to Mr. Neville's place in Harp Hill?"

"Are you kidding? He'd have freaked out."

"Who said that?"

"Tara."

My heart rate quickened, beating a tattoo underneath my ribs. There was no subtle way to pose my next question. "You never noticed anything going on between Tara and her dad?"

He inclined his head, breathed in; sniffing the air as if I'd waved a dead rat underneath his nostrils. "Like what, tensions?"

"Tensions, yes." I failed to contain the strain in my voice.

Sharp as a viper-strike, he said, "That's not what you mean."

"I—"

"You asking me if she had a thing for her daddy?" he snorted as if I were nuts. Inside, I shrieked with horror. "Is that what you're asking?" Realising I was deadly serious, he narrowed his eyes in disbelief.

"I'm not trying to put words—"

"She always was a daddy's girl, but, hell," he said astounded. "You really think…" His voice trailed off. "Some secret, huh?" he said, failing to conceal his shock and disgust. "Nah, couldn't be. I'd have known. For sure."

Twenty-Three

Relief made me giddy. Jordan's defence of Archie meant I no longer had to stare into a sickening and twisted vortex of dark imaginings. I bolted from the prison, called Allan Dukes the minute I boarded the bus, and broke the news that I'd seen Jordan.

"Great," he said. "Really great. How was he?"

"Holding up."

"Did he talk?"

"Yes."

"And?"

"I think he's innocent of Tara's murder."

"Thank God."

I could hear a faint wail in the background—Asher. "Is the baby all right?" I stabbed with anxiety; Jordan's warning sending chills deep into my veins.

"A bit colicky, nothing serious. Dionne's with him. You virtually pass the door coming from Bristol. Why don't you call in and tell me all about it?"

I longed for a hot bath. My skin crawled with the smell of captivity and despairing humanity. I needed to process my thoughts and work out a way forward. Wouldn't I feel awkward about tipping up at Allan Dukes's home?

"I might even cook you tea," Allan pressed. Tea was what my mum and Tiff called an evening meal. They thought me stuck up for saying *dinner*. I tried to remember the last time someone had cooked for me other than my mum.

"Honestly, it's kind but not necessary." I couldn't work out whether he was a nice guy or needy or worse, manipulative, and then I checked myself. How would I feel if it were my son rotting away in prison for a crime he didn't commit? Wouldn't I want someone on my side?

"I'll be with you in around an hour."

Allan gave me directions. I picked up the Mini and clattered up the motorway. Snatches of the exchange with Jordan flitted into and out of my mind. *I didn't do it. Nah, couldn't be.*

As I turned off the motorway at junction 11A, my stomach gave a queasy lurch. Why had Tara called her secret dirty? Had she done something of which she was ashamed? I was as sure as a mother could be that she'd been a virgin up until meeting Jordan. Now I wished I'd asked him.

The Dukes family lived in a crescent of Thirties-style bay-fronted houses. As I parked in the drive next to Allan's builder's van, I thought how prosperous it looked: nice red brick, detached, roomy, with an attached garage large enough for several cars and with a high council tax sure to be band F. It came as a surprise. I'd imagined weeds running riot in the garden, dirty broken blinds at the windows, garbage littering the drive; in short, a run-down dwelling, bleak and tainted by criminality. It was hard to imagine that the house had been subject to a full forensic search and that police had visited with prosecution in mind. I fleetingly wondered what the neighbours had thought, how they'd reacted to the family that had spawned a murderer. Did they walk on the other side of the road? Did they hurl abuse at the schoolgirl with the baby, or the man who couldn't keep his family in check? How did that feel? Ashamed, I realised that I, too, secretly thought these things.

I rang the bell and a girl I assumed to be Dionne answered the door. She had coloured beads woven into her straightened hair. Her wide smile and fine features and skin tone were similar to her brother's, although her nose was more upturned at the tip, her brows more finely drawn and framing eyes that were like great pools of molten chocolate. She wore a front-loading sling from which the top of Asher's head was visible. From the lack of movement and sound, I deduced he was asleep. The thought of them being harmed, burnt Jordan had said, was harrowing.

"Come inside," Dionne said. "Dad's cooking up a storm."

I followed as she sashayed through the hall. When the door swung open into the kitchen I was almost blinded by steam and heat, and the sharp savoury smell of unfamiliar spices and herbs. A big pot boiled away at a furious rate on the hob. Allan was fiddling with a big purple-skinned vegetable, like an oversized potato. He turned in apology as I entered, wiped his streaming eyes with the back of one hand which he then wiped on a navy and white stripe butcher's apron. Perspiration spotted his brow. "Bonnet peppers," he explained. "They're more effective than tear gas."

"Is it usually this frantic?" I said with a half smile.

"Only when we have guests, not that that's happened lately," Dionne said, her answering smile vanishing in a film of mist. "Hope you like Creole cuisine."

Allan's face fell in alarm. "You're not allergic to peanuts, are you?"

"Erm … no, but really I didn't expect … "

"You have to stay," Dionne said with a grin. "We'll be eating jerk chicken for weeks otherwise."

The carnival atmosphere baffled me. These were serious times. A boy's future lay in the balance, a killer was at large. Was I the only person to care? Then I got it. I was their best hope of getting Jordan Dukes off a murder conviction and out of prison. Cause for celebration.

Not so fast, I thought.

"Take Grace's jacket and show her through to the lounge, Dionne," Allan said. "I'll be with you in a minute. Do you want a drink, glass of wine, elderflower presse?"

"Elderflower would be lovely, thanks."

I don't know what I expected. I suppose, if I were honest, I thought a man on his own with two teenagers, and now a baby, would live in chaos. Unless they'd both spent the past hour vacuuming and cleaning, the sitting room was show home clean and, although I detested the black floral-patterned wallpaper on one wall and wasn't quite sure about the print of cheap primitive art over the fake fireplace, it was more stylish than I'd dreamt possible. Furnishings had come straight out of an IKEA catalogue. The TV and sound system displayed up-to-the-minute technology, a Moses basket in the corner of the room the only giveaway that there was a baby in the house. On the light wood sideboard were photographs of Dionne and of Jordan—no trace of Allan's wife or, indeed, any other female. I glanced at Jordan Dukes as a gummy kid in football kit; lanky and all legs as a boy on the cusp of adolescence with a hint of facial hair above his upper lip; the mean and moody stance of a rebellious teenager without a cause. Why in God's name Jordan had turned his back on a comfortable home life, forsaking his family, preferring to hang out with a nasty crew of violent individuals defied me. Perhaps if I'd had a boy and not a girl, I might have had a better handle on it. And then, with a pang, I realised that Jordan's dance with the wild side was no more inexplicable than Tara's with him. It's what kids did.

"Make yourself at home," Dionne said.

She watched me as I sat down with what I could only describe as fascination, as if I were some strange, rare breed of wading bird. "Dad says you saw Jordan this afternoon."

"Yes." I didn't really want to get into conversation with her until I'd had a chance to talk to Allan first. "Have you seen him?"

She glanced down at Asher and swayed her hips, rocking him. "Not since the beginning of the trial."

"Of course, silly of me."

"I don't think Dad's keen."

"No." I flashed a smile of understanding.

"It's bad inside, isn't it? Especially for mixed-race kids. I read up about it on the Internet."

"It's not a very nice place. I suppose that's partly the point."

She frowned. "He's not a bad boy, Mrs. Neville."

"Call me Grace, please."

"He's wayward, got a mind of his own, but he'd never hurt Tara."

"Did you meet her?"

At this, she beamed a smile, her teeth white and perfect. "Such a laugh, really pretty and fun, not like that other girl."

"Dax?"

"A right jealous bitch, two-faced, too. Smarmy to your face and stick a knife in your back. Sorry," she said, covering her mouth with her hand.

Jealous enough to hurt Tara in spite of Jordan's assurance, I registered.

"Here you are," Allan said, planting a tray of drinks down on the coffee table. "Dionne looking after you?"

"Thank you," I smiled. I felt like a visiting dignitary. Allan sat down, handed me a glass, and chinked his with mine. I wondered what DI Dunne would make of it if he knew. Consorting with the enemy, most likely.

Dionne gently placed Asher in his basket.

"So," Allan said, pitching forward, intent, "what did Jordan tell you?" He said it like a man prepared for the worst and hoping for the best. I'd not forgotten the expression on his face when he last came to the apartment. He had the same look now.

I glanced nervously at Dionne, who sat down next to me on the sofa. Should she hear what I had to say?

"We have no secrets in our house, Grace, if that's what's worrying you," he said.

At the mention of secrets, my stomach curdled. I took a calming breath, started with the easy stuff—Jordan's claim of innocence and the way in which his account of what took place that night appeared to support it.

"Are you saying he was involved in killing that boy?" Dionne burst out, her eyes springing angry tears.

"Hush, Dionne," Allan said. "You'll wake Asher. I know Jordan had something to do with it."

"But it's not true," she wailed.

"Jordan denies carrying the knife," I said.

"He said that?" Allan interjected.

"Yes."

"So he *was* there. It's as bad as I'd thought."

"No, Dad," Dionne protested.

"He could have been a witness," I pointed out, feeling as if I were trying to broker a deal between them and failing miserably.

"Or an accomplice," Allan said, anger in his voice.

"Shut up, Dad," Dionne exploded. "He wouldn't. Jordan isn't like that."

I exchanged glances with Allan. We both knew that it was a possibility. "Perhaps he deserves to be in prison then," he said wearily. His entire body sagged with the weight of what his son might have done. Defeat shadowed his eyes. I realised that Allan had used me to confirm his suspicion and uncover the truth. I wished he hadn't.

"Whatever Jordan's involvement, he's been forced into silence."

"I knew it," Dionne said. "By Dax?"

"Uh-huh."

"What did they say they'd do to him?"

I wanted to grasp Dionne's small hand in mine, or put my arm around her shoulder, but I didn't know her well enough. "Not to him; to you and Asher."

Colour drained from their faces faster than a riptide. Dionne pulled away, jumped to her feet, and, crouching down, checked on her baby as if someone had already made good on the threat.

"I'm sorry," I said.

"Dad, we have to go to the police."

"And tell them what?" Allan's voice cut with cynicism. "To reopen the investigation on my say-so?" He shook his head. "They've got what they wanted."

And he was right. Overturning a conviction would be a huge uphill struggle even with evidence. In the slim event that the police could be persuaded, would they offer Asher and Dionne protection while an investigation took place? It seemed unlikely. As far as Dunne was concerned, the Dukeses were trailer trash. "Jordan warned that if you make any approaches, you're putting Dionne and Asher's lives in danger. I believe him."

"So I'll damn well talk to Dax," Allan said. "I'm not afraid. I'll find the evidence to make sure they pay, and Jordan, too, if he's found guilty."

"It's too risky," I pointed out.

"You expect me to do nothing?" he roared. His hands balled into fists. "Whatever Jordan has done, he has to face up to it, but I will not let my daughter and grandson..." He pitched forward covered his eyes with the heels of his hands. Grim, obliterating silence invaded the room. I wanted to tell him that there had to be a way despite any and every path seemingly paved with obstacles.

Dionne got up and put her arm around her dad and squeezed his shoulder.

"I can't stand by and do nothing," he said, looking up into my eyes, begging me to understand. Tired to my bones with thinking, I didn't know what to say. This wasn't my fight. I owed Allan Dukes nothing, and yet I couldn't simply walk. We were inextricably linked. Clearing his son's name was dependent upon my daughter's real murderer being found. That was the only kind of silver bullet to which the police would pay attention.

"Is there somewhere Dionne and Asher can go, an aunt or close friend who could look after them?"

"I don't want to go anywhere," Dionne protested.

"Only for a short time, until it's sorted out."

"For the next eighteen years, do you mean?" The surly note in her voice reminded me of her brother.

"Dionne," Allan said, "don't be sarcastic. Let Grace speak."

172

"If you could find a place of safety for them," I said, addressing Allan, "I'll go to the police."

"You?" he said, dumbfounded.

"If I go, it will carry more weight. I've a decent relationship with Detective Inspector Dunne. I'll tell him about the threat to Asher and Dionne and how the Stringers played a part in Tyrone Weaver's death."

"It won't save Jordan," Dionne said sadly.

"Maybe that's as it should be," Allan said, grim-faced. "Maybe that's what my son deserves."

Twenty-Four

I didn't stay. The threat of violence coupled with the confirmation that Jordan was associated, however tenuously, with the death of Tyrone Weaver killed everyone's appetite.

Allan saw me to the door. I hovered on the threshold, breathing in the clear night air. It felt good after the cloying and heavy atmosphere inside the house. "I'm sorry," he said.

"For what?"

"For getting you involved in a fight that isn't yours."

"But it is, kind of, isn't it?"

"You could walk away from us. I wouldn't blame you."

He was right. I *could*, but knew I wouldn't. It was too late to save Tara, but not too late to prevent further violence and injustice.

"Do you think you can persuade Dionne to go into temporary hiding?" I said.

Allan let out a frustrated sigh. "It will take some doing. She's stubborn."

"I'd feel a lot more comfortable talking to Dunne if I knew she and Asher were safe."

"Leave it with me."

"Okay," I said slowly, "but the sooner I talk to Dunne the better."

"Agreed." With so much at stake, I got the impression from the tone of his voice that Allan would insist and get his way. I was banking on it.

Bonded by mutual interest, we fell briefly silent.

"Looks nice and sedate and suburban out there, doesn't it?" Allan said, gesturing towards the sleeping row of houses on the other side of the road. "I've had strangers spit at me, friends walk on the other side, and I've lost jobs through all this."

"I'm sorry."

"Not your fault, Grace."

"Not yours, either."

"Isn't it?" He looked at me with soulful, searching eyes. "Why did our lives become so ugly?"

I patted his arm, felt the tight musculature beneath the shirt. Electricity flashed through me on a basic, instinctive level that took me by surprise and which I quickly suppressed. "Look, must go, I'll give you a ring when I've spoken to Dunne. Let you know what happens."

He nodded sadly, obviously expecting no more from the exchange than me.

I drove home lost in thought, my mind glazed with confusion. Archie's name still popped up too often. He was in the mix somewhere; not in the way I'd feverishly imagined, perhaps, but something wasn't right. I wondered what had transpired on the eve of Tara's death and what they had rowed about.

———

Contact with the police at any time is unsettling, even when you've done nothing wrong. To be intimately involved in a murder investigation is beyond strange. As a parent of a victim, initially you're treated with compassion, and next as if you are a cog in a machine and will fit in without question. You never quite get over the basic lack of trust such a system elicits, or the nasty sour feeling in your mouth after a bland response when challenging a line of questioning or investigation. As a parent of the deceased, you remain one step removed from the action and, even though a family liaison officer is appointed to ostensibly guide you through an investigation and answer all your queries, there is still a sense of isolation and exclusion, as though you are only privy to what the police see fit to release. You may have parented your child for the best part of two decades, yet this counts for nothing; your child is no longer yours, but the property of the state and its representatives. You don't play a part in the decision-making, whether it's post mortems or the date a body can be released for a funeral. Handed scraps of information for which you are supposed to be grateful, you are left alone to conjecture their meaning and how they connect. Joined in a mutual desire to catch a killer, you're not exactly batting on opposite sides, but neither do you work together, or even in tandem. It's simply not possible because there is an eternal truth and it's this: long after the crime scene examiners have packed up their kit and gone, and the police have moved on to the next case and another set of tick-box requirements, you are alone. Picking up the pieces. Surrounded by death and ashes.

With all this swilling around inside my head, I put a call through to DI Dunne the next morning. From the sound of his opening gambit, he believed I was signing up to play a part in the knife amnesty. I hastily corrected him.

"Sorry, it's something else. Could I drop over to the police station?"

"I can come to you, if you like."

"Well …"

"I'm on my way," he said with cheery persistence.

True to his word, Dunne turned up ten minutes later. "You sounded worried on the phone. Is everything all right?"

"No," I said bluntly.

His eyebrows arched in surprise.

I began by telling him about an uninvited visitor, how Tara's things had been pored through. He stopped me right there. "Who else has keys to your apartment?"

"No one."

His face softened as much as his granite features allowed. "Could you be mistaken? You've been under a tremendous amount of pressure."

"There's no mistake."

He stared at me for longer than was comfortable, then returned to business mode. "You've had the locks changed?"

I assured him I had. When asked to continue, I told him that I'd discovered the reason why Jordan Dukes had kept his silence and described the threat to Asher and Dionne

This time, his eyebrows worked in inverse motion. "How do you know?"

"Because I spoke to him."

He gave a start. "How? When?"

"Yesterday."

"You visited him in prison?" His voice was a roar.

"I did."

"Why in God's name?"

"Because he wasn't with Tara on the night she died. He was with a gang involved in the murder of Tyrone Weaver."

Dunned looked as if I'd smacked him over the head with a baseball bat. "The Stringers?" he stuttered.

"That's how they're able to blackmail him."

His expression said it all. It was preposterous and I was deranged. "You're flying in the face of the evidence."

"The evidence used to fit the crime?" I hadn't meant it to come out like that, but Dunne was so closed to any other interpretation, it shook me and I needed to express it. For God's sake, Dionne and Asher have been threatened, I wanted to insist.

"I'm going to forget you said that," he said, jaw hard, eyes harder.

"Can't you at least take another look? Can't you pass on the information to the team investigating Weaver's murder?"

"I can."

"Good," I said with relief.

"But it doesn't matter. A man was arrested only a few days ago."

"For Weaver's murder?"

Dunne gave a self-satisfied nod.

"A gangster?"

"No," he said.

"But that means … "

"You've been played, Mrs. Neville. You can't believe a word of what pours out of Jordan Dukes's mouth. I'd reflect on that if I were you," he added as he got up and left.

I had a storm in my heart and it was blowing a gale. Misery blasted through me, so acute it stole my breath away. I had no idea how I was going to carry on. What was the point? Anguished tears streaming down my cheeks, I phoned Allan and was pleased the line rang out and went to voicemail. In a voice I barely recognised, I left a short message and drove over to my Mum's. The sky, grey and smudged with rain, reflected my mood.

Taking a circuitous route, I pulled up outside the ratty hotel where Tara had breathed her last. Gazing up at the cracked rendering, crumbling cornices, and filthy windows, I thought my heart would explode and shatter. Tara, my only child, had died such an ignominious death with nobody to cradle her or hold her hand; nobody to absorb her fear and pain; nobody to stay with her, to listen to her last breath and see her into the next world or life or infinity. I had a fleeting image of Jordan Dukes, the sincerity in his eyes, the way his expression tightened at the memory of finding her, and his socking revelation of a dirty secret. Why would Jordan create a lie like that? Wasn't it too elaborate? And why didn't he fuel my suspicion about Archie if he wanted to "play" me, as Dunne had suggested? It would have been so easy.

Mum let me in, took one look at my face, drew me to her, and gave me a hug. "There, Gracie," she said. "Bad day, love? Come on, I'll put the kettle on."

Sniggering over a private joke, Doug and Graham were in the kitchen when I arrived. One look at me and they sprang apart. Graham hurriedly snatched a piece of paper off the worktop and scrunched it up.

"What's that?" I said.

"Nothing." Graham avoided my eye, his expression sheepish.

"Take no notice," Mum said. "Boys will be boys."

"Graham?" I persisted.

"Go on, show her, Gray," Doug said with a sly grin.

Doug's little acolyte, Graham did everything Doug told him, however reluctantly. He opened out the sheet, smoothed out the creases, and laid it flat. I stared at two circles, one bigger than the other, uncomprehending.

"See," Graham said, pointing with a nicotine-stained fingernail. "The first circle is an arsehole. The second is an arsehole after eighteen years in prison."

"Graham," Mum said, "that's really not very nice."

Alarm jolted through my body as strong as a power surge. I gaped at Doug and Graham and the stupid, ugly expressions on their faces, the same repugnant twist to their mouths as I'd seen plastered on Dunne's.

"Sorry, Mum," I said, turning on my heel and chasing back out of the house.

"What's the matter, Gracie?" Doug yelled after me.

"Now look what you've done," I heard my mother curse.

But it was too late. I couldn't stand to be in the same room and breathe the same polluted air. I felt surrounded by sick people. I climbed into my car, blew a kiss to my poor mum standing outside in the spitting rain, and drove half a mile down the road. Shaking with distress, my hands welded to the steering wheel, knuckles shiny and white, I pulled over and bellowed for my loss. I cried for my broken marriage. A human blur of misery and self-pity, I sobbed for the leftovers of a life I didn't want and had utterly rejected.

After a while, spent, my breathing slowed. I got a grip and took out my phone. Two missed calls from Allan Dukes. I deleted both and contacted Archie.

"Are you at work?"

"No."

"I need to see you."

"Why?"

Did I imagine a thread of fear in his voice? "I'd rather not go into it on the phone." I have to see your face.

"It's not convenient. We've got viewers this afternoon."

"All afternoon?"

"If this is about the money, I thought I'd made it clear that—"

"It's not about the money." Why would he say that?

"Well, I still can't—"

"If you won't agree to see me, I'll turn up anyway." That should knock a few grand off the asking price.

"You wouldn't."

"Try me."

"Grace, this doesn't sound like you."

I said nothing. Now that I had the equivalent of my foot on his throat, I wasn't going to relieve the pressure. Archie *did* know something and I had to know what it was.

"Tonight," he said, caving in. "At yours."

"I'd prefer to meet on neutral territory." I named a bar in Clarence Square. We agreed on a time. At last, if only briefly, I felt as if I were getting somewhere.

Twenty-Five

At 7:45 p.m., Archie was late by fifteen minutes. I took another sip of Prosecco, feigned interest in the red and cream furnishings, picked up the drinks menu, put it back down. The bar bubbled with conversation, mainly from diners.

Strategically placed, with a good view of the entrance, I hoped to see the expression on Archie's face and take a punt at what he was thinking the second he stepped inside. With each minute that ticked by, his guilt in my mind grew to unfathomable proportions.

Dirty secret.

Whose?

What?

Footsteps grabbed my attention. I listened and, with a disappointed sigh, dismissed them. The *click-clack* of heels striking pavement belonged to stilettos.

Irritation pulsing through me, I bent over to retrieve my phone from my bag when a familiar voice spoke my name.

I looked up, mystified. "What are you doing here?"

"Archie's not well, a migraine."

I straightened up. He never had so much as a headache when we were married. Kristina swept back her long blonde hair and sat down. The epitome of chic in her soft leather dove grey jacket, slim black trousers tucked into knee length boots, every eye was upon her. "Stress," she explained with a short smile. I didn't believe one word of it. "Moving and work, you know how it is."

"Why didn't he phone and cancel? Why send you?"

"He didn't send me," she said, horrified by the notion. "I offered."

"Then you've had a wasted journey. I want to talk to Archie, not you."

She leant forward, smiled sweetly. "Grace, I'm not here to argue. Would you like me to freshen your glass?"

"No, thank you." I felt hot with anger. I did not relish a cosy chat with the woman who had spirited my husband away from me. I could only assume one thing: Archie had something to hide. That's why he'd pulled a sickie.

"Mind if I have one?"

I shrugged a *whatever*. Kristina glanced at the barman, who just happened to be looking in her direction, alongside every red-blooded male in the room. "Champagne," she said. "Are you really sure, Grace?"

"Certain," I said.

She eyed me with another smile. Viper, I thought. "Archie told me about Allan Dukes," she began, delicately solicitous. I said nothing. "Naturally it must be hard for him, but it's quite appalling that he should—"

"Archie told me you'd had personal problems."

She blinked in surprise. "Did he? I can't imagine why. We're extremely happy. Obviously, there's been a degree of strain, what with the trial and—"

"No, this was before."

"Before?"

"A few years ago." I quoted Archie word for word.

The champagne arrived. Kristina took a sip. Her manicured hands didn't tremble. Her voice didn't shake. Her knee didn't jackhammer. Cool, so cool, in a way that I could never attain. "I'm really not sure what he meant. All couples have their tricky moments, of course. Oh well, whatever it was, all in the past." She beamed a kilowatt smile that would short the grid.

"And did he have a *moment* the night before Tara died?"

Two tiny dots of colour punctured her smooth pale cheeks. She took another swallow of champagne. "There was a quarrel," she admitted, eyes blink-blinking.

I waited for her to elaborate. She didn't. I'd always thought that conversing with Kristina was like eating a complicated fruit, like a pomegranate. You had to dig deep to winkle out and catch what she really meant.

"About?" I pressed.

"Jordan Dukes," she said. "Archie never approved."

"Why?"

"Isn't that rather obvious? Most parents don't want their daughters consorting with gangsters."

"He didn't know about the gang until after Jordan was arrested." Neither did I.

"Well, anyway," she said, breezy with it, utterly unflustered, "he thought him dubious. As it happened, he was right." More punch in her voice than was warranted; she intended it as a criticism of my judgment. "I'm not entirely certain where you're going with all this, Grace. Surely, you don't think Archie was somehow responsible for what happened. He feels guilty enough already."

"Guilty?" I almost screeched.

"His last words to Tara were thrown in anger. He blames himself for playing it all wrong and driving her closer to Jordan. What he really wanted was to prise her away. They had such a strong bond, Tara and her dad. Fathers and their little girls." She flicked an indulgent smile that made the blood in my veins congeal. "So you see, Archie was always going to worry about boyfriends. I think he found it particularly painful when she hooked up with Jordan."

Reasonable and credible, but why did I feel an inexplicable wave of deep unease? Sitting with the gorgeous Kristina, her make-up skilfully applied to highlight her beauty, it was hard to imagine Archie having an affair while shacked up with Kristina, let alone doing something illegal. Although, I had to admit, he'd strayed before—from me. Once you've committed adultery, it must be easier to repeat the process.

But I wasn't talking about adultery.

"Kristina," I said, "did Tara ever confide in you?"

"Me?"

"I won't be hurt or jealous, but I need to know."

"Why would she confide in me when she had you and Archie?" It was a good question and one I couldn't answer. It was also a damn fine response. "Grace, I know you won't believe this," she continued, "but Tara and I were really not that close. She tolerated me because I was her father's partner. She already had a mother. She didn't need a pale imitation."

"Yes," I said, dully and pathetically grateful.

"She really loved you."

"She told you that?" Despite my best endeavours, there was crying need in my voice.

"She did."

"I thought she only liked being with you."

"Rubbish. You know what kids are like." Kristina's accompanying smile was expansive, lighting up the entire bar. "They play one against another. Sure you won't have that drink?"

I hesitated because I badly wanted to be convinced that I was being overly dramatic. I wanted to be told everything was within the realms of normality. I didn't want to entertain scenarios I couldn't hack.

"Okay," I said. "Thanks." Goodness, wouldn't Archie be proud?

Kristina ordered the same again. "It's nice here, isn't it?" she said brightly. "I don't think I've been before."

Our drinks arrived and she raised her glass to mine. "Futures," she said.

Easier said when you have one. Taking a long deep swallow, I retreated to safer ground and asked how the viewings were going.

"As far as one can tell, fine. No offers yet, early days, but I think one couple were serious. I'm not sure the other lot could afford it."

"Is it that easy to tell?"

"One look at the car they drive is usually a good indicator," she said in a matey, girls-together tone. Shamelessly I took advantage and struck.

"Kristina, when did Archie meet Jordan?"

"I'm not sure I remember, exactly. Is it important?"

"Difficult to have a view on someone you barely know."

Her eyes flashed concern. "Oh, I see what you mean." She thought for a moment. I thought how impossibly long her eyelashes were, same as Archie's. "I think they met a couple of times at that new pizza place in town."

Awkward silence descended. I guessed we'd both run out of conversation, run out of road.

"What are you going to do, Grace?"

"Do?"

"Archie told me about the settlement."

"I suppose I should thank you for that."

Kristina frowned. "Wasn't my idea. All Archie's, I'm afraid. Not that I begrudge you a penny," she added quickly. "Why not take a holiday, somewhere warm and exotic, feel the sea breeze in your hair?"

I nodded blindly, not really listening. Why had Archie lied to me?

"We're so glad we had a break," Kristina prattled. "Moving is so stressful."

"Yes," I said. "How long have you known Archie's parents?"

Despite my best efforts to catch her off guard, Kristina was impossible to unbalance. "A while," she replied.

I muted a startled response. "I thought it a recent introduction."

"Known them for years now. His mum is such a sweetie. You never met them, I gather."

Kristina rattled on about her design business, the difficulty of shifting everything to the New Forest and having to start over again, her *conservative*, as she put it, plans for her forthcoming wedding. "Here's me droning on," she said. "I seem to have done all the talking. Another?" She gestured at my glass.

"Thank you, but no." I stood up and, with a wafer-thin smile, gathered up my coat and bag like a soldier reaches for his rifle. "Can you give Archie a message for me?"

"Of course."

"Tell him I hope he feels better soon."

"I will." She beamed.

"And let him know that I visited Jordan Dukes in prison yesterday."
Before Kristina could react, I strode out of the bar.

―――

The phone rang as I walked through the door. I smiled. Archie. Wrong.

"Mum told me what happened," Tiff said.

"Tiff, I'm really tired."

"You've seen him, haven't you?"

"If you mean Jordan, yes, I have."

"Fuck, Gracie, what were you thinking?"

"If you've called to give me a hard time, forget it."

"I'm coming round."

"No, Tiff—" Too late, she'd gone.

Half an hour later, Tiff sat on my sofa with a cup of coffee in her hand. The heady smell of horse manure and saddle soap filled the room despite me insisting she take off her boots and leave them outside the front door.

"They'll get wet," she'd complained.

"I don't care. They're not coming in."

I told her about my visit to the prison, the reason Jordan refused to offer a genuine defence, and the fact that I'd warned the Dukeses of the threat to Dionne and the baby. She'd learnt from our last exchange not to interrupt, although her facial expressions were mobile enough for me to divine what she thought, which was strong disapproval. Next I told her about approaching Archie, him agreeing to meet me only for Kristina to show up.

"Fucking coward," she concluded.

"Do you think it significant?"

Tiff blew on her coffee. "I don't believe he had a migraine. He's hiding something."

Time to drop my tiny bomb. I mentioned Jordan's remark about Tara's secret.

Her brown eyes shot wide. "Dirty?"

"That's what he said." Then I told her about my meeting with Thea and what she'd inferred about Archie. I'd expected a "Bloody Norah" response, but for once, Tiff was silent, her expression dazed. Frankly it worried me far more than an angry, accusing knee-jerk reaction.

"The dirty secret kind of fits with Thea's remark," I said, uneasily edging up to what I really meant to say.

Tiff took her time before opening her mouth. "Nothing shocks me, Gracie. Actually, that's not true. Doug shocks me every flipping day. But, Jesus, Gracie, what you're talking about is incest. Do you honestly think Archie had a thing with Tara? Is it really possible?"

I spread my hands. Archie's lies confused me. The more he lied, the more anything seemed possible. It was like discovering your favourite celebrity had been knocking off little girls and boys for decades. How did they get away with that? And yet... "That's why I want to talk to him."

"You're going to confront him?" Tiff said in amazement. "You never do things like that."

I do now, my expression said. Tiff took a slurp of coffee and scrutinised me warily, as if I'd announced I was about to head to Antarctica and study penguins.

"Word of advice," Tiff said. "Leave the Dukes clan to work out their own problems. You don't want to get involved. If Allan Dukes thinks his son didn't do it, that's down to him to prove, not you."

"But—"

"No, Gracie. Not your call. You've already done more than you should, and you were plain nuts to go to the cops. Anyone could have told you that Dunne or whoever would close ranks. As far as they're concerned they've got their man. Job done. Box ticked. And don't you be going all soft on me about it," she said, trying to play down the sisterly lecture with the hint of a smile.

I knew she meant well. I knew she was right, yet the idea of abandoning the Dukes family left a bitter taste in my mouth.

"It's not as if Jordan Dukes is pure as the driven snow," Tiff said, spotting my reluctance. "He killed that lad, Gracie."

"You can't say that. He says he didn't."

She pitched forward. "He was *involved*. They've passed a new law and that means if Jordan was there, he's guilty."

"How come you know so much about it?" I sharpened. Tiff never followed the news.

She flicked a grin. "Doug, the Mr. Big of Birmingham and West Midlands crime lord."

"What? Is he?" My turn to be shocked.

"Dunno, but I wouldn't put it past him, what with his dodgy contacts. Do you ever wonder how he made his fortune?" Her eyes flickered pensively.

"I try not to."

The landline rang. I pulled a face. Past eleven, who'd be ringing at this time?

"Archie?" Tiff said. "Want me to get it?"

"Would you?" Tiff was dying for an excuse to stick her hooter in and right now that suited me.

"Yes? Who? Calm down, take a breath."

I put down my mug. Straightaway I thought about Mum and searched Tiff's face in trepidation

"Say it again, slowly," Tiff said, eyeing me. "Okay, I'll get her. It's Dionne," she said, clamping one hand over the receiver. "Not making a lot of sense, but she said something about a fire. I think her dad's been hurt."

Everything swirled around me. The walls closed in. The air exited. Someone had drained me of blood and filled my veins with lead.

Because she'll burn you, burn everyone, Jordan said.

And now Dax had.

Twenty-Six

Too shaken to drive, I let Tiff take me in her car, a lime green Nissan Micra, more motorised food whisk than vehicle. The funny thing about my sister, whatever she felt about the Dukeses, and specifically my connection to them, she always delivered in a crisis.

It seemed to take forever to get there. I blinked ahead into the darkness and shining lights, imagining the worst. Dionne was crying so hard at first I thought something terrible had happened to Asher. Only when she calmed down did I get a handle on what had happened. Following my call, Allan must have stewed for the rest of the day and into the evening before paying Dax and her crew a visit that night, with unpredictable consequences. Alarmingly it transpired that Dionne was on hand because she'd flatly refused to leave her father. I'd definitely got that wrong. Had I known, I'd have stalled talking to Dunne.

"How badly is he hurt?"

"They busted his nose and beat him. He lost consciousness. By the time he came round, the extension to the house he was working on was alight."

"They set it on fire?"

"If they didn't, who did? Firemen are there now."

"This it?" Tiff said as we swung into the crescent. Lights blazed from every room in the house.

"Yes."

"Do you want me to come in?"

"I don't want you getting uppity in there."

"I didn't get *uppity* driving you here."

I flashed her an apologetic look. "Okay then."

"I suppose I'll have to take my boots off here, too," she grumbled as we crossed the drive.

Dionne let us in. Drawn and with her cheeks flecked with smuts of mascara, she held Asher, squirming and grizzling in her arms. I introduced her to Tiff. "Here, let me," I said, taking the baby from her. Immediately I felt Tiff's death stare bore into the side of my head.

"Thanks for coming," Dionne said. "I didn't know who else to call. I was so scared. I'm really sorry about … " She burst into tears, her shoulders shaking. In unison, Asher's mewl turned into a full-throttle wail.

"Hey," Tiff said, putting an awkward arm around her. "Here," she said, extracting a tissue from her jacket and handing it to Dionne. I waited while Dionne mopped her face and blew her nose.

"I told him not to go, but he wouldn't listen," she sobbed. In that moment, I saw from where Dionne got her stubborn streak.

Tiff glanced meaningfully at me. I couldn't tell whether she thought Allan unhinged or heroic. "Where does this bitch, Dax, hang out?" she said, spiky-faced, meaning trouble ahead. I had horrible visions of my sister taking Dax on in a cat brawl.

"There's an old youth centre in Podsmead, closed down now," Dionne replied.

"And *she* beat up your dad?" I couldn't imagine anyone easily knocking Allan Dukes about. Muscular, fit, and no doubt strong from days spent on building sites, he would have put up a fight. The odds must have been overwhelming.

"She doesn't do the dirty. Gets others to dish out beatings."

"Including Jordan?" Tiff said pointedly.

Dionne scowled. "*Not* including Jordan. My brother's mixed up, but he isn't a murderer or an enforcer."

Tiff opened her mouth to retaliate but one look from me and she stopped in her tracks.

"How much longer do you think your dad will be?" I said, rocking the baby, heading off a bust-up.

"Depends on the police."

Tiff shot me another sturdy glance.

"Will he tell them the truth?" I asked.

"I don't know. He doesn't trust the police, especially not after what happened with you and Dunne."

Cold and clammy, guilt curled up and nestled against my chest. In trying to help, I'd made matters worse.

"Can I get you a drink?" Dionne asked. "Coffee, tea?"

I looked at Tiff, who shrugged she was fine. "Tea would be nice, thanks," I said.

We followed Dionne through to the kitchen. Tiff scrutinized the appliances, the range cooker, taking it all in, making mental judgments and calculations, calibrating how much it was all worth, working out that Allan Dukes was doing all right considering his son was a criminal. I threw her a stare that told her to back off and wind her neck in.

Dionne made a brew. Precise and methodical, she was keen to be busy, I guessed, and eager to escape the weight of motherhood, worrying about her brother and now her dad. Her sixteen-year-old shoulders stooped, buckling under the load.

We were settling down when, at the sound of a key in the lock, we collectively held our breaths and heard the front door swing open, followed by a man's slow gait down the long hall. Allan Dukes appeared at the doorway, his face grimy, hair flecked with soot. There was a rip in his jacket. The heavy odour of bonfire, smoke, and ashes clung to his clothes. Shattered and defeated, he stood, one hand gripping the frame, knuckles skinned. His right eye was swollen and shiny, almost closed, his skin beneath the grime bragged a mass of purple, livid bruising. A nasty cut above his left eyebrow, as if someone had glassed him, seeped fresh blood, and his lips were cracked and torn. He grimaced a greeting, his expression betraying shame and defeat.

"Dad." Dionne started forward and threw her arms around him.

"Steady." He winced.

I caught his eye. Immediately he looked away, avoiding my gaze, closed off, and I realised that I shouldn't have come, that I was no longer welcome. It was them and us and always would be. Tiff sensed it, too. I could tell by the way she was looking at me, wildly grimacing for us to leave.

"Thank you for coming," he said stiffly. "Sorry for your trouble."

"It was no trouble," I said. "I was worried."

"We're all right now. Everything will be all right," he repeated. Failure and shock threaded his voice. Unnaturally brittle.

"If you're sure." I felt awkward. I don't know what I imagined, but it wasn't supposed to be like this.

Tiff tugged at me. "Hand the baby back. Let these people get some sleep."

I didn't budge. "Allan, did you talk to the police?"

He turned to me with a dead to the bones expression. "About the fire, yes. About this"—he pointed to his face—"no."

"Whyever not?"

He issued a sad, cynical smile. "Because they wouldn't have listened."

Feeling small, I handed Asher back to Dionne and said good-night. Almost out of the door, I heard Allan's voice, clear, strong, and true. "They called him a glass jaw."

I turned in puzzlement.

"A coward," he explained. "That's what that bitch called my son. Said he'd *dissed* them by trying to talk them out of *shanking* Tyrone Weaver."

And then they'd threatened him.

Tiff drove me home in silence. Almost two in the morning, she crashed at mine and slept in my bed while I slept in Tara's. Except I didn't sleep at all. I thought about lies and deception, about Kristina and Archie, about casual violence and blatant disregard of the law. I thought about me swimming against a tide of intrigue and murder and secrets, and drowning, disappearing into the murky depths unseen and unheard.

Around five I heard the front door open and close. Tiff leaving for the stables. We'd barely spoken on the way back. *Not your call. Not your problem.* If anything, coming face-to-face with Allan Dukes had hardened her view. Her final words to me before we turned in were, "Take it as a warning."

"But Jordan ... "

"Forget him."

Twenty-Seven

"*F*or goodness sake, Tara, can you play something else for a change? It's so depressing. And what are you doing brooding in the dark?" I blundered in and tore open the curtains to let in daylight.

"Aw, Mum," she protested, curling up on her bed. Protective. Defensive.

"Why don't you go out and get some fresh air? It's a lovely day."

"Because." She unfurled, reached up, and punched a pillow to make the point.

Giving up, I headed back out. Before I got to the door, Tara called after me.

"Yes?" I turned.

"How do you get rid of stuff, you know, documents?"

"What documents?"

She rolled her eyes and exhaled an enormous sigh. "I meant as an example. Private stuff."

"Shred it."

"Where could I do that?"

"There's a shredder at the gallery. Is there something you want me to get rid of?"

"Nope, only wondered." Swinging her body round, she planted her feet firmly on the floor and stood up. "Think I'll take your advice and get some air."

"Want some company? I'm not busy."

"No thanks."

I limped around the house all Sunday morning. Not five minutes passed when I didn't think of Tara, of Jordan, and of my ex-husband and what he might or might not have done. Against this, Tiff's warning boxed my ears.

Archie called three times and, after a brief tussle with my conscience, I deleted every message from him and, in frustration, switched off the phone. Bored and restless, I went over to Mum's for lunch. Unusually, Tiff and Gray were out. About to sit down to eat, the doorbell rang a tacky rendition of a classical piece of music.

"I'll get it," I said.

A short, wiry guy stood outside. He had a flat nose that looked as if it had been broken several times and badly set. His thin mousey-coloured hair was plastered to his scalp with gel apart from a weird sticking up bit in the middle, like a duck's bum. He had a fresh cut over one eye that looked sore. For a crazy moment I thought he was one of Dax's minions until he opened his mouth and said in a broad Black Country accent, "Is Doug in?"

A shadow darkened the wide hall as Doug lumbered up behind me. "It's all right, Gracie," he said, his voice a rasp. I backed away and headed to the kitchen, but not before I'd heard Doug snarl, "What the fuck do you think you're doing coming to my house?"

"Who was that?" Mum said, pouring gravy over her meal.

"Someone for Doug."

"A friend? Why doesn't he bring him inside? There's plenty to go round."

"Not that kind of friend, Mum."

She held my gaze for a moment, a trace of mute understanding passing between us. "Right you are," she said. "Do you want horseradish with your beef?"

I shook my head. Doug reappeared and sat down. When my mum pressed him about his unexpected visitor, he said, "Nothing to concern yourself with, Doll." And that was that.

On Monday, I dragged myself back to work.

"Intravenous coffee," Vron said, plonking a mug on the desk. We were sorting through a data list of buyers who'd been unable to attend an exhibition at our sister gallery in Cirencester the night before. With some pieces left over, unsold, we were matching these requirements from previous buyers so that we could approach them with a carefully crafted email, the intention to close a deal.

"Had a drink with Seb last night," Vron said shyly, her white as ice skin gleaming.

"Did you?" How was I supposed to react? I wasn't into condoning an affair in spite of thinking Seb's wife a world-class cow.

"Mmm," she said dreamily.

"And?"

"We talked. Nothing more," she added quickly, darting a look, "other than a swift peck on the cheek."

"Vron," I began, breaking off as a silhouette caught my peripheral vision, a customer, or so I thought. "Don't you think—"

"Oh hi, Archie," Vron exclaimed.

He jogged up the steps to the second floor and gave her an easy hug. "How's the lovely Vron? Looking good, darling."

"Not so bad yourself." Vron's droopy expression indicated that he'd overwhelmed her with his flattery and charm. Archie tended to have this effect on women, although it had never infuriated me before. Women, I thought with a jolt. Not girls. Not our daughter. Not…

He looked over Vron's shoulder. Deliberately. "Hi, Grace."

"I'm working," I said. "Whatever it is will have to keep."

"I'm sure Vron here won't mind?" He gave her the benefit of his full-beam smile, seductive and deeply sexy and a masterstroke of manipulation. Had he transgendered into his future wife?

"Of course not," she said, obviously melting. "Take as long as you like, Grace."

"I don't get paid to chat to my ex-husband."

Vron's lips twitched at my wretchedly unkind response, for which I was sorry. Vron wasn't winding me up. It was all Archie's fault.

I stood up, threw Archie a glassy stare, marched across the gallery, and stepped outside into the spitting rain. A blast of wind gusted across the street and I wished I'd put my jacket on. Despite it being April, it was cold and bitter and grey. Fingers of damp clawed at my neck.

Archie drew up alongside. He took my elbow and pointed to an empty bench on the other side of the road in front of the war memorial. Dodging a bus and a Bentley purring down the street, we darted across and sat down. He turned in, close to me, conspiratorially. I drew away, hunched my shoulders, shivering.

"Grace, about last—"

"Are you better now?" My voice was scathing.

"You don't believe me, do you?" He tilted his head, smarting, unable to fathom my sarcasm.

"There's a lot I don't believe, Archie."

He sighed in irritation. I'd rattled the bars of his damned cage and it pleased me. You don't know how to handle me anymore, do you, I thought?

He leant back, flicked both palms up. "Truce?"

I hiked one shoulder. Whatever. "Shouldn't you be at work?"

"Worked out my notice, packed it in."

"I see."

"Don't look at me like that."

"Like what?"

"As if I'd announced taking up arms with Islamic State terrorists."

I wanted to say it then, give breath to the sneaky voice creeping around inside my head, blurt it out, accuse him. But the words wouldn't come. Secrets by definition were not supposed to be busted open or dragged out into the screaming light. I needed to be subtle, to act the diplomat, to assume a delicate approach. How to do this beat me.

"Kristina passed on your message," Archie said. "I don't understand why you did it."

"Because Jordan is innocent and Tara's killer is out there." I tipped my chin, gestured towards the crowds of people and shoppers strolling along the Promenade as if any one of them could be guilty.

"Innocent?" Archie jeered.

"Don't you care? What's the matter with you?"

"As innocent as his father, you mean?"

Something inside me shifted. Archie saw it and closed in with a superior expression. "Allan Dukes isn't quite the golden boy you take him for."

"What the hell are you talking about?"

"Didn't he tell you about his past, about why his wife left?"

I couldn't speak, couldn't utter a sound.

"Thought not," Archie gloated. "Any man who hits a woman should be locked up in my book."

"No," I shook my head. "This is crap, Archie. If Allan had done something like that he would never be allowed custody of his children."

"Allan? That's pally. Rules are made to be broken, Grace, and if you don't believe me, ask him."

Twenty-Eight

I spent the rest of the afternoon in a haze. Every painting on the wall screamed in my ear and mocked my gullibility. When Vron went downstairs to telephone clients, I went onto the Internet and Googled Allan Dukes, only this time I added "charged with assault" and estimated the year in which it might have taken place. Nothing specific came up. I quickly found myself amid a screed of sexual offences, kidnappings, and gang-related violence. Had Archie created a smokescreen designed to bamboozle my thinking? If so, it worked. When I'd demanded to know how Archie had stumbled across this nasty nugget of information, he told me he'd heard it from Allan's next-door neighbour.

"You've been snooping?" I'd said, aghast.

"Obtaining information. No more than you're doing," he'd added with a sly dig. And, of course, now he'd have bags of free time at his disposal.

As I left work for home, my temple throbbed, which no amount of painkiller could cure. Blind with double-vision and pain by the time I staggered into the apartment, I slipped down onto the sofa, jacket still on, kicked off my shoes, lay flat out, and closed my eyes.

Uninvited, I remembered Archie the first time we met. I'd spotted him before he noticed me. Talking to a dark-haired girl, far prettier than anyone else in the room, a model, perhaps, he leaned towards her, eyes intent on hers as if she and him were the only two people in that crowded room. I'd observed from a distance, with longing. I don't know what made me do it—nobody dared me and it wasn't some personal challenge—but I plucked up enough courage and sauntered over. He tilted his head, dark eyes dissolving into mine, and broke into a starlight smile. The brunette glanced sharply up at the intruder I was. Not that this fazed Archie. When he asked me to join them, she got up, stalked away, never to be seen again, and then it was the two of us in our own private, secret world, him and me forever.

I must have drifted off to sleep because I woke with a start. Thinking I'd received a text on my phone, I swung my legs round, reached for it, and checked. No calls. No texts. Yet, deep in my bones, I sensed something had happened, but couldn't work out what it was.

Nervously, I checked each room and window. Not a cushion or furnishing moved or out of place. No sign of forced entry. To be sure, I looked through the window to the courtyard. No shadows lurking. To be really sure, I opened the front door and stepped outside, shivering a little in the reduced temperature. The security light flicked on, illuminating the steps, pots and plants, and the fig tree that was growing like mad and had cost me a packet. Relieved, putting my jumpiness down to

Archie's little bombshell, I turned to go back inside and noticed a bin liner full of rubbish dumped on top of the wheeliebin in the corner. Cheek, I thought, remembering it was collection day in the morning. Picking it up and chucking it in with the rest of the rubbish, something wet and leaking dripped down my new stone-coloured work trousers and onto my shoes. I cursed aloud, slamming down the lid, retreating. Staring down to inspect the damage, I noticed that my trousers were smeared in red paint, as were my hands. Except the consistency was thinner, viscous. Prickling with alarm, I rubbed the pad of my thumb against my fingers and raised them to my nose. Sickening realisation piled into me with the full force of a cyclone. Blood. I was covered in blood.

I sped back inside and into the bathroom, stripped off my clothes and threw them into the bath. Shivering with fear, I washed and scrubbed my skin until it stung, slung on a pair of jeans, reached for the first sweater I could lay my hands on, and pulled it over my head. Armed with a torch I kept for emergencies, about to go back outside, I stopped stock-still.

Are you out of your mind? a voice inside me said. What if it contains bits of a body? Shouldn't you call the police? What if the perpetrator is lurking around the corner? What if it's bait designed to trap you and he, whoever he is, is waiting to pounce?

I shot into Tara's room, dug out the rape alarm, briefly switched it on and was rewarded with a high-pitch noise loud enough to burst eardrums and disable the most determined attacker. Shoving it into the pocket of my jeans, I tugged on the pair of rubber gloves I used for washing up and forced myself back into the dark before my nerves failed me.

Rolling the bin into the middle of the courtyard, underneath the full glare of the security light, I flipped open the lid and gingerly removed the offending bin bag, and laid it on the stone. Roughly tied with orange twine, it stank of meat and carcass and a rank odour I couldn't place but associated with death and—God help me—remains. My head snapped up at the sound of footsteps on the pavement above. I froze, not daring to breathe, one hand against the pocket of my jeans resting against the alarm, the sturdy torch, gripped in my hand, a makeshift club. The footsteps receded and it was back to the grisly cargo and me.

I fumbled with the tie, struggling with first one knot and then another. Would the police accuse me of contaminating a crime scene? Would they care? I thought, almost taking leave of my senses. At last, the twine undone, I parted the opening and gawped inside. My brain absorbed it in random order: hair, blood, bone. Green eyes. Pointed ears, soft and smooth as felt. Pink tongues protruding through tiny teeth. Severed heads. Cats. Kittens.

Jesus fucking Christ.

I dropped the bag and tore inside, slamming the door hard after me, the wood rattling in the doorframe. My back pressed against the cool wall, I ripped off the gloves and sank to the floor.

This *was* madness. I was mad.

Who would do something like that? Dax? Hadn't she done enough damage already? I wanted to call someone. Tiff, I thought, but recalled it was her night with Graham and it would take them ages to get here and the last thing I needed was his gormless face in mine. Worse, he might even tell Doug about it. Blind-sided, I did the unthinkable. I did the absurd.

My hands trembled as I punched in the number. "Archie?" I panted. "Can you come? Can you come now? Quickly."

Twenty-Nine

"There," he said, handing me a glass of the brandy I only kept for culinary purposes and for when I'd run out of wine and still needed a drink.

Hand shaking, I lifted the balloon to my lips and sipped. Liquid fire slid down my throat, warmed and anaesthetised my tummy and then what remained of my brain.

"I've double-wrapped the bin liner and shoved it in the back of the Discovery."

"Nice present for Kristina," I quipped, feeling giddy.

He half smiled. "I'll bury it in the garden. Nobody need know a thing about it."

"Except me and you, our secret." I looked into his eyes for a long moment. In the early days of our relationship we had gazed at each other for what seemed like hours, to the point that it had almost physically hurt me when Archie or I had to go to work. I couldn't bear to be without him—we'd been that close, spiritually, mentally, sexually. It was the same for him. Wherever my feverish imagination took me, through whatever dark and dangerous doors, I could never deny those intimate and memorable moments in time. It seemed impossible that they had counted for nothing as far as he was concerned.

Archie was first to look away.

"What now?" I said.

"You go to bed. You sleep. You get up in the morning and forget it ever happened."

"Forget? Do you realise some bastard actually trapped and killed those poor creatures? God, they could be someone's pets."

"There are a lot of sick people in the world, Grace. It's their idea of a joke."

"You really believe that?"

"Why not?"

"You don't have to be a criminologist to know that people who hurt animals often graduate to hurting people." And why dump them on me?

"*I* didn't."

Goggle-eyed, I gripped the glass so hard it was in danger of shattering.

Archie flashed a smile. "Don't look so shocked."

"But—"

"Hey, I've just noticed. You're wearing my old sweater."

Was I? I looked down, distracted. What had I been thinking? That was the trouble. I wasn't thinking at all. Looking back up into his eyes, I wondered whether he'd drawn my attention to it to distract me. Swallowing hard, I said with as much strength as I could muster, "Tell me what you did, Archie."

He tilted his head, settled down in his seat, in storytelling mode, at ease. "A few years before I met you, I had a girlfriend," he began slowly. "I thought she was the one."

Not me? I jolted inside. I'd always thought *I* was *the one*. Flayed with disappointment, I mumbled, "You never mentioned her."

"No," he said shortly and in a way that I found earth-shattering. Shouldn't he qualify it? Shouldn't he say, *Because she wasn't important? Because it wasn't serious. Not like you, like us?*

"I wasn't very proud of what happened," he continued with a penetrating stare that frightened me. "We lived together in some god-awful hole near Paddington station. I was studying and so was she. We were stupid, young, and in love and we'd barely enough money to feed ourselves."

"In love?" I murmured, but he didn't pick up on it. It was as if our conversation was taking place in stereo. He had his soundtrack and I had mine.

"You know how cats adopt you? Well, this cat moved into our place. We called her Smutty. She had a white face with black patches." His eyes warmed and he briefly smiled at the memory. "One day, out of the clear blue, she produced six kittens. We could barely feed ourselves. We couldn't afford to keep them."

The air bloated around me, as if filled with a noxious substance, like chlorine gas or something that incapacitated the senses. I tiptoed up to the words on my tongue and whispered, "You got rid of them?"

"Drowned them in a bucket of water."

"Jesus, Archie."

"You've no idea how awful it was," he rushed on, desperate to reduce my horrified reaction. "They really didn't want to die, but it was the kindest thing to do."

Kind? I sat frozen. You gutless bastard, I wanted to say, but I couldn't speak. Archie was so caring. Archie would never have done something as monstrous as this. Not the Archie I knew. And yet he had. Did I know this man at all? And why reveal it now?

"You're right to think badly of me," he said, preempting my response, "but we were kids. I'm ashamed of myself, still."

"So you should be." Rigid with revulsion, I crossed my arms.

"But I'm not responsible for what happened tonight, Grace."

"Is this why you're telling me? In case I find out and think the worst of you?" He had no idea how low my worst actually was.

"I'm simply explaining that it isn't significant."

"I think I'll decide about that, if you don't mind."

"You're angry." He looked troubled, as if he realised too late that he'd overplayed his hand and misjudged my likely reaction. Too damn right.

I didn't let him off. I regretted asking him round, and I wanted to erect a ring of razor wire around me to protect myself from him. Archie sensed it because he reached out, took my stiff hand in his, and fixed me with another impaling gaze—only this one was ringed with concern, fake or genuine, I no longer knew. "I'm worried about you Grace."

I wrenched my hand away. "So you've said. There's no need."

"You're on self-destruct. No good can come of raking over and digging up the past. We've got a conviction, Grace. Justice has been done. You need to move on with your life, the same way I need to."

"Is that what this marriage and the move is all about?"

"In a way." A flicker of light behind his eyes told me no, or at least, it wasn't the whole story.

He took my hand again. He'd always been tactile. I tried to resist and pull away, but he hung on, turned it over, and studied my palm, tracing the lines. He'd once told me that my heart line extended from my index finger sweeping down to the side of my palm. Mine was like a chain, which denoted I was highly strung, common in creative types, or so he'd informed me. "Do you remember how we used to be into all that horoscope stuff?" he said with a grin.

"You had a chart done," I said primly. At the time I thought it fun. Now I thought it ridiculous.

"Still got it somewhere, although I might lose it before the next move. Kristina wouldn't approve," he added, a naughty telling-tales curl to his lips. How dare he play the conspirator with me?

"Did it foretell the break-up of our marriage?"

He let my hand drop and, with it, his gaze. "I didn't plan it, Grace. I wasn't looking for someone else. It simply happened. There was a connection I can't explain. I still can't," he said, glancing up at me with a beseeching expression, which I found distasteful. I didn't want to hear about his blasted "connection."

I took another swig of brandy. For courage. For Tara. "But something went wrong, didn't it?"

Archie *never* flushed and I'd only ever seen him perspire twice, once when he was shifting a bush in our garden and once when he'd run all the way home because I'd gone into labour. He did both now.

"It was nothing, a blip, unimportant."

Then why do you sound so brittle? "And Tara?"

This time he paled. "What's Tara got to do with it?"

"I don't know. I was hoping you'd tell me."

His gaze transferred to the contents of my glass. Either he was wondering quite how much I'd drunk or was longing to take a slug himself. "You're talking in riddles, Grace."

"Do you know anything about a secret?"

"Whose?"

"Tara's. She had a dirty secret, Archie."

He shook his head. Perspiration beaded his brow. "Who told you this?"

"Does it matter?"

His face contorted. "Of course it fucking matters."

I drained the glass, reached for the bottle, felt Archie's hand shoot out and grip my wrist. "Tell me."

"Let go."

He did as quickly as if he'd touched a naked flame. "Sorry," he muttered. "Shouldn't have done that."

I silently agreed and poured myself another drink. "One of Tara's friends, Thea."

"Thea Molyneux?"

"Yes."

"What did she say exactly?"

"She said that before Jordan came along, Tara was secretive. She attributed it to you."

His eyes shot wide and his jaw went slack.

"She thought it wasn't healthy," I said, never dropping my gaze. Deadly.

"Me, no shit?" Archie's widened eyes closed and crinkled at the edges. Shoulders shaking, a deep laugh frothed up from inside him and erupted into a peal that would shatter titanium. I watched stupefied. Had I been too subtle? Did he know what I meant? Why would he find something like that hilarious? "I'm sorry," he said, wiping his wet lashes with the back of his hand. "She thought ... No, I can't get my head around it. It's too ludicrous. Tara and I were close ..."

"How close exactly? What did you row about the Friday night she stayed over, before she was killed?"

The smile fled. "Fucking hell, Grace, you never believed her, did you? You seriously thought ... " His voice slunk off and died.

I sat up straight, raised my head. I was drunk, but not that drunk. "You lied to me over and over. You said nothing about a quarrel. You lied to me about it being Kristina's idea to give me money, about your parents and God knows what else. You kill kittens because they're an inconvenience. I don't know you, what you're capable of. I'm not sure I ever did." My voice soared and ricocheted off the tiny walls and sliced through the fetid atmosphere.

He jumped to his feet, tight-jawed, mouth flexed with fury. His hands balled into fists in the same way as Allan's, except his had been in anguish not temper.

"You're cracked."

"Rather that than depraved."

"And sick," he raged. "You think I'd harm a hair on Tara's head, our daughter, our baby? You think … " He screwed his eyes shut, jaw grinding, then snapped them open. Bulging. "You're right, Grace," he snarled. "You don't know me at all."

Thirty

Archie stormed out. I finished my drink, replaying the footage in my head, revisiting the sound of his voice, examining each nuance from every angle. The way he'd laughed out loud, almost with hysteria, at my warped suggestion reassured me on one level. On another, I was confounded. Was it possible that Tara's secret was due to someone else? Had she threatened to reveal it? Was that why my girl was killed? And did the killer believe that, somewhere in her belongings, Tara still had the power to expose from beyond the grave?

Brain-dead, I went to bed, slept the sleep of the inebriated, and woke up too early and with a pounding headache. The variation on a hangover theme was along the lines of a heavy metal band playing a gig in my frontal lobes. Downing a couple of painkillers, I returned to my duvet, pulled it up over my head, and slept for a couple of hours. Headache tamed, I got up and gently floated around the living room in my dressing gown with a mug of tea and did my best not to think about blood and fur, pink ears and dead eyes. It didn't work. I couldn't help but dwell on Archie's hideous revelation. I was like a lost soul wandering through a winter forest of dripping trees, marsh and bog beneath my feet, with absolutely no idea which path would lead me to safety.

Disquieted, I switched on the radio and tuned into the local station. Hitting it on the hour, it went straight to the news:

"Police have released a man arrested in connection with the murder of Tyrone Weaver, the twenty-year-old stabbed dead in Gloucester almost…"

A charge of revelation pulsed through me. Seemingly snookered by Dunne's information, I hadn't been "played" at all. My mood lift lasted mere seconds.

"Suicide and murder rates in prison have reached their highest level, a new report states. Averaging at a rate of six suicides a month, only last night, an inmate at HMP Bristol attempted suicide…"

I froze, my mind homing in on Graham and Doug's despicable little joke and Jordan's claim that someone had tried to "jump his bones." How many inmates were there? Six, seven hundred? Could be any inmate, couldn't it? Jordan was all right, wasn't he?

If I contacted the prison would they tell me? Don't be daft, of course not.

I phoned Allan. His mobile was switched off. Maybe he was up a ladder or in a mobile black spot. I paced. *What I believe is you're on self-destruct,* Archie had said. *Leave the Dukes clan to work out their own problems,* Tiff advised. But what if Jordan was dying slowly in a hospital bed, wired up to machinery, stomach packed with charcoal to counter the effects of an overdose? Or maybe he'd tried to hang himself with his own sheets, or slit his wrists, or hurl himself down a flight of concrete steps. My mind raced and sprinted away with me. In a strange, indefinable way, if Jordan Dukes teetered on the black wavy line between life and death, then so did I. In truth, I'd been edging towards flatlining since Tara had been taken from me.

I dressed, tried Allan's number again, this time left a message. I graduated from tea to coffee, washed up mugs and glasses, flicked through a magazine, not reading the words, not seeing the pictures, waiting and waiting. When my phone rang around mid-day, I almost accidentally cut the call, so great was my haste to answer it.

"Yes?"

"Hi, Grace, sorry I couldn't get back to you sooner." Allan didn't offer an explanation and I didn't ask for one.

"Did you hear the news this morning?"

"The lad who tried to top himself? Rushed to Frenchay hospital in the early hours, poor beggar."

Almost keeling over with relief, I felt foolish and overdramatic and all the things that Archie thought I was. "You know the police have released the man suspected of murdering Tyrone Weaver?"

"When did you hear this?"

"First item of local news this morning. Don't you see, the police will be looking elsewhere."

Allan fell silent.

"You still there?"

"I'm not sure whether that's good or bad. Unless there's categorical proof of Jordan's non-involvement, he can still be found guilty."

"I understand, but don't you remember that Dax called him a coward? She said he tried to talk them out of it. The police might be prepared to check it out now that—"

"We've already done this. If the police put the squeeze on Dax and her gang, God knows what she'll do. You saw what happened to me."

I flashed with fury. "But what about Jordan? You can't give up on him."

Stony silence indicated I'd caused grave offence. Who was I to accuse Allan of deserting his son? I tried again. "How old is this Dax kid?"

"Old enough to have a guy twice her age beaten up."

"But the fire?"

"Covered by insurance, thank God, and the damage isn't as bad as I'd first thought."

Without a trace of irony, I said, "That girl should be feeling the heat, not you. And Dionne and Asher, how are they?"

"She hasn't been back to school. Too shaken up." Grim finality inhabited his voice. "What about you?"

Apart from a parcel of severed cats' heads, the fact that my daughter's killer is free to do as he pleases, and that my ex-husband is and remains a conundrum, I'm fine and dandy. I made a noncommittal remark.

"It was nice of you to call, Grace. I'm sorry about the other night. I was tired, upset, not myself."

"Please don't apologise. I shouldn't have come."

"I'm glad you did."

I blinked, felt a warm thrill. Archie's voice dripped in my ear, *wife beater.*

"It would be easier for you if Jordan had killed Tara, wouldn't it?"

Floored, I didn't really know how to answer. "I suppose you're right, yes."

"I'm sorry." He let out a dry laugh. "We seem to spend a lot of time apologising to each other."

"I know."

"Look, feel free to pass on it, but would you like to come to dinner to make up for the other night? We could talk things through."

"A council of war?"

"Something like that. Perhaps." He didn't sound certain.

"Well, I ..."

"I promise not to cook. We could have a takeaway. Something easy."

On the verge of declining, I thought about Archie's accusation. This would give me an opportunity to discover the truth. "What time?"

"About seven."

———

"Stan Getz," I said.

"A fellow music-head," Allan grinned. Close-up, I could see that he had slightly offset features, not like Archie's.

"My ex-husband introduced me to jazz a long time ago. I love a mellow sax."

"Would you like some more?" He pushed a tray of duck in plum sauce towards me.

"No, thanks, I can't move." I grinned.

Dionne was safely upstairs poring over homework. Asher snoozed in his basket. For the past two precious hours I'd really laughed, like I hadn't in ages. It seemed weird, yet I didn't think people who haven't been caught up in tragedy really understand that, however bad things are, it's hard to despair 24/7. It's the mind's way of saying you can't take it. We didn't talk about murder and prison, cats and killers, beatings and fires, or the threat of imminent destruction. I'd noticed that Allan continued to talk with his eyes long after he'd stopped speaking, and I was forced to admit that this gently spoken man with a beaten-up face privately fascinated me.

It didn't anaesthetise me from guilt.

The devil on my shoulder demanded to know why I should smile, let alone laugh. Joy or a deep feeling of pleasure would never be mine again. Why should I forget for even a fleeting moment that Tara was dead and her killer was free?

Deliberately shooting a line, I spoke to Allan about Archie—how we'd met, how I'd loved him, and how he'd left me for Kristina. I spoke nothing of suspicion or dirty secrets. I did not confess that I spent way too much time walking around inside my own head or that I kept the forgotten remnants of Archie's aftershave in a box marked KEEPSAKES and still wore one of his sweaters, sometimes without even realising it. That was too personal.

"The man's a fool." Warm-eyed, Allan said it as if he meant it. It made it easy and natural for me to ask him about his wife.

"Makeda," he said, splashing more wine into his glass. Silence descended, casting shadows.

"What went wrong?" I murmured.

"What went right?" He took a deep swallow. A distant light entered his eyes. Our conversation had taken a left turn and there was a nasty undertow. My pulse raced. He pulled an apologetic smile. "That's not quite fair of me," he said. "Despite everything that happened, the kids we got right."

"That's what Archie always said."

"You're not really over him, are you?" It wasn't an accusation. He spoke solicitously, as if enquiring about an affliction I'd recently weathered. I suppose that's exactly what Archie was—an affliction. In nearly five years, there had been no other men in my life. I remained in chains. But chains were for breaking.

"That obvious?"

"You talk about him all the time. Perhaps you don't even notice." He broke into a lovely smile. "I'm not being unkind."

"I know."

"You must have really loved him."

"I did." I do, or I do as long as he hasn't done what Thea thought he has.

"It's true what Archie said about Tara." He smiled. "She was a great girl. She'd appear wherever we had a job on. I used to shoo her away, sometimes, when she was bunking off school." He stalled, taken aback by my shocked expression. "You didn't know?"

I shook my head. How come I was unaware of something as blatant as her truanting? Tears prickled my eyes. And how would I ever discover her deepest secret when there were so many lesser and more mundane ones to reveal? It reminded me of the wooden Russian doll she'd bought for me when she was about ten. Three inches tall, it came apart to reveal a smaller version. Unscrew that, and a baby nestled inside.

He closed a solid hand over mine. Strong and calloused, the thumbnail blackened by injury, a fading bruise on the back close to the edge of his shirtsleeve, it felt different than Archie's smooth cool touch. "It only happened once or twice, honestly."

I didn't move my hand away. I liked the weight of his on mine. I liked the connection. It felt more solid, reliable, and dependable than Archie's. "Your wife," I began again.

"What you're really asking is, did I hit her?" His steely expression locked onto mine. "You're a smart woman. You've done your homework. It's no secret that there were problems."

"You hit her?" With a stomach-turning sensation, I realised that this very hand, parked on top of mine, had slapped or punched a woman. I quickly withdrew.

"To my shame, I did. Once."

"Why?" My voice emerged as if scraping through the edges of a tunnel.

"She was having an affair and threw it in my face, threatened to take the children with her even though she was a lousy mother. When I cut up rough—"

"Whoa," I said, putting up my palm. "What exactly do you mean?"

"I yelled at her."

"Lost your temper?"

"Nah. Not my style."

I blinked. I didn't know what his style was. From the little I knew Allan struck me as a quiet man, in control, his reactions within the wide spectrum of emotional responses. I had no sense of simmering violence underneath the composed exterior. But I could be mistaken. Hadn't I been utterly wrong about Archie?

"When she came at me with a knife, yes, I hit her in self-defence," he explained. "Cut my arm, but at least she dropped her weapon. I admit she sustained quite a bruise."

"And you got custody." It was more statement than question.

"Would you leave your children with a woman who brandishes a blade?"

Thank God, I thought, feeling the tension seep out of me. Thank God.

"Anyway, Makeda didn't want them," he continued. "She only threatened to take them because she knew how much it would destroy me."

"Did Jordan witness it?"

"Afraid he did. You'd think it would act as a deterrent."

"Who knows what kind of effect that has on a small boy."

"Whatever he's done or hasn't done, I can't deny the police found his knife in this house. He wasn't carrying because he planned on taking up wood carving," he said without smiling.

I fell silent. Now I understood his resistance. How I longed for clear lines, the equivalent of a smoking gun, a sign that pointed unmistakably and categorically in a single direction marked THIS IS ME. I KILLED YOUR DAUGHTER.

Allan touched my arm. An electric charge shot underneath my skin and into my veins. "I've never asked, but..."

"Allan, I have no idea who killed Tara."

He flicked a smile. "How did you know I was going to say that?"

"I read it in your eyes."

"We must be in tune with each other." I smiled back. He made it so easy to like him. "Where do we go from here?" he said.

Mired in events I couldn't control, I shook my head and thought about Archie, drowned kittens, denials, and lies. Was I somehow getting close? I shrugged.

"I can't see the police reopening the file unless new evidence is found," Allan said. "At least that's what I've been told."

"You've seen a lawyer?"

"That's where I was when you tried to phone me. If we find out who killed Tara, we have a shot at clearing Jordan's name."

Air seeped out between my lips. "It's not that simple, is it?" If you only knew how complex it is, I thought. "I ought to go," I said, taking fright.

"So soon?"

"It's past eleven and I'm working tomorrow. You must get up early, too."

"Five thirty," he said with a mischievous grin.

"Nice in the summer, hideous in the winter, I'd imagine."

He laughed in agreement. We both stood up. When he guided me to the front door, he rested a hand briefly on the small of my back. It was done with the lightest of touches, like a feather glancing off naked skin.

I waited awkwardly on the doorstep, not sure whether to kiss him on both cheeks or touch his arm and leave. Alan took control. He took my hand, raised my wrist to his lips, and kissed it once, softly. Breath fluttered shallow in my chest. "You take care," he said, releasing me.

Silhouetted in the doorway, Allan waved me good-bye and I drove away, my thoughts scrambled all over the place. One little kiss and I fizzed with surprising pleasure. Feelings I'd long denied and buried flooded through me, as if I were on the brink of something new and sensational. If anyone could have seen me, they'd have spotted the big smile. And then just as quickly it expired.

It was plain wrong, inconceivable, to be attracted to Allan Dukes. There was no substance to it. Mine was nothing more than a purely physical, instinctive reaction to my barren emotional existence and events that had conspired against us. It was probably the same for him. It didn't matter that his eyes consumed me, that his strong hand felt safe on mine, and that he was kind and quiet in a way that Archie was not. If we'd met in other circumstances, perhaps it would have been fine, but not in these. It was all too perverse, too weird.

A car drove up fast behind me, flashing its lights. I slowed, thinking it was a police car. Cursing and wondering what offence I'd committed, I waited for the sound of a siren indicating for me to pull over. There was no siren. The lights flashed again on full beam.

I flicked the rear-view mirror to reduce the glare and wondered if I'd inadvertently cut a driver up, or failed to close my boot properly, or made a turn without indicating. Unrelentingly, the vehicle bore down on mine, its lights piercing the glass, illuminating the inside of the Mini, lighting me up like a target.

Grimacing, I put my foot down, the Mini spurting forward. In response, a loud throaty roar erupted from a massively powerful engine and the car behind me glued itself to my rear bumper. A shudder of fear rippled through me. Disorientated, I realised that instead of turning onto the right road I'd taken the wrong route. Houses and leafy suburbia mysteriously disappeared. The road widened. Without street lamps, it was difficult to work out where I was. On both sides were blocky shapes, metal fences, low and high buildings like sleeping monsters that, at any moment, would stir, lash out, step on my car and squash me.

I glanced in the rearview mirror again. My pursuer was dangerously close. If I braked, he'd be joining me in the passenger seat. Frightened, my hands fused to the steering wheel, my heart pounding, I realised that I had to do something dramatic to stand a chance of throwing him off. Spotting a turning, I signalled left, slowed, and then pressed my foot to the floor.

The sudden increase in speed bought me a few precious seconds, nothing more. This time, the driver swung out, the car drawing low and level with mine. Rap music spat out of its speakers, a big bass beat throbbing and ricocheting off the tarmac. A young woman hung out of the open passenger window, her face coarse and gnarled with anger, snarling, cursing, and gesticulating. Sneaking a terrified glance, I estimated there were at least three of them in the vehicle, maybe more.

Rigid with fear, my throat closed and I fixed my eyes on the vanishing road and oily night. Panic raced inside me and I braced for the sudden impact of metal grinding against metal as they ran me off the road. Spotting another turning, I signalled right and swerved left. The pursuing car flew on, its lights disappearing.

I travelled down the road like a blind man desperate to feel a way to a fire exit. Hope burst forth, bright and alive, and died. Ahead was a red brick wall and dead end. Desperate, I reversed onto a forecourt, crunching the gears, and tore back towards the main road. Approaching the junction, my jaw dropped open. Side-on, a car blocked my way. Four figures ran towards me, their voices whooping, dancing and shrill.

Cornered prey, I locked the doors. Knee hammering, tongue stammering, terror clutched my heart. If I cried out, nobody would hear. If I pleaded for my life, nobody would care. Alone and defenceless, tears streamed down my cheeks and my teeth chattered in my jaw. A solid silver flash caught the moonlight and something hard and heavy struck the windscreen. With three powerful blows, the length of lead piping shattered the glass, and I screamed.

Thirty-One

Powerful hands reached in, released my seat belt and yanked me through the empty space. Resistance pointless, I let them jerk and bump me out of the car, clothes ripping, skin tearing.

Someone flashed a searchlight. My eyes scrunched against the powerful beam, half blinded. I couldn't move because two men, fresh out of their teens, had me pinned on both sides. Their bodies, lean and lanky, crushed against mine. They wore thin T-shirt vests despite the chill of night and reeked of tobacco and weed and clothes that stank of sour feet. A short stocky lad wearing a hoodie over a baseball cap prowled, his fist repeatedly striking the open palm of one hand. Beyond him, I vaguely made out a young white woman, hair in dreads and, similarly immune to cold, wearing only a thin see-through vest over a black bra. Her skirt, worn like a belt, revealed drug-spindly legs. She rested her lower back against the side of the car. I was in no doubt as to who she was.

"Let me go," I shouted, twisting and squirming. "You won't get away with this." Even as I said it, I thought they might.

She slid off the car, walked slowly towards me, and pushed her feral face into mine, booze on her breath. "Fucking fizz bitch."

I stared back into eyes that were beyond deep. At one time the razor sharp cheekbones and full mouth would have been pretty. Not anymore.

"And now she's our bitch," the lad in the hoodie leered. He seemed younger than the rest, unpredictable and dangerous.

"Fuck you," I muttered under my breath.

A hand shot out, grabbed a fistful of my hair by the roots. "You do not know how to conduct yourself. You be what I say you be."

If I hadn't been scared, I'd have sneered at her stupid hip-hop slang. "What do you want?" I gasped, wincing with pain.

"You been aksin' too many questions. You let that sonofabitch do the time for the crime," she said in a singsong. "You stay away from his daddy. You shut your fat bitch mouth about Tyrone Weaver and we straight, feel me?"

I nodded. Extending her arm, she swung it across her body and then powered back, striking me on the mouth with the back of her hand. My lower lip split and blood trickled down my chin. In agony, I was sure she'd loosened a tooth.

"Speak," she said, threatening to swing her arm back a second time. Astounded and terrified, I reached into the back of my throat, found the word for *yes*, and ejected it.

"I didn't hear you."

"Yes," I mumbled again.

"Make it loud, bitch. Make it MASSIVE!"

"Yes," I screamed.

227

"DO NOT FUCKING SHOUT AT ME!"

"Please," I said, my throat tearing. "Please let me go."

With a laugh that sounded like a dirty guitar riff, she turned to the prowler. "Shall we gut her, Rube?"

"Be my pleasure. Do I get to do her first, babe?"

My legs buckled, unlike my voice, which erupted from desperation and nascent rage. "Like you did Tara?"

The blow came out of nowhere, straight to my stomach. Pain shattered and splintered through me. I pitched forward, vomited my recently eaten dinner onto the road. Choking and spluttering, I heard her voice scratching in my ear. "You don't want no beef with me. Jordan Dukes banged the filthy slag. We did not touch your whore daughter."

"Bitch and whore," the boy called Rube chuckled.

The pressure on my arms tightened as I was dragged upright. I could hardly stand. My tender stomach felt as if it had swelled to twice its size. If they hit me again, I thought a major internal organ might rupture.

Shapes shifted in the dark. Hoping the clarity of night would sharpen every noise, I listened for a passing car, someone out walking a dog. There was nothing—not an owl, not a tree shuddering in the breeze. All was silent aside from a car boot opening and shutting followed by the graunching sound of twisting metal. Without warning, a familiar everyday smell assailed and engulfed me in bright deaf and dumb terror.

My captives sprang apart with choreographed precision. I shut my eyes tight and the full force hit my face, invading my nose, soaking my hair, clothes, and shoes. I stood paralysed apart from my bladder.

"Fuck it, Dax," Rube said. "She's pissed herself."

"Got your lighter handy?" one of the others jeered. "Probably shit herself too, dirty bitch."

"Please," I screamed. "Please. I promise you. I'll go away. I won't say a word. I won't ask questions. Please," I pleaded hysterically, really sobbing now. Raw, visceral, gut-wrenching fear snatched hold and would not let go. With it, the dread of burning, of torment and agonising pain, from which dying would be a mercy.

Dax stood back. Between her thumb and forefinger was a box of matches, which she shook, the noise like a death rattle. "You breathe one word, we'll get you and then we'll burn the rest, too, including that bastard baby."

"Go on, Dax, torch her," one of the youths dared her.

Everything slowed. Dax invaded my terror zone, stalked and owned it. A shroud of cold sweat enveloped my body. My breath vanished in the damp night air and soon, I realised, I would disappear, too. *Puff.*

Then the most extraordinary thing happened.

One by one, they turned, Dax last to move. Mute with shock, I watched as they took their time climbing into the car, laughing and joking as if they'd emerged from the pub after a fantastic night out. The engine revved and roared. Dax slid down the window, stuck her head out. "You get out of my crib, bitch woman, and you stay the fuck out." Then they tore off up the road, leaving a vapour trail of death and destruction behind them.

Crazed with fear, I stripped down to my bra and knickers, kicked off my shoes and staggered to the car. Clambering over the bonnet, skinning my knees, I climbed in through the shattered windscreen. The smell of petrol overpowered me, seeping into my skin and bones. I imagined a flash of white heat and flames, my body alight in a grotesque act of self-immolation, sizzling flesh and muscle and then my bones, reducing my DNA to an unrecognisable black and sticky mess.

It took three gos to start the engine without it stalling. When I finally got the car running, my foot kept slipping. I could barely engage the clutch. After a couple of false starts, I found the will to live and drove.

Everything depended upon it.

Thirty-Two

"All right, all right, keep you hair on, I'm coming."

The lights flashed on in every room in the bungalow. I hunched, arms crossed over my chest in a vain attempt to hide my near nakedness. My knees clanked. I could do nothing to control them. The soles of my feet hurt from racing across the gravel and I stank of petrol and piss.

The door swung open. Nostrils flaring, Doug towered over me in his pyjamas and dressing gown. One sharp look and his entire face slackened. "Bloody hell, Gracie. " He twisted round, shouted an order. "Put that fucking fag out, Gray."

"What?" Graham said, emerging blearily into the hallway, tapping out a length of ash.

I let out a howl and scuttled back towards the bushes edging the front garden.

"Give it to me, you daft sod," I heard Doug yell as I cowered in the shrubbery. "Now go and wake Dolly and Tiff. Tell them to run a bath. We'll need plenty of washing up liquid."

Seconds later, Doug's slippered feet crunched across the drive. "Gracie," he called as if searching for a dog. Next I felt a soft, warm texture against my skin. Strong arms gathered me up and carried me back into the house, Doug hugging me to his barrel chest.

Inside whirred with activity. Doug barked orders. My mum's voice called for more towels, high pitched with distress against the lower sound of running water. Tiff raced through the hall with only a stunned backward glance in my direction, a bottle of Fairy Liquid in one hand, a plastic bag in the other. Graham was dispatched to the kitchen to make hot sweet tea.

Doug manhandled me to the opposite end of the bungalow and into a bathroom thick with heat and steam, where my mum waited for me. One look and I thought her heart would explode. "Your face, Gracie, your beautiful face."

I burst into wretched swollen tears.

"There, there, you're safe now," my mum said, patting me awkwardly, as if worried that getting too close would trigger an explosion.

"She won't bite, Doll," Doug snapped. "Use plenty of washing up liquid, like this," he said, squirting it over my head and rubbing it vigorously into my hair. "My apologies, Gracie," he said for the personal incursion.

"Will that do the trick?" Mum asked with frightened eyes.

"Works a treat," he said, as if talking about adding fabric conditioner to the weekly wash. "Then we'll talk," he said, wiping his hands on a towel. His tone, which was uncompromising, underlined that telling the truth was my only option. I shrank inside.

Tiff joined us and gingerly touched my arm. Her eyes met mine. She'd worked out exactly what had happened. "You going to stand there Doug?" she said pointedly, brandishing a sponge.

He gave her a hard stare. No fool, he'd obviously spotted our complicity and he wasn't a man who liked to be kept out of the know—not when it threatened his interests and the people he cared about. "Make sure you put her underwear in the bag and hand it to me, Tiffany," he said, edge to his voice. "One spark to that little lot and we'll all go up like a flaming comet. Right," he said, grinding his jaw, "I'll leave you girls to it." He closed the door and I heard him padding back down the hall.

"Come on, let's get this lot off you," Tiff said, slipping off Doug's robe. "Oh fuck," she said, staring at my midriff. An angry nucleus of red the size of a fist sat centrally underneath my ribs. My mum was speechless. Tears sprang to her eyes.

"Mum, why don't you sit down and talk to Gracie?"

"I'm all right, Tiffany," Mum said, stoically squeezing liquid onto a damp flannel and gently wiping my face. "Is your lip sore, lovey?"

"Stings," I mumbled. From my cheek to my jawline, it hurt a lot. I remembered the shock of Dax lashing out and splitting my lip. "Have you got any mouthwash?" The taste of blood and neat gasoline was like a force of nature in my mouth.

"I'll get it," Tiff said, rummaging around in a mirrored medicine chest that hung over the sink. She poured out a measure as though dispensing vodka and handed it to me. I pushed it between my cracked lips, slooshed it around my mouth, and spat it out.

Between them, they peeled off my underwear, soaped me all over, like a couple of handmaidens preparing me for marriage to a prince, and lowered me into the bath.

"Not too hot for you, Gracie love?" Mum said.

"Fine," I said indistinctly. My tears had dried and my skin felt raw, as if rimed with hoarfrost. Fear abated. At any second, it could roll right back in. I wanted to feel anger, cold and dark, something solid I could work with and use as a weapon to defend myself, but I was too numb to feel. My overriding emotion, as much as I had one, was grief. Why had my life come to this?

I took a deep breath and slid down under the suds, ears popping, mouth stinging, as water washed away the final vestiges of benzene and ethanol. I stayed like that for as long as I could stand and then sat back up with a loud splash and clambered out of the bath. "I can dry myself," I said, suddenly embarrassed by my nakedness in front of my sister and mother.

"Are you sure?" Mum said, handing me a soft warm towel. Now that I was all shiny and new she wanted to pat me dry and hug me as she had when I was little.

I nodded with a shy smile.

"Pop on the robe hanging on the back of the door."

"We'll see you in the kitchen later," Tiff said, folding her arms under her breasts, large and loose without the constraints of a well-designed bra underneath her pyjamas. I knew what she was thinking. Doug was about to interrogate me.

I took my time, applying body lotion, rubbing it deeply into my skin. I could still smell petrol even though every last trace had been removed. I put on the robe, squeezed toothpaste onto my finger, and did a makeshift job of cleaning my teeth. Another quick swill of mouthwash and I was ready to face questions for which I had few answers.

They all sat around the kitchen table. A big pot of tea sat in the centre, like a crystal ball at a séance. My mum had got her best cups and saucers out, the ones with roses on them. God knew why.

Graham looked up, jittery, probably because his nicotine fix was denied. He grunted a stock "All right?"

"Sit down, Gracie." Mum pushed a cup of chewy-looking tea towards me. I took a sip. It was tooth-shattering sweet and there was too little milk, but it tasted good.

"Who did it?" Doug said, searching my face with a *don't lie to me, girl* expression.

"Give her a chance, Doug," Tiff said, strained.

"I am giving her a chance. Nobody gets petrol slung over them by accident. It's as rare as blue lobsters. Now who fucking did it?"

"Doug," Mum began, before withering and retreating from Doug's hostile gaze.

"If I tell you, other people will get hurt, including a baby." My breath caught at the prospect. I fleetingly thought of Allan at home, oblivious, probably thinking about his nice evening and looking forward to the next.

Doug snorted in derision. "This to do with that lad?"

"Which lad?" I said wide-eyed.

Doug's smile glittered like ice over a frozen stagnant pond. "Playing stupid doesn't suit you, Gracie. We both know who we're talking about, Jordan Dukes."

Graham's mouth dropped open, exposing a crooked row of teeth. My mum's complexion shrank from pink to grey. Tiff threw me another desperate glance. I swallowed. Being questioned by Doug was akin to taking part in a triathlon when you had a crucifying hangover.

"Doug," I said, pleading with him, "I can't."

"You can and you will."

I shrivelled under Doug's laser glare. Bloated with threat and revenge, he seemed capable of anything.

"I'm sorry," I murmured.

"You will be."

"Don't you damn well threaten her," Tiff snapped.

"Other people will suffer, Doug," I said, trying to make him see sense. "Don't you understand?"

"I understand, all right, which is why something needs to be done about it and fast. Got any names? What did these bastards look like?" He pronounced *bastards* with an aggressive short *a*. "I'm waiting, Gracie." He didn't drum his fingers on the table, but he might as well have done.

How I wished Doug would wave a wand and magic it all away. In my heart, I knew he was more likely to wield a hammer. An image of the magpie with its head smashed in flitted through my mind. I remembered the guy with the broken face at the door—one of Doug's employees, maybe, or someone who owed him? Tiff and I recognised that Doug had a nasty side. We'd never witnessed it but somewhere under that semi-civilised exterior lurked a barely housetrained thug. My mum mistook it for strength of character.

"Dukes was innocent, wasn't he?"

My mum shot Doug a horrified look. "What do you mean he's innocent?"

"Always had my doubts about that boy's guilt. Someone did a number on him. Clear as the mole on my arse. Nobody facing a murder rap stays that schtum without a damn good reason. So, Gracie," he said, hard eyes darting back to mine, "are you going to tell us the truth, or do I have to drag it out of you?"

Mum spread her hands. Her bottom lip wobbled. She was having trouble keeping up with Doug's relentless pace and she wasn't the only one. I wasn't sure whether it was tactical on his part or whether this was how he always operated under pressure. "Grace is a victim, not a criminal, Doug," she pleaded.

"I know that, Dolly," Doug said menacingly slow, "but we're dealing with hard-arsed bastards and nobody got anywhere by being nice and poncing around the edges. I'll ask you one more time, Gracie."

"You're bang out of order, Doug," Tiff flashed, racing to my defence.

"And so are you," he hit back, a dangerous glint in his eye. "I've watched you going out to the garden for your cosy little chats. You knew all about this, didn't you? If you'd said something when you should have done, this would never have happened."

"Why do you always fucking blame me?"

"That's not fair, Tiffany," Gray waded in. "Doug's only trying to help."

"Doug doesn't need a fucking poodle," she roared.

"For God's sake, will you all shut up?"

Every face in the room fixed on mine. A suggestion of a smile glanced off Doug's mouth before he assumed an inscrutable expression once more. "All right," I swallowed. "I'll tell you, but if there is any collateral damage, if anyone dies," I said, looking directly at Doug, "I'll go to the police and shop you myself."

"Fair dos," he said, as though we'd shaken on a deal to run a car dealership.

I focused on the Dukes family. I told them of Allan's approach to me less than a week after the trial, my subsequent visit to Jordan in prison, and the threat against him from Dax and the gang. I mentioned that I'd appealed to DI Dunne but he'd dismissed it. I said nothing of the break-in, severed cats' heads, or Thea's insinuations. Keep it simple, I told myself. Don't overcomplicate it.

"So you see, Jordan didn't kill Tara," I concluded.

My mum pressed her hand to her mouth, veins raised blue against her liver-spotted skin and swollen joints. She'd nearly passed out when I said I'd visited Jordan in prison.

"Then who did?" Graham gawped, twirling an unlit cigarette in his fingers.

"I don't know."

"Best left to the police," Mum said, a warning note in her voice.

"Only if we can persuade them that Jordan was elsewhere on the night she died."

"We'll persuade them," Doug said. In spite of me skirting facts and editing my account—something I'm sure had not escaped him—he'd remained ominously quiet, tuned out almost, as if he had a plan that he was none too keen to share. "Where does Miss Thinks She's It hang out?"

I started. "Doug—"

"An old youth centre somewhere in Podsmead," Tiff cut in.

"Thank you," he said in a dry tone. "Most sensible thing you've said all night."

Tiff glowered, although this time she kept her mouth zippered.

"What are you going to do?" My bruised stomach contracted in fear.

"No need for you to worry about that," Doug said with a closed expression. Graham glanced at him, a moment of silent and creepy understanding passing between them that made me shudder.

"You get hold of Allan, Gracie," Doug said, "persuade him to bring his family here."

"Here?" Mum yelped in alarm.

"Safest place for them to be."

"I'm not sure he'll—" I began.

"Do it, Gracie. No time like the present. We're sorting this tomorrow night."

"But ... " I floundered. With Doug involved, God only knew where it would end.

He leant towards me, clasped my hand as if we were going to arm wrestle. "Do you trust me?"

Did I? I looked into his eyes, which were cool and grey and deadly. The sheer physicality of the man overpowered me. I was a mouse and he was a cobra. I knew he would act and inflict potentially lethal violence. I didn't trust him to make things better, yet what choice did I have? He must have registered my doubt and fear.

"Gracie, you have my word nobody will get killed."

"I should hope not," Mum said with shock.

"Quiet, Dolly. It's important that Gracie here understands. Me and Gray are going to have a gentle word with Dax and her crew. We get this little misunderstanding cleared up. The police get back on board and then we leave them to get on with the job, exactly as you said," he added, stealing a fond glance at my mum. "You good with that, Gracie?"

I nodded dumbly even though I thought Doug's interpretation of *gentle* was different than mine.

"Marvellous. You talk to Allan in the morning. I want names and descriptions."

"It was dark," I said.

"Allan Dukes knows who these little shits are. He'll be able to help on that front. Me and Gray will work out the fine detail."

Gray flicked his tongue, lizard-like, and nodded, barely able to contain the excitement of being Doug's right-hand man and lieutenant.

"In the meantime, I suggest we all get some shut-eye."

Thirty-Three

Allan got to me before I got to him. Deeply asleep, I shot out an arm, scrabbling on the bedside table to shut up the noise chiselling its way through my eardrums. Through several layers of slumber, I registered it was a few minutes past eight. I'd been asleep for less than five hours. Everything hurt. My face. My stomach. My ribs. I felt a hundred years old.

"Mmm?"

"Did I wake you?" he said.

"Nnnrgh."

"Won't you be late for work?"

"Oh God," I said sitting upright, throwing back the duvet, the previous night's events thwacking me over the head. I needed to phone in sick. I needed to explain to Allan. I needed to keep Doug in check, a hopeless task. Panic seized me.

"Shall I call back?"

"Yes. Scrap that, no."

"Grace, is everything okay?"

I closed my eyes to stop a sudden flood of bitter tears. Petrol mixed with the heavy tangy odour of fear flooded my olfactory senses. Dax's twisted expression floated before my eyes. In my ears, I heard the shrill rattle of matches shaken against cardboard; the raw thought of what might have been: unendurable pain.

Allan let out a low moan as I stumbled through what happened, explaining how I'd fled to my mum's for sanctuary and been forced to reveal the truth to my family, or the bits of the truth I wanted them to hear. With a voice ringed with concern, he asked how I felt. I didn't know whether he meant physical, mental, emotional, or all three. I made out that I was better than I was.

"Who is this Doug character?" Allan asked warily.

"My mum's partner." It was how she liked to describe him to anyone interested enough to ask.

"I meant what does he do?"

"This and that, scrap metal, mostly," I said, cagey and vague.

"Sounds like a mafia don from what you've told me."

"Pushing it." A bit.

"Not a man to cross up though?"

"No."

"Then I'd like to get to know him better."

I jolted. Why did men think that to defeat violence you needed to inflict more? "Not a good idea, Allan."

He fell heavily silent. I'd offended him. I could tell. I pitched in with Doug's plan to bring Allan's family to the bungalow.

"I can protect my own," Allan said, a stony note in his voice. And why did men get all territorial when offered help?

"They'll be less of a target here at my mum's. Dax knows your house. She's watching it. Think about Asher and Dionne, their safety."

Another silence. I could almost hear the struggle going on inside his head.

"If Doug can sort Dax—"

Allan laughed without humour. "How old is he? I hope he can run fast."

"If you met him, you'd understand."

"Yet you told me that's not a good idea," he said, throwing my own words back at me.

"I don't want you getting mixed up in something potentially criminal," I protested.

"But you're happy for your mum's elderly squeeze to take the law into his own hands. What the hell happens if he screws up?"

"Doug can take care of himself." And take his chances.

"Whereas I can't." I pictured Allan's beaten up face after Dax's crew had got their hands on him. In his eyes, he felt inadequate, a failure and angry. A mess of bruised pride, no doubt.

"Will you at least think about it?" I entreated him.

"I have." He made his excuses, which I thought lame, and cut the call.

I pummelled my forehead with my knuckles. I wanted it to be yesterday, Allan's hand on mine again, to feel mellow and believe that, although my life would never be the same, I had a shot at happiness, at sorting things out, finding Tara's killer. But now it was all gone.

I phoned work, got Seb, and lied through my teeth. "I've caught a horrid stomach bug."

"Best keep away," he said. "Can't have you passing Montezuma's revenge on to the clients."

"That's what I thought. Will you be able to manage?"

"I guess."

241

"You don't sound sure. Isn't Vron in today?"

"Erm … no."

"Seb?"

"She handed in her notice in this morning."

A weary sigh escaped from between my lips. I didn't need to ask why. I already knew.

"It's complicated," Seb said.

No, it's really very simple. You won't leave your wife and Vron can't bear to work with you another minute. Poor Vron. It made me feel mean for being so short with her last time we spoke.

"Better go," Seb said, eager to get off the phone.

"You'll pass the message on to Michael?"

"Sure. I've got a customer." Code for *go away*. He hung up.

Without clothes, I dragged on a robe and walked like a mechanical toy along the thick pile carpet towards the kitchen. Voices, sharp and insistent, cut down the hallway. I stopped, listened.

"You swore you wouldn't say anything to her."

"I'm a man of my word, Tiff. Are you really telling me Grace didn't know?"

"Of course she didn't."

"Turned a blind eye, more like."

"That's a shit thing to say, Gray."

"It's the truth. I'm not blaming her or nothing, nobody wants to think that their other half is having it off with … "

I fled, humiliated, stayed in my room and waited until Gray and Tiff left for work. This time when I ventured out, Doug was talking in low tones to Mum. They sprang apart as I walked in.

"You spoken to Allan Dukes yet?" Doug said.

"Yes," I said, thin-lipped.

"Won't play ball?"

I shot Doug a caustic look. "Not keen on playing nursemaid."

"Fancies his chances with them, does he? What's his number? I'll talk to him."

"He's a proud man. It's not a good idea."

"Did he say that?" Doug's grey eyes searched mine with such intensity I squirmed.

"Look, Doug, I've been thinking."

He rested his big hairy hands on my shoulders. "You don't have to think. That's the beauty of it. You leave everything to me and Gray."

"He's right, Gracie," Mum chipped in. Doug must have spent the rest of the night getting around her, not that she'd take much persuading. She idolised him.

I sat down defeated, muscles complaining, bruises hurting, and changed tack to more practical matters. "I've got nothing to wear."

"Tiff's probably got something in her wardrobe."

"Nothing that fits." Like a petulant teenager, I felt sullen and angry and wanted to make a big issue of it. "And what about my car?"

"Already sorted," Doug said. "Got a man coming to fix the windscreen and valet it." He glanced at his watch. "Should be here in twenty minutes."

He seemed to have an answer to every question bar the one I most needed answering.

"Tea's in the pot," Mum said brightly. "Help yourself and then I'll cook us a bit of breakfast."

"I'm not hungry." Which was true.

"Got to keep up your strength," Mum said. "Trouble attracts trouble," she added, rolling her eyes as if it explained the meaning of life.

I went through the motions and let her fuss. Inside I was a mess. The numb sensation had worn off, replaced by an uncontrollable urge to lash out and hurt—so much for my rejection of violence—and it scared me because it felt alien and immoral. Overnight I'd changed, shifted my position on everything I stood for. I was muddled and edgy, as if every one of us were heading off through the fog, about to shoot over the cliff edge and tumble onto the craggy rocks below.

After forcing down a piece of toast simply to please, I went into Tiff's room and rifled through her drawer, pulled out a sweater and a pair of baggy trousers that were at least three inches too short and an inch too big around the waist. Thick socks were easier to accommodate, unlike shoes. She had small feet for a woman her size and build. Mine were size seven. I'd have to chance driving with bare feet again.

Allan's rebuff unsettled me. I tried several times to call. Each time it went to voicemail.

A man came and repaired the Mini's windscreen. Plugging in a piece of high-tech machinery and using a product called Snow Foam, he valeted it, removing every trace of petrol and without asking awkward questions. When I offered to pay, Doug told me to put away my purse and handed the man, someone he knew, cash. In an offbeat moment, I wondered what this man also did for Doug. Crush cars? Get rid of evidence? Solicitous towards me, Doug seemed remarkably cool and controlled, his anger, if he felt it, contained and hidden in a deep vault inside him. Having no experience of such matters, I'd expected him to be on the phone all morning, calling in favours, organising backup, quizzing me again about the events of the previous night, choreographing moves. Instead, he drifted around the house in his pink sweater and grey slacks, ate a bacon sandwich at a leisurely pace, drank mug after mug of sweet tea, and read the newspaper. I found his calm approach disturbing.

An overheard phone call to Graham provided the only clue to what Doug had in mind. He asked to meet at six that evening for what he called a board meeting. A "reckoning" was mentioned. Meanwhile,

Mum treated me as if I'd come out of hospital after a major operation. By afternoon, I was stir-crazy with thinking and frustration and, yes, taut with random terror.

"Think I'll pop back to the apartment," I said, "and pick up some clothes."

Mum reached for her coat. "I'll come with you."

"Silly of us both traipsing over. I won't be long."

Her eyes filmed with tears. I saw that she wasn't as young and robust as she used to be. The grooves under her eyes seemed deeper and darker. I realised then that, since Tara's death she, like me, had aged.

And now this.

"Let the girl go," Doug said, sliding an arm around her shoulder. "They won't try anything in broad daylight, not this soon. Why don't you bake a cake, lemon drizzle, my favourite?"

She nodded, flashed a forlorn little smile. I kissed her good-bye and promised I wouldn't be long. Doug followed me out onto the drive. Over the past twelve hours, he seemed to have grown in size and bearing, his presence overshadowing me like an eclipse. There was more spring in his step. He was like a man who, forced into retirement early, had been offered a prime job doing what he knew, what he'd worked his whole life for, and was glad of a fresh opportunity to prove himself. Or, more appropriately in Doug's case, like an elderly safe cracker engaged in one last job for the pension pot, one last hurrah.

"You're coming back, aren't you?" he said, drawing up alongside me.

"Yes."

"Your mum's not one to make a fuss and she wouldn't say anything, but she's not been too clever."

"She's not ill, is she?" I couldn't bear it. *Trouble attracts trouble.* Was that what she was alluding to? Was she sick?

"Worn out with worry, to tell the truth. She had a shock last night. I know you did, too, but you'll survive."

"Will I?" I wasn't convinced. Tired out, I couldn't see a way clear.

"Course." He grinned, putting a firm hand on my shoulder. "You're strong. You're bloody clever and nobody's fool. We'll get to the bottom of it, promise you. Law of averages." He paused, briefly glancing up into a blue sky daubed, it seemed, in white paint, like a painting by Monet. "Anything you haven't told me?" He gave my shoulder a squeeze.

I blushed and smiled. "Like what?"

"Put it this way," he said, his eyes stripping away any false veneer, his hand still resting on my shoulder. "How long have you suspected Jordan Dukes was innocent?"

"A little while," I admitted.

"And have you been sitting around on your duff waiting for the killer to pop up?"

I muttered a bland response. Doug sniffed, released his grasp, and stared down at the gravel. He scuffed it with the sole of his shoe, crushing it into the dirt. The highly polished leather cracked. I wanted to get away, to climb into my car. The force field of violence with which Doug occasionally surrounded himself would not allow it. He might as well have had me caged. When he met my eye once more with his intimidating gaze—no way could I escape, not unscathed, at any rate.

"I've had a lot of life experience, Gracie, some of it not good, some of it downright nasty. I know what makes men tick, especially bad men. I don't reckon some random stranger killed our kid. If she'd been raped, something sick like that, I'd take a different view. But she wasn't."

I tensed, pain digging its bony fingers into the muscles in my neck and shoulder.

"Someone close, Gracie," Doug said, eyes burning into mine. "Mark my words."

Nauseated, I nodded in silent resignation, opened the car door, and climbed inside. The interior, all shiny and freshly valeted, smelt of orange flower with a subtle hint of vanilla. It did nothing to reduce either the stench of fear clinging to my skin or the ache in my back.

Doug tapped on my window. I lowered it. He bent down so that his eye-line was level with mine. "Watch your back, Gracie. Don't break your mother's heart."

Thirty-Four

Doug's words jangled in my brain. Someone close. Someone with a secret. Someone who'd kill to protect it. Tiff thought it was Archie, as did Graham, and now, mystifyingly, so did Doug. Worse, they thought I'd turned a blind eye. Blood popped in my veins.

Against my will, my mind flashed back to the morning Tara had disappeared for a walk, returned with a swollen lip, flushed with radiance, and pushed me away. She'd spent an age in the bathroom, soaping and washing, and …

Incest, for Christ's sake. My ex-husband having sex with Tara. I had to almost say it out loud to calibrate the enormousness, the *enormity*, of what I was thinking. Archie had marvelled at Tara's blossoming beauty in the same proud way any parent thinks their child is gorgeous, but not like *that*, not like he fancied her.

Had he?

Next, as if my brain had frog-marched my thoughts down a dark alley, I remembered something I'd long ago chosen to forget.

It had started as an off-hand remark. Tara was quite small and was over at my mum's. We'd had a lovely Saturday, pottering around the house, nice dinner with a bottle of wine and Archie suggested we went to bed early, code for making love. Afterwards, lying in his arms, he said, "You're not as tight as you used to be. Must be childbirth."

I braced, speechless.

"We could do something about that."

"Pelvic floor exercises," I mumbled in humiliation.

"What about anal sex, Gracie?"

I shot out of bed, dragged on a robe. "No."

"What's the matter? It could be liberating."

"For you, maybe. Don't ever mention it again." At intervals, he'd suggested it and, on one painfully memorable occasion, came dangerously close, before I'd made my opposition clear by insisting he sleep in the spare room. He apologised afterwards, never brought it up again and our sex life got back to what I regarded as normal. But a young girl would be perfect, I thought, my mouth dry and tasting of dead leaves. She would be tight and malleable and…

Shaken, I cast the memory back into the deepest, darkest crypt within my mind.

The apartment was exactly as I'd left it. No nasty surprises, only a telephone bill, a flyer for a pizza delivery service, and a request for quality clothes from a registered charity with an accompanying plastic bag.

I checked the phone for messages, none, and dragged an overnight case from off the top of the wardrobe, which I packed with underwear, toiletries, a long-sleeved T-shirt, and a pair of pyjamas. I showered, changed into my own clothes, took one look in the mirror and recoiled at the bruising to my face and damage to my mouth. I tried to contact Allan again, but my call went straight to voicemail. At a loss, I called his landline. No reply. A lick of fear crept up my spine. I toyed with driving over, changed my mind, changed it back and, finally, sacked it off. If I brazenly went to the house, Dax might get wind of it. For once, I could do nothing, as hard as that was.

Before I left, I sneaked into Tara's bedroom, stood in the middle of the carpet, held my breath in concentration. Her secret was leering at me, darkly anonymous, taunting me from all four walls, and with it cold condemnation for my utter failure to protect her.

I'd been through her things in obsessive detail, but I went through them again, beginning with every pocket of the clothes that hung on her rack. I ripped open drawers, chucked the contents onto her bed, raking through like a tramp rifling for a dog end. I knelt down on the carpet, knees cracking, pulled everything out from beneath her bed. I pushed her keepsakes to one side and piled anything she'd written in or on—exercises books, jotters, and random scraps of paper—into a heap. Sitting on the floor, I went through them methodically, Tara's words speaking to me from the grave:

I'm worried about my boobs. What if they don't grow? What if I don't take after Mum?

Sadie wouldn't speak to me today. Right cow.

Thea stuck up for me. That's what best friends are for.

When I grow up I want to marry someone rich and famous like Jonathan Rhys-Meyers, sooo hot, and live in New York. Odd choice, I thought. Wouldn't she have chosen someone nearer her own age, like Aaron Paul, or one of those young and up-and-coming actors that play small roles but you sense deep inside are destined for stardom?

Must remember swimming kit for school tomorrow.
I love Amy Winehouse. She's so cool.

Nothing jumped out at me. The huge handwriting suggested Tara must have been thirteen or fourteen at the time of writing. I searched for hidden clues in mathematical equations, not Tara's strong suit. She'd always leant more towards the arts, although even that dropped off her radar during the last two years of her life, from the time Jordan Dukes stepped into it. She wasn't one of those girls who'd chosen a career early on and stuck to it. At ten years of age, she'd expressed a typical little girl desire, "I want to be a vet," until she learnt that she was hopeless at maths, physics, and chemistry. She'd variously aspired to be a model, a beautician, a fashion designer; the last for which I'd offered encouragement.

The final note on the random scraps of paper pile read: *Jonathan Rhys-Meyers looks like my dad.* My skin prickled. Lots of little girls worshipped their dads, I told myself. Hadn't Annie Jacks, a keen art collector and friend of mine, laughingly joked that her daughter once told her she wanted to meet and marry a man just like her own father? Annie had quipped, *"I'd think twice about that if I were you, darling."*

Determined to squash the thought before it bloomed again into something vivid, full-grown, and monstrous, I picked up Tara's sketchpad and flicked through.

The later fashion designs were more confident, fluid, with flair and creativity. Layouts were professionally presented and she'd taken great care to draw outfits from different angles, detailing the precise cut of a sleeve or the way a scarf should be tied around a neck or waist. She'd included fabric boards, swatches of silk and chiffon, poplin and jersey. She'd drawn bodices and hats, sleek dinner jackets for women, whacky trousers in big check, dresses with high waistlines, cloaks and outfits that would need scaffolding to climb into, any trip along a cat walk a threat to health and safety. My eyes blurred at the thought of all the waste and the might-have-beens, for her and for me, the fact that I would never meet the man she'd marry or see her walk down the aisle, or hold her child and my grandchild in my arms.

Right at the back was a single swatch taped to the notepaper. Against a cream backdrop, red flowers the colour of garnets on long stems. Pretty and fresh rather than floral and old lady, it would have looked gorgeous on her. With her dark looks, variations of red had always been Tara's favourite colour. I fingered the luxurious fabric, a richly sumptuous mix of cotton and embroidered silk. Unlike other swatches in her collection, there was no accompanying note to explain its origin.

No wiser, I pushed everything back in its place, straightened the cover on the bed and, with a final visual flourish, picked up my bag and drove back to Gloucester where my mother was waiting, face at the window, anxious for my return. As soon as she saw the car, her eyes lit up and she waved, the relief and delight in her expression reminding me of Tara's when she was little and I'd arrive to pick her up at the school gate. Wondering how long Mum had been planted there, I waved back, eased my car next to Tiff's clapped out Micra, and went inside.

Thirty-Five

Tiff sat in the sitting room, the television on, watching *Pointless*. TV was her god, soaps her favourite, another difference between the two of us. She barely glanced up as I walked in.

"All right?" she said, eyes stuck on the telly.

I nodded. "Where's Doug?"

"In his quarters, having a powwow with Gray."

Doug's "quarters" consisted of a small room at the back of the bungalow. Masculine, with black and grey striped wallpaper and thick pile carpet, it contained Doug's pride and joy: a humidor, the contents of which he lovingly tended like a gardener nurtures his prize onions. The air was often thick with the savoury and spicy odour of cigar smoke. Mum disliked him chugging anywhere else at home, but here Doug was king. His throne, a big power chair in tan leather, sat behind a huge desk on which there was a telephone and separate phone line. There was no computer because Doug "didn't hold with them" or technology in general because, I suspected, it left too much of a digital footprint. Every time he paid for anything it was by debit card or cash. Anything online "could go to hell," he'd say and he said it often. Having wondered for a long time what Doug got up to, now I thought I knew.

I walked down the hallway, heard the thrum of two male voices speaking in confidence about things I couldn't hear or want to picture in my head. Pausing outside, I knocked twice on Doug's door. That was the other thing. You never entered his lair without knocking first. Tiff had only ever done it once. We all learnt from her mistake.

Graham came to the door, opened it a crack and, seeing me, let me in. I was immediately enveloped in a cloud of finest Havana.

"Your man turned up yet?" Doug said, mobile lips working their way around the words while his teeth gripped a fat cigar. He'd changed into a black polo neck sweater and denims. I wasn't sure I'd ever seen Doug in jeans before. It made him look harder and less elderly.

"I don't think he'll come."

"He will. You'll see."

"What if he doesn't? What will happen then?"

"We stick to the plan. Nothing you need trouble yourself with," he added, wrapping up the conversation.

"He's right, Grace," Graham chipped in. "What you don't know you can't gab about."

"All you have to do is sit tight, look after your mum and that baby when it comes." As if Doug had the gift of second sight, the doorbell chimed. He threw me a *told you so* expression.

I hurried down the hall, beating Tiff to the front door by a squeak, and discovered Dionne cradling Asher in her arms. Nervous and confused best summed her up. Allan, inscrutable, stood behind her holding an overnight bag.

"Here, I'll take that,"' Tiff told Allan, taking charge. "Want to come through, Dionne?"

"Tea, everyone?" Mum said, sprightly. She'd obviously been well briefed.

"In a minute, let everyone settle. Why don't you go and help Tiff?" I said pointedly. Mum's quite biddable, particularly if a baby is involved, and off she trotted. Watching her made me think my world had taken a surreal left turn.

Left alone, I turned to Allan who gulped at seeing the damage to my face. Embarrassed and awkward, it made me awkward, too. I touched his hand lightly. "Hi," I smiled.

Eyes creased with concern, he smiled back, unsure for a second, then his lack of certainty vanished and he drew close, a breath away. My heart lifted in my chest. I knew what would happen a second before it did. I couldn't stop it and didn't want to. When he slipped his arms around me I thrilled as he held me tight and I burrowed my face into his sun-kissed neck. He felt reliable and decent in a way that Archie did not. "I'm so sorry, Grace," he said, his voice husky.

My laugh was giddy. "We said we had to stop apologising to each other."

He drew back a little, smoothed a lock of hair away with his firm fingers, one hand resting in the curve of my back, his eyes tracing the bruising on my cheek and the swelling on my lip.

"What made you change your mind?" I whispered.

"You," he said as if it were blatantly obvious. "I'd never seen you smile until you saw Asher. Every day you sat in that courtroom you looked so desolate and sad. That's why I didn't recognise you when I came to your flat. It wasn't your haircut. It was you, Grace. It was always you."

Warmth spread through my body. My face softened mirroring Allan's. I needed him. I couldn't fight it.

"I phone you," he murmured, "simply to hear your voice. You're one hell of a woman and Archie Neville must have been touched in the head to desert you."

My spirits soared. I wanted to stay like this forever, to forget about threats and secrets and the prospect of incest and what might happen after tonight. Like a blade in the darkness, I remembered Tara and pulled away as Doug's voice boomed down the hallway.

"Are you going to introduce us? Haven't got all bloody night."

I shot an apologetic look at Allan, who seemed less disconcerted by Doug's manner than I'd expected.

"Down there, is it?" he said.

"Last door at the end."

"Go and see if Dionne's okay." He flicked an easy smile, his way of saying that he was quite capable of an audience with Doug without me flapping about.

Tiff and Dionne were laughing. The TV was still on, the sound turned down, flickering images on a screen. Mum sat in her favourite chair, cuddling Asher in her arms. He was wide awake and Mum was baby gazing, dreamy and soppy, Asher gazing back adorably, with a puzzled, slightly bemused expression on his little face.

"Your mum's a natural. She can have him any time," Dionne grinned at me. She sat cross-legged on the floor between Tiff and Mum. I'd never understood a teenager's attraction to the ground when there were perfectly good chairs to sit on. Tara had been exactly the same, I remembered with a pang.

I joined Tiff on the sofa, stared ahead as if in concentration, thought about Jordan Dukes, wondered what he was doing, whether he had a clue that so many people were secretly rooting for him, including his former accusers.

After a short time that felt like a long time, the door swung open to reveal the good, the bad, and the ugly standing in the doorway. Allan slipped inside and onto a chair nearest me. Doug, wearing a tan three-quarter length leather jacket and pair of black leather driving gloves, and Graham, a beanie hat clamped onto his thin head, which made him look skinnier than ever, were obviously about to go out.

"Allan's staying here with you," Doug announced. "We'll be back later." He strode across to my mum. She tilted her head towards him, a mixture of apprehension and adoration on her face. With fingers thick as black pudding, he stroked the top of her hair and delicately kissed her forehead. Foreboding exploded inside me. What were we all thinking? Shouldn't I say something that would keep Doug at home safe with my mum, Gray with Tiff? Would a young woman like Dax be as awed by Doug as I was? My body language must have communicated it because Allan found my eyes and held my gaze and imperceptibly shook his head.

"Don't I get a kiss?" Graham said to Tiff.

"What for?" Apart from her mouth, she didn't move a muscle.

I'd no idea what kept my sister and her boyfriend together. Their relationship seemed fuelled by a mutual lack of respect.

"For luck?"

Tiff huffed, got up, and pecked Graham on the cheek. He looked as pleased as if he'd had a scratch card win.

Then they were gone.

I formally introduced Allan to my mum. Most women would have found the scenario too bizarre. My mum was not most women. Benign to her core, she thought the best of the worst. How could she have taken up with Doug otherwise?

"Have you lot eaten?" Tiff said. "I'm starving."

Dionne looked cautiously to her dad. "If it's no bother," he said.

"Plenty of cold meat in the fridge and there's eggs," Mum pointed out. "I'm all right here," she said, looking lovingly at Asher. I left Allan with them and offered to help Tiff in the kitchen, the first time we'd had a proper chance to talk after the previous night's events. She chucked me a potato peeler and a bag of spuds. "Ham, egg, and chips, all right?" If the bungalow were burning down, Tiff would finish her dinner before she made an exit.

"Perfect."

"About last ... " we both spoke in unison and broke off with a laugh.

"That's better." Tiff grinned. "You've been as tight as cheese wire."

"Hardly surprising."

Tiff didn't do sympathy but she viewed me with genuine concern. "You took a nasty smack to your face."

"It will heal."

"Doug's really pissed off with me," she said glumly. Although she fought like a tiger with him, Tiff was as fond of Doug as he of her. She hated being in his bad books.

"That's my fault."

"No, I should have told him. He's right. If I'd let on about Dax, you wouldn't have come to within an inch of your life."

"Wasn't your place, Tiff."

She took a piece of cooked ham from the fridge and slapped it on a carving tray. "You realise he'll sort it once and for all?" Which, if we were incredibly lucky, would open up possibilities and get Jordan off the hook for Tara's murder. But where did that leave Tara and me?

Tiff picked up a fork and stabbed it into the meat. "Seen Archie lately?"

I flinched. "Yes."

"Is he still planning a fast getaway?"

"I think the move has been in the pipeline for a while."

"At least a year," she said with a cool look. "Have you talked to him about Thea?"

"He was livid."

"What did you expect, a confession?"

"Tiff," I said in exasperation, "it's a serious allegation."

"Yes, it is."

"He's not a pervert," I blurted out, "and I'd really appreciate it if you didn't go spreading that kind of rumour to someone as voluble as Graham."

She paused, jabbed the knife in my direction. "You were listening."

"Listening?" I smarted. "I'm surprised you weren't heard in Cheltenham."

"You had no right, Grace."

"I knew the man. I loved him." If he did what I suspected, I couldn't live with myself, I wanted to say.

"Have you ever thought how many loyal wives have said the same?" Her voice was hard and resistant.

"I have absolutely no proof. And neither do you."

Jonathan Rhys-Meyers looks like my dad.

Tara had a secret, a dirty secret.

My stomach roiled with nausea. I felt cold, clammy and weak-kneed. The floor beneath my feet revolved and shifted. Walls swayed. The contents of the room slipped and slid and, finally, blurred. Then everything went black.

Thirty-Six

"Gracie, can you hear me?" Shapes, greys and blacks rippled at the edges of my consciousness until Tiff's face swam in front of mine. My eyes fluttered open, tried to focus. Like looking through an incubation tent. Mum and Allan bent over me flat out on the kitchen floor. She had a glass of water in her hand. The back of my head throbbed. I could hear the sound of a baby crying and Dionne's urgent voice trying to shush him.

"Here," Allan said, putting something soft, a cushion maybe, underneath me.

"Ow," I let out.

"Drink this, Gracie." Mum tilted the edge of the glass to my lips. I took a few tentative sips. Water trickled down my chin. Thankfully, the crucifying nausea had passed, although I was still whoozy.

"She's very pale," Tiff said to Mum.

"Better off in bed," Allan murmured.

"Can you stand, Gracie?"

"Christ, Mum, she's not deaf," I heard Tiff say.

"Here," Allan said, sliding his arms underneath me. "I'll carry her."

Hoisted up, my cheek slipped against Allan's chest, my free arm hanging down, deadweight.

Mum and Tiff scuttled ahead. A door flung open. Covers rolled back on the bed. Me laid down, mattress surrendering.

"Take her clothes off?" Tiff said.

"No," I shouted.

"Let her lie still awhile," I heard Allan say.

A discussion broke out about calling a doctor. I declined both. "Can I have another drink, please?" I jacked myself up on one shaky elbow. The walls seemed to have calmed down. Less drift and shift. Less motion.

"What happened?" Mum said. Aimed at Tiff, there was a faintly accusing edge to her voice, most unlike her. "What did you say?"

I dared not breathe. Panic quivered in my chest. I silently offered up a prayer. *Please don't say anything, Tiff. Please don't tell.* And then I understood. Wasn't this how secrets were kept? Because people like me colluded?

"I didn't say anything," Tiff said.

I turned my face to the wall and shut my eyes. Allan asked if I wanted him to stay.

"I think I'll sleep for a while, thanks."

"Right you are." I felt subtle pressure on my shoulder. "You do that. I'll pop in later, see how you're doing."

I heard the door close behind him. My thoughts switched to Archie. What was it about him? What set him apart that made me deify

261

him in my mind? Was it his voice, the way he looked, his style? When others viewed him, did they see what I saw? Undeniably handsome, a caring individual, cultured, socially at ease, he'd always attracted the eyes of the opposite sex. Michael liked him, too. He was as popular with the male of the species as with female. Rare men have that special magic charisma and Archie had it in spades.

Did it make me deaf, dumb, and blind?

Swallowing hard, I analysed what was going on in my head by returning to the very beginning. Archie had provided me with an escape route from domestic mayhem. He'd believed in me like no other, not like my mum who was soppy and believed the good in everyone. Archie's faith in me held the ring of authenticity and for that I'd loved him endlessly, given him my heart and my soul. I'd planned on growing old with him. It never occurred to me that he would leave. I never saw it coming and I mourned for our love, which he'd so easily discarded and left behind. He had ruined me and ensured that I would never fall for someone else, even someone as decent as Allan. As dreadful as it was to admit, by comparison, other men would always feel second best.

But would I have missed the signs of a sexual relationship with Tara? Truth was, divorce guaranteed my absence. How could I spot something like that when I rarely saw father and daughter together?

Without answers, I fell into a scratchy sleep. Sometime later, the door swished open. Footsteps. The bed yielded underneath the weight of a man. Expecting Allan, I opened my eyes.

"Doug," I exclaimed, stirring.

"Your mum told me you'd had a turn."

"Nothing serious." I stared up, raked his face for signs of cuts and bruises. There were none. I glanced down at his big hands. The nails were intact, knuckles unscathed. "You didn't find them?" The biggest part of me felt a flood of relief. Best left or, as Mum would say let sleeping dogs lie. Or, least said soonest mended.

"We did." He flicked a deeply satisfied smile. I'd seen the same on terriers after they'd caught and dispatched a rat or baby rabbit. "They won't be troubling you or the Dukes family ever again."

"My God, Doug. What have you done?" I elbowed myself upright.

"Taken care of things."

A knot tightened in the pit of my stomach. "How?"

"You don't need to know."

"I do. You could get us all into trouble." I was beside myself. Doug had made a terrible situation one thousand times worse. What had he pitched us into? Visions of bloody retribution from Dax and her crew, or, if Doug had behaved in the way I suspected, police officers swooping down and us all hauled in for questioning. Hadn't I pointed Dunne in the gang's direction? Now he'd think I'd given the order to have them removed. What would happen to Mum and Tiff? And then there was the money. Forty thousand pounds I'd lifted from Archie. What might I want that kind of cash for, Dunne would be entitled to know.

Doug grinned, playing with me. "Gracie, I don't know what you think I've done."

"You mean you haven't … " I couldn't bear to say it out loud.

"Rubbed them out?"

I bit my lip, nodded.

"No, my girl. Made them see sense, that's all."

All? "How?"

He tapped the side of his nose with an index finger. Enigmatic. Exasperating.

"Is Graham all right?"

"Sound. Good man to have on your side in a scrap."

I made a mental note to quiz Tiff. If anyone could get it out of Graham, she could. "What time is it?"

"Twenty past two."

"Where's Allan?"

"Taking the kids home."

"It's safe?"

"As GCHQ." Stationed up the road in Cheltenham, the British Government's ultra-secure Communications Headquarters was widely regarded as the third wing in British Intelligence. He grinned, barracuda teeth glittering. "That Dax might have thought she was the dog's bollocks, but, put it this way, I've seen bigger bollocks on a dog."

I narrowed my eyes, not because of the crude way in which Doug spoke, something to which I'd become accustomed, but through morbid curiosity. For the millionth time, I asked what the hell had Doug done? Did I even want to know?

"I've explained the position to Allan," he said. I lifted an eyebrow. How about explaining to me? But Doug ignored it and got up. "Said he'd call you in the morning. Get some rest, Gracie. It's going to be fine. Perfect, in fact."

Bewildered, I lay awake, counting the hours. I pictured all kinds of things, each one a more violent scenario than the first. Giving up on sleep, I got up, slipped through to the kitchen and made myself a drink. Half an hour later, Tiff joined me. Her hair stuck up, all pointy bits, and she had a big red sleep-crease down one side of her face. Attractive.

"Crashed out until Gray came back," she explained. "Now I can't sleep and I'm frigging wide awake. Shouldn't you be tucked up?"

"Doug came to see me. Couldn't drop off after that. What did they do exactly?"

"Dunno, but it must have been bad. I've never seen Gray chug on two fags at the same time."

My mind briefly spun at the image. "You didn't get it out of him?"

"I tried, trust me, threatened him with all sorts and promised him all sorts," she said, a sexually predatory look in her eye, "but he wouldn't budge. All he admitted was they dropped Dax and another kid at A&E."

"A&E?" I gasped. "Was that wise? Won't Dax go straight to the police?" Talk about brazen. I briefly closed my eyes to relieve the pain gathering inside my left temple at the thought of what might have been done.

Tiff threw me a look with which I was fast becoming familiar. It said *Are you out of your tree?*

"Tiff," I said. "She'll demand payback."

"Not after what Doug did, according to Gray."

I shook my head. This kind of stuff happened to other people, in another walk of life. My stomach somersaulted when I remembered that I'd said the same about Tara's murder.

"There's a twenty-four-hour deadline. If Dax doesn't comply ... " Tiff broke off, rolled her eyes, and drew an index finger along her throat. And she dared to call me theatrical.

"What does she have to do?"

"Search me. Graham looked very smug, though. Said it would be a nice little surprise for you."

"For me?" I didn't like the sound of that. Tiff shrugged, flicked on the kettle. The kitchen clock registered four in the morning. I reckoned in an hour I could safely text Allan.

"Are you feeling better?" Tiff said.

"Heaps." Untrue.

She rifled through one of the cupboards, took out a tin, and lifted off the lid. After last night, she was nervy around me. "Biscuit?"

I shook my head. Tiff took two, a custard cream and a chocolate digestive, made us both a cuppa, and sat down. "About earlier, I shouldn't have pushed you."

"No, you were right."

"You think?" she said, guarded.

"I've cut Archie slack for too long."

She dunked the custard cream into her tea. "What are you going to do about him?"

"We've already *done* this," I said, short with her. To tell the truth, I didn't know what I could do. How could I prove it?

"Okay, no need to bite my head off." As if to make the point, she lifted the biscuit to her open mouth. Childish of me, but I grinned as half of it dropped off, plopped into and capsized beneath the surface of her tea.

"Fuck it. And you needn't look so pleased." She grabbed a spoon, plunged in, fished out the soggy remains, and shoved them into her mouth.

"I don't know how you can do that," I said in disgust.

"Don't be so stuck-up. I'll bet Allan Dukes dunks his biscuit," she said with a sly grin.

"What's Allan got to do with it?"

"Don't go all big-eyed on me. He's sweet on you."

"I don't know what you're talking about."

"And you're sweet on him."

"Rubbish," I said. Defensive.

"Be careful, Grace," Tiff said, suddenly serious.

I pushed back the chair, stood up. "I've been careful all my life, Tiff, and look where that got me."

Thirty-Seven

I'M AWAKE. NEED TO TALK. I sent the text at 5:30 a.m. By 6:30 I'd showered, dressed, left a note for Mum, and was heading out to my car. Allan phoned as I parked along Lansdown Terrace half an hour later.

"I miss you," he said.

Tiff's remark flashed through my mind. I blushed and, coward that I am, sidestepped Allan's endearment and enquired about the children.

"Still asleep," he said.

"What did Doug say exactly?"

"I'm not altogether sure. He was fairly cryptic."

"Typical Doug." I told Allan the little that Tiff had wangled out of Graham.

"That figures. Doug advised me to make an appointment with Jordan's solicitor. Said there should be breaking news later today and that the police would have to reopen the case."

"He actually used those words?"

"He did."

"What's he up to?"

"He wouldn't say, other than it would blow the case wide open."

I wanted to shake the truth out of Doug. Frustration tossed me about. Something else, too: uncontrollable, snarling fear. Doug had warned me to watch my back. Someone close. There was only one person who fitted that description. Was I in danger from Archie?

"Can I see you tonight?" Allan said, hunger in his voice.

Cagey, I didn't want to commit. I didn't want complication. I was twitchy and neurotic and unanchored. It was like looking through a heat haze, knowing that a clear view lay beyond, staring you in the face yet out of reach. I needed to let bright sunshine in, to smarten up the focus, to recalibrate my mind and see things clearly. "I'll have to work something out, get back to you later." I blended more vitality into my voice than it warranted. When Allan said good-bye he sounded crushed.

My fault.

Back at home I went straight to Tara's room, retrieved the box containing her notes and sketch pad, and went through them once more, touching the script, hoping to crack a code, attempting to channel her words and their meaning. I rubbed the swatch of material against my fingers, the weave a talisman against my skin, wondering if the absence of a reference in her notes was significant, or whether it was a simple omission. How well do we really know our children? I thought of the parents whose son is radicalised and becomes a terrorist or suicide bomber, the children who get into drugs on the quiet, those who join cults or pretend they are in gainful employment or at college or university when they aren't. I thought of the countless young men who smile at their parents, say that they are fine, that their world is cool and then kill themselves hours later.

So much heartache and chaos and pain in the world.

I remembered Allan's comment about Tara bunking off. I'd been blissfully unaware. What else had happened in her secret universe? It came back to the unthinkable. I could no longer pretend that I believed in Archie as Mr. Nice Guy. I should have stopped denying it days ago.

My stomach rumbled with hunger. Although I had little appetite, I needed a sugar boost to offset the dizziness and shore up my dwindling physical resources. If I were to act, I had to stay strong.

Sweeping Tara's things aside, I went through to the kitchen, pushed two slices of bread into the toaster, took fresh orange juice, butter, and raspberry jam from the refrigerator, and laid it out properly with a plate, knife, and spoon. When the toast was ready I flicked on the radio for company, half listened to a programme, and made myself sit down and eat, slowly and methodically. Feeling more sorted I pushed the last crumbs into my mouth when there was a tremendous noise, as if someone were using a battering ram to burst through the front door.

My first reaction was *Police*. I spun out with possibility. Gangland Murder. Accusation. Arrest. Questions. I pictured Detective Inspector Dunne's granite features white with condemnation, Doug and Graham stone-faced in an interview room next-door offering "no comment" as Jordan Dukes had done before them. I thought of my distraught mum, her homilies ineffective against Doug's epic crimes and the combined forces of law and order. All of this travelled through my mind with the velocity of a shooting star and still the door rattled with rage.

I darted out into the hall, called out, "Who's there?"

"Thea," a voice shouted back, "Thea Molyneaux. Mrs. Neville, for God's sake, let me in."

I opened the door. Scared and furious, Thea darted inside. Without make-up, she seemed younger and vulnerable. Her clothing consisted of leggings and a floppy tracksuit top and I had the impression that she'd thrown on the first clothes that spilled out of her wardrobe. I ushered her through to the sitting room, invited her to sit down. She did, clasping her hands tight together as if to stop them from shaking.

"You betrayed me," she exploded.

"What?"

"You talked. You told Mr. Neville what I said."

My pulse stammered. "Why don't you tell me what this is all about," I said as smoothly as I could.

She snatched at her bag, unzipped it, and plunged inside. Drawing out a sheet of A4 lined paper, she thrust it under my nose.

SEE NO EVIL, HEAR NO EVIL, SPEAK NO EVIL

"It was addressed to me, delivered by hand and shoved through our letterbox. I found it on the mat this morning."

I read it twice, overwhelmed by the implication. I'd only told Archie and Tiff, and now this. Who else was to blame if not him?

"I'm not sure it has anything to do with our conversation," I said, scrabbling for a more plausible explanation.

Thea's features hardened. "Yeah, right. You talked to him," she sneered. "You dropped me in it."

My gut felt full of stones, earth in my mouth, no, couldn't be. Surely? Not Archie, because if it were him then he was guilty, and if he were guilty he had a motive for murder, and if he had a motive for murder, I'd have to face the unpalatable truth. "Do you have the envelope?"

"Here," she said, slapping it into my hand. The accusation in her eyes whipped through me.

Big capital letters in an unformed hand. Not Archie's writing. Relief rushed out of me so fast I was light-headed. I handed the note and envelope back and told Thea this. It made no difference. "I don't damn well care," she said, shaking the note at me like some evangelical pushing the Bible in the street at a reluctant shopper. "You opened your mouth and now someone has threatened me."

"Could it be a misunderstanding with a friend?" I knew what girls her age could be like.

"You told him, didn't you?" Her green eyes were dark with tears of rage and fear.

"I…"

She stood up. "You tell that sicko to keep away from me."

Sicko? "Thea, I'll sort it. I promise. I really think you've got it all wrong. Would Archie be stupid enough to threaten you so openly and like this? Honestly, it's the kind of thing kids do, not grown men."

Already Thea was heading for the door. She took one long last look back at me, her features distorted with disgust. "Why do you collude with someone as perverted as that?"

My mouth dropped open with shock. "I'm not," I protested.

Thea wasn't finished. "Prove it. I don't know what's going on in your sordid little world, but if he sends me anything else, or threatens me, I'm going to tell my parents and they'll go to the police."

The door swished open and slammed shut. Every muscle in my body contracted. I could no longer run or hide or pretend.

Thirty-Eight

I reached for a jacket, grabbed my keys, and ran down the road to the car. I was too angry to feel sick or afraid. Everything dropped into place. The fierce denials, the sweet talk and concern about my sanity and emotional well-being, the cats, and the bloody advice to drop it, *let Jordan take the heat* and, oh my God, what had the boy endured inside? And now I knew why. Jordan was the perfect dupe, but Archie wouldn't get away with it. I'd nail him and then go to the police myself.

Snarled up in traffic, I zipped in and out of cars, cutting up, overtaking when I shouldn't, and chancing my luck with my life and the law. Horns blared. Drivers gesticulated. Well fuck you, too. I didn't care. When I chicaned past the For Sale sign and swung into the drive at Harp Hill, stones spat from beneath the Mini's wheels and smacked against the paintwork.

Unsurprisingly, my arrival didn't go unnoticed. Archie was already out of the door, rushing down the stone steps, to my mind a man in a hurry to avert trouble. Displeasure curled his top lip. "What the hell—"

"You filthy dirty bastard," I shouted. "I know what you've done and I know what you did to protect your grubby little secret."

Archie's eyes flitted from me to the tree line and back again. He shot out an arm and grabbed hold of my elbow, attempting to propel me forward. "Let's go inside."

I shook him off. "Afraid the neighbours might hear? That would screw your precious sale, wouldn't it?"

"I want you to calm down." His jaw flexed and his words came out staccato and stern.

"That's right, can't have me emotionally disturbed."

"I didn't say that."

"You inferred it."

"All I want is for us to talk rationally."

"Rationally?" I screamed. "Can't wait to see Kristina's face when she finds out that her future husband has been screwing his daughter."

The slap took me totally by surprise. Raw and hard, my cheek stung, teeth rattled. Shock rendered me temporarily silent. Archie had never raised a hand to me, not ever. I put a hand to my skin and stared into the eyes of someone I no longer recognised.

Colour bled from Archie's features. He looked old and gaunt, as if middle age had deserted him. I had a sudden insight into how he would appear in his seventies. His lower lip trembled. "I'm so sorry, Gracie. I'm terribly sorry. I shouldn't have done that. I snapped. Unforgivably. Are you all right?" He took a step towards me, one arm raised, this time reaching instead of striking.

"Don't step any closer," I sputtered. My face burnt with heat. My voice shook and a single solitary tear fizzed onto my skin and zipped down my inflamed cheek. So it was true. Oh my God.

"We need to talk," he said, letting his hand drop. "It's not what you think."

I held his gaze, trying to fathom an alternative, more palatable scenario that made sense. I came up empty. He must have known I'd keep digging until I discovered the truth. It was inevitable. How could he prepare for a confrontation like this? Ignoring the dubious sensation in my stomach, I nodded my assent.

He turned reluctantly on his heel and, shoulders hunched, body bowed, returned to the house. I followed at a distance. Each pace felt as if I were one step closer to my own execution.

Inside, I walked past packing boxes, past the big expansive drawing room with the piano near the window, and into a snug, its reduced size all I registered. I had no time for interiors; show home style, or the way the damn cushions were plumped or flat. I wanted answers and explanations, nothing more, nothing less.

"Sit down, Grace."

I perched on the edge of a repro Regency-style library chair. Archie took the sofa. We were two metres away from each other. It might as well have been the Grand Canyon.

"What happened to your face?"

"You hit me, remember?"

He blanched. "I meant the cut to your lip."

"Doesn't matter. Get on with it."

Briefly confounded, he pitched forward, an urgent expression in his eye. "I want you to hear me out. It's been extremely difficult for me, for Kristina, too," he said. "I hope you'll understand that I kept quiet for the best of reasons, to protect Tara's memory."

Heat and fear swept through me in equal measure. I had a bad feeling and knew that once Archie spoke there was no going back, no retreat. This was it. A tiny part of me felt a swell of vindication quickly followed by one of abject terror. With dread, I took a breath, nodded.

"I admit, I tried to dissuade you from uncovering Tara's secret."

"Why?" I said sharply.

"Because it would have hurt too many people."

"You mean you?"

"Not me. Tara."

I didn't understand. But I had an idea. "You threatened Thea, didn't you?"

He didn't blink, didn't waver. "I don't know what you're talking about."

"Don't dare come the innocent with me. It's true, isn't it, you fucking pervert."

His eyes shrank to two black orbs. "Will you stop calling me that and making wild allegations? I did not threaten Thea."

"You didn't send the note?"

He frowned. "What note?"

It was hard to know what to believe. Archie kept lying but his face, his body language suggested that he was telling the truth. This time. I fluttered my fingers in dismissal, gestured for him to continue.

"You have to understand that it was a phase in Tara's life, something that a lot of young girls go through." Experimenting with drugs, I thought, my heart sinking. "Something," Archie said, struggling to find the right words, "that was silly and got a little out of hand, admittedly, but passed."

I screamed exasperation. Why did I *have to* understand? Why, if it was silly, did it need to be kept secret? Was it another boy? Oh Christ, she didn't get pregnant, did she, and have an abortion? With Archie a nurse, perhaps she'd confided in her dad. Was that why she'd come to me about going on the Pill when she met Jordan? Yes, that gelled. I asked him.

"No," he said with a tight smile. "Nothing like that. It was more subtle."

"Archie, you're talking in riddles."

And then he came out with it. "Tara had a crush on an older woman."

I started and pulled a face. It sounded so far from left field I didn't know what to make of it. "An older woman?" I repeated dumbly.

"Yes."

Was that so bad? Lots of girls had crushes. It was part of growing up. I mumbled the same.

"This was more serious."

"An affair?" I whispered.

He held my gaze, eyes saying it all and, when he could no longer look at me straight, he glanced down at the thick pile carpet. My vindication felt short-lived. "That's ridiculous. I don't believe it."

"It happened."

"What are you saying, that she was gay?" I wouldn't have minded, but it didn't ring true. I knew Tara. I knew how she lusted after young men. How did being gay stack with her relationship with Jordan?

"No, no," Archie said. "It was something she really regretted."

"Bisexual then, is that it?"

"I don't think so, no."

I still didn't get it. Confusion made me hasty and jealous. "And you knew? Tara confided in *you*?" Hurt scorched my voice, sending it up a scratchy octave where it missed and hit a bum note.

"I knew about it, yes."

"And you didn't think to tell me?" Or the wretched police, I realised.

"Tara was ashamed. She asked me not to."

"Did you always do as she said? I had a right to know. I was her mother. I had custody." Flashing with fury, I slammed my hand against the arm of the chair. "What else have you kept from me?"

"Nothing, Grace, honestly." He spread his hands. I'd never seen him look scared before. Archie was invincible; he looked absolutely petrified.

My breath came in spurts, hot through my nostrils. Damn him. Damn his lies.

"I know it's come as a shock." The smooth, conciliatory note was back in his voice. This was what he did best, Archie the healer, the carer, the liar.

"Who was this woman?"

He blinked twice. "I don't know."

I didn't believe him. "When did it happen?"

"Tara was thirteen or fourteen at the time," he said vaguely, "a fairly typical age for that sort of relationship."

"Infatuation is one thing, an affair isn't. This is not typical."

"It's not unusual," he said quietly, averting his gaze. Playing with semantics, as far as I was concerned.

"Conducted a study of it, have you?" My voice was excoriating. "How long did this *thing* last?" I could barely string a sentence together. Cool, collected Grace, *not*.

"A couple of years on and off."

In the piercing light of revelation, Tara's moodiness, her unpredictability made sense. The time she'd snuck out and come back five hours later, her lips full and bruised, complexion glowing, suddenly dropped into place. Was this what she wanted to confess to Jordan? Had her lover found out and killed her before she had the chance to expose her?

"Did you report this to the police?" My voice was cold and hard, not like mine at all.

"No."

"Why the hell not? She might have killed Tara to shut her up, don't you see that?"

The whites of his eyes shone bright and frightened. "Jordan Dukes killed her."

"No, he didn't."

Archie stared at me for a long moment. I could see his chest rising and falling beneath his shirt. I could virtually feel his racing pulse. "Even if Jordan wasn't guilty," he conceded awkwardly, "what you're suggesting is impossible."

"Is it? At the very least, this bloody woman should be on the sex offender's register."

"It was a one-off, a passing thing."

"How do you know, Archie? You stated that you have no idea who she was."

"I … " He pitched forward, face in his hands. He let out a moan, almost a sob.

I gaped at him. "Tell me, damn you."

His shoulders shook and his hands dropped away. There was a terrible beating in my heart. I could barely look at this wreck of a man, and husk of my ex-husband. Tearing my gaze away, I fixed on the furnishings, the way everything meshed together, everything perfectly placed, the Old English white and vivid reds, the …

My eyes locked onto the drapes. The drumming in my chest thundered. The fabric. The swatch in Tara's sketchbook. It matched. How could I have missed it?

I heard a movement behind me, felt the air disturb. I swivelled round.

"It was me, Grace," Kristina said. "I was the woman."

Blood rushed through my temple. I gripped hold of the arm of the chair. "But I thought you loved Archie."

"I do," she said. "But for a very short time, I was in love with Tara. I'm so sorry."

Thirty-Nine

I wanted to pick up something hard and heavy and hurl it through the Grade II sash window, or at the large effortlessly cool mirror. Anything that would crash and shatter and express my hurt and rage.

"In love?" I yelled. "What would you know about that? In lust, more like."

"It wasn't sexual," Kristina claimed in a piping voice.

"Next you'll be telling me that Tara was your muse. You're a liar."

I felt as if a huge wave had washed me up onto a spit of land and I was stuck there alone, without food or water. This was so dysfunctional.

Springing to my feet, I pushed past Kristina, banging her as hard as I could with my shoulder. She cried out, "I'm sorry. I'm sorry. Please forgive me." I didn't want to hear it. I didn't want to dispense absolution. I fled through the downstairs rooms, wrenching open every door in search of the cloakroom. I found it in time to throw up in the lavatory. Afterwards, I ran the cold tap; splashed my face and the back of my neck with water. My mirrored reflection stared at me, drained and un-comprehending.

Physically, emotionally, spiritually, it hurt me to move, but move I did. I'd entered one door, pitched into the chasm, dropping, twisting and tumbling through empty space and into another dimension.

Kristina had risen to prime suspect spot. She, not Archie, had most to lose from Tara exposing her, and now me. What I didn't under-stand, what I truly could not get my head around, was why Archie had protected Kristina? Was it shame, collusion, or had I missed a crucial point? And when did he find out? How long was he ignorant of what was going on right under his nose?

I considered all the women, and they were mostly women, married to men who betrayed them. Did the wives of serial killers ever sense their husband's murderous predilections and proclivities? Had they sat across the dinner table without having the slightest inkling of their spouse's dark imaginings? Easy for me to cast Archie and Kristina in the roles of Mac-beth and Lady respectively, but who was I kidding? Hadn't I been a willing dupe where Archie and affairs of the heart were concerned?

I straightened up, dry-eyed and, despite my trembling knees and the fact that my feet felt as if they were encased in concrete boots, returned to the sitting room with as much poise as I could marshal.

Kristina sat in the chair I'd vacated. With her wounded looks and pre-Raphaelite beauty, she looked more victim than perpetrator. How well she played the martyr. Archie hadn't moved from the sofa on which he sat mute, one hand covering his mouth, the skin around his eyes creased in despair. There was no show of unity, no joined hands, no sign of them about to sing from the same frigging hymn sheet.

The air crackled with static as I crossed towards the Victorian fireplace and stood with my back to the grate. As shaken as I was, I realised that I had the drop on the pair of them and the power to destroy. All my venom focused on Kristina. I'd deal with Archie afterwards.

"You told me that you weren't close," I said, clipped and controlled. "You said Tara tolerated you because you were her father's partner. You're a liar. What else have you lied about?"

She chewed her bottom lip. "I don't understand."

"Yes, you do. Jordan Dukes is innocent."

"God," Archie said. "When will you get it through your—"

"He didn't kill Tara." The authority in my voice hit home.

"You mean …" Kristina began, stung by my implication. "I didn't hurt her. I swear. It was a mistake, an aberration, but I wouldn't have harmed—"

"Spare me the fucking platitudes. You had a motive."

"No," she wailed in desperation. "Tell her, Archie," she said, appealing to him. "Tell her that it was over."

I remained implacable. "If this got out, you'd be finished. Think what a dirty rumour like that would do to your precious design company." My brain revolved inside my cranium. That's why they were running away, to escape their pasts before word got out.

"She didn't kill Tara, Grace," Archie pitched in. "Kristina has a cast-iron alibi." Muscles tightened in his jaw. I read much in his expression—suffering and grim acceptance mostly, the kind you see in women whose husbands repeatedly stray or abuse and, after offering vacuous promises that things will get better, are welcomed back with open arms. I was surprised he hadn't buckled under the weight of such a secret. He'd not lied when he'd told me of the problems in the relationship, something he'd assured me was consigned to the past.

Archie, I realised, would have been the first to suspect Kristina when Tara was murdered, the first to check out Kristina's alibi.

"That's right," she leapt in. "I was in London at a design conference. At least a dozen people vouched for me."

"Mates, were they?"

"The police cleared her, Grace." Ancient, used up and spat out, a dreadful world-weariness inhabited Archie's voice.

"But they didn't clear her of sexual offences with a minor because they didn't damn well know."

Kristina was all big eyes and pallid complexion. Fat tears rolled down her cheeks. Her lip quivered and her fingers with her manicured nails shook. I hated her and I wanted her to die slowly and in unspeakable misery. The strength of my feelings should have rocked me. They didn't.

"It wasn't like that," she whispered, crumbling under my vicious glare.

"What was it like?" I said. "Actually, I don't want to know. You took advantage of an impressionable young girl on the cusp of womanhood. You exploited her when she was confused about her sexuality. And you," I turned to Archie, "let it happen. How the hell do you live with yourself? What happened to your protective parental instinct, your moral compass?" I didn't wait for an answer. "You must live in a duplicitous little world." My eyes swivelled back towards Kristina. For all her beauty, I thought her the ugliest person on the planet. "Wasn't it good enough that you stole my husband from me?"

"Grace, it wasn't—"

"Shut up, Archie. I'm sick of your excuses. Did she have to have my daughter, too?" My voice cracked.

"I'm sorry. Really," Kristina gulped. "I can't explain it because I don't understand it myself. It was just one of those one-off connections, pure—"

"Pure?" I roared. "You've taken everything from me." Unable to mask the heartbreak in my voice, I trembled from head to toe.

"I can't bear for you to feel the way you do, to hate me so." Concern tightened Kristina's eyes. Fear, too.

"Well, you'll have to endure it, won't you?" My whole life these past years had been a feat of endurance, thanks to the miserable woman sitting in front of me.

A crushing silence built up around me, bricking me in. The air stank of misery. Kristina assumed a tragic pose. I looked at Archie. "Is that what the row was about, the one you had with Tara before she died?"

He lowered his gaze. "I didn't think it wise of Tara to tell Jordan."

"You bastard," I said. Then I had another thought. Tipping my head in Kristina's direction, I said, "Do you still love her?"

He held my gaze. "I do."

An incredible stillness swept over me. I stood tall despite the tightness in my throat and chest. I had one last question.

"Kristina, did Tara give you a key to our home?"

"Yes," she admitted quietly.

"So it was you who broke in?"

"Broke in, why?"

"To look for and remove incriminating evidence," I said, raising my voice.

"What evidence?"

"I don't know," I said exasperated. "Messages."

"We never left messages." She spread her hands. "And I don't even have the key anymore."

"Did you give it to someone else?"

She blanched. "Of course not."

"Where is it?"

"I lost it."

Archie flashed alarm. This was definitely news to him.

"What are you going to do?" Kristina said, nervously hunched in the chair, arms crossed, her hands clutching her elbows, desperate to give the impression of control and keeping things together.

"What *he* should have done," I flared. "I'm going to the police."

"Grace," Archie started, "it will do no good. It won't bring Tara back. It will only hurt you."

"Hurt me? What about other young women who need protecting?"

Kristina's chest rose and fell in double-time. "You have my word," she begged. "Nothing like that had happened to me, to us, before and nothing since."

"It's true, Grace," Archie said, scrubbing at his face with his hands.

"You choose to believe her lies if you want to. Not exactly good for your street-cred, is it, having your girlfriend conduct an affair with your daughter? Don't bother getting up," I said, crossing the floor.

I did not go to pieces. After the rankness in the house, I felt neither clean cool air against my face nor remembered my journey home. I felt the kind of dead numbness that only bad news can evoke. Only when I was back inside my own four walls did I allow myself to falter and fall. I was a fool and a failure. My own daughter and I'd been unable to protect her. What did that make me?

Lost, I didn't talk to Allan and I didn't talk to Tiff. I thought about infidelity, Archie betraying me, and Kristina betraying him. I did not begin to understand how he could forgive her. For me, my child had always come first in my life. Anyone who'd exploited Tara in the way that Kristina had done was answerable. Perhaps mother love was stronger than a father's. Perhaps I was doing Archie a disservice. He'd played the episode down, treated it as a natural part of Tara's adolescence. But how he factored the affair into his relationship with Kristina I couldn't begin to imagine and didn't want to. It was too perverse, too much outside my experience and emotional make-up. For that I was glad. I daresay he thought me unsophisticated.

Whatever had transpired, I was left with three unresolved questions.

Who had entered my home? Who had threatened Thea? And who had killed my daughter?

Were they connected or coincidental?

When the phone rang I ignored it. I closed my eyes and conjured up Tara's voice in my ear, evoking a sea of memories. I talked out loud to Tara's pictures and photographs. I could because there was nobody there to deny me, no husband to accuse me of madness, no friend to tell me, erroneously, that I would one day get over it.

There was only one truth: you never get over something as monstrous as this. Whether your child is small, a teenager, an adult, the agony of loss remains the same. Always.

I sat alone until the afternoon turned to evening and the evening turned to night. Only when there was a knock at the door did I stir. I had no need to view my visitor through the spy hole. Resigned to my fate, I knew who it would be.

"Hello, Detective Dunne," I said as I threw open the door.

Forty

With a briefcase tucked underneath his arm, Dunne advanced into my small home like a man selling me financial services. To his credit, he cut to the chase. "There's been a fresh development."

I inclined my head and assumed a neutral expression—not easy. I've never been good at deception, other than deceiving myself.

"We've had a confession." My pulse rate skipped, hammered, skipped again.

"For the murder of Tyrone Weaver," Dunne continued. "According to my colleague working the investigation, Denise Saxon and her crew came forward first thing this morning."

"Is Denise Saxon also known as Dax?"

Dunne nodded. He coughed and cleared his throat. I'd never seen him look so uncomfortable, which I guess explained why he didn't think to ask how I knew Denise Saxon's soubriquet. I wondered whether the man seated before me had a wife or significant partner at home. Was he a walking cliché, a divorced copper with only a bottle and TV dinner for company when he returned after a hard day at the coalface of crime and at some ungodly hour? I blinked back to the present.

"What does this have to do with me?"

"Saxon admitted that Jordan Dukes is innocent. It's alleged he tried to stop the gang from carrying out the attack on Weaver."

"Alleged?"

"We're still carrying out an investigation," Dunne said, deadpan. "But evidence indicates that she is speaking the truth."

"What evidence?" I thought of Allan and Dionne, how overjoyed they'd feel, how their journey would come to an end while mine soldiered on. "So?"

"Dukes was locked in the boot of Ruben Monk's vehicle between the hours of eleven p.m. on the Saturday night and just after two thirty a.m. on Sunday morning. We have a witness who attests it," he said, shame glancing across his craggy features. "If you recall, the post mortem report suggested that Tara had been killed between one thirty and two thirty on Sunday morning, the same time Weaver was killed."

I think Dunne expected me to express dismay, clap a hand to my mouth, and collapse with hysteria. Calm enveloped me. I was right. I was in control. I had more knowledge at my fingertips than the highly trained police officer sitting opposite me. I felt no sense of triumph. Inch by inch, I was slip sliding towards the truth. I could feel it with every beat of my heart, with every breath I took.

"Have the Dukes family been informed?"

"There are procedures in place," Dunne said, mealy-mouthed. I guess it came as a grave disappointment to have his judgement questioned and the prospect of a conviction overturned. He'd been gunning for Jordan from the start. "Last time we talked," he said, moving clumsily on, "you mentioned the flat had been entered."

I recalled without rancour how Dunne had given the impression that they were the febrile ramblings of a grieving mother. "Yes," I said. To add to his humiliation, I told him about the delivery of freshly severed cats' heads.

Colour deserted his face. "Why didn't you inform the police?"

"Do you really want me to explain?" It came out tetchier than I'd meant. I was so damn tired of justifying myself and explaining my actions.

"What did you do with them?"

"I got rid." Which wasn't true but I didn't think involving Archie was a great idea at this particular juncture. It would only undermine what I wanted to say later.

"Might be an idea to get forensics to give your place the once-over."

I nodded wearily.

"Have you any idea what someone might be looking for?" he said.

"Not exactly."

"But?" He raised an eyebrow.

I gave him a straight account of Tara's relationship with Kristina. I described it as a "fling" to protect Tara's memory. It did nothing to lessen the impact. His head snapped up. His face twisted. "How did you come by this? When did you find out?"

I told him the truth. I didn't need to point out that Kristina had a motive.

"And Mr. Neville was aware?"

"He found out. I don't know when. You'd have to ask him."

He thought for a moment. "You'll give a statement?"

"I can, but I don't think Kristina killed Tara." He raised an eyebrow again to underline that he, not me, was in the best place to make that kind of a judgement. With satisfaction, I pictured the knock at the door at the big house on the hill, the police officers' request to speak to first Kristina and then Archie, the fear and embarrassment it would provoke. Might they deny it? With Tara dead, it would be easy enough; my word against theirs. Dunne's next question held the same precision as a laser beam.

"How would Mr. Neville react to Miss. Beaumont conducting an affair? Quite a slap to his manhood, isn't it?" A weak light shone behind Dunne's pupils. "Going off with another bloke is a fairly bog-standard occurrence. A full-on affair between his girlfriend and his daughter, now that's a completely different hornet's nest."

My eyelids flickered. The tip of my tongue caught the corner of my mouth, which was dry and crusty. "It was, apparently, brief," I pointed out, my composure slipping.

"That what they told you? How old was Tara at the time?"

I coloured and repeated what Archie had told me.

"She was a minor, Mrs. Neville. Kristina Beaumont broke the law."

"I understand that." Mortified, I realised the full implications and wondered what kind of mother Dunne thought I was.

"And your daughter was the only person who could expose her, expose them," Dunne said with emphasis.

I thought of Archie's answer to my question. *Do you love her?* I'd asked. *I do,* he'd replied. There had been no change to his marriage plans, no change in his feelings towards her. Why the hell not? Dunne's suggestion took me to an alien and forbidding place in which Archie, or both he and Kristina, had plotted and killed Tara. Insanity grasped hold of me and spun me around. If I didn't break free and cling to a different truth, it would destroy me.

"I noticed when I came in you have quite a bruise to your face," Dunne said,

"I slipped over in the courtyard."

The way he studied me, I knew he didn't buy my lie. "Can I get you a glass of water? You're rather pale."

"That would be good, thanks."

The chair creaked as Dunne got up. I felt vacant, tuned out. The next I knew, cool glass on hot hands. I sipped. Nothing could expunge the acrid taste of betrayal. Diminished, I looked up at him, searching his face. "What happens now?"

"The investigation into Tara's death will be reopened. The team will be briefed and Mr. Neville and Miss Beaumont will be called in for questioning."

"You'll let me know?" I stood up on weak legs that threatened to give way at any second.

"Will do. Have you got anyone to stay with you, your sister, Mum, someone close?"

I told him I'd contact them. "One thing before you go."

"Yes?"

"Denise Saxon," I said as casually as possible. "I'm curious, what made her confess?"

"Someone got to her."

"Oh?"

"I'm guessing one of Weaver's friends."

I frowned as if I didn't quite understand.

"Took a blunt instrument to her hand. Two of her fingers smashed, not that she's saying who was responsible, but you don't wind up with that kind of injury by tripping up in the garden, if you get my drift." No more than slipping over in the courtyard, his expression implied.

Forty-One

I felt ill and feverish the next day. My head throbbed and no amount of painkillers could shift the ache. This was becoming a horrible habit. I stayed huddled under the covers until gone one o'clock, getting up only to teeter to the bathroom and pour the odd glass of water from the kitchen tap. My mobile rang twice, once from Tiff and once from Archie. I ignored both. Eventually I got up, showered, and dressed. When Allan phoned me that afternoon, I picked up.

"I've seen Jordan," he said. "Have you heard the latest?"

"About Dax?"

"She handed herself in." He was ecstatic. "How did you find out?"

"Dunne told me. I'm glad for you, Allan, glad for Jordan, too." I pushed the ethics of Doug's behaviour right out of my mind and recalled what might have been: me as a human torch.

"They're reopening the case, Grace."

"Yes," I said, my pleasure bittersweet. "Will Jordan be released? I'm not sure how it works. Dunne was pretty guarded."

Some of Allan's joy faded. "Unfortunately, it's not straightforward. Getting into prison is a whole lot easier than getting out even if a conviction is quashed. There will probably be a retrial and it could cost."

"I've got a little money saved. If you needed help with legal bills, I'd be happy to help out."

"After all you've done already, you'd do that for us?" Wonder filled his voice.

"It's what Tara would have wanted."

"I don't know what to say."

"Thank you is fine."

"Then thank you," he said warmly.

Silence encircled us. I should have hung up, would have been easy to wrap up the call and say good-bye. I didn't want to. Not yet. Couldn't explain. Lonely, I longed for company, specifically Allan's. I'd be safe with him in a way I never was with Archie. When Allan smiled, I knew it was for me alone. With Archie, he only gave the illusion of intimacy.

"It's so good to hear you," Allan said. "I thought you'd deserted me."

"I had a few things to think through." Strain washed through my voice, staining it grey.

"Are you feeling better?" He said it like he really meant it. I hesitated. How to answer? Blandly, misleadingly, the truth? "Only I wondered," Allan began, "if you're not busy, if you'd like to ..."

"Yes," I said.

He laughed. "Now?"

"Why not?"

"Great," he said. "That's great."

And it was.

Almost out of the door, my landline rang. Curiosity always trumped caution. Half of me wondered whether it would be Archie. In her inimitable sisterly style, it was Tiff checking up.

"A lot has happened," I gabbled, giving her a highly edited rundown of the most recent turn of events.

"Lord alive, I'll be over in fifteen."

"Can't. I'm on my way out."

"Where?"

"Like I said, out."

"You never go out."

"Don't be soft."

"Where then?"

"To see Vron." Deception seemed easier.

"Vron?" she said suspiciously. "How long will you be?"

"Can't say."

"You're bloody lying, Grace."

"How about tomorrow, a walk or something?"

"What are you up to?"

"Nothing." My stomach churned. My sister knew me too well.

"I'll be straight over after I've mucked out in the morning. Be ready." It sounded more a threat than promise.

━━━━━

I reached Allan's place in time for an early dinner. "I wasn't sure if you'd eaten," he said. Wearing sand-coloured chinos and a navy and white stripe shirt, he'd taken care with his appearance, yet the effect was casual and unstudied. "Cold meats, salad, and bread," he said temptingly. "Glass of white wine, if you'd like one. It's chilled," he added.

"Lovely, thanks."

"Take your coat?"

I slipped it off and handed it to him, automatically smoothing down the nonexistent creases in my skirt. I'd been impulsive, reckless, and my nerves kicked in. "Where's Dionne?" I watched as he uncorked the bottle and poured out two glasses.

"At a friend's."

"And Asher?"

"With her."

"You're not at work." I immediately cursed myself for stating the obvious.

He passed my wine, fingers grazing mine. "Not today. Too much to do."

"Oh," I said, "if this isn't the right ..."

Putting down his glass, he looked calmly into my eyes and rested both hands lightly on my shoulders. The gesture reminded me of Tiff gentling a skittish horse, whispering and listening, calming it down, gaining its trust. "Do you realise how much I miss you?"

"Allan, I'm not sure this is a good ..."

"Shhh," he said. "Does it have to be good or bad? Can't it simply be?"

"I wouldn't want you to hope," I said clumsily. "With so much going on, so much unresolved, I'm unable to give ..."

"Nobody is asking you to give a thing." His smile knocked me out and made me ache inside. "We're two people simply reaching out to each other."

"I'm beyond reach," I said sadly, my eyes filling with tears, my throat constricting. "No good can come of it. It's too complicated, too weird. Archie has scorched me," I blurted out.

"I know he hurt you, but you're not lost, not with me around."

I shook my head. There were things nobody could protect me from, from death and grief, from a broken heart. I'd get through, for sure, but I'd never get over. Nobody ever did.

"Never let the past take the present prisoner," he said.

"Not that easy," I mumbled.

"I didn't say it was," he smiled gently. "Sit down awhile, sip your drink, and talk to me."

So I sat and talked and told him everything.

Forty-Two

"Tara and Kristina?" he gasped in astonishment.

"It's hard to get my head around, but yes."

"You don't think … " his voice trailed off.

"It's down to the police now. I told Dunne yesterday."

We talked all that evening and night until dawn broke and a pink tinged sun shed its hesitant rays on the morning. It wasn't a confessional or monologue. I told him how my heart had been split in two, that the anguish resulting from Tara's death, I feared, would never lessen or leave me. In return, I learnt a little more about Allan's former wife, the good and the bad, the struggles of single parenthood, the worry of Jordan running so far from the tracks he'd no idea how to reach him, the constant nagging fear that when his son went out, he might never return, and the prejudice against the family in the light of the murder conviction.

"I love that boy," he declared. "The thought of him in that place," he said with a shudder, "makes me writhe inside."

"Which is why we have to get him out."

I admitted to Allan things I'd never told anyone, not even Archie because with Archie I'd wanted to be the new Grace, the aspirational Grace, the Grace who strived for a better, more meaningful life with money and nice things and proper holidays and cultured friends. Some men would have thought me shallow. Allan didn't.

"Nothing wrong with wanting to better yourself."

"There's a fine line between ambition and turning your back on your roots."

I told him about my childhood, the relentlessness of moving from one home to another, one town to another, and the ceaseless procession of different men in Mum's life, dads and partners and lovers, and the sisters those relationships created.

"Don't get me wrong," I said. "Through it all, my mum was solid and constant, always putting a bright spin on things."

"But?" he said with a mild smile.

"None of it made up for the fact that at times we didn't have enough to feed the meter, or buy the pair of shoes I'd always wanted, or have a party for friends who would not be my friends the following week because we'd be gone." I confessed to feelings of anger, long suppressed, the way grief for the loss of a child incubates and gnaws through you from the inside out. I admitted that I concealed it all with a bland smile and a pleasant and reasonable disposition while inside I was raving, and the deception was slowly killing me. He never offered a word of judgement, no more than I judged him. When the clock finally struck five, we went to bed as if it were the most natural thing in the world. In every sense, he felt different than Archie—his limbs, his body, his skin, his touch. I felt joyous, like the warm glow you get from the sound of rain pattering against glass. Some time later, we fell asleep.

A soft kiss on the back of my neck woke me up. I rolled over and gazed into Allan's soft brown eyes, crinkled at the edges with smiles. I smiled back, sleepily bemused before guilt threw its long dark cloak over me.

"Oh God, what time is it?"

He perched himself up on one elbow. "You have to be somewhere?"

Naked and exposed, I shot out of bed and grabbed my clothes. "Tiff, I promised I'd meet her."

"Phone her," he said.

I hooked up my bra, plunged both legs inside my knickers and then my long skirt, and ran my fingers over the buttons of my shirt, doing them up with the same dexterity as if I were playing a wind instrument. "Can't," I said.

"She wouldn't approve?"

"Something like that." I charged towards him, bent over, went to kiss his cheek. He was too quick for me. Hooking a hand behind my head, he tilted his face to mine and kissed me long and slow. My skin tingled.

"Will you tell her about us?" he murmured.

"Sixth sense, she probably already knows."

"And Archie and Kristina," he said, serious now, "will you tell her about that?"

"She has a grasp of the broad outline, not the fine detail." I ran my finger down his cheek. I really didn't want to leave him. "I'll call you later," I promised, pressing my lips to his once more.

Predictably, Tiff beat me home. She stood, her back against the black painted front door, one leg straight, the other bent, her boot leaving a muddy mark on the rendering. Sour-faced, she glanced at her watch. "What time do you call this? I have to be back at the stable in a couple of hours for a vet's visit. Got a mare with suspected laminitis."

"Sorry."

"And why don't you answer your frigging phone?"

I pushed past her, plunged the key into the lock.

"Bloody hell, you smell of sex."

"And you smell of horse muck. Take your boots off if you're coming inside."

She shut up for a full thirty seconds. I told her to put the kettle on while I showered and changed. "Did you sleep with Allan?" she bawled unrestrained, opening the bathroom door a crack.

"For goodness's sake, shut it. There's a draught."

Newly soaped and in fresh clothes, I sat down, sipped the mug of tea plonked in front of me, and squirmed under Tiff's accusing glare.

"Give," she said.

I took a sip and revealed my visit to Archie and Kristina and what had transpired.

"Christ on a crutch," she said, goggle-eyed. "Kristina and Tara?" So much for being unshockable, I thought. When I outlined subsequent developments she flapped for a second time, mouth opening and closing like a goldfish snatched from a pond and dumped in the rockery by a cat. "And Jordan? But that means ... " She ran out of steam, which is fairly unusual for my sister.

"It means the killer is still out there. And knows what I'm up to. Why else the grim feline message?"

"Kristina," Tiff spat, slapping her meaty thigh. "Has to be."

"I don't think so."

"Archie then."

I shook my head.

Her brow furrowed, snapping her dark eyebrows together. "Then who?"

"If I knew, I'd tell you," I said, rolling my eyes. "Look, I need to clear my head. Shall we go for that walk?"

"Suits me. I could do with some fresh air," she agreed. "As long as I'm back on time."

We went in Tiff's car. It was a good spring day, plenty of sunshine, little cloud and the air fresh and astringent with new growth.

Parking in a gateway close to Dowdeswell Reservoir, we climbed out and followed a wide path, passing a couple of houses until we joined a steep single-file track favoured by serious walkers. With a view of fields on one side, woods carpeted in bluebells on the other, I followed Tiff at a brisk, lung-bursting pace. Conversation was impossible; it suited the pair of us.

Partially blotted out by an overhang of trees, the sun broke through, its light mottling the slippery earth in patches of green and gold. Another season, another spring, and a shot at fresh chances; not least to bring Tara's killer to justice.

We climbed higher and higher, stopping once to get our breath before moving on and out through a gate onto a road signed for Andoversford and Ham in one direction and Cheltenham the other. Tucked into a gateway was a 4x4 similar to Kristina's.

Breath back, and on a wide even stretch, Tiff said. "Did you sleep with Allan?"

I let out a sigh. "What if I did?"

"God, Grace, you hardly know the guy."

"It's none of your business." The edge in my voice prevented further discussion. Tiff got the message and we kept walking. Finally, she broke the enforced silence.

"I've been thinking, that break-in, what were they after?"

"No idea."

"You quizzed Kristina?"

"She said she no longer had a key and wasn't responsible."

"Believe her?"

"I *think* so."

We walked on. I could tell Tiff was still chewing it over, probably in the same way she was mithering about Allan and me. She had a special way of walking when she was thinking: hunched shoulders, hands deep in her pockets, face angled towards the ground.

"Did Tara keep a diary?" she asked.

"No. I've been through all her stuff. The only clue was the swatch of fabric."

Tiff shuddered. "Creeps you out, doesn't it?"

I nodded. "Not that I have a problem with gays."

Tiff shot me a look. "That's not what I meant. It's the whole idea of Kristina taking advantage of Tara when she was underage. Hell's teeth, what was she thinking? Had she ever done anything like that before?"

"Not according to her." It seemed like a one-off from the way she'd reacted, although I had to admit that Kristina was a more accomplished liar than I'd previously thought.

We arrived at a five-bar gate that opened out onto a farm road flanked by pylons. Electricity crackled loudly in the breeze.

"You first," Tiff said, holding it steady as I scurried over. She followed, dropping down next to me, like a piece of rock. "Hell, I'm getting too old and fat for this malarkey."

We followed the road and then turned left back into the woods again. Tiff fell silent. I could practically hear the synapses snapping in her brain. "Have you been through the junk in Mom's garage?" she said.

"For God's sake, give it a rest. I've had other stuff on my plate in case you hadn't noticed."

"Don't bite my head off. I meant have you been through it, you know, to search for clues."

I screwed my eyes up against the sun. "Is it likely?"

"The cops never searched it, did they?"

"Why would they? It was Tara's junk from years before, after me and Archie split and we moved into the apartment." As soon as the words were out of my mouth, I felt the thrum of impending revelation. Tiff caught it, too.

"Fits the timing. Might be worth a peek," she said. I clapped a hand around her shoulder and squeezed. "What's that for?"

I grinned. "For not being as thick and stupid as you look."

"Cheeky mare," she said, slapping me on my arm with a laugh.

The way became dense with foliage again as we picked up one of the lower tracks. I took the lead, Tiff clonking along behind. About to head downhill to open countryside, the sound of voices drifted at first and then cut through the woods.

Sometimes, in the early hours of a Saturday or Sunday morning, I'd hear odd shouts of revelry slicing through the night air from Montpellier. Occasionally, the shouts turn ugly as, stewed with booze, tempers erupt, fists are thrown, and young men shout and women scream. Nine times out of ten, it's followed by the sound of police sirens. The voices I heard now were like that. Raised, one higher-pitched, sibilant and shrill, the other older, emollient, playing peacemaker or mother, or both. I stopped abruptly. Tiff cannoning into me. "Shit, what's the matter?"

"Hush, listen."

I half turned, watched Tiff's face, one ear cocked. Impossible to make out the words, the intonation and rhythm of speech throbbed with agitation, climbing anger and, unexpectedly, frustration and tears. I craned forward, tried to make out exactly where the sound was coming from. It seemed to travel from the other side of the broken-down fence, deep within the trees, rebounding off bark and wood.

Tiff poked me hard in the back, urging me forward. Reluctantly I edged along, every step unfeasibly loud, twigs snapping, leaf rustling, my breath bursting, almost a pant, and the small of my back slick with moisture.

"I did it for you," a girl's voice cried. "You can't leave me now. I won't let you."

"You have to let me go," a voice said, soft and low. "I can't protect..." Frustratingly, like a mobile phone losing signal, the rest of the conversation disappeared.

"Is that who I think it is?" Tiff said, eyes wide.

"I don't know," I whispered back. I thought of the 4x4 parked up on the road.

Without warning, noise, like the sound of a pheasant breaking cover and eager to escape the hunter's gun, erupted, followed by a cry of "Come back!"

From nowhere, a figure burst onto the path lower down, hoodie half up, face obscured by a curtain of red hair. Wearing jeans, slim-hipped but with an unmistakable female curve, the lone young woman cut down the track and tore off, earth and loose stone flying. I froze, turned towards the woods, scanning the line of beech, peering into where the trails petered out and lurched into the black expanse that loitered between tree and undergrowth.

Tiff tugged on my arm. "Can you see Kristina?" I shook my head. She must have moved off immediately. "Any idea who the youngster was?"

Muddled, I tried to shake sense into my head. Female. Young. Red hair. It was only a glimpse, but somehow the figure felt oddly familiar. Only one person fitted that description, to my mind. "No," I said, my voice thick with deceit.

Did *what* for you? I thought.

Forty-Three

You can't easily run down a steep incline, and yet Thea Molyneaux must have descended with the agility of a mountain goat. Tiff and me slithered and slid crab-like and in tandem, Tiff bumping into my heels and cursing. By the time we tumbled to the bottom and raced back to Tiff's car, there was no sign of Thea or anybody.

"Drive to Harp Hill?" Tiff said, as we climbed into the Micra.

"No."

"Call the police?"

"And say what?"

"Tell them what we overheard." Her voice was laced with aggression. "You must have Dunne's number on speed dial."

I turned to Tiff. "What did we overhear exactly?"

"Why must you be so bloody reasonable?" she flashed. "We heard a row. We heard Kristina."

"The police need hard evidence. They don't react to hearsay."

"Well, it's about time they did." Which was Tiff's standard response to any argument she was losing. "We know, *you* know, that Kristina is up to her neck in something. Why else would she be having that kind of conversation?" She drummed her stubby fingers on the steering wheel. "If only we knew who the other person was."

"Haven't you got to be getting back?" I said pointedly.

"Fuck," Tiff let out, checking her watch and starting up the engine. "I'll be shot if I'm late."

"Drop me in town," I said smoothly. "I'll find my own way."

Tiff glanced across. "You seem very together. Are you okay?"

"Fine," I said. In truth, I was, and a million miles away from how I'd felt during my conversation with Archie and Kristina. With each revelation, Archie had done the equivalent of pushing my face into the mud. Each time I raised my head, his boot had pushed me back down. This was different. If I were right, Thea Molyneaux was involved in a way in which I could only speculate. I'd believed the girl when she'd answered my questions. I'd believed her when she'd shown me the anonymous note. Based on fragments of overheard conversation, it now seemed that she had deliberately deceived me by pointing the finger of blame in Archie's direction, not Kristina's. So what the hell was her connection to Kristina? She was Tara's closest friend, or so I thought. But how close? As I stared into the void, I twisted inside. Thea held the key.

I shot out of Tiff's car at a set of traffic lights and tapped the roof in a gesture of good-bye. Tiff hooted in reply and sped off. As I watched her little car disappear into the traffic I had an urgent desire to phone her, to tell her about my suspicion, to beg her to come back and come with me. The moment passed.

Thea lived with her parents off Selkirk Street and within walking distance of Pittville Park. It was a lovely period town house with Cheltenham spike railings and three stone steps up to a glossy black front door that resembled Number 10. I admit it was the kind of home I'd once fondly imagined living in.

As I turned the corner off Prestbury Road, I saw the flash of police lights from a stationary vehicle in a resident's permit parking bay directly outside the Molyneaux house. Dunne must have joined dots I hadn't even begun to put onto the board. Were the police moving in with the intention of taking Thea in for questioning?

I stopped walking and, positioning myself on the other side of the street, pulled out my mobile phone, pretending to make a call. A few minutes later, the front door swung open and Mrs. Molyneaux stepped out, flanked by a WPC and an older male officer. Another middle-aged woman wearing an apron hung back in the doorway, her face a picture of voyeurism and morbid concern. She stood and watched as Mrs. Molyneaux, red-haired like her daughter, walked unsteadily down the steps and path. The tip of her nose and the rims of her eyes were bright red, in livid contrast with the pallor of her face. Both police officers were solicitous, the man touching her elbow lightly, as he guided her to the waiting police car.

Pain cramped my stomach. The dynamics were all wrong for what I'd imagined. Mrs. Molyneaux had the alabaster complexion of a woman in deep shock, an expression I recognised only too well. There is nothing like bad news about your children for eliciting that type of intense physical response.

I waited until the police car had driven off and then approached the house and rang the bell. The woman with the apron came to the door. Her face pinched with suspicion straightaway. "My God, you people don't hang about, do you? Making money out of other people's grief. I've got nothing to say."

Staggered, I said, "I'm not from the newspapers. I'm Mrs. Neville. Thea was my daughter's friend."

The hard edges around her mouth and eyes slackened. "Oh my, you poor woman. I always said lightning never strikes twice."

I shot a hand out to the wall to steady myself. "Has something happened to Thea?"

"Some thug hit her over the head this morning while she was jogging through the park. Dragged her into the bushes, apparently. You've missed the police. Mrs. Molyneaux is on her way to the hospital now in Gloucester."

This morning ... jogging through the park ... Then she couldn't have been the redhead arguing with Kristina, I realised.

"Do the police know who it was?"

"Got to be a man, hasn't it?" she sniffed, folding her arms.

"Will Thea be all right?"

"I don't know, love. Didn't sound very clever to me. Do you want to come in? I was making a brew. Looks like you could do with one."

I snapped a smile. "Thank you, but no, I need to get on."

I blundered down the steps and lurched back home. I remembered nothing of my walk, who I saw, or what was going on in town. I could only think of the mystery girl with the red hair. Who was she? Why was she upset? What was her connection to Kristina? A daughter nobody knew about, a friend, a *lover*?

What was patently obvious, Thea hadn't been with Kristina. The timing didn't match and that meant only one thing: Thea was telling the truth and someone had made good on a threat.

I pressed a hand to my forehead, which felt cold and damp. Back home, I stumbled across the courtyard, half expecting a figure to explode from out of the walls. Plunging the key into the lock, I entered my basement flat.

Tara was dead.

Thea had been attacked.

Why not me next?

Drifts of conversation cut through my mind with the same precision as a blade through flesh: *I did it for you … You can't leave me now. I won't let you.* If the girl was Kristina's lover and vying for her attention, Archie, I suddenly realised, was in danger, not me.

I picked up the phone, called his mobile. As soon as the line connected, and before I had a chance to say a word, he launched in.

"Satisfied now? You've put the pair of us through hell."

"You did that all on your own, Archie. You lied to me, to the police, and to yourself."

"Having thoroughly explained the situation, we're cool with the police," he said bravado in his voice.

"What?" I didn't believe a word of it. "Have you any idea where Kristina was this morning?"

"She went for a walk near the reservoir, what's it to you?"

"She met someone."

"So what?"

"Someone who was pretty upset."

"How would you know?"

"I was there."

"Snooping again. You're a woman with an obsession."

"Wanting to know who killed our daughter is *not* an obsession."

"How do you expect me to believe you?" He didn't jeer. It was more like the weary resignation adopted by parents when their teenage sons and daughters tell them a lie so blatant and glaring they can only admire their audacity.

"It's true," I said, stung. "Kristina's affair with Tara wasn't a minor lapse. Don't you see, she's involved with someone and that someone killed our daughter and attacked Thea Molyneaux?"

"Thea?" he repeated.

"Someone got to her this morning. She's in hospital. Maybe they were in it together, Archie. Maybe you're next."

"For God's sake, Grace, when are you going to stop muckraking?"

"When you stop deceiving yourself," I yelled.

"There's only one person doing that—you."

He cut the call. What to do now? Should I drive to Harp Hill, as Tiff suggested? Would Archie even let me in? And what if I were mistaken? Should I call the police? What if Archie was right and they had somehow persuaded Dunne that I was the one with the problem, not them, that in my grief I'd come up with an outlandish story of sordid affairs? But they couldn't challenge what had happened to Thea, I reminded myself.

Unless it was one of those random stranger attacks you hear about in the newspapers.

Squirming with fatigue, I sank down onto the sofa. Everything was going wrong. Feeling needy, I punched in Allan's number then baulked and cancelled the call. If anyone had asked me to explain I would have said that no way could I get him involved in this, yet I had a deeper reason, one I hated admitting to myself.

Archie had been as much deceived by Kristina as the rest of us, his love for her borne of a dark destructive passion, one I knew so well because Archie, the man I'd fallen in love with, lurked intoxicatingly below the surface of my skin. Allan was lovely and dependable and considerate and all the things I should want in a man. Archie was ...

I closed my eyes, tried to work it out. Archie and me were like the kind of stories depicted in a Jack Vettriano painting, one of dependency and drama, seduction and enigma. The kick was in the not knowing where I stood. I hadn't even after thirteen years of marriage. It had blinded and corrupted me. Faced now with the monstrous, impenetrable

309

possibility that if it had not been for Archie leaving us, Tara would still be alive, was like someone let loose in my sitting room and coating the walls in vantablack, the world's darkest material, a colour so deep it looks like a hole. Contemporary artists and sculptors had seized upon the blackest black with an enthusiasm normally reserved for the discovery of something like Einstein's Theory of Relativity. My discovery was quite different, a flash of self-awareness and one that I had to crush and destroy.

Archie hadn't killed Tara. But he'd aided and abetted in it, unwittingly, perhaps, and I had to face up to, confront and overcome my squeamishness and break his contemptible hold on me forever.

My resolve stiffened, I jumped up, grabbed my car keys, and drove to Mum's.

Forty-Four

Doug was out and Mum was pottering in the garden tying up a rambling rose that had broken free from the trellis. She straightened up as I walked through the wicket gate.

"Hello, Gracie, love. My, you look tired. Not sleeping too well?"

"Not really," I smiled uncomfortably. "Would it be all right if I go through stuff in the garage?"

She frowned. "Has Tiff been on at you again? Honestly, Gracie, I love her to bits, but I'm not sure I want her under my feet, let alone gormless Graham."

"Nothing to do with Tiff. I want to have a rummage, find out what I've got stashed away in there. It's hard to keep tabs on it all."

She viewed me with a probing expression. At times my mum surprised me. Sleepwalking through life, she could unexpectedly display flashes of insight that proved she was very much awake. I fleetingly wondered how much Doug had told her about Dax and how much my Mum knew about Doug. Like women and men the world over, did she accept what he did because she loved him? I experienced a twinkling light of self-awareness go on in my brain. "You'll find your things stacked against the back wall nearest the door to the garden," she said.

I went inside and closed the door after me. The garage had an old-fashioned ironmongers' smell that I found reassuringly timeless. More of a storage facility than a place to stow a car, there were great pots of paint and creosote, ladders, tins of nails, lightbulbs, gardening paraphernalia, cases of booze (possibly knock-off), a chest freezer, a tumble dryer and an old fridge. Heartbreakingly, a high chair and baby's cot stood in lonely isolation. Immediately, I remembered my mum's son, my little brother, the one who'd died. So much tied up in the things we keep, mementoes of the dead, reminders that one day we will join them.

There were seven big storage boxes, three belonging to me, four to my mother. Bone-dry, the garage was the perfect place for Mum to keep her stash of old photographs and LPs, which she sometimes fished out to play when she was feeling sentimental, or pissed, or both.

I made a space and lifted the first box off the top and hefted it down onto the floor. It contained mostly my junk, wedding photographs and reminders of my relationship with Archie, including a vintage '50s evening dress in ballerina print, pink and blue against a black background. For a few seconds I closed my eyes, burrowed my nose into the fine fabric and dwelt on ecstatic times when my life was sweet and not blighted by death, lies, and deceit. The garment no longer fitted, much the same way as my current existence.

Sadly, I reached down the second box off the pile. Containing Tara's things, it looked more promising if haphazardly packed. I could tell from the way it was all bunged in that she probably hadn't enjoyed being asked to divide her belongings into stuff for the flat and less immediate items to be stored. Smiling at her legendary impatience, I pulled out soft toys, favourite clothes she'd grown out of and refused to throw away, a pair of whacky Wellington boots in pink with yellow flowers, books, pens that had run out of ink, a couple of board games, pieces missing, jigsaw puzzles, exercise books, and dozens of plastic folders of printed material for school, most of it nicked off the Internet by the look of them. Setting these aside, I continued to plunder her belongings and unearthed a throwaway camera, the sort you're handed at weddings, and a tin containing school photographs.

Perching on an old garden chair, I sat amid the wreckage and went through exercise books scant in content that held nothing other than what you'd expect. The majority of her schoolwork from thirteen years of age onward resided within the folders. These I scoured with painstaking attention. Yards of stuff on World War I; a suspense novel, an abbreviated classic, and a book of modern poetry; the UK climate, industrialisation, Germany between 1918 and 1945; crime and punishment during the Tudor and Stuart dynasty—I remembered that one because Tara had been appalled at the unspeakable tortures devised to extract so-called confessions from prisoners. There'd been much debate in our house about the Judas Cradle and Crushing Rock and whether torture ever got to the truth or was a barbarous device to make a crime fit a suspect. How bloody ironic, I thought, chucking it back into the box and reaching for another folder labeled PERSONAL, SOCIAL HEALTH AND CITIZENSHIP EDUCATION. I yawned, dragged out the contents and, as I parked them on my lap, a sheaf of hand-written sheets dropped onto the dusty floor. Stretching down, I picked them up, shook them, and noticed that the text was littered with capital *K*s drawn in pink. They stood out from Tara's writing like sequins on a piece of naïve art. In random order, I read.

Friday:

K always said I was special from the moment I walked into the art gallery. OMG! Makes me feel weird and a bit shit. Poor Dad. I love him and I never want to hurt him but me and K are so, dunno, I can't find the right words, cool and special and lovely. We live in our own little world. My mum would go mad if she knew. She'd really freak out. I know she would because she's always been jealous of K. She wouldn't get that it's not a crush. It's way bigger than that. I love K and K loves me.

Thursday:

We've been together ten whole months, but I don't know how much longer I can keep it secret. I thought about telling Thea but she wouldn't understand. I can't tell Mum because she'd go ballistic. Obviously, I can't tell Dad. I feel soooo bad for him. I'd like to tell someone because I'm confused and guilty. I can't help my feelings for K but I know that it's wrong and it's not as though I don't like guys. K understands that but K made me swear. K would get into a lot of trouble if people found out. Special K, I call her, like the breakfast cereal, ha-ha!

Monday:

It's our thirteen-month anniversary today. Can't believe it! Woo-hoo! K says Dad will be out working a night shift so I can go to theirs. I still feel bad about Dad. K says that we're not doing anything wrong. She says I mustn't worry because everyone has different relationships with different people and you can love more than one person and, in any case, she isn't married. I kind of get that because I like boys, but all I can think of is K, the way she touches and makes me feel.

Tuesday:

I had a horrible time last night. K was acting all weird. She wasn't nice at all. I'm scared she's met someone else. I don't want to go on holiday with them anymore. That will pay her back. I hate her.

Saturday:

Two weeks with my mother—boring. I missed K every single day, but when K came back we got together at our special place. Ha-ha! Special K in a special place. K was HOT for me. K told me so. That's the nicest thing anyone has ever said. We had a lovely sexy time together but I was worried when I got back home because Mum noticed, I know she did. I think she suspects something.

Sunday:

I'm scared and confused. K doesn't love me anymore, well, not in THAT way. K says I will always be important but that it's time to move on. It will be good for Dad. Part of me feels glad that I don't have to lie any more. Dad is nuts about Special K. But I think K has someone else now. I tried to find out, but K wouldn't tell me. She's probably prettier than me, younger, too. K always likes young girls and I'm too old now. I feel ugly and fat. So unhappy.

P.S. I also feel dirty and ashamed and guilty. Poor Dad, I can't look him in the eye anymore. Wish I could talk to Mum about it because I love her and she loves me.

Tears careened down my cheeks. Everything clicked into place. Scalded by the thought that, if only Tara had talked to me, she would still be alive, I stuffed the sheets back in the folder, the rest of the printed text unread. Next I ripped open the tin of school photographs and plucked out single pictures of toothy Tara from primary school days, and group photos at secondary school. Discarding the earlier prints, I sifted through those taken later. I found one that depicted a drawn Tara, loaded down, confused by rejection and riddled, no doubt, with guilt. She must have felt truly awful about betraying her father, but I couldn't find it in my heart to condemn her in the way I'd condemned Archie. She was, after all, only a kid. Her expression epitomised the clash between child and woman: outwardly sassy, yet deeply insecure and vulnerable inside. I wondered whether the photograph coincided with the timing of the last entry.

Another picture showed Tara around sixteen. More confident and cheery, she had the gleam back in her eye, her thirst for life and adventure reawakened. She was more like the daughter I remembered and loved, my girl—and, yes, Jordan's girl, too.

My fingers tiptoed over her smiling face, Thea's next to hers. I scanned to the end of the row, silently naming Tara's friends and schoolmates, my eye travelling to and probing the next line down when my breath stalled and fell away. Nimble thoughts snapped and bit into my brain.

Red hair, pretty face in spite of the smile marred by a set of braces. Oh my God, how could I have been so blind?

Forty-Five

I didn't say good-bye.

I tore out of the garage and, under a bellicose sky, ran to the car and drove back towards Pittville Park. I sped into the Smith-Arrows' drive as light drizzle turned with awesome speed into fat cold droplets.

The housekeeper who'd answered the door with glacial disdain weeks previously dished out more of the same treatment. "The Brigadier and Mrs. Smith-Arrow are out."

I cast my eye over her shoulder. "I want to speak to Ruby."

"I'm afraid that's not possible."

"Why not? I know she's in."

"I have my orders, Mrs. ... " She searched over my shoulder as if my surname would suddenly materialise from where she could catch hold and smack it on her lips.

"Neville," I said.

"I'm sorry, but—"

"To hell with this," I said, shoving past. "Ruby," I bellowed, angling my head toward the galleried landing. "Ruby."

A firm hand gripped my arm. "Mrs. Neville, I really must insist."

I whirled round. "Let go of me. Either I speak to Ruby this minute or I'll call the police and let them do it for me. Your choice."

Mystified and knowing that I was deadly serious, she was rendered momentarily speechless. I bet she wondered how Ruby's parents would respond to a visit from the cops. Not good, judging by her frightened rabbit reaction. She nodded curtly. "Upstairs, second room on the right."

"Thank you," I said.

I took the stairs two at a time, didn't knock, and went straight in. I was struck first by the stylishness of the room—not a swag, drape, or floral print in sight. Over the bed a print of Audrey Hepburn on a wall that was Tiffany blue. A decorative dressmaker's tailor's dummy sat in one corner close to a wall unit displaying a fine selection of vintage and modern handbags. Next to this, a little black dress hanging from a picture rail like a piece of conceptual art, reflecting the fashionista theme. White linen with black motif complemented the teenage chic meets funky bedspread. Not for one second did I suspect Mrs. Smith-Arrow or Ruby's hand present in the interior's creation. Kristina Beaumont ran through every aspect, even down to the metallic blue desk with the state-of-the-art Mac, the leather-bound notebook, and the carefully chosen literature on the bedside table that included chick lit, psychological thrillers, and a recent copy of *Cosmo*.

Ruby sprang from the bed. Her mud-spattered jeans left a dirty smear on the ferociously white bedding. Her arms hung loosely at her side, unlike her hands, which were thin and tight. My eyes travelled to meet her red-rimmed green-eyed gaze and porcelain features, lips cracked and dry, her expression neither belligerent nor mutinous, but simply and unmistakably scared. A tendril of red hair escaped from behind an ear and plastered itself against skin damp from crying. She looked more child than woman, as if her young mind couldn't cope with the violent acts she'd inflicted.

"What are you doing here?" Fear stalked her features.

"You know why I'm here, Ruby."

"If this is about me breaking into your flat, I'm sorry. I was only trying to protect everyone."

"Protect? How?" My cutting look made her stammer.

"I-I thought Tara might have written about me, in a diary, or something like that. I thought, if I could find it, then nobody need know. I didn't take anything, I swear," she said plaintively. "You're not going to tell my parents, are you?"

"About what exactly?" Realising that she'd revealed too much already, she chewed her bottom lip. "Your parents are the least of your problems, believe me."

Her face collapsed into an ugly expression. "I was nice to you," she whined, hurt, as if I'd betrayed her trust and deserved to be punished for it. "I stuck up for you against them."

"This has nothing to do with your mother and father. This is about Tara. You killed her, didn't you?" Despite my loathing for Ruby, I said it as non-threateningly as possible, as if making a bland statement.

The mention of my daughter's name had a dramatic effect. "No," she recoiled. "Of course I didn't. How could you say such a terrible thing?"

"Because you're in love with Kristina."

319

Ruby's jaw clamped shut, concealing her perfectly straightened teeth. Nothing could still the tremble in her dimpled chin or prevent her green eyes from filming over with self-pitying tears. "It wasn't my fault. None of it was my fault," she cried. "She didn't have to die."

"But she did," I said quietly.

Ruby stared at me as if I were deliberately missing the point. "But *I* didn't do it."

"Then who the hell did? Kristina?" My voice rattled with anger. I couldn't hold it in.

"I don't know. Honestly," she snivelled, flashing with anxiety. "I didn't even know about Tara until … " She stopped, realising again, too late, that she'd said too much. And then I got it.

"Kristina told you."

"Kristina *warned* me, that was all. She said Tara had threatened to tell Jordan about them, about us."

And so you killed her. I could barely contain my frustration and anger. "You were jealous of Tara, weren't you? In your warped little head, you didn't understand that, whatever ridiculous infatuation she'd had with Kristina, it was over. She had a boyfriend and a life and you took it."

"That's not true." Spots of colour seeped through and dotted her pale cheeks. "Tara would have ruined everything, but I didn't … "

"It was already ruined. Kristina doesn't care a damn about you."

"You're lying," she said, her voice tearing.

"She only cares about herself. She's getting married, Ruby, or had you forgotten?" In that moment, I registered that Kristina was using Archie to cover her tracks. What was it about this woman that so captivated, that inspired that brand of devotion? She might not have wielded the knife but, to my mind, she was as guilty as the child/woman standing before me. How I recognised the pain of obsession in Ruby's eyes, the desperate need to cling on in the bitter face of both rejection and God's honest truth.

"Shut up," she snapped through a blizzard of furious tears. "I won't have you speak to me like that." My mind flicked back to Ruby's father, the sneering way in which he proclaimed and gave orders, as though he were better than everyone else.

I lowered my voice. "Tara was about to blow wide open your secret affair with Kristina, and then your parents would have found out, right?"

"My dad would have killed me," she wept, her voice a plaintive howl. "I'd have been cut off without a penny."

I virtually had to pinch myself to remind me that I was talking to a teenager. Money, the oldest motive in the book for murder.

"Is that why you sent an anonymous note to Thea?"

The sobs came thicker and faster. "I didn't mean any harm. I was just trying—"

"And attacked her, like you attacked Tara?"

Her jaw dropped open mid-sob. "Why are you saying these terrible things?"

"Did you attack Thea this morning before you saw Kristina?"

"How did you know I was with Kristina?"

"I was there, walking in the woods. What did she tell you, Ruby?"

Her green eyes spurted with fresh tears. "She told me that she was leaving, that she was going away, that she had a new life to begin." Unsteady on her bare feet, she swayed in anguish. "She said we wouldn't be seeing each other again." Then Ruby broke down entirely.

I waited for her to recover. "Ruby, do you think Kristina capable of murder?"

Her swollen eyes met mine. When she spoke her voice was thin and tinder dry. "I don't know," she whispered.

Forty-Six

I raced to Harp Hill as if my life depended on it. Driving with one hand, I pulled out my phone with the other and called the house and then Archie's mobile, both of which went to voicemail. In desperation, I called Dunne. The call got routed to a recorded response. Spotting a police car driving towards me in the opposite lane, I garbled a message and threw the phone down into the passenger foot-well from where it stared back at me, blunt and redundant.

I didn't hack up the drive in the Mini. I dumped it on the roadside and hurried the rest of the way on foot, the lawn springy beneath the soles of my shoes. Rain gushed from the sky, pinning my hair to my scalp. I rolled the collar of my jacket up in a fruitless attempt to restrain it.

Kristina's 4x4 was absent. Ahead, parked to the side, was Archie's Audi. A shiver rippled through me at the sight of the front door wide open, as if someone had left in a hurry. Gathering my courage, I sped across the gravel and darted inside.

There was no sound, no breath, as if the house had gone into cardiac arrest. With my heart thundering in my chest, I cruised softly through downstairs rooms stripped bare and gaunt, their remains bundled into dozens of packing cases, lifeless and long dead. The stark, minimalist kitchen seemed the only place to escape the ravages of people in flight, although it was difficult to tell. It lacked ordinariness. Few household items on display, no homey tea towels hanging from a hook or shelves full of cookery books. No clutter. No soul. Which was probably why I spotted the plain white envelope lying facedown in the middle of a granite-top work surface. I stretched out towards it when a creak from the floor above, almost imperceptible, stopped me in my tracks.

I lifted my head, listened. Having never been past the downstairs, I didn't know the layout, but Tara had once mentioned that Archie and Kristina's main bedroom and en suite were over the kitchen. It would make sense with the plumbing. I crept back towards the wide staircase. Looking up, I felt briefly dizzy. Ascending would be like climbing K2 without crampons or breathing equipment.

Trembling with cold and fear, I slipped off my shoes and, cushioned by thick pile, padded up towards the next floor. Tiff once told me that I had the weak heart of a guinea pig while she had the heart of a lion. She was right. Any shock and I'd keel over.

With every step I braced, expecting raised voices, Kristina to explode in front of me brandishing a knife.

Only ticking silence.

Sweat trickled from every pore in my body. I felt old. Stale.

Yet there was no turning back.

I inched my way quietly towards the only room where the door was not flung open and pictured the scene behind it: drapes drawn, in semi-darkness, Archie's dead body offered as a human sacrifice and token of a perverted form of love like the prone figure in Munch's *The Murderess*. Instinctively, I knew that once I crossed the threshold my life was in mortal danger. I kept going for one reason only—not for Archie, but for Tara.

With a beating heart, I stretched out, grasped the handle and, depressing it, pushed the door open. It swung back slowly as if on castors and, aside from the drawn curtains, the interior wasn't as I imagined at all. No body sprawled on the white linen duvet and duck-egg blue Jacquard throw. Softened by lamplight, shadows played across the eau de nil painted walls. Friendly.

Emboldened, I stepped inside. Subliminally, I noticed fine art prints on the wall; the desk that doubled as a dressing table; a twelve-inch-high bronze sculpture of a young naked woman; a gilt-edged Art Deco mirror; the bookcase, every spine so vivid it burst with colour and class and style, and authors I'd heard of, some I'd read. Everything sharp and finely delineated; every edge, plane, surface, and curve. With a soft tread, I walked towards the window.

Mistake.

The door swung back behind me and clicked shut.

I spun round and opened my mouth to speak, but no words emerged. Face-to-face with Roland Smith-Arrow, I was seized by a spasm of terror.

In one hand, he gripped a boning knife, the blade narrow, razor-sharp and pointed at the tip. I knew without the slightest doubt that this was the weapon used to stab Tara. My eyes travelled to meet his thin, glassy, ice blue gaze.

"You shouldn't be here." The tight, skeletal lines on his face contracted, giving him the appearance of a blind man.

I swallowed. Fear defiled me. "Why are you here?" I said stupidly, already knowing the answer.

"That perverted bitch ruined my daughter's life. I warned her. She promised she'd leave Ruby alone, but she didn't. She kept on and on with her sordid declarations of what she calls love, completely brainwashed Ruby, as I daresay she did your daughter."

"Then why kill Tara? Why not Kristina?"

"Kristina gave me her word, not that it counted for anything." His thin top lip kinked with distaste. "But I'm afraid your daughter threatened to expose the pair of them, to tell the whole sordid story. I had no choice," he said as though it was stunningly obvious and he'd taken the most sensible course of action. "Think of the shame. Think of the damage to my reputation."

"*Your* reputation? You murderous bastard."

His eyes chilled. He straightened up, to attention. "I have spent my entire life serving my country. I've enjoyed a distinguished career in which duty, tenacity, and honour are treated with the respect and reverence they deserve. You don't think I'd let some chit of a girl ruin everything, do you?"

Words failed me. "You must understand," Smith-Arrow continued, "at the time I'd no idea that Kristina had broken her promise to me. They were clever, cunning, secretive," he said issuing a nasty smile that left no trace of warmth in its wake. "We suspected Ruby was truanting, but we didn't realise until it was too late that she'd taken back up with that detestable woman."

"How did you find out?" I stammered.

"Ruby's leather notebook. Full of revolting drivel, there for the world to see. Always had a bent for words, my daughter. Could make something of it if she doesn't get any more deviant ideas."

"And that's how you knew about Tara, that she was going to tell Jordan," I said more to myself than to him, the final piece slotting into place.

He nodded once. Slowly.

He'd struck a deal with the devil, as far as I was concerned, and when that devil—in the form of Kristina—betrayed him, he killed to protect a reputation.

And now he was going to kill me.

I stared into his monstrous, jagged face and felt an adrenalin rush of undiluted hatred that made me bold.

"Put down the knife."

A smile skidded across his lips, twisting them into a sneer. "Or what? You'll rush me, put up a fight? I don't think so." Desperately, I glanced around the room. Two exits, one blocked by Smith-Arrow. Jerking his chin towards the en suite bathroom, he must have read my designs.

"It's locked. You had your chance. I warned you, but you wouldn't back off."

"The cats' heads," I gasped in realisation. "It was you."

He blinked slowly, the light behind the ice blue deadly with recollection. "A meddler, you had it coming to you."

Dazed, I thought of Dunne and wondered how long it would take for him to arrive. Had I even told him the essentials? Had I in my panic instructed him to go to my place instead of here? How long before he even listened to my message? Oh God, oh Christ.

I ran my eye over the contents of the room, urgently looking for a means to defend myself. I was younger and more agile than Smith-Arrow, but he was a military man. He knew how to stalk, trap a quarry and kill. Against a knife, I was powerless. One thrust was all it took to dispatch my lovely daughter. He wouldn't hesitate to do the same to me.

He must have read this in my expression because he raised the blade, lunged, and jabbed within a metre of my face, silvered metal

326

catching the light, glittering and deadly. I think he would have come straight at me had it not been for Archie's voice.

"Kristina, for Chrissakes," he yelled. "Are you upstairs?"

We both froze. "If you scream, I'll gut you first," Smith-Arrow threatened, edging several paces back towards his hiding place behind the door.

"Kristina," Archie called again, closer, louder, distress in his voice. "You can't walk out. We need to talk."

I heard Archie's tread on the stairs, his footsteps like hammer blows, deafening above the sound of Smith-Arrow's breathing and the drumming in my ears.

Smith-Arrow's callous eyes locked onto mine, held me in a vise-like grip, leaving no doubt in my mind that he would spring and strike if I uttered so much as a sigh.

I stared straight at him, spread my fingers wide towards the bed, touching and silently threading the silk throw between them, scrunching up the fabric. Archie called again, nearer now, on the other side of the door, an angel's breath away. At any second ...

"ARCHIE," I screamed, ripping the bedspread off and, like in a magic act, threw it over Smith-Arrow as he advanced. Still he came, roaring and lashing out, flinging off the cover. I felt a sharp sensation in my left arm, material tearing, blood spilling, and yet I felt no pain. I was too busy looking for something, anything with which to defend myself.

Intense with shock and fury, Archie flew into the room, made a grab for Smith-Arrow, briefly pinning his arms to his side. Smith-Arrow swivelled and turned, breaking free, the blade silver-white and lethal in the lamplight. Panting, he licked the corner of his mouth, narrowed his hooded eyes, which burnt with desert heat and anger. He darted a look from me to Archie, sizing us up. We circled, cornering him like a dangerous wild beast. Archie was pitched forward, sweat beading, fists up; me, searching the room for something to destroy the man who had killed our daughter. I understood now what Tara had faced. She hadn't stood a chance.

Smith-Arrow feinted one way, then another, sweeping the blade in a wide circle. A yell sliced through the air. Mine. The knife missed my right eye by a feather's depth. Archie moved in. Smith-Arrow carved and jabbed. Archie jack-knifed, danced back out of the way. Smith-Arrow lunged again. Archie sucked in his lungs, his body concave, less of a target. Or so I thought…

Blood bloomed on his shirt. Archie grunted, dropped onto one knee, the expression on his face one of bewilderment mixed with horror.

Smith-Arrow's smile was a weapon as he moved in for the kill. His arrogance cost him. Glancing to my left, I swept the bronze statuette from the bedside table in both my hands and charged. Swinging it high, I smashed it smack against the side of his head. Like a building under demolition, Smith Arrow collapsed, out cold, blood issuing from his temple.

"Archie," I cried, rushing to his side, the tang of fresh blood strong and filling the room with foreboding. Kneeling over him, I tore open his shirt. Ashen-faced, eyelids tinged an alarming blue, he let out a groan.

The wound was smaller than expected but it bubbled with blood around the entrance. "For God's sake, tell me what to do."

"Phone in pocket," he said haltingly. "Ambulance."

I slipped it out, my hand shaking, got through to the emergency services, gave instructions.

"Your arm, Gracie," Archie wheezed, wincing in pain as I finished the call.

"Doesn't matter," I said. "None of it matters."

"I was always better with you," he rasped. "Sorry."

"Stop it, Archie." My voice was thick with tears. "How bad is it?"

"Can't see, but it's deep. Air in the chest cavity," he mumbled, nostrils flaring, perspiration exploding across his brow. "Needs pressure."

I raced back to the bed, grabbed a pillow, stripping it from the pillowcase, hurled open the wardrobe and plucked out a tie. Back to Archie, I gently placed the pillow beneath his head and shoulders, made a pad with the case and pressed it to the wound. He grunted in pain and more blood seeped through. I tried to tie it around him, but gave up. Minutes passed like hours.

I heard noise downstairs. I didn't budge but maintained pressure. "Stay with me, Archie. Don't you go dying on me, you stupid bastard." Footsteps next. Hard and fast. I was still speaking to Archie as Dunne and two paramedics barrelled through the door and charged into the room.

Forty-Seven

Paramedics held off Dunne, listened to Archie's ragged breathing, then stabilised him and shunted us both into an ambulance, from where I called Allan. Those kind of phone calls never strike the right note. *Hi, it's me. I'm in an ambulance. I've just critically injured the man who killed my daughter.* Of course, I didn't say it like that, but it came close.

"Good God, are you okay?"

"I need stitches."

"I'll come straight to the hospital."

Feeling a little whoozy, I smiled. Allan had all the proof he needed that Smith-Arrow, and not his son, had killed my daughter. "It's going to be all right," I said, feeling stupidly sentimental. In spite of my interior moral compass playing right or wrong with my emotions, I had a deep sense of justice done. I suppose

I should have been worried about the damage I'd inflicted on Smith-Arrow and the consequences. Would it count as reasonable force? I hoped so. "Can you call Tiff for me, let her know?"

With sirens blaring, I sat with Archie all the way. Vulnerable and badly injured, an oxygen mask clamped over his face and an IV line pumping God knew what into his stuttering system, he looked deathly. As his clammy hand rested in mine, I wondered how the heck it had come to this. If he'd only stayed and not deserted me, our lives would have turned out so very differently and Tara, my darling daughter, would be alive. The thought killed me.

"You all right, love?" one of the paramedics said.

I wiped away the tear sliding down one cheek with the back of my hand and nodded.

"He'll pull through. He's strong."

I nodded again through another blur of tears. Archie, I thought, you stupid bloody fool.

I had a horror of being treated in the same hospital as Smith-Arrow although I needn't have worried. Carted off to Gloucester, from where he was transferred to Bristol, Smith-Arrow wound up safely out of my airspace, miles away. Archie, amid lots of activity, with doors opening and slamming, trolleys and people running, went straight to Gloucester and into an operating theatre. Last to leave the ambulance, I stepped out into the dying light and blinked. Without the natural anaesthetic of adrenalin, a tidal wave of pain washed fast over my arm and then over my entire body.

I saw Allan before he saw me. Standing at the entrance, deep in thought, he was gazing the other way. My heart lifted. As soon as he spotted me, he darted forwards, eyes heavy with concern.

"Grace, sweetheart," he said in consternation. I could tell he wanted to hug me but didn't dare for fear of hurting me further. I stretched out my right arm and he took my hand, raised it to his lips, and kissed it.

Inside, a jolly nurse took charge.

"Can my boyfriend come into the treatment room with me?"

"Of course," she said.

Allan whispered into my ear with a barely disguised laugh, "Boyfriend?"

"Sounds naff at our age but it's the best I could come up with."

"Don't worry, I quite like it."

A doctor inserted fifteen stitches. The injections were the worst part. A reassuring presence, Allan didn't smooth-talk, patronise, fire a volley of questions, or press me, as Archie would have done. He sat calm and composed, his expression letting me know that we'd talk about everything later when I was ready and the storm of activity died down.

I asked a passing doctor about Archie.

"Still in theatre. No news," she said.

Realising his parents should be informed I gave their name and city to a nurse. What would they think of Kristina now?

Walking wounded, I insisted I wanted to go home, or more correctly, back to Allan's. The nursing staff were probably glad to get rid of me. The phone call to Tiff had triggered a gathering of the clan. As soon as my family clapped eyes on me, it turned into a free for all.

"Gracie, love, whatever's happened to you?" Mum stared at my bandaged arm as if I'd never be able to use it again. Tiff was more explicit.

"Fuck's sake, Grace, what were you thinking?"

"Leave her alone," Doug said. "The girl done good."

"Nobody asked for your opinion," Tiff bridled. "And you can't smoke that in here," she snarled at Graham, who rotated an electronic cigarette between his fingers as if he were a cheerleader twirling a baton.

From where he was skulking around Reception, Dunne shot across and practically had to fight his way through to gain an audience.

"What are you doing here?" Doug said, surly.

"I need a word with Mrs. Neville."

"Well don't take long. The girl needs peace and quiet." Not a visit from the law, his glare conveyed.

"Will you be all right?" Allan looked at me, ignoring Dunne. Enmity crackled between them. I couldn't blame Allan. Dunne's certainty and prejudice had got Jordan convicted for a crime he didn't commit.

I assured him I was up to it and followed Dunne through the door to a side room where he gallantly drew up a seat for me. I sat down and faced him as he perched on the edge of a consulting couch. He crossed his arms and viewed me with sympathy.

"Sewn up okay? It looked pretty nasty."

"It will heal." The second time I'd made such a claim in recent days.

"I'll need a statement from you," Dunne said. "Sooner rather than later, while it's fresh."

"Tomorrow?"

"That would be fine."

"Will I face charges for injuring Smith-Arrow?" It was the one thing that gnawed away at me.

"Self-defence, wasn't it?" he said, no smile. Next he told me about Thea. "She regained consciousness."

"Thank God."

Dunne fixed me with one of his speciality stares. "She identified her attacker."

"Kristina Beaumont?"

His eyes gleamed like oysters in a shell. "You knew?"

"Process of elimination."

"And Smith-Arrow?"

"That, I didn't know until roughly an hour ago."

"You believe he killed Tara?"

"I do." I told Dunne what Smith-Arrow had told me. "So you see, he had a primary motive, saving face," I said with dry emphasis.

"We'll get a sample of his DNA and see if it's a match."

"You're not sure?" I frowned.

Dunne flicked a smile. "We need evidence."

"Like you did with Jordan?" My voice was deliberately empty and dull, knocking the smile from his face.

"It was an honest mistake."

I said nothing. He didn't deserve my absolution. Dunne cleared his throat. "Think Smith-Arrow will confess?"

I nodded. A military man, Queen and Country and honour, why not? I had other, more pressing matters on my mind. "What happens to Kristina? Have you found her?"

"She was picked up late this afternoon about to board a flight to Spain."

"Arrested?"

"And charged."

"She admitted it?"

"She did."

Poor Archie.

Agreeing with Dunne to make a statement the following day, I emerged to find an argument underway. For a change it wasn't internecine and it wasn't familial.

"She's coming home with us," Tiff said, bullish.

Allan looked over her shoulder and earnestly at me. "Here she is. Let's ask Grace what she wants to do."

"I'm coming back to yours, aren't I?" I said, holding Allan's gaze.

"You can't," Tiff spluttered.

"Why not?"

"We're your family," she said, spelling it out as if I'd been clubbed over the head and didn't know my own mind. "You belong with us."

"If it's a matter of space, Gracie," Mum waded in, "I can make up the bed in—"

"Nothing to do with space. I want to go back to Allan's."

"But Gracie, you really—"

"God save us," Doug burst out. "How old are you, Gracie?"

"Wrong side of forty."

"There you go. An adult. She wants to go to Allan's. That's what she's going to do."

"But Doug," my mum protested.

"Will you come and see me and your mum tomorrow?" Doug cut in.

"After I've been to the police station," I said.

"Satisfied?" Doug said, clapping his big hairy hands together. "Can we go home now, cos I'm bloody starving."

Forty-Eight

In the week that followed I was spoilt and wrapped in a fine cashmere cloak of love. Allan picked up my clothes from the apartment while I gave a statement to Dunne. It was all very formal. Smith-Arrow was still in hospital, although not considered to have life-threatening injuries. He'd been charged and hadn't denied what he'd done. Dax and her crew were on remand and a plea date had been set in which they were expected to plead guilty for the murder of Tyrone Weaver. I visited my mum and Tiff, who interrogated me with the same determination as an intelligence officer from MI5.

"How did you know it was Smith-Arrow?"

"I didn't."

Mum placed both hands against her temples and massaged with her fingers. "Let me get this straight, first you thought it was Archie, then Kristina, then Ruby, then ..."

"Yeah, we know all that," Tiff snapped.

"*You* might know all that, Tiffany," Mum said in her sternest voice. "But I'm still trying to catch up."

Eventually, she did *catch up*. "Bitch," Tiff said about Kristina, rather predictably, I thought, although I could only agree. "And Archie, miserable tosser," she continued with a vindictive expression.

Tiff followed me out to the car. The purposefulness in her stride convinced me that she wasn't quite finished.

"Do you have to go?"

"I want to."

"It's Allan, isn't it?"

"If you mean, am I staying with Allan, then yes. He's a good man."

"And we're not good enough for you?"

"Change the record. And don't be so immature. For goodness sake, Tiffany, I'm tired of being alone."

"You're not," she protested, her voice blazing with frustration. "You've got me and Mum."

"And you've got Graham and Doug. Look, I've never been very good at being on my own. It's been over four years. I'm not getting any younger."

"So you're grabbing the first bloke that comes along?"

"That's not fair."

"I know it won't work."

"What?" I snorted. "Did someone hand you a vision into the future?"

"There's too much baggage surrounding the pair of you. Gracie," she said, touching my arm, "I don't want you to get hurt. None of us do."

I let out a derisory laugh. "What makes you think anything or anyone can hurt me after what I've been through?" Life had thrown the very worst it could at me. I'd get through, not intact, but I would survive.

Rattled, I opened the car door and climbed inside. Tiff tapped on the window. I put the key in the ignition, turned it, pressed the switch to slide down the window, and glanced up at her.

"We care about you, that's all."

"Right," I said stiffly.

"Allan isn't Archie," Tiff said. "You know that, don't you?"

I started the car.

"He won't electrify you the way Archie did."

I didn't say a word and drove away.

———

Dionne and little Asher stayed with friends while Allan and I kept tabs on progress with Jordan's solicitor and the police investigation. Meanwhile, we fell into an easy pattern. We walked and talked and then talked some more.

News travels fast. I'd barely had time to get my bearings when Michael, my boss, called.

"Where the hell are you?"

I glanced across at Allan, who was driving. "Currently en route to prison."

"Are you serious?"

I laughed and explained.

"Had me worried for a moment. But isn't that young man released yet?"

I let out a sigh. It had been an enormous source of frustration for both Allan and myself. Jordan's case had been referred to the Criminal

Cases Review Commission, whose job it is to examine individual cases independently and refer those appropriate to the Appeal Court. I told Michael this.

"Well, let's hope they get a move on."

"To be fair, I think heaven and earth is being shifted."

"Hmm," he said. "Where exactly are you hiding out?"

I told him.

"Does it have an address?"

"Why?"

"Because we want to send you something."

"Sounds mysterious."

"A vast bouquet of flowers," Michael said in the no-nonsense way so typical of him.

"A form of bribery?" My shave with death had made me skittish.

"Do you mean are we surviving without you?"

"Well, are you?"

"Strangely, the answer is yes. Vron's back."

"You're kidding."

"Sebastian has left Arabella."

"You mean … "

"Funny old world, isn't it?"

"Goodness," was all I could manage.

"Any news on Archie?" Michael enquired.

"Discharged today, I believe."

Surgery had saved Archie's life. I hadn't visited him in hospital, although we'd spoken briefly once on the phone. Despite their grand age and his dad's indifferent health, his parents had kept a virtual bedside vigil. Archie spoke guardedly. I got the message: don't come. I also got the message that he didn't want to discuss Kristina. I couldn't blame him. He sounded lost and alone and for that I was sorry.

"Thought I'd pay him a visit," Michael said.

"I'm sure he'd appreciate it."

"Grim business."

An understatement.

———

Jordan had more fullness in his face. He looked less edgy and not as if he were expecting a blow from behind at any second. He beamed as we sat down. This time his knee didn't jink when we spoke to him. Even the room seemed more hospitable. The deadly fragrance of boiled cabbage and disinfectant had magically diminished, too, or perhaps it was symptomatic of my upbeat mood.

"Hello, Mrs. Neville."

"Grace, please," I said. "Hello, Jordan, and before you say a word I want to tell you how sorry I am."

"What for?"

"For this," I said, my eyes darting to the nearest prison officer.

"Wasn't your fault. You listened when others didn't."

"That's generous of you."

"It's the truth. If it hadn't been for you I'd be locked up for the next eighteen years. Isn't that right, Dad?"

"It is," Allan replied, casting a loving smile in my direction.

Jordan watched us for a moment, almost shy. I wondered if he were thinking what I was thinking—that we'd endured more in our lives than we'd ever wanted to.

He flicked his head. "That git, the army guy, has a lot to answer for, yeah?"

"Don't you go getting any ideas, son," Allan said in a cautionary tone. "Once you're out of here, you're to stay on the straight and narrow."

"From what I hear, Smith-Arrow is looking at a long stretch," I pointed out.

"Won't be enough though, will it?" Jordan said.

"Yeah, well never mind about him," Allan said, eager to move on. "The point is he's guilty and you're innocent." And that's the way it is going to stay, his tone implied.

"Why did he do it?" Jordan said. "I heard it was something to do with a row between his daughter and Tara."

"Yes," I said, keeping my eyes doggedly fixed on Jordan. "I believe so."

"Any news on your case?" Allan said, following my lead.

"Had a visit with my brief this morning."

"Mr. Alexander," Allan said in reproof.

"Yeah, well, whatever, anyways he said that things were moving as quickly as possible. The Commission have got a ton of outstanding cases, he said, but my case has gone through the screening process and it's gone into the fast-track queue."

"That's great." I beamed.

Allan clamped a hand to his mouth. Jordan's face clouded. "You all right, Dad?"

Too choked to speak, Allan reached out and squeezed Jordan's hand.

"Shall I leave you to it?" I said.

Allan shook his head. "I'll be fine. It's such a relief."

"What are you like?" Jordan grinned. "It's me doing the time."

"That's the point, son. So how long will it all take?"

Jordan hiked a shoulder. "Dunno, but Mr. Alexander," he said, pausing over every consonant, "reckoned that once it's through, the Appeal process would be a lot quicker."

They talked some more. I listened and ached. For me, my parenting days were over.

About to leave, Jordan said, "Mind if I have a word with Grace, on her own, like?"

Allan raised his eyebrows in an *Are you cool with that?* gesture. I assured him I was.

Once he was out of earshot, Jordan said, "Will you be visiting the cemetery soon?"

I told him I was.

"Can you put some flowers on Tara's grave for me? She said she liked sunflowers."

"Of course." My heart creased.

"I'll pay you back."

"Don't worry."

"No, it's important. It has to come from me, do you see?"

I smiled. "I'll keep a receipt." I went to move.

"Wait," he said, looking at me expectantly. "Did you ever find out Tara's secret?"

I looked into his eyes and prayed he couldn't hear the pounding in my chest. I could lie. I could say that we would never know. I could pretend to myself that it was for the best to say nothing, but then I remembered that Tara hadn't wanted to keep her secret. I remembered that the one person she'd needed to know was the young man sitting in front of me. I owed it to both of them to tell Jordan the truth. So, as gently as I possibly could, I explained. When I finished I told him how sorry I was and how confusing it must be for him.

He sat for what seemed like a long time. I thought how impossibly young he seemed. When he finally spoke he was more measured than I thought possible. "I guess she was finding out stuff about herself, about how she connected to other people." He ran his fingers through his short hair, rubbing his scalp, eyes wide. "To be honest, I'd never have guessed if you hadn't told me."

342

"The point is, Tara was going to tell you. Not me, not her aunt, or her grandmother, but you. She loved you enough to be honest."

"Yeah," he said. "I get that. And," he said with a sad smile, "it was me she chose in the end."

"Yes."

He waited a beat. "Does everyone else know?"

"Only those who count and they won't say a word."

"For the best," he said.

"I think you might be right."

Forty-Nine

Dionne was back, Asher jiggling on her knee. He seemed to have doubled in size since the last time I saw him. We were sitting in the living room having a drink before dinner when my mobile rang. I shrank when I read the number. "I'll take it upstairs," I said with false brightness.

Allan looked but didn't comment. He probably thought it was Tiff.

"Hello," I said, my voice low.

"Grace, I've been meaning to phone you."

"How are you, Archie?"

"Mending well."

"I'm pleased."

"I wondered if it would be possible to talk?"

"Fire away."

"Not like this. I mean in person. Could you possibly come to me?"

Déjà vu assailed me. I glanced at the door, God alone knew why. I think I instantly sensed that Allan would perceive a meeting as a threat to us. Less easy to assimilate, it flagged up a subconscious fear that, if I saw Archie, I'd be sucked back in. "I'm not coming to the house."

"No, I thought somewhere nice, private."

"I don't know. It's not that easy."

"I really wouldn't ask if it weren't important." Such a plea in his voice, I found it hard to resist. I let out a long prevaricating sigh. "I know I don't deserve it," Archie said in haste, "after all you've been through, but please. I'm beg—"

"Okay," I snapped. "Where?"

"John Gordon's."

A cosy bar in town that specialised in whisky and wine and where you could also get a decent cup of coffee. "When?" I said.

"Tomorrow?"

"Morning. It has to be morning." The a.m. signified business, clear thinking, and straight speaking.

"Ten thirty?"

"I'll be there."

"Everything all right?" Allan said as I returned.

"Sure."

I think he knew then that Archie had phoned. I wasn't sure why or how, intuition maybe, but he was smart enough not to pursue it.

I didn't sleep. What did Archie want to discuss? In danger of imploding, I didn't think I could stand any more revelations.

Allan stirred drowsily beside me. "What's the matter, sweetheart?"

"Nothing."

He stretched, rolled over, encircled my body with his arm, and drew me close. A thread of moonlight lit up his face, his eyes shining bright, like a star in the night. "Which is why you haven't slept a wink."

"Sorry," I said. "I didn't mean to keep you awake."

"Doesn't matter." He smoothed away a lock of hair from my forehead, searched my face, looking for clues. "Is this connected to the phone call?"

"Allan, I don't … "

"Ssh," he said. "I'm not asking you to explain. All I want you to know is that whatever you do next, you do what's right for you. Do you understand what I'm saying?"

I knew then what Archie wanted to ask of me. My eyes filled with tears. "Thank you," I said.

"Now," he whispered, nuzzling my ear, "go back to sleep."

Allan left for work around seven the next morning. Before he went he placed a mug of tea on the bedside table, leant over, and kissed me once. He didn't ask me what I was going to do for the day as he usually did. Somewhere inside he already knew.

I waited until Dionne had used the bathroom, got Asher ready for the child-minder, and then dragged myself out of bed. I showered and dressed, throwing on a favourite vintage '70s green maxi skirt and blouse, topping it off with a loose-fitting faux fur jacket that didn't snag on my recently dressed arm. Scarf or no scarf? I tried with and without. Definitely with.

"Just off," Dionne said, easing Asher in his buggy out through the front door. "See you later."

"Have a good day," I called after her. I made myself sit down and eat a breakfast that I didn't want. I cleared away, washed up, padded around my temporary home, and looked out onto the garden bursting with tulips and irises, reminding me of Renoir's *Flowers*, an exquisite oil on canvas, Impressionistic in style, dated around 1902, and now in a private collection. Tara loved flowers and planning to drive straight to the cemetery after I'd finished with Archie, I set out early, stopped off at a florist and bought an armful of forget-me-knots and sunflowers, remembering to keep the receipt.

Finding a rare parking space and with five minutes to spare, I slowed my breathing and checked my make-up was still in place and I hadn't left traces of toothpaste on my lips. Then, straightening my shoulders, I got out and crossed the road and then doubled back past Blanc's Brasserie on the opposite side and to John Gordon's. With no sign of Archie, I wandered back outside to the covered courtyard. It was monastically quiet and I caught Archie's eye immediately. He stood up with a nervous smile and beckoned me to join him.

"I've ordered cappuccinos," he said. "Shall I order pastries?"

"No, thanks, not for me." I unravelled my scarf and awkwardly shrugged off my jacket.

"Here, let me," he said, unusually attentive.

"I can manage, Archie." My voice sounded brittle, an intruder.

"Sorry, sure you can." Flustered, he forced a smile.

We both sat down. He did a mini drum roll on the tops of his thighs, like an anxious teenager. "It's nice here, isn't it?" he said, glancing towards a waiter heading our way.

"Mmm," I said, sitting back as proper brown lump sugar was set on the table alongside two frothy coffees. Archie helped himself. I watched his every move. His hands trembled and I didn't think it was connected to the injury from which he was recovering. Only when he pushed my cup and saucer over towards me, like he was playing draughts, did it feel as if he regained a modicum of control.

I glanced down at the foam, parted it with a spoon, as if entranced by the dense liquid lurking beneath, and reluctantly returned my solid gaze to him. I didn't speak. He'd got me there to talk, so talk he would.

Leaning in, he fixed me with his eyes, so dissimilar to Allan's in spite of being brown, and rested his hands, palms facing upwards, on the table.

Meant as a gesture of love and a kind of *we're in it together,* it provided my cue to place mine on his. We used to do it a lot when we first met. In the current circumstances, it was a calculated move and one hard to resist. Archie was like a scab inside my heart that needed to be picked.

I shook my head minutely. Archie dazzled me with a magnetising smile, withdrew his hands, no big deal.

"I have made so many mistakes," he began. "And my biggest was to leave you."

"Your biggest was to leave Tara," I said softly.

His face fell. Lines on his face deepened. "I need to explain something to you, Grace. Remember when you last came to the house, you asked me what had happened to my protective instinct? Don't you see that it was *because* of my love for Tara that I kept quiet?"

I understood why he would say this now. How else could he live with his guilt and the horrible truth that he'd failed her? I picked up my coffee cup, pressed it to my lips, and sipped. It tasted good, earthy and bitter, to complement my mood. I returned it to the saucer and did not waver. I'd only ever have the chance to say this once.

"I need to explain something to you, too."

"Yes," he said, smiling encouragingly, face, limbs and body relaxing.

"The nature of mother love, what it means and how it feels."

"Grace, there really is no need. I know how much Tara meant to you. I know how much she loved you, too. Nobody could doubt—"

"Enough," I said. If I didn't shut him up, he'd do what he'd always done: electrify and bedazzle me with one of his oratories. "Every mother encounters the sheer bloody terror and dread of thinking their most precious gift of life will be taken. There are so many countless ways that Fate can snap its fingers, through illness, through accident, through self-destructive addictions, all those desperately sad yet banal and everyday packages of pain that life has in store for the unwary, but no, Archie, it didn't happen like that with Tara. We did it. *You* did it."

His eyes bulged with indignation. "How can you say that? It wasn't me who wielded the knife. If anybody was responsible for setting the terrible train of events in motion, it was Kristina. She's to blame."

"No, Archie, it was *your* fault our daughter became a memory. And it wasn't only us who suffered. There's Jordan Dukes, a young man serving a sentence for a crime he didn't commit."

Archie spread his hands. "He's no angel, Grace."

"And he's not the devil either. Another family, Archie, another set of people who've had their lives smashed, and all because you couldn't keep your dick in your pants."

He blanched. Had I plunged his hand into boiling oil, he could not have looked more shocked.

"That's the way it is and how I feel, and it's no use you blaming someone else," I said conclusively, unable to speak the wretched woman's name.

The air throbbed. My breath came in shallow bursts. I felt the walls compress and close in despite sitting outside with my back to the street. I watched Archie's face as the full reality of what I'd said hit him and, to be honest, me. He looked as if he were struggling to breathe.

"I'm so sorry," he whispered, anguished, close to tears. "I'm really, really sorry."

"I know you are," I said softly, my voice tired and so very weary.

"Will you forgive me?"

I wanted to speak the truth, to say what was really in my heart, that one day I might, but that day wasn't now. I did what I always did and told him what he wanted to hear. "Yes."

He looked as if he might burst with relief. "Thank you, Grace, I'll make it up to you, I promise." I wasn't sure how, but I nodded. "It's why I want you to come with me to Hampshire."

Stunned, my lips parted in disbelief, not because I was surprised by his declaration, but because of his audacity. "What about ... ?" My voice ran out of steam.

"Kristina?" His face darkened. "We're finished. Through. I can't stand by her after what she's done."

"Days ago, you told me you loved her."

"Obsession, codependency, it wasn't true love. I recognise that now."

Patience that I'd kept in check for a lifetime snapped. "Then why the hell did you let her get away with what she did?"

"Grace, Grace," he repeated, leaning towards me, snatching hold of my hand. "We've got a terrific opportunity to make something of our lives. There's a great little business to run. My parents are cool with it. You've been discussed. It's all fine."

I snatched back my hand. "You've talked to them about *me*?" You're sick. You're all sick in the head, I thought.

If Archie recognised how insulted I felt, he seemed oblivious. "It's a measure of how serious I am. You can have a lovely house, a garden, too. If you want, you can have your own gallery. It could be a really exciting time, a brand-new chapter."

I gazed up at the convex ceiling, the glass and terra cotta patterning, trying to control the flood of misery in my chest and failing. Tears seeped out of the corner of my eyes and trickled down the sides of my face. How could I have a brand-new chapter when I couldn't even turn the page?

"Oh, Grace, please don't cry. It's you I want, always has been, always will be. We're so good together," he insisted.

I lowered my gaze, a smile fleetingly breaking through my glassy expression. How often I'd longed to hear those words and now I wondered why.

"Have you never fallen in love with someone you shouldn't have?" he said, appealing to me.

I let out a sob. "Only you, Archie. Only you."

He stared up at me hopefully as I scrambled to my feet, his expectant look expiring as I grabbed my jacket and bag.

"Is there someone else?" he said, a frantic note in his voice. "Have you met someone? It's not that bloody man, Dukes, is it?"

I didn't look back. I walked and kept walking.

Fifty

I drove to the cemetery and visited Tara's grave as planned.

The sky was a radiant blue. There was warmth in the sun. One of those lone, unique days when the world blossoms with possibility, or so it seemed to me then, for I hadn't cherished hope in a while.

I arranged the flowers in the vase near the headstone, whispered to Tara that they were sent from Jordan with his love. Sweeping my fingers over the cool grey-blue surface, I wept for all that I'd lost, unashamedly and unchecked. With fervour, I told my daughter how much I loved her, as if words and thoughts and prayers could cross the great divide and reach the dead.

I told her that Jordan would soon be free. I said that his dad was a good man, kind and honest, and that, although I didn't know what the future held, he made me happier than I'd been in a very long time. Then I simply sat in the sunshine and tried to let go of my disgust, despair, and anger towards those I felt had hurt me so badly.

Afterwards I phoned Allan. He picked up immediately, strain in his voice. "Grace, I'm so glad you called. I've been worried. Where are you?"

"I'm on my way back."

"Yes?" He sounded wary.

"There's no need to worry, Allan. I'm coming home." I tipped my head to the sky, let the sun's rays fall on my face, and smiled without guilt. "I'm coming home to you."

About the Author

Eleanor Gray (England) has written nine novels under several pseudonyms. She began writing after a successful career in public relations and raising five children. She has published articles in *Devon Today* magazine and had a number of her short stories broadcast on BBC Radio.